Kashmir

Advance praise for *Kashmir: Book 3 of The Partition Trilogy*

'*Kashmir* makes for a compelling read. The book examines the tumultuous occurrences during India's partition in 1947, shedding light on the relatively lesser-explored consequences of this partition on the enchanting Kashmir valley. The book skilfully highlights the striking contrast between Kashmir's renowned beauty and the harsh realities of war, violence and chaos that unfolded alongside the Partition.'

– **Rana Safvi**, author of The Delhi Trilogy

'In her last book of The Partition Trilogy, Manreet deftly dips in and out of decisions made in palaces, recording, with rich detail, their devastating repercussions on ordinary lives—giving us a gripping and panoramic view of one of the most important periods in the subcontinent's history.'

– **Farah Bashir**, author of *Rumours of Spring*

Praise for *Hyderabad: Book 2 of The Partition Trilogy*

'Hyderabad! A liberation? A tragedy? The result of the Ironman's will and Nehru's vision to build a nation? The daydreams of a Nizam? The diplomatic strategies of Nehru and Dickie? Dreams of a Communist revolution? The common people's struggles and sacrifices for land and a fistful of grain? But everything finally ends with a never-ending, silent violence on women's bodies in the formation of a state. This is well-researched history woven as a thrilling novel by a terrific novelist, Manreet Sodhi Someshwar.'

– **Volga**, author of *Vimukta Kadha Samputi*

'Politics, rebellion, conspiracies, spies, weapons, jewels and the recalcitrant Nizam of Hyderabad pitted against stalwart Indian leaders, Manreet Sodhi Someshwar's novel *Hyderabad*, part two of her Partition trilogy, has ample fodder for the imagination … A momentous time in Indian history is captured well.'

– *The Tribune*

'*Hyderabad*, a novel about a state's quest for self-rule, is a fine balance of fact and fiction. Someshwar entwines the rhetoric and machinations of state and statecraft with the lives of the ordinary. The violence inherent in the trauma of the Partition often played out on women's bodies, turning them into a battlefield. Someshwar's novel takes cognisance of the physical and psychological violence performed on women.'

– Scroll.in

'India has a ton of Partition and Independence literature. The elements that make *Hyderabad* distinct are the amount of research involved, and the multiple plot lines where the writer switches from a chapter on Nizam to that on Patel and Nehru to that on common communists with sophisticated ease. There is no hero here either, but characters navigating their way through what they mean by independence and nationhood. The short chapters, crisp language, and a deep dive into the Hyderabad culture, from Osmania biscuits, the university to its writers and poets, keeps one hooked.'

– *Financial Express*

'Mention "Partition" to the average non-Hyderabadi Indian, and chances are the associations will be of mass exodus, violence and horror along the Pakistan borders. Sodhi Someshwar, with *Hyderabad*, fills that gap and reveals some of the oft-ignored aspects of Partition. This novel shines the light on the nizam's Hyderabad, with the tensions and stresses, both political and personal, that tugged it in different directions.'

– *Open*

'Like the first part, *Lahore*, the second part, *Hyderabad*, too, has a love story as nut graf, while the real backroom drama, politicking and courtly intrigue play out on the side. The author is in her element when she describes events inside a drawing room or the political intrigue as she flits between Delhi and Hyderabad. It is in the Nizam's household that she lets her imagination fly and brings alive the characters who surrounded Mir Osman Ali Khan as he played a diplomatic game to outsmart the British and Indians to stay independent.'

– *The Hindu*

Praise for *Lahore: Book 1 of The Partition Trilogy*

'As the men fought over religion and maps, the Partition heaped unspeakable atrocities on women. Manreet's book is a faithful, unforgiving look at what was and also what shouldn't have been. Lahore is breathtaking in scope, painful yet gentle to the touch.'

– Taslima Nasreen, author of *Lajja* and *Shameless*

'Vivid and atmospheric. By deftly weaving the personal and the political, Manreet Sodhi Someshwar transports us to the uncertain months leading up to the tragedy of Partition.'

– **Aanchal Malhotra**, author of *Remnants of a Separation*

'A timely reminder of what differences and divisions can do .... An engaging read that tries to humanize the politics of the Partition. Current, relevant, and important. This is a voice which makes you question, rethink and reimagine the past as the future and the future as the past. A voice to pay attention to in these times of rising intolerance and right-wing extremism. A voice of reason and reckoning.'

– **Sabyn Javeri**, author of *Hijabistan*

'Tension pervades this first part of Manreet Sodhi Someshwar's Partition trilogy. It wafts through the corridors of power, penetrates bonds between friends and lovers, and befouls the earth itself. Without releasing the reader from its ominous undercurrent, Manreet deftly weaves the big strands of history with the finer threads of human feeling, reminding us of a calamity that tore apart not just nations and states but also the heart and spirit of a people.'

– **Manu S. Pillai**, author of *The Ivory Throne: Chronicles of the House of Travancore*

'The value of Lahore lies in how it does not let the subaltern disappear into the shadow of giants like Jawaharlal Nehru and his socialist dream, Vallabhbhai [Patel] and his tremendous contribution to the task of the consolidation of the nation, the statesmanship of Lord Mountbatten and the effortless charm of Lady Mountbatten.'

– Scroll.in

'Clearly a passion project, this first book of an ambitious trilogy on Partition is all heart, and brilliantly traces our heritage.'

– *Deccan Herald*

Kashmir

III
THE
PARTITION
TRILOGY

MANREET SODHI
SOMESHWAR

HarperCollins *Publishers* India

First published in India by HarperCollins *Publishers* 2023
4th Floor, Tower A, Building No. 10, DLF Cyber City,
DLF Phase II, Gurugram, Haryana – 122002
www.harpercollins.co.in

2 4 6 8 10 9 7 5 3 1

P-ISBN: 978-93-5699-540-6
E-ISBN: 978-93-5699-541-3

Typeset in 11/15 Berling LT Std at
Manipal Technologies Limited, Manipal

Printed and bound at
Replika Press Pvt. Ltd.

MIX
Paper from responsible sources
FSC® C016779

This book is produced from independently certified FSC® paper to ensure responsible forest management.

For

Kashmir and Kashmiris, everywhere

The Hun so loved the cry, one falling elephant's,
he wished to hear it again. At dawn, my mother
heard, in her hospital-dream of elephants,
sirens wail through Manhattan like elephants
forced off Pir Panjal's rock cliffs in Kashmir ...

– 'Lenox Hill', Agha Shahid Ali

Garah wandai gara sasah,
Bareh nerahah nah zah.

O Home, for you I sacrifice a thousand houses,
I can never leave you behind.

– Kashmiri proverb

About The Partition Trilogy

Set in the months leading up to and following India obtaining freedom in 1947, The Partition Trilogy is an exploration of the events, exigencies and decisions that led to the independence of India, its concomitant partition, and the accession of Princely States alongside. A literary political thriller that captures the frenzy of the time, the series is set in Delhi, Lahore, Hyderabad and Kashmir. Covering a vast canvas, Jawaharlal Nehru, Vallabhbhai Patel and Dickie Mountbatten share space in the trilogy with the ordinary people from the cities that were affected by the partition and the reorganization of the states.

Backed by astute research that ensures the authenticity of the political thread, this trilogy will take readers back into a world of great political upheaval and churn. In its fresh, incisive, and insightful portrayal of a cataclysm that haunts us to this day, The Partition Trilogy is both spellbinding and believable – a remarkable feat.

Cast of Characters

His Majesty's Government

(London)

King George VI, King of the United Kingdom and British Dominions, and Emperor of India

Winston Churchill, Prime Minister of the United Kingdom, 1940–1945

Clement Attlee, Prime Minister of the United Kingdom, 1945–1951

British Empire in India/The Raj

Lord Louis (Dickie) Mountbatten, Last Viceroy of India (1947), and the first Governor General of independent India (1947–1948)

Edwina Mountbatten, wife of Louis Mountbatten, and the last Vicereine of India

Pamela Mountbatten, younger daughter of Louis and Edwina Mountbatten

Mizzen, Sealyham terrier belonging to Edwina Mountbatten

Lord Archibald Wavell, second-last Viceroy of India

Lionel (Pug) Ismay, chief of staff to Lord Mountbatten

Alan Campbell-Johnson, Mountbatten's press attache

Claude Auchinleck/The Auk, commander-in-chief of the Indian Army

Roy Bucher, first commander-in-chief of the Indian Army

Sir Robert Francis Mudie, Governor of the West Panjab

Maharaja Hari Singh, His Inner Circle and Staff

(Jammu and Kashmir)

Hari Singh, Maharaja of the Princely State of Jammu and Kashmir

Maharani Tara Devi, Maharaja's wife

Tiger/Karan Singh, Maharaja's son and heir apparent

Thakur Nachhint Chand, Maharaja's household minister

Rajguru/Swami Sant Dev, Maharaja's spiritual guide

Captain Ranjit Singh, Maharaja's aide

Victor Rosenthal, jeweller and Maharaja's friend

Mehr Chand Mahajan, the prime minister of Kashmir

R.L. Batra, the deputy prime minister of Kashmir

Political Leaders of the Subcontinent, Their Families and Staff

Gandhi/Mahatma/Bapu, leader of the Indian National Congress

Mohammed Ali Jinnah/the Quaid, leader of the Muslim League, Pakistan's first Governor General

Jawaharlal Nehru, first Prime Minister of independent India

Indira (Indu) Gandhi, Jawaharlal's daughter

Rajiv and Sanjay, sons of Indira

Vallabhbhai Patel, Deputy Prime Minister and Home Minister

Manibehn, Vallabhbhai's daughter, assistant and housekeeper

Vidya Shankar, Vallabhbhai's confidential aide

V.P. Menon, Secretary of the States Department

Baldev Singh, Defence Minister

Maulana Azad, Education Minister

Colonel Sam Manekshaw, India's Director of Military Operations

Liaquat Ali Khan, first Prime Minister of Pakistan

Mian Iftikharuddin, president of the Panjab provincial Muslim League

Sheikh Abdullah, leader of the National Conference and head of the Emergency administration

Begum Akbar Jahan, Sheikh Abdullah's wife

Common People

(Jammu and Kashmir)

Zooni, young Kashmiri woman

Mouj and Moul, Zooni's mother and father

Masud Ahmed, Zooni's husband

Koko Jan, Masud Ahmed's first wife

Jugnu, young boy

Rani, Jugnu's mother

Kashmira, Zooni's older sister

Gul, Kashmira's son

Safina, Kashmira's daughter

Bilquis, Kashmira's mother-in-law

Ali Dar, Kashmira's husband

Hassan Dar, Ali's younger brother

Margot Parr, American journalist

Larry Collins, English journalist

Abdul Aziz, thekedar

Durga Mehra, widow, mother and refugee

Zulekha/Madhu, refugee

Havildar Fateh Singh, Indian Army

'Boi', Gul's bird

Junior Commissioning Officer Naik Singh, Indian Army

Others

Sardar Ibrahim, formed the first provisional government in Muzaffarabad

Sardar Shaukat Hayat Khan, minister in the Pakistan government

Akbar Khan/General Tariq, director of weapons and equipment at GHQ, Pakistan Army

Khurshid Anwar, leader of the kabailis

Captain Alamgir, Pakistan Army

Staff Officer Kamil, Pakistan Army

Brigadier General L.P. Sen, Indian Army

Brigadier Harbakhsh Singh, Indian Army

Second Lt. Jabar Jan Singh, Indian Army

J.E. Brown, Tiger's tutor

Freda Bedi, wife of B.P.L. Bedi, confidante of Sheikh Abdullah

Philip Noel-Baker, commonwealth secretary

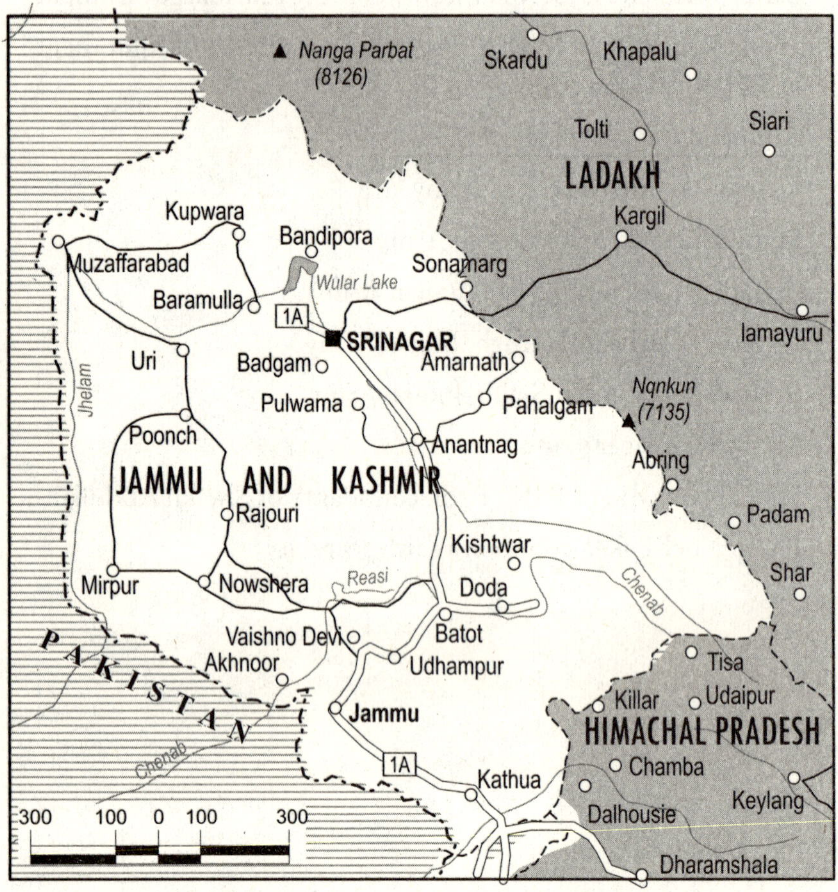

Nanga Parbat
(8126)
Skardu
Khapalu
Tolti
Siari
LADAKH
Kargil
Kupwara
Bandipora
Muzaffarabad
Sonamarg
Wular Lake
Baramulla
1A
SRINAGAR
Iamayuru
Uri
Badgam
Amarnath
Jhelam
Pulwama
Pahalgam
Nqnkun
(7135)
Poonch
Anantnag
Abring
JAMMU AND KASHMIR
Rajouri
Padam
Kishtwar
Shar
Mirpur
Nowshera
Reasi
Doda
Chenab
Vaishno Devi
Batot
Tisa
PAKISTAN
Akhnoor
Udhampur
Killar
Udaipur
Jammu
HIMACHAL PRADESH
Chenab
1A
Chamba
Kathua
Keylang
Dalhousie
300 100 0 100 300
Dharamshala

Baramulla, Kashmir (October 1947)

The crisp autumnal air smells spicy sweet. The land is dressed in red, gold, mauve. The men in lorries, ancient trucks, juddering buses, lying on the roofs, sitting on the engines, hanging on to the mudguards, armed with rifles, daggers, axes widen their eyes and begin to sniff like hounds. They register the change. Two large towns they ransacked en route – the border town of Muzaffarabad and the bowl-shaped Uri, its walls made from steep hills – the tribesmen are familiar with. But *this*, this earth dressed as a bride and smelling like a houri, intimate, inviting, *this* is what they have been promised? The fertile valley of Kashmir, bounteous and beautiful?

Baramulla is indeed where the Kashmir valley begins. The rich loamy soil springs forth orchards. A brisk trade in apples, grapes, walnuts makes the riverside town bustle. It even boasts a Catholic mission, St Joseph's, complete with a chapel and a dispensary.

As the odd cavalcade lumbers down the only road towards town, the *crunch-crunch-crunch* of fallen chinar leaves alerts the family gathering saffron flowers in their field of mauve. A hand stills, another clasps a mouth and the buzzing of honeybees feasting on saffron blossoms drowns in the clamour. Men loading a lorry with rosy apples stop to watch. The driver of the lorry, a turbaned Sikh, emerges having filled petrol—

Balwallah kuffar!

A bloodcurdling howl rips the air.

As if it were a war cry, the tribesmen explode out of their assorted vehicles and rain down upon Baramulla.

In a barn, a woman sits down to milk her buffalo. She sings to the crooning of the Jhelum river in the background, her deft hands tugging the teats, her earrings swinging playfully, arrows of velvety white milk shooting into the pail—

Which is grabbed by rough hands … A bearded man hoists the pail and starts to dunk the milk into his yawning mouth. Riveted, the woman watches as rivulets of milk run down the man's matted beard, leaving wet tracks down his coarse clothes. Before she can begin to comprehend the situation, she's screaming in agony as a hand grabs her earrings, tearing her earlobes. The buffalo snorts, ears raised. Her screams draw her husband, who hurries in from the sheep pen at the rear of the barn, trailed by his young son. With his shepherd's staff, he lunges at the black-turbaned assailant. Who shoves a dagger into his throat. And hurls the boy against a wall with force. The boy slides to the floor like a rag doll, his face frozen in shock. As the shepherd crumples to the ground, clutching his neck, the first Pathan burps, flings the pail aside, and yanks the woman by her hair. The irate buffalo swings and lands a forceful kick with her hind legs on the Pathan's back. He collapses. His comrade, having robbed the dead peasant of his rings by chopping off his fingers, helps the man up. But not before he shoots the buffalo and the woman. He spits, latches the barn door shut and sets it afire.

By now, fires are burning across Baramulla. The air is thick with fumes. Tribesmen are hunting from door to door, helping themselves to the loot they have been promised – wealth and women. Wives, mothers, daughters who escaped being butchered are streaking to the Baramulla bridge to hurl themselves into the Jhelum. At the Catholic mission, the tribesmen are meting out justice to those kuffar, too. A nun is raped, the Mother Superior shot, a British army officer and his pregnant wife killed, the chapel desecrated ...

One wealthy household, though, welcomes the liberators sent by Pakistan. The Kukroo family hosts a lavish dinner for the lashkar. A commander is feted with a garland of red koshur gulab, rare because the season has ended. The lashkar attacks the food with gusto. The commander sits at the head of the table, whilst Kukroo stands in waiting. Watching his men eat, the commander begins to rip petals off the roses strung around his neck, until the garland is a bare string, the petals heaped on the floor. His tough, leather footwear creaks as he slips his feet out to rest them atop the pile of shredded roses. His men begin to rip silk carpets from the floor and walls, grab carved walnut chairs and tables, round up brass samovars and oil paintings. Then they stride to the zenana. A terrified Kukroo folds his hands, falls to his knees, begs and pleads as the hysterical cries of his womenfolk radiate outwards.

Too late. The kabailis are blades without handles.

Prologue

In the sack of Baramulla, its population of 14,000 was reduced to 1000. Muslims, Hindus, Sikhs and Christians were pillaged and killed without distinction. Those who survived bore chopped noses, ears, wrists – the kabailis too impatient to extricate their gold ornaments. Having taken the same route as Alexander's army in 325 BC, and the one used by many invaders thereafter, they made fast work of the invasion and decided to linger in the picturesque town. Making St Joseph's their military base, they hauled iron and steel beds from the dispensary to roast cows, and chamber pots to cook rice; strung a local revolutionary to a post in the town square, a tin plate nailed to his forehead reading: *The punishment of a traitor is death*; whilst the few survivors huddled in smouldering buildings.

From the Pakistani perspective, the lashkar was wasting precious time. Time in which Srinagar, that lay trembling down the road 35 miles away, could be captured.

Time in which Maharaja Hari Singh, his Dassehra Darbar disrupted, signed the Instrument of Accession to India and fled

Gulab Bhavan to Jammu with his royal entourage, bursting with jewels and precious palatial wares.

Time in which 1Sikh of the Indian Army could land at the Srinagar airport and begin mounting a defence of the Valley. But we are getting ahead of ourselves.

Most people make the same assumption about Kashmir that the kabailis did: The Valley *is* Kashmir. The populous Valley, because of its peculiar beauty and fecundity, could be considered the *heart* of Kashmir. It is not, however, the *entirety* of Kashmir. Which consists of Jammu, Ladakh, Gilgit, Baltistan, besides the Kashmir valley. The state, with a 77 per cent Muslim population, was diverse in its own unique way. Jammu, in the south, was nearly half-Hindu. Ladakh, to the east, was majority Buddhist. The residents of the Valley, majority Muslim, practiced a version of Islam influenced by Sufism. The western regions, Muzaffarabad, Poonch, Reasi, Mirpur, were ethnically close to western Panjab. Gilgit, Baltistan were sparsely populated.

Another reigning assumption is that the trouble in Kashmir *began* with the invasion by kabailis in October 1947. *No*. The trouble started earlier, in the spring of 1947, in Poonch in western Jammu, where the residents – a large number of whom had returned from fighting World War II for the British, were up in arms against the Dogra Maharaja's new tax policy. Under which, just about everything they possessed was being taxed – including additional wives and widows even!

A chain reaction started.

Maharaja Hari Singh's troops responded with force … the Poonchis sent protest telegrams to Jinnah … cross-border raids began … refugees poured into Jammu … a Poonchi named Sardar Ibrahim went to Pakistan seeking weapons and volunteers for revolt against Hari Singh …

To understand it all, we need to roll back and start afresh.

Shall we?

1

Srinagar (June 1947)

'What will the future of Kashmir be?' Dickie Mountbatten gazed earnestly at his host.

The Viceroy's question arrested in mid-flight the spoon ferrying fragrant chicken curry to the lips of Maharaja Hari Singh, who was hosting the banquet in honour of his esteemed guest.

'Accession to India or Pakistan? Your Highness must establish the will of the people to decide either way.'

Dickie returned his attention to his plate to allow the spoon, stalled in Hari Singh's right hand, to complete its journey. From the corner of his eye, he caught Edwina's meaningful look. Yes, he admitted, it wasn't appropriate dinner-time conversation, but the Maharaja had left him with little choice. Since they had arrived at the sprawling English manor–styled palace and been greeted with a thirty-one-gun salute, the Viceroy and Vicereine had been plied with a series of garden parties and receptions amidst the lush gardens overlooking the splendid Dal Lake, met countless people, eaten lavish meals – all very charming, but Dickie had not been able to get a moment alone with His Highness. He turned to his host, who appeared to be contemplating the grilled rainbow trout festooned with lemon slices on his wife's plate. The Maharani and Edwina sat across, heads dipping as they ate and conversed softly. Should Dickie whisper in the Maharaja's ear? Amidst the banquet-table babble and tinkling silverware?

Dickie cleared his throat ostentatiously. Which drew him a glance of concern from Hari Singh. Good. Dickie praised the succulent chicken curry. A smile of relief broke on the Maharaja's broad bland face, before he returned to spooning more curry into his mouth.

Dickie was aware of the shock that had ricocheted amongst the princes upon the announcement of the 3rd June Plan. The news that the Raj would end and that each Princely State must join one of the two new dominions of India/Pakistan by 15 August was still being digested. Bhopal had been aghast that the British would not provide rulers with resources to stand comfortably on their feet and leave them instead at the mercy of their erstwhile enemies! Nawab Hamidullah Khan had rejected the entire notion saying, *I don't believe the British will actually leave*. Maharaja Hari Singh too appeared to be labouring under the same delusion.

Dickie cast a look around the room, thick with multiple heady aromas. A live band waited in a discreet corner as fragrant dishes wafted out of the kitchen. Accession was in the best interest of the rulers, he was convinced. No Princely State would be able to stand alone in the world, least of all Kashmir, which had been sliced from the Panjab Durbar and sold to Hari Singh's ancestor by the British to create a buffer from Czarist Russia. How was he to get the Maharaja's exclusive attention?

Stretching his leg beneath the table, Dickie leaned into Hari Singh. His knee came up against something, a tinkle sounded, before a bell rang through the banquet hall. Immediately, the notes of 'God Save the King' started to fill the room. Which arrested banqueters mid-course through the chicken curry and set off an almighty scramble: silverware clattered, napkins were scuffed, chairs scraped as diners struggled to stand. A fit of giggles erupted from across the table. The Yuvaraj, Tiger, couldn't mask his amusement even as the Maharani glared at her son. Edwina was doing her best impression of the stiff British upper lip, which was quivering nonetheless in concealed merriment. Beside Dickie, Maharaja Hari Singh looked mortified, his jowls red. Things had not worked as planned. Dickie had accidentally hit the bell which was clearly meant for the Maharaja to signal the end of dinner with a play of the national anthem of the British Empire.

Dickie swept his arms out in an expansive embrace of the banquet, before clasping his hands together in appreciation and beaming at his host. 'EN-chanting!'

When they were back in their rooms after the eventful dinner, Edwina let off a mighty yawn. 'Such splendid rich food … I could fall into a trance, still smacking my lips.'

'Well, now you have the perfect remedy for your lack of sleep from migraine,' Dickie grinned.

'Think the Maharaja will loan me his chef?'

'In his current mood, he'll loan me anything. Provided, I promise ALL remains the same.'

Edwina paused in slipping off her heels. 'Doesn't Hari Singh want independence? Like Hyderabad and Bhopal and countless others?'

Dickie probed the corners of his pursed mouth. 'I have a feeling that he is loath to take *any* decision. So, status quo.'

Edwina rolled her eyes. 'Exactly the kind of behaviour Jawa accuses the princes of.'

Dickie padded across the thick carpet to the window. In the dark, he could discern the silhouette of the massive plane tree native to Kashmir. What did they call it? Ah, *chi*-nar. Persian for 'blaze' because the tree turned crimson in autumn ... Jawa was a native Kashmiri, too, but his socialist leanings were at odds with the princes. Dickie was glad that the realist Patel was in charge of the States Department. He turned to his wife who was tracing one hand along the intricate tapestry hanging from a wall.

'Mr Patel was quite convinced that Hari Singh would put Jawa in jail if he visited. Considering that Jawa's friend, Sheikh Abdullah, is already imprisoned, I'm glad I offered to come instead, but the Maharaja is not playing ball.'

Suddenly, Edwina's eyes lit up.

What, Dickie queried with raised brows.

'Imagine the fit Jawa would have thrown if he'd been here! An endless rollout of rich food—'

'An army of attendants in shiny gold-and-maroon uniforms!' Dickie chimed in.

'All the vale's beautiful people—'

'Standing in attention to "God Save the King"! While the Maharaja has a fit.' Dickie shook his head. 'Let's hope Ismay can engineer a quick meeting out of the extravagant schedule of receptions and parties.' He knew few men more tenacious than General Hastings Lionel Ismay, his chief of staff, who was accompanying them.

'It'd appear,' Edwina said as she headed for bed, 'that the "King" that needs saving is not your cousin George, but the Maharaja himself.'

A flight of ducks across the Hokarsar Lake, emerald-green necks stretched against the cloudless azure sky. A loud crack rent the air. Two birds dropped like stones from the sky. Plop. Plop.

Maharaja Hari Singh's double-barrelled Webley & Scott shotgun had found its mark.

Having fired the first gun, the Maharaja handed it over to the man standing to his left and took a loaded one from the man to his right, and fired again. The flight of birds was overhead now; two more birds plumbed the blue waters. Passing the empty gun to the left loader, the Maharaja grabbed the reloaded shotgun from the right, took aim at the mallard ducks that had passed him overhead and brought two more birds down. A sharp click followed each bird plopping into the Hokarsar, the Yuvaraj keeping count of the number of kills.

They paused to eat.

Bearers laid out the packed lunch and proceeded to serve Maharaja and Yuvaraj mutton kantis, chicken patties, walnut fudge and a teapot of steaming nun cha. The shimmering waters of the Hokarsar, towering distant pines, birdsong ... none of it was distracting Hari Singh from the pressing matter of Mountbatten. As he chewed on the kebabs, he wondered how the Viceroy's fishing trip was going. He had sent his royal guests to the most scenic spot in his kingdom where the Lidder river came down from Pahalgam; the crystal-clear stream literally flowed through the garden – one could get up and catch fish for breakfast! Indeed, Hari Singh had meticulously planned the Viceroy's entire trip after His Excellency had finally accepted the long-standing invitation: ceremonial arrangements, programmes neatly printed and bound in golden paper with a maroon bow, guest lists and menus worked down to the last detail ... And yet! His cheeks flushed with the embarrassing memory of the band bumbling the British anthem at the banquet. Tch! He turned to his son.

'What did you think of the Viceroy?'

Tiger's eyes sparkled over his plate of patties. 'A handsome couple, nothing stuffy or formal about either of them. I loved how they addressed me as "Tiger"!'

'Because that's how I introduced you,' Hari Singh grunted.

'Sure, Father, but you'll admit the glamorous Mountbattens are a contrast from the last Viceroy.'

'Lord Wavell could be dour.' Hari Singh waggled the fingers of his right hand and a bearer started to pour nun cha. At a shake of the imperious head, the bearer stopped and another stepped in with red wine which he duly served to the Maharaja. Hari Singh took a long sip and sat back in his chair, legs splayed. 'But Lord Mountbatten comes with disturbing tidings ... Do you think the British will leave India?'

Tiger was surprised enough to choke over his bite. As he coughed to clear his throat, a teacup was immediately brought to him and the Yuvaraj took a grateful sip. But the Maharaja was not waiting for his son's answer.

'The Viceroy thinks that now that he's announced pack up, things will automatically fall into place. I accede to Pakistan or India, anger my Dogra base or alienate my Muslim subjects – already they are agitating against tax in Poonch! – but I must do it either way, because independence is not an option. Why, I ask.' Hari Singh fulminated at the horizon. 'I was part of Churchill's War Cabinet during WWII. Kashmir supplied troops for the Allies, troops that helped win the Great War. And *this* is my reward?'

Tiger, meanwhile, ate quietly and kept his counsel. He was aware that his birth in 1931 had made the British unhappy: An heir in place negated the use of 'Doctrine of Lapse', which the Empire had used to annex several Princely States.

'Why should my kingdom be parcelled off to either of Jinnah or Nehru?' Hari Singh quaffed his wine and held up the glass for a refill.

Tiger sipped on his nun cha and listened to his father, whom he used to find absolutely formidable as a child. But at sixteen, he had begun to discern the cracks in that facade. As Tiger chewed on the crushed almonds and pistachios that topped the creamy pink tea, he did think that arresting Pandit Nehru during his last visit to the Valley had been a blunder. The writer of the *Discovery of India* and the leader of the national freedom movement, a native Kashmiri at that, was a man to be befriended—

A loud honking punctured the stillness. The Maharaja rose abruptly, plunking his glass and sloshing red wine on to starched white table linen. A team of geese was approaching the wetlands. An extended right hand beckoning his son, Hari Singh strode forward to where his man stood with a loaded shotgun. Tiger, in awe of his father's shooting skills, grabbed the gold counter and hurried after him. As he took aim, the Maharaja dismissed Mountbatten from his mind. The Viceroy would return from Thricker tomorrow and he would deal with him then. Plop. Plop. Empty gun to the left loader, new gun from the right loader. Plop. Plop.

Thus the relay continued: a whole day spent massacring duck of various species – including wild geese and chakor, the Kashmiri partridge – Tiger clicking the gold counter in tandem. The Maharaja was a crack shot.

The car purred to Srinagar airport, its English occupants quietly nursing their thoughts. Gulab Bhavan had been left behind, its splendour in stark contrast to the dwellings that could now be seen on the banks of the Jhelum river. Crimping into each other, the squalid houses looked set to topple into the river any moment.

'Hari Singh's subjects,' Edwina commented aridly. 'Now, if *they* were seized by colic, I'd understand.'

Dickie, sitting next to her, grunted.

'Say, Pug,' Edwina addressed the chief of staff whose bulldog jaw had earned him the nickname Pug. 'Didn't you start your career with the Indian Army in Jhelum?'

From the front seat where he sat beside the driver, Pug Ismay swivelled to face the Vicereine. 'Jhelum *city*, in Panjab, set on the right bank of this very river downstream. An ancient city, apparently the site of the famous battle between Alexander and the local ruler.'

Dickie turned to his fellow passengers. 'You think Dear Old Blighty is old and then you come to India, which is like an onion with layer upon layer of history and conquest. That's how a Hindu Dogra king ends up ruling a Muslim-majority kingdom. Just about everything is ancient and complicated, even the grudges.' He snorted. 'It's clear to me that Kashmir should accede to Pakistan, just as Hyderabad to India, with perhaps a partition of the state that ensures the smaller Hindu section of Jammu goes one way and Kashmir proper the other. If only the Maharaja weren't so fickle! A colic attack!'

Dickie's five-day visit, packed with fun and festivities, had ended as a political failure. After the banquet, Hari Singh had packed the Viceroy off to a prolonged fishing trip to Thricker with the promise of a meeting just before Dickie's departure to Delhi. Fishing the famed trout and skinny-dipping in the emerald waters had refreshed Dickie. The Maharaja, however, had suffered a suspicious colic attack that ended all hopes of a meeting. Disappointment hung heavy in the purring car.

Edwina rested her right palm on Dickie's thigh. 'Downright foolish of him to abandon this chance for a meaningful discussion.'

'Rather typical of all these rulers; they will do anything to avoid facing a difficult situation. Ostrich-like.'

'Or a fiddling Nero,' Pug said wryly.

The allusion to the emperor who fiddled while Rome burned was not lost on the group.

'Hmm,' Edwina acknowledged. 'That's a bit dire, isn't it?'

Pug rubbed his jaw, his eyes distant. 'I wonder if we have lost our chance of working out a viable political settlement … The Maharaja sits on the fence with dreams of Switzerland for his kingdom. And Mr Jinnah is insistent that the army must be partitioned on communal lines before 15 August. Two new dominions with newly divided armies and an undecided Himalayan kingdom smack in the middle …' Pug massaged his neck and turned to face the front.

The car had left the city of Srinagar behind. Outside, lofty Himalayan peaks pierced the bright sky, a brook tumbled through a meadow dotted with flowers and grazing sheep, a shepherd lay napping in the shade of a chinar. Inside the car, the words of the man who had served as Churchill's chief military assistant during WWII hovered ominous as a thunder cloud.

2

Jammu (July 1947)

Zooni held the Y-shaped frame at arm's length, tucked the rough stone in the rubber holder and pulled the strings taut as she aimed at a bunch of jamun. A cluster of purple berries fell on to the cloth below, strung between the hands of two eager boys. Scouring the rough earth, Zooni grabbed another pebble and shot. Eyeing the bunch as it descended, the boys darted left to catch it, a gaggle of eager onlookers swaying in their wake. Zooni perambulated the base of the tall jamun tree, letting loose clumps of the tart berry which the neighbourhood boys scooped, until their fruit hammock sagged to the ground. Then, it was time to gorge.

When the boys returned home at dusk – fingers, lips, tongues stained indigo – their mothers pretended to berate them, threatening no dinner unless they washed up. *This Zooni*, they clucked. The mothers were envious as well because Zooni Aapa was as popular as the madari that came to their Reasi with a bear that performed tricks. At least, they didn't need to shell out money to Zooni!

Giddy with their loot, chanting thank yous, the boys now swept to a hillock to start the feast. A grinning Zooni made her way down to the riverbank with some jamuns she had grabbed from the hammock. Her favourite spot, where she could dangle her legs and watch the bubbling brook below, reminded her of home: the low-roofed house in Baramulla she had left eight months ago as a bride, her bamboo-slim body clad in red silk, as tall as the groom, who was twice her age and had the spent look of an ex-soldier. It was a good match. Zooni's parents were poor, Masud Ahmed had a pucca house in nearby Reasi and a desperate need for a young second wife, the mehar adequate. In her mind, Zooni wandered to the yard where her parents reared buffalo, sheep and goats, to supply milk to the city from their village on the Jhelum. In Reasi, people spoke Urdu-Panjabi, not Kashmiri: Moul was Abba, Mouj Ammi, even the river was called Chenab. But the rivers were all one. Moul said they tumbled from high up in the mountains and spread out to water the land before ending up in the ocean. That comforted her, now that she was at a remove. Zooni bit into a jamun, reliably tart, and sucked her teeth. She had seen the river all her life; placid on some days, roaring on others, it spoke to her.

Her mind wandered to the small plot of land where her Gujjar family grew chillies, tomatoes, capsicum and onions, that she tended. Greedy birds she scared away with her trusty catapult, the one she had carried with herself to her husband's house. The thought of Masud Ahmed soured her little idyll. She spat the jamun out whole.

The evening light would fade soon. Zooni should be heading back. She had cooked dinner, cleaned the kitchen, swept the courtyard, filled the earthen jar with water, but still Koko Jan would find some fault. Even though their husband wasn't expected till late that day. He had gone to Poonch for some meeting with his ex-comrades, other demobilized soldiers of the Great War. A crusty man, he usually returned sour and angry from such meetings. *The Maharaja was a tyrant, he was looting them in broad daylight, he had raised taxes yet again, the men must band together to fight!* After dinner, he would go to the rooftop to smoke a hukkah whilst the women finished up. Then he would descend upon Zooni on the bedroom cot, a rough hand playing with her golden hair, grunting and thrusting till his seed was poured into her. When he rolled off and started to snore, Zooni would rise gingerly to rub butter on her bruised thighs and bitten lips before wearing her salwar. Masud Ahmed was in such a hurry to sire a son that Zooni got no off-days except when she bled monthly. On those days, it was Koko Jan's turn to receive his seed, and hope to get lucky and trump the new young bride. Thus far, no luck for either woman.

Zooni sighed and stood up. As she brushed her kameez, a head popped out from behind the mulberry tree. 'Why are you hiding?'

The boy smiled shyly. Five–six years of age, probably. Grabbing the catapult, Zooni walked up to him. 'Can't speak?'

He shook his head, then pointed with his right index finger to the catapult. Before lifting his arms to mimic the slingshot action.

'Go ahead.' Zooni held out the catapult.

The boy took it gingerly, examined the base, the rubber tubes, pretended to aim, but he clearly had no idea how to use it.

'Tomorrow, I can show you how it is done.'

He hopped in delight.

'Okay.' Zooni set off with a wave of her hand. She traversed the undulating ground until she reached the pond beyond which was a clutch of houses, including hers. Birdsong and woodsmoke was in the air, the sky starting to blush. Fireflies flickered in the weeds that rimmed the pond. Zooni was at her wooden door when she heard running feet. Swivelling around, she realized the boy had been following her all along. With a quick smile, he darted into the neighbour's house, a firefly in his wake. A large Hindu family lived there, multiple adults, many children, but she hadn't seen this child before. Visitors, perhaps? Mulling over this, she opened the door and stepped into the yard. A shudder swept her spine. Koko Jan was by the earthen stove, dutifully stirring the milk cauldron. Masud Ahmed sat cross-legged on the cot eating dinner. His eyes bored into her.

'Marjani! What kept you so long?' Koko Jan thrust the ladle in her direction.

Zooni, eyes lowered, head hastily covered, hurried into the kitchen. The catapult, clutched against her chest, she kept hidden under the folds of her long mulmul dupatta. She could feel Masud Ahmed's eyes on her.

'I send you to deliver the atta in the next lane and it's like you went to Sialkot!' Koko Jan continued with her rant.

'Where had you sent her?' Masud enquired, his voice that of a thanedar.

Koka Jan smacked her forehead with her left palm. 'Afshana Bibi, the Chaudhary household, had some grain she wanted ground fresh. For the baby who's recovering from dysentery. So I put this stout filly to work. Didn't her mother say Zooni is fit as a fiddle because of grinding grain on the chakki and churning milk every morning?'

In the kitchen, Zooni set about stacking the washed vessels. With a toss of her chin, Koko Jan indicated the roti basket. Zooni approached her husband with it.

'Fit to deliver an army of children, supposedly, which is why I married the filly,' Masud Ahmed retorted as his eyes roamed over his young wife's supple body. Zooni offered more roti, but he pushed his plate away. As she began to gather the utensils, he grabbed her wrist and locked eyes with her. 'The fertile older sister has delivered three, four, children, I hear … I'm hoping the old Gujjar hasn't saddled me with a barren filly.' He let go of her hand and began to massage his whiskers, twirling the pointed ends.

Birds flew across the darkening sky as the two wives finished their chores. Meanwhile, Masud Ahmed stretched out on the cot and spoke his thoughts aloud as he habitually did upon return from a meeting with ex-soldiers. 'Something big is coming … The Angrej are going to leave soon; Hari Singh is losing his guarantor… Angrej Sarkar has given him permission to join India or Pakistan. Now, Hari Singh the Hindu will obviously join the Gandhi topiwale, but we Poonchis have brethren in Pakistan …'

The two women exchanged looks. Zooni massaged the red ring on her wrist before starting to ready the hukkah, as Koko Jan ladled roti-sabzi for the two of them. Her nose-pin glittered in the dim light. With a gulbadan like Koko Jan at home, Masud Ahmed had settled for Zooni, the bamboo with golden hair. Because Koko Jan, despite her obvious beauty – doe eyes, dewy lips, body like a rose – had not carried a baby, not even a stillborn one, after eight years of marriage. Baanjh, the word was hissed when the neighbourhood women spoke of her. But Zooni and her saut, recipients of their joint husband's nightly exertions, shared an unspoken thought: Who was sterile really?

'LISTEN!'

The women stood to attention. Clearly, they had missed replying to some loud rumination. Masud Ahmed indicated the neighbour to their left and lowered his voice conspiratorially.

'Keep your distance from them. They have relatives … newly arrived from Laur, carrying stories of Muslim atrocities …' He spat on the packed mud floor, bunched up his tehmet, and swung his legs off the cot. 'In any case, they are not our type. Just stay away.'

The women gulped, nodded, and huddled down.

Masud Ahmed yawned. He climbed the steps to the rooftop and Zooni trailed behind with the hukkah. A waft of jasmine arose from the harsingar tree in the courtyard. She set the water pipe beside a low-slung chair and made to turn when her husband spoke again.

'Have the bed ready.'

3

Srinagar (August 1947)

Hari Singh rolled the die and mechanically moved the checkers on the backgammon board. But for the sudden rain, he would have been at Dachigam before sunrise – the cold air fragrant with the aroma of pine, his pulse quickening as they made their way through the forest in search of the hangul. It was rutting season, the best time to catch the magnificent Kashmir stag, which was notoriously shy. A sixteen-pointer would make an excellent wall mount in the recreation room—

'Father,' Tiger grinned, 'you aren't going to last long if you play without focusing on the consequences!'

Hari Singh grunted, eyed the board, the raindrops bouncing off the paved walkway, before exhaling wearily and sitting back in the chair. India and Pakistan had become independent, yet Pakistan's citizens were pouring into Kashmir. What was the point of this freedom?

'Jammu on your mind?' Tiger's voice broke into his thoughts.

'Hmmm ... Jammu's becoming a refugee thoroughfare as Panjabis flee both sides, carrying their stories of violence ... infecting us with their communal virus.'

Tiger who felt a familiar urge to scratch his leg, damn that cast, clenched his fist and tried to distract himself. Intelligence reports arriving from the frontier areas of Poonch and Mirpur, as well as the Sialkot sector, were speaking of massacre, loot and rape of their villagers by aggressive hordes from across the border. Father worried that they were losing control of the outer areas as Mother hovered about wanting to know more. Yesterday, Father had handed a report to him and asked him to explain it in Dogri to the Maharani. Tiger felt the back of his neck growing warm at the recollection: He was trying to find an acceptable equivalent for 'rape' when Mother had enquired why he had turned the colour of ripe shahtoot!

Meanwhile, at a flick of the Maharaja's hand, a bearer had surfaced with a silver case from which Hari Singh had withdrawn a cheroot which he puffed desultorily.

'But the Valley continues to be peaceful, right, Father?' Tiger attempted to buoy up his father's mood. 'And Gandhiji himself said that in the darkness engulfing India, the only ray of light seems to come from Kashmir.'

Father grunted. The smell of tobacco and wet earth wafted over them. Tiger angled his chair to stretch out the leg in plaster. He recalled Bapu's visit on 1 August at 5 p.m. Mother, Father and he had met Bapu under a tree in the garden. In a low, lisping voice, Bapu had urged Father to ascertain the wishes of his people, take the people into his confidence and to align himself *with* rather than *against* them. It was a monologue, and after about ninety minutes, Gandhiji had got up to go. Mother had pressed him to partake of some milk and fruit, but he declined because it was not his eating time—

'So he did,' Father said, thrusting his cheroot in the air as he made his point. '"The Maharaja must take the will of his people into account" – so the departing British and the arriving Indian government have decreed. Did the British consult the people of Kashmir when they sold the state to my ancestor Gulab Singh for 7.5 million Nanakshahi rupees? Hmmm? Because kings and queens and maharajas rule by diktat! What's this newfangled nonsense!'

Tiger was sixteen, his hip cast in plaster, education disrupted on account of ill health and yet … yet Tiger felt that Father was not grasping what had begun to be evident to him, clear as the crystal waters of the Lidder, that contemporary reality was shifting. But it was not something he could voice, so he attempted afresh to bolster his father. 'We have signed Standstill Agreements with both India and Pakistan.'

Hari Singh blew a ring of smoke and returned his gaze to his son. 'With Pakistan, yes. But Jinnah is not satisfied, clearly. He's begun squeezing essential supplies to force my hand … An economic blockade. And India wants me to send a representative for further discussions. Talk, talk, talk!' He snorted.

A rustle and Thakur Nachint Chand entered the room with a summon. The only person who could summon the Maharaja was the Rajguru, of course, and the Thakur's prime responsibility of late had been as the intermediary between the Rajguru and the King. The Thakur was the Maharani's brother – Maharani Tara Devi was deeply religious, and Hari Singh had watched with some dismay as the brother's influence had mounted. It was now at the point where Rajguru Swami Sant Dev, whom Hari Singh had banished when he ascended the throne, had staged a mysterious comeback and was now installed in Chashmashahi Guest House in Srinagar.

Backgammon having been abandoned already, the cheroot having burnt to a glowing stub, Hari Singh stood up. His brother-in-law grabbed the handles of his nephew's wheelchair and began to steer it down the hallway, following at a discreet distance behind the Maharaja.

Whilst feigning attention to his uncle's useless patter on rainy weather, hip pain, and the chanting of certain mantras, Tiger tried deduction. An only child, and not a particularly fit one, he was accustomed to solitary pursuits of the mind. A non-religious man had become a devout disciple of Swamiji, sitting for long periods on the ground before him, never smoking in his presence. How?

The party entered the cavernous hall. Swamiji, pink-complexioned, forehead glowing, sat in his customary place atop a cushioned dewan. Mother sat by his feet, head covered with her saree pallu. She turned at their appearance and smiled briefly, before concern filled her eyes at her son's debilitated appearance. Maharani Tara Devi seemed to take Tiger's use of the wheelchair as a personal failing and held Doctor Mirajkar, the eminent Lahore surgeon, culpable for her son's conversion to a cripple. Tiger hated having the hard cast, which started at his waist and went all the way down to his toes, the itching underneath for which there was no relief, and needing assistance to go to the lavatory ... What was worse though was the grief in Mother's eyes and the injured pride in Father's. Sigh!

'Come, son,' Swamiji hailed with an extended arm.

Maharaja Hari Singh bowed low, hands clasped, and squatted at his guru's feet, across from his wife. Tiger's cast spared him from having to sit cross-legged on the floor.

'You look troubled,' Rajguru surmised.

Hari Singh nodded. 'The state is in trouble.'

'Pray how?'

Swamiji's eyes crinkled with humour – or was it inner wisdom? Tiger couldn't quite fathom. Often the guru appeared to be afloat in some spiritual realm unconnected with earthly matters. Perhaps it was the opium he consumed regularly? But Swamiji had managed to bring down Father's smoking and drinking and anger, and also brought his parents closer together.

'*How?*' Father couldn't hide his incredulity. 'Kashmir is caught between India and Pakistan; surely you are aware.'

Rajguru smiled benignly. 'And you, son, you are caught, too?'

Hari Singh shrugged.

Rajguru looked up, swung his head around the room, taking in the distant vista of the snow-capped Himalayas, shimmering in the misty air. His eyelids drooped, and he went into dhyana.

Sometimes his head started to nod as he meditated. Tiger waited, as did his parents and uncle. A bulbul tweeted with maddening insistency. The air of the hall, incense-laden, fragrant with roses, felt oppressive. The itch crept up Tiger's thigh.

'I see a vision …' Rajguru's dulcet voice floated down. Everyone perked up.

'A powerful, beautiful, soulful vision … A vision that sweeps me from our Valley, over glacial Himalayas, adrift over our Jhelum–Chenab, from tall chinar trees and flower gardens, cherry orchards and saffron fields to wheat and mustard fields, to the grand plains of Panjab criss-crossed with five rivers, to the great city of Lahore … Where your great ancestor Maharaja Gulab Singh strode with pride a century back. Hari Singh,' Swamiji's eyes blinked open, 'you recall?'

Hari Singh smiled and nodded. 'And his illustrious brothers, Raja Dhyan Singh and Raja Suchet Singh.'

Tiger knew the story, having heard it on numerous occasions. Gulab Singh was the founder of their Dogra dynasty. He had such influence in the court of the Sikh Maharaja Ranjit Singh that his brother Dhyan Singh was the prime minister of the Sikh empire—

'And what do I see?' Rajguru's eyes were wide open. 'I see the Dogra flag flying in Lahore, all the way from Srinagar, the whole swathe under you.'

The Maharani couldn't contain her excitement. Clasping her hands together, she gushed at Swamiji's vision. 'Such an auspicious sighting must be celebrated!' Tara Devi cast a happy glance at the menfolk, her eyes sweeping past her husband and brother until they settled on Tiger. '*Jaijaiwanti*, son?'

Swami Sant Dev, a connoisseur of classical music, favoured that particular raag. He also liked it when the Yuvraj, devoid of the plaster, would visit him frequently and regale him by singing that song.

As Tiger wondered what would be easier, to rehash the raag or demur, Swamiji urged him on and, in anticipation, closed his eyes. Tiger launched into *Jaijaiwanti*. As he sang the lilting and lively raag, punctuated with sombre notes, he couldn't help recalling that the song conveyed the double-edged nature of achievement: For every joy, there was a compensating sorrow. To get his young charge to understand the complex emotion, his guru had explained: *Imagine a King who learns that he has won a mighty battle, but also lost his son on the battlefield.*

Meanwhile, Father's eyes were heavy-lidded as he allowed himself to revel momentarily in Rajguru's vision.

4

Jammu (August 1947)

The tick in Masud Ahmed's left cheek got more pronounced with agitation.

Right now, it hopped like a caged bird as he supervised his wives wrestling with the vast iron trunk that sat on four bricks in the storeroom amidst assorted household items: a sewing machine, earthen pitchers, spare string cots inclined against a wall. Thick winter quilts were being dug out on a monstrous summer day when the heat in their hilly region rivalled that of the plains. Sweat beaded Koko Jan like dew on a rose as she strained to hold the heavy lid upright. It ran in rivulets down Zooni's bamboo body, curling her golden hair into tendrils that escaped her thick braid, as she dug out the padded blankets.

'Stop!' Masud Ahmed commanded.

Gingerly, he lowered a rifle wrapped in sheet on to a quilt, grabbed another quilt and spreadeagled it atop the gun. Patting it, he grunted for Zooni to layer yet another quilt on top. Then he took another smaller gun, wrapped in one of Koko Jan's dupattas, and repeated his steps. As Zooni grabbed the remaining quilts, folding and arranging them all to fit within the trunk, Koko Jan groaned and Masud Ahmed frowned. Finally, when the lid wouldn't close, he ordered his wives atop the trunk as he latched and locked it. Tucking the keys in a crevice inside the sewing machine, he ordered everyone out and locked the storeroom, too. That key he pocketed in his shirt.

'Not one squeak,' he commanded his wives before heading out purposefully, his leather juttis rustling on the parched courtyard floor. Gone for the night for another mysterious meeting. The women slumped down on the cot. Six in the evening and the cloudless sky was still ablaze. Grabbing the handheld cloth pankhi, Zooni fanned Koko Jan and herself. 'You think other men are hiding their guns, too?'

'If they have sense enough. Our Shahji always says that a soldier and his rifle are meant to be together. Like a needle and thread. What sense is there,' Koko Jan blew air through her mouth, 'in handing guns over to the Maharaja's police? If the Dogras have all the weapons, how will we stay safe?'

'But if the police takes all the guns, then there will be no weapons left to fight with,' Zooni countered.

Koko Jan smacked her forearm. 'Entire Jammu–Kashmir is smouldering like a dung pat! Don't you listen to anything Shahji says?'

Zooni paid no attention to Masud Ahmed's declamations, nor addressed him reverentially, as if he were the lord of the house or herself. Eyes lowered, mouth shut, legs splayed was how she dealt with him. Koko Jan's reservoir of affection for him intrigued her. Maybe the older woman had known him when he was as fresh as puffed bread; Zooni was only acquainted with a crusty bajra roti.

'Tch! So many Poonchis, Mirpuris, Reasis served in the Great War that the Maharaja is alarmed they will fight him. Like they fought the increase in taxes. So take away their weapons and render them useless, eh? And guess what?' Sotto voce, Koko Jan confided, 'Yesterday night, after Shahji had finished his business, he told me. A group of ex-soldiers is going to Rawalpindi to speak with the Muslim League in order to plan for the days ahead. They suspect,' she cast a quick look around before hissing, 'that the confiscated guns are being given to Hindu–Sikh families for self-defence. Hain! What about our defence?' Her eyes glittered.

Zooni wasn't impressed with Masud Ahmed's pillow talk, even less with Koko Jan's giddy assessment. Before she could reply, the older woman dismissed her.

'Get me a bowl of buttermilk, ni.'

Zooni was in the kitchen when a head popped over the courtyard wall that was common with the neighbour to the left. Bibi Pyari, gold earrings swinging, greeted Koko Jan who sat fanning herself on the cot. 'How are you, sister? It's been a while.'

'God's been merciful,' Koko Jan beamed.

As the women exchanged banalities, Zooni detected the brittleness beneath her saut's demeanour. There was past acrimony between the two women unrelated to Masud Ahmed's recent injunction. Had Bibi Pyari, matriarch of a large family, been the one to label Koko Jan baanjh, saddling her thus with the ultimate sin of her gender? As Zooni stepped into the yard Bibi Pyari clucked at her.

'What magic have you cast upon our little one? He returned crying from play because his gulel instructor didn't turn up. Here,' she hoisted the boy over the wall, his legs dangling, a catapult clutched in one hand. Handing the bowl to a bemused Koko Jan, Zooni hurried to catch the boy. Bibi Pyari disappeared with alacrity. Koko Jan sipped the buttermilk and cast dagger eyes at her.

'So?' Zooni jogged her brows at the boy. 'Have you been practicing?'

Nodding, he dug pebbles out of his kurta pocket and started to aim at the wall. A hail of pebbles clinked in the yard. Zooni sat down on the cot, feeling the need to explain. 'Jugnu here is very keen to—'

'Jugnu!' Koko Jan scoffed. 'The mute's name is Shokey.'

'Shokey?' Zooni considered this. She recalled the firefly trailing the boy that first evening she'd met him. 'I like Jugnu better.'

'Well, you're not his mother.' Koko Jan smacked her lips, thrusting the empty bowl into Zooni's hand. 'And I'm relieved to know that you aren't meeting a secret lover the evenings you venture out, like some lissome lass still eligible for marriage!'

Zooni twisted her mouth. Koko Jan didn't understand her need to get out and sit in solitude by the river, but she didn't stop her as long as the chores were done. On some days, she even saved Zooni from their husband's wrath. Meanwhile, Jugnu was waiting for her. Zooni showed him how to perfect his technique by keeping both rubber strings equally taut. She adjusted his arms, making them parallel and he giggled, wiggling his thin body. With a stern face, Zooni caught his upper arms and started to tickle him, vigorously. Shrieking, he squirmed and tried to escape. His puny arms were no match for her as she hoisted him up and swung him in the air, their laughter filling the courtyard. Reminding Zooni of her Boi, born to her mother in dotage, as Moul joked with great affection, his eyes fixed on his young son who tailed Zooni everywhere. Koko Jan, stretched out on the cot, swivelled to watch them, a smile escaping her. Before she started to wrinkle her nose and snuffle.

'Zooni, ni, did you leave the stove—'

A crackling sound erupted as the pungent smell of burning floated through the air. Koko Jan bolted upright. From outside came shouts, hurrying feet … Gunshots ripped the air! Zooni hurried with Jugnu to the wall and hoisted him to his side where people scampered in panic. From her elevated position, she could see the clutch of burning houses in the distance. Koko Jan was bolting the entrance door. Breathless, the two women sought the safety of the master bedroom. At the threshold, Zooni caught the older woman's wrist.

'What if they set our house afire?'

Koko Jan gulped. Their breathing shallow, both women scoured the house. *Courtyard? Rooftop? The shed?*

The shed! With its rear door, which was seldom used because it opened on to hilly scrubland where foxes roamed. Grabbing their footwear and dupattas, in case they needed to escape, the women took shelter in the dark shed, their hearts rattling as shots punctuated the gathering dusk.

5

Murree (September 1947)

Akbar Khan, director of weapons and equipment at GHQ, Pakistan Army, shook his head in disbelief.

Three weeks into Pakistan's independence, its critical organ was dangling outside as if the new nation was an invalid soldier whose intestines, gutted by shrapnel, had spilled out. Kashmir was an integral part of Pakistan: not only did it account for the 'K' in the nation's name, it was the essential buffer the fledgling needed from its imposing neighbour. One glance at the map was sufficient to show that Pakistan's military security would be seriously jeopardized if Indian troops came to be stationed along Kashmir's western border, the vital 180-mile long road and rail route between Lahore and Pindi forever exposed!

He had driven up to Murree from his office in Rawalpindi for a critical meeting. Summer was over; yet, the hill station near the Kashmir border was swarming with people carrying tales of woe. The Maharaja's state troops were committing atrocities against Muslims, forcing them to flee to the nation created anew. But Jammu–Kashmir *was* Muslim-majority

– surely non-Muslims should be the ones seeking refugee? Akbar Khan snorted as he ascended the steps to the tea room. A bearer bowed deferentially as he made enquiries. The high-ceilinged room smelled of tea and butter. Several tables were occupied by English ladies, conversing over scones and cucumber sandwiches. Akbar Khan couldn't help noticing the incongruity of his situation. He was meeting a Kashmiri subversive in a genteel relic of the Raj over high tea! Absurd, but practical. Sardar Ibrahim and he were unacquainted, the meeting arranged by a common friend, the spot was always busy, which offered little chance of being eavesdropped upon. Now, Akbar Khan strode towards the table at the far corner where an earnest young man, clean-shaven, with thick wavy hair, sat with his fingers crossed on the table.

Sardar Ibrahim Khan was not a man for small talk. 'The time for peaceful negotiations is over, Akbar Bhai. Every protest is being met with repression. You know what happened in Bagh on Pakistan Day? People who raised the flag of Pakistan—'

Tea arrived, as ordered by Akbar Khan upon entering. Sardar Ibrahim tapped his long fingers as the waiter served them and bowed away.

An impassioned Sardar Ibrahim ploughed on. 'And why not? Isn't Kashmir part of Pakistan? Wasn't that the promise? So Baghis who celebrated our new nation were shot at by the state troops! They fired on crowds in Poonch, Reasi, and burned houses indiscriminately ...' His agitated hand almost knocked over the tiered serving tray with its pastries and mini sandwiches.

As he sipped on fragrant tea, Akbar Khan studied his companion. Ibrahim was unknown in Pakistan, but the other known leaders of the Muslim Conference were all rotting in the Maharaja's jails. And the Lincoln's Inn–trained lawyer was the one behind the July resolution, which had called for the state of Kashmir to join Pakistan. Because of Hari Singh's chicanery – signing a Standstill Agreement with Pakistan and terrorizing Muslims in the interim – people had risen in revolt! He well understood the sentiment of Sardar Ibrahim Khan, a Pashtun like him.

'We need weapons to protect ourselves, our women and children …' Ibrahim ran an anxious hand through his hair. 'Otherwise, the Maharaja will hand us over to India!'

Returning the cup to the saucer, Akbar Khan asked, 'How many rifles do you need?'

'Five hundred, to begin with.'

Akbar took a deep breath and exhaled. Ibrahim might be a Sadozai Pashtun descended from the legendary Ahmad Shah Durrani, but he had no idea about actual fighting. Five hundred rifles would barely liberate a village, leave alone the largest Princely State of India. But, he massaged his chin, procuring even that number was difficult …

'So, can you help?'

'Brother Ibrahim, I certainly intend to. However, the big question really is whether our government can be moved to take an active hand in this affair—'

'*Tch!*' Sardar Ibrahim shook his head. 'Kashmir is linked with Pakistan, like azaan is with a mosque. Inextricable. Indivisible. Kashmir's only trade route, open through the year, is the road coming into Pakistan at Kohala and Muzaffarabad. Kashmir's timber, our main source of income, goes by the Jhelum river to Pakistan. Kashmiris, an overwhelming majority of whom are Muslim, want to join Pakistan. What then is the government of Pakistan waiting for? For Kashmiris to leave their homes in kafilas?' He shifted his gaze to the Mall Road below, crowded with refugees – a sight unimaginable three weeks earlier, when the premier artery road was forbidden to non-whites.

Sardar Ibrahim pursed his lips and leaned forward to make his closing argument. 'A merchant is not a merchant without goods to trade. A Jatt is no Jatt without land to till. A Pashtun is no Pashtun without guns to fight with.' He paused, his nostrils quivering.

A wail rent the air. On the Mall Road, a woman, surrounded by bundles and baggage, was beating her chest with her palms as she mourned some loss.

'So, I ask again,' Sardar Ibrahim hissed, 'can the director of weapons help me procure guns?'

Back in Pindi, Akbar Khan made enquiries about weapons that could be obtained. There was no time to squander; yet, the Muslim League was vague about the exact nature of the support it could offer. A large part of the Pakistan Army's share of the reserve stock of weapons and ammunition was still lying in India. Had the stock been in Pakistan, there would still be no possibility of parcelling out some for the Kashmir cause unless the government ordered the commanders-in-chief to do so. But the chief was English and not to be taken into confidence. What then?

Akbar Khan cranked his network for information. Colonel Imtiaz of the Ordnance Corps popped up with a name: *Malik*. A soldier who fought in WWII, he had organized various militia run by his former colleagues, and was the man credited with fuelling the arson and attacks in Lahore. Unlike other armed bands, whose leaders called themselves general or field marshall even, Malik was just 'Malik': a shadowy figure who wasn't into self-promotion or meetings. But could he deliver?

Akbar Khan didn't want to be saddled with weapons purchased from the NWFP arms bazaars instead of military-grade rifles. Plus, he had a sizeable order, ten times what Sardar Ibrahim had requested. The Maharaja's army was estimated to be 9000 strong, of which the 2000 or so Muslims would desert – or stay passive – once an armed revolt was launched. The remaining 7000 troops were scattered through the large state. Sardar Ibrahim and his fellow Kashmiris, many of whom were ex-soldiers in west Jammu, armed with 4000–5000 rifles would be able to overcome the state troops. His own WWII experience with the 14th Battalion in Burma at the crossing of the Irrawaddy had taught him the value of the whole nine yards. Choppy waters, snorting mules, night skies lit up with flares and gunfire ... The British were advancing upon the Japs, who had pulled back into Burma after failing to invade India and the great Irrawaddy river was the largest natural obstacle in their path. With no specialized transport available, the army had to cross with crude rafts in short order as the Japs counter-attacked. In the end, it was the longest opposed river crossing attempted in any theatre of WWII – and that had won Akbar a distinguished service award.

Akbar Khan insisted on meeting Malik. Colonel Imtiaz, who had seen action in Egypt with Malik, arranged it. Malik chose the location: an abandoned cowshed on Ferozepur road, ceiling blackened, pillars charred. The stench of burned flesh pervaded the humid air. In a brick room, with a lone lamp waging a battle with dusk, sat the cryptic Malik, his face in the shadows. Akbar Khan greeted him, got no response, so he perched on the lone chair there and came straight to the point.

'You have 4000 military rifles for sale, I believe?'

Malik watched from the moorah on which he sat, his legs wide open, taking up space.

'Rifles that were condemned as unfit for military use.'

With no answer forthcoming, Akbar Khan cleared his throat. This man used silence as a weapon. He had no option but to persist. 'Colonel Imtiaz of the Ordnance Corps—'

'What's your interest in faulty weapons?'

Malik's voice was unexpectedly soft. Akbar leaned forward, resting his elbows on his knees. 'But the weapons aren't faulty, right? Just condemned. Old stock? A clerical error?'

'What makes you think so?' So soft, like a Burmese python moving noiselessly through the jungle.

'They were waiting to be transported to Karachi to be thrown into the sea. Yet, you secured the stock.'

'It's a large consignment. And an expensive one.'

So it was. But Mian Iftikharuddin of the Muslim League was keen to get Kashmir's accession to Pakistan, and had committed support. A horn blared from the roadside, intruding upon the gentlemanly dance going on in the room. You first. No, you first. Neither man showing his hand. Akbar decided it was time to ram through.

'We need it in order to support Kashmir. Our Kashmiri brethren are under attack from the Maharaja and his Dogra troops. Don't you want to help?'

'Everything's fair in war … And love, eh?' Malik gave a hollow chuckle, full of self-loathing.

Akbar Khan recalled hearing something about star-crossed lovers … How Malik's fiancée had died in sectarian killing, precisely the kind he was facilitating now.

'There are two sides to every war,' Malik said. 'Yet, each side believes it is right. What is fair, what is just, what is not …

Too much confusion. So, I leave wants and wishes and hopes and pieties out of this business. The business of killing.' Malik shifted on his moorah. 'You know the price. Colonel Imtiaz will have instructions for the exchange.'

The director of weapons knew when he was dismissed. 'Inshallah,' he said and arose.

'Why bother god with everything?'

Malik's laconic voice followed him as Akbar Khan strode out.

'Some tasks are best left to men.'

6

Srinagar (September 1947)

The chinar trees had turned russet, living up to their name, setting the whole of Kashmir ablaze. This year though the metaphorical fire – which had greeted invading Persians the autumn they entered India, duping them into thinking they were riding into a blaze – was literally raging in the state.

In the eastern wing of Gulab Bhavan, Maharaja Hari Singh, Maharani Tara Devi and Thakur Nachint Chand sat listening to the radio. Normally, the centre of activity – where courtiers and advisers assembled, and where the family of Maharaja Hari Singh spent the balmy autumn days playing ludo, backgammon, or rummy – today, the room was bereft and a sullen air prevailed.

Discontent is growing … The Jammu and Kashmir state forces are dangerously over-extended … Mirpuris and Poonchis are tied to West Panjab through family and faith …

'Ji,' Maharani Tara Devi addressed her husband, 'please reconsider what Thakur Nachint Chandji has advise—'

'Just as he advised me to believe wholeheartedly in Swamiji's visions?' Hari Singh snapped.

Nachint Chand extended a conciliatory palm. 'Perhaps Rajguru made an error … Swamiji sees a lot and knows a lot, but things are also happening so fast … besides, you haven't met him in weeks now, perhaps he has a new vision to share—'

'No! No more visions.'

'Okay, then how about exploring the option of acceding to India?'

Hari Singh watched his brother-in-law with narrowed eyes. 'How is that advice different from Kak's?'

Aghast, the Maharani tugged on her pallu and said briskly, 'Prime Minister Kak was advising us to accede to *Pakistan*! Advocating treachery to our faces! Which is why you had him resign and—'

'And now he's secure under house arrest and no more a menace to us,' Nachint Chand concluded. 'However, we must decide to move firmly to India's side. What do we have in common with a Muslim nation?'

'Besides our very large number of Muslim subjects?' Hari Singh enquired softly.

Nachint Chand wiped his chin and pursed his lips.

'Seems to me you are in need of a lesson, Nachint. Kashmir is a complex state, geographically and socio-culturally. We have boundaries with India, Pakistan, Afghanistan, Tibet … and we are within kissing distance of Russia. Why were the British so vested in Gilgit, you think? As far back as 1935, they pressured me to lease Gilgit Agency to them for sixty years!' Hari Singh locked his gaze with his brother-in-law. 'Hmm?' When no answer was forthcoming, he stood up and started to walk, hands locked behind his back.

'To complicate matters further, we have diverse ethnic and religious groups: a majority of Sunni Muslims in the Valley, Sunni Muslims and Dogra Hindus present equally in Jammu,

Buddhists in Ladakh, Shia Muslims in Gilgit. As long as Pakistan was just a thought, we could continue as usual. But now the virus that was wrecking India is destroying the state forces, too! Regiments composed of Rajput Muslims from Poonch and Mirpur have gone to the side of Pakistan; the remaining are strung out in penny packets along the hundreds of miles of state borders from Gilgit in the north to Mirpur in the south. Reports have come in that Pakistani nationals are entering our borders and preaching revolt in the name of Islam; Sattis and Sudhans, whom we had disarmed, have suddenly found themselves new modern rifles! And Hazara tribesmen are surfacing in Poonch for jehad against Kashmir!'

Hari Singh signalled for his cigar case and lit a cheroot.

Tara Devi exchanged a look with her brother. Patting her multi-strand pearl necklace, she sat up. 'The storm, as you rightly say, is directly over our heads. With Kak, Pakistan thought it had Kashmir in its pocket. Now that you have sent a clear signal, the Pakistanis are stirring up trouble. Which is why we need a new Prime Minister, a wise counsel, one respected by India's leaders, who can present our case to Panditji.'

She paused to assess the impact of her delivery. Hari Singh puffed briskly on his cheroot and nodded.

'You recall, I journeyed to Lahore in April to sound out Justice Mehar Chand Mahajan for the position of dewan of Kashmir?'

'Mahajan refused,' Hari Singh said with a brusque wave of one hand. 'After which, he was made a member of the Panjab Boundary Commission.'

'Yes. With Independence, the commission was dissolved.' The Maharani licked her lips. 'So I wrote to the justice and invited him to visit us—'

'Here! In Srinagar?'

'Ji. The rains have played havoc, but he arrives tomorrow.'

Hari Singh went still, cheroot smouldering in hand, eyes narrowed. Then hurriedly snuffing out the cigar, he clapped his hands, strode towards his companions, pulled up a chair and sat down abruptly. 'Excellent! Excellent! Justice Mahajan will be just the right person to convey my message to India's Prime Minister. Which is that India must accept Kashmir's accession *without* insisting on a referendum or any other step of internal administrative reform. The first is of immediate necessity; the second, we will choose a suitable time.'

'Maharaja,' Nachint Chand cleared his throat, 'will the justice be able to convince Panditji, who is adamant that Sheikh Abdullah be brought into the government?'

'Ah!' Hari Singh beamed and draped an arm over his brother-in-law's shoulders. 'Which is where my household minister comes in. You are already accomplishing the initial task of moving the leader of the National Conference from jail to one of our very fine bungalows – Sheikh Abdullah will no more be an enemy, but an esteemed guest. Right? Now why do you think I ordered that?'

A bearer entered to announce that Victor Rosenthal had arrived.

'Ah, Victor!' Hari Singh's face lit up at the mention of the man who handled much of his jewellery and foreign investments. 'Tell him to wait ... And yes, inform Tiger – likely Victor has some books for him.' Turning to his companions, he again queried, 'Why? Why this leniency towards a man who has been stirring up trouble for me since the year an heir to the throne was born?'

Thakur Nachint Chand listened with a bowed head. The Rani watched with furrowed brow.

'Because with the Muslim Conference in Kashmir styling itself on the Muslim League, the peace of Kashmir will be disturbed as they poison the minds of the public. However, the other party, National Conference, is allied with the Congress. And its leader, Sheikh Abdullah, is friends with Prime Minister Nehru. Whether we remain independent or join India, we *will* need the Sheikh's cooperation.'

Hari Singh sat back in his chair, massaging his hands. Rain was drumming the rooftop, striking glass panes, sloshing down drainpipes. He turned to the Thakur.

'Which is why, as household minister, you must ensure that Sheikh Abdullah is appeased enough to write a letter to the Prime Minister of India stating that he's reconciled with us. Jolly him along while we wait for the storm to pass.'

7

Lahore (September 1947)

The fact that Akbar Khan had managed to source 4000 rifles had won him an invitation to meet Prime Minister Liaquat Ali Khan at Government House at 6 p.m. The major came with his plan: 'Armed revolt inside Kashmir.'

He had prepared it at the behest of Mian Iftikharuddin, the influential president of the Panjab provincial Muslim League. Iftikharuddin had returned from Kashmir convinced that Kashmiris were unlikely to be able to freely exercise their choice – in which case, the Muslim League *must* act to help them. Akbar Khan had consulted Sardar Ibrahim as he fleshed out his plan. Any action would have to be of an unofficial nature, no Pakistani troops or officers could take active part.

At the conference, Akbar recognized Sardar Shaukat Hayat Khan, a minister in the Panjab government. Beside him sat Zaman Kiani, a senior member of the former Indian National Army. Copies of Akbar's plan were already in the hands of some, he noticed. As the tea service ended, Liaquat Ali Khan walked into the conference room and took his position at the head of the table.

'Sardar Shaukat Hayat Khan,' the Prime Minister extended his right arm at the minister, 'will you share your plan with the team?'

Akbar was taken aback. *Another* plan? He tried to catch Mian Iftikharuddin's eye, unsuccessfully.

'The plan,' the minister rubbed his hands together as he spoke, 'is two-pronged. One: Incursions into Jammu from across the Panjab border. Two: Raise a tribal force to attack Kashmir from the north. Now, the incursions will be led by ex-INA soldiers under the command of Mr Zaman Kiani.' He indicated a man who sat across from him, knees splayed, head cocked. 'And north of Rawalpindi, the sector will be under the command of Mr Khurshid Anwar. The operations in two sectors will be under my overall command.'

Akbar listened with interest. The minister had seen action in the Middle East theatre with the British Army during WWII, and was a well-known favourite of the Quaid. Additionally, his mother was Kashmiri. Qualification enough, Akbar guessed, to lead the operation. But the reason Akbar was also seated at the table was because *someone* was interested in *his* plan, too. That someone had to have Liaquat's blessing. It was critical that Akbar married his plan to the minister's. Clearing his throat to draw attention, he addressed the Prime Minister directly.

'Sir, I commend Khan saab's plan to strengthen the Kashmiris internally. An open interference by Pakistan is undesirable, so our efforts ... *incursions* ... must be to equip the local Kashmiri effort. Sardar Ibrahim has been in constant touch with me and he appreciates that we will be equipping his fighters with rifles.'

The Prime Minister was studying a file, Khurshid Anwar quelled a yawn whilst Zaman Kiani spun a pen.

Akbar paused to drink water, unsettled by the casual air of the conference.

Mian Iftikharuddin checked his wristwatch and declared, 'Time for another round of tea–coffee.' He beckoned the bearer standing quietly by the closed door.

Akbar resumed. 'I must emphasize that there are *two* items which need our serious consideration: the Kathua road and the Srinagar landing ground. Here's why. As we begin assisting the Kashmiris, it is critical that the Maharaja is not reinforced by India. Therefore—'

The door swung open and a couple of bearers entered with trays. As they set about serving tea or coffee, Akbar Khan sat down stiffly. Snacks accompanied the hot brews: a plate of cocktail samosas and another laden with barfi. The Prime Minister's personal assistant entered, whispered in his ear and the two left the room. Small talk that the conference members were engaged in grew louder as they partook of sweets and savouries and sipped tea like they were at some wedding reception. Finally, Liaquat Ali Khan returned and the meeting resumed.

'You were saying, major,' the Prime Minister gazed at Akbar Khan, his bald pate shining in the tube light.

Scraping his chair back, Akbar Khan held up his plan and pointed to the map. 'The road from Kathua to Jammu is an unmetalled fair-weather track through broken country. A determined band of guerrillas could prevent the passage of armed civilians. Organized movement of Indian troops, however, would be a different matter—'

'As yet, there appears no likelihood of that.' Liaquat Ali Khan frowned.

'Sir,' Akbar Khan acknowledged.

With a raised arm, Zaman Kiani asked to intervene. 'In a month or so, the area will be muddy with rains, and then in December the snow in Banihal Pass will block the entrance to the Valley. Should we then be so concerned?'

Akbar Khan slapped his right palm on the table. 'Precisely why it is critical that we make this road inaccessible to India for the next few weeks. If India misses that window of opportunity, it is out of action for months! Srinagar airport – that's the second thing we should consider. A couple of hundred armed men, with good sniper skills, will seriously discourage the landing of Indian transport aircraft—'

'Do we have that many rifles for distribution?' Khurshid Anwar squared his shoulders as he sat upright, elbows on the table.

'Out of 4000 rifles, I propose we send 1000 for the Kathua road, 200 for Srinagar, and the balance 2800, we distribute over the rest of the area adjacent to Pakistan's borders.'

'Excellent plan, major,' the Prime Minister declared. Adjusting his round-framed glasses, he gazed at the seated men.

'Inshallah, we shall rescue Kashmir from India!' Shaukat Hayat Khan added.

Akbar Khan liked the enthusiastic response as he sat down. The minister now broached the allotment of funds and how much was to be allocated to which efforts. Iftikharuddin voiced concerns over the allocation to the National Guards and sought Liaquat Ali Khan's opinion. As the three men deliberated over funds, Akbar Khan, Khurshid Anwar and Zaman Kiani exchanged looks. It was nearly 9 p.m. and they were yet to discuss the many operational details of the campaign plan.

Akbar decided on a toilet break. As he washed hands at the sink, his face stared back at him: bushy brows, heavy-lidded eyes, long slim nose, small mouth, the overall dreamy look he tried to mask with a thick moustache and a stiff demeanour. He was wiping his hands when Khurshid Anwar walked up to him. 'I thought you should know. I have no intention of accepting any orders from Shaukat Hayat Khan.'

'Wha-*aa*t?'

Anwar dipped his hawk-like brow.

'But that will lead to complete chaos! The only way this plan works is if we have complete cooperation between all the moving parts … Which are too many to begin with.'

Anwar stroked his moustache. 'I understand your concern, brother, but leave my part to me. I know what I am doing.' Saying this, he strolled back to the conference room.

A disgruntled Akbar returned to find the leaders still debating fund allocation. Civilians overseeing a military operation was not looking like a sound idea …

Finally, the Prime Minister addressed the room. 'Shaukat Hayat Khan and Major Akbar Khan will jointly plan and pursue the operation which will be a great success, inshallah …'

He droned on, and Akbar Khan realized that the nitty-gritty of military op, ammunition, communications, and command and control would not be discussed. The conference ended with much bonhomie and the men headed to their official cars. Shaukat Hayat Khan beckoned Akbar Khan to walk with him. Head dipped conspiratorially, he confided, 'Since we are to work together, I thought you should know that I have absolutely no confidence in Khurshid Anwar.'

Akbar's jaw fell open. Ahead of them, Liaquat Ali Khan was getting into his car.

'We need to immediately stop the Prime Minister and get someone else in place of Khurshid Anwar!'

Shaukat Hayat Khan sucked his teeth. 'Just understand that Anwar is the choice of the concerned authorities ... Nothing can be done at this stage.'

'But, Khan saab, how will we succeed without—'

The minister patted Akbar's upper arm benignly. 'Such pessimism, major. We have just wrested independence from the British after a hundred years. And we have achieved a new homeland. Any minor hindrances, we'll overcome.'

In the car ride back to Pindi, Akbar Khan rubbed his chin. There were serious problems with the operation even before it had even begun. Too many cooks were meddling with the plan for armed revolt within Kashmir ... And the cooks had knives buried in each other's backs!

8

Srinagar (September 1947)

'The Treaty of Amritsar was a sales deed. With the ending of the Raj, the deed is terminated – meaning the people of Kashmir have the right to decide their own sovereign.' Sheikh Abdullah studied the brick floor, a sprig of grass escaping from a crevice.

'It is not *I* who needs convincing.'

Seated across from him on a wooden chair, Begum Akbar Jahan regarded her husband.

Abdullah snickered. When the Maharaja and his Prime Minister had clamped him in jail and launched an offensive against his 'Quit Kashmir' movement, how had the Begum answered? She had stepped out of the seclusion of home and begun touring villages, keeping hope kindling in the hearts of Kashmiris. He raised his head.

'No, not you, my love. I hear entire villages turn out to listen to you.'

'Now, now, don't go about trying to win me with flattery,' Begum Jahan chortled. 'We all know who the orator in the family is.'

'All because of Ammi.' Abdullah sighed, a distant look in his eyes. 'My earliest memories are of my mother sitting on the prayer mat, hands raised in prayer. How pure and innocent she looked; after namaaz at night, she would tell me stories of emperors and fairies, and I would ride the clouds with them, scaling the heavens, savouring another world, not one more beautiful than ours – no, what can be? – but one where people got to eat wheat, not chaff!'

Begum Jahan reached out to touch her husband's forearm. Mothers were precious to all, more so to a boy who never knew his father, dead two weeks before his birth. 'She'll be happy to know the path she set you on has brought you to great heights—'

'Detention camps of Maharaja Hari Singh himself!' Abdullah chuckled.

'Sher-e-Kashmir! What the ordinary Kashmiri – shawl-weaver, saffron farmer, houseboat-owner, shepherd, shopkeeper – calls you.'

'Which is why I should be out with the people. Our stance is perfectly valid, legally just and morally correct. And the reason why I launched the Quit Kashmir movement. Instead, here I've been for the last fifteen months – Military Hospital, Badami Bagh, where the Maharaja detains those who disagree. How intimately I have got to know it over the years!' Abdullah snorted. He didn't know where to even begin from when enumerating the injustices the average Kashmiri suffered. Being called a Hindu state when 85 per cent of the population was Muslim. Being hailed as a paradise by the world, yet Kashmiris having to flee to the dusty plains of Panjab to eke out a living. Being master craftsmen, yet penurious. As the son of a shawl-weaver, he had first-hand knowledge of the sub-human existence that Dogra domination had wrought through heavy taxes on artisans.

'It's *because* the Lion of Kashmir is imprisoned that the valley of flowers is afire. More and more Muslims are courting arrest.' Begum Jahan shook a rueful head. 'The whole state is a prison now …'

'People realize the unfairness of the transaction of one hundred years ago – Kashmir was sold for 75 lakh Nanakshahi rupees to Raja Gulab Singh. Less than 5 lakh pound sterling changed hands and sealed the fate of over 40 lakh men and women, and their land of milk and honey. Imagine! All the National Conference is doing is to—'

'—challenge the political and moral status of this sale deed, this instrument of subjugation, handed by the East India Company agents to a bunch of Dogras.'

He turned to his wife, admiration in his eyes.

'You've trained me well,' she giggled, the rickety chair with a loose back creaking as she shifted her weight.

'Yet, here I am, incarcerated in jail for nine years … well, three consecutive terms of three years each.'

Outside the corridor where they sat on two chairs, bulbuls hopped in the puddles of rain left from the morning showers. Abdullah shook his head. 'Tell me about the children. How is my dearest Khalida?'

'Missing you, as always. There's something to be said about a first child. She's been managing the household since I started venturing out. And Farooq is her right hand, of course.'

The father smiled as the mother shared snippets about their five children, ordinary acts which a regular father should not miss out on account of being imprisoned. But ever since

1931, when the Sheikh had launched the movement for the independence of Kashmir, he had become a regular in Hari Singh's prisons. In 1931, 13 July had the same impact on their movement that the massacre at Jallianwala Bagh had on the movement of Indian independence, as the Sheikh liked to say. The Dogra rulers had unleashed a reign of terror: martial law imposed, hundreds thrown in prison, people made to crawl on their bellies …

Begum Jahan cradled her husband's hand, coarse as rough-hewn wood. '"Quit Kashmir" is spreading in the Valley like wildfire. Even Bapu was encouraged by the spirit of our people.'

He smiled. When Gandhiji had visited some weeks back, not only had Begum Jahan attended his prayer meeting, she had participated in it by reciting the Quran.

'Gandhiji's advice to me was simple: Courage.' Begum Jahan sucked her teeth. 'I remind myself daily of that.'

The lump in her throat returned as she studied her husband in his shabby prison clothes, days-old beard, permanently creased forehead. She lowered her head. What if the tall, handsome science graduate from Aligarh Muslim University had been able to find a government job in Kashmir? What would their lives have been like, today? The commanding presence – six feet, four inches, marvellous at oratory, incapable of obsequiousness – had instead steered his way into political activism, challenging the Dogra regime on behalf of his oppressed people. As her husband liked to say: He had no choice in the matter, destiny had intertwined his future with Kashmir.

'Begum?' Abdullah enquired softly.

He couldn't help noticing the sniffle that his wife had masked by rubbing her nose. She was his true friend and comrade. Patiently facing all the trials he had brought her way, running the house single-handedly, never complaining. When the granddaughter of the Swiss proprietor of Srinagar's prestigious Nedou Hotel tied the knot with the Valley's revolutionary, did she know that Abdullah would one day be this towering leader? If the children completed their education notwithstanding his continued absence from the domestic scene, he would owe it to her. Content to be a homemaker, she had now been dragged into politics.

Begum Jahan smoothed the kameez over her lap, as if ironing out her life. 'News from my parents in Lahore confirms that Panjab is passing through hell. And refugees are pouring into Kashmir. Jammu is particularly—'

'The Poonchis are fighting to have their grievances addressed. And the Maharaja refuses to listen. Typical of him. The question, however, remains: Should Kashmir accede to India or to Pakistan; or should it maintain its independent identity?'

'What do you think will happen?'

Sheikh Abdullah raised his hands skywards.

'If we accede to India, Pakistan will never accept our choice, and we will become a battleground for the two nations. Besides, the Muslim League is dominated by feudal elements which is an anathema for our peoples' vision of a "New Kashmir", where every man and woman, irrespective of religion, is equal and must have the same chances. But India is different. There are individuals in India – Gandhiji, Jawaharlal Nehru – whose views are identical to ours. By acceding to India, then, wouldn't we move closer to our goal? The third choice obviously is an independent Kashmir. But to keep a small state independent while it is surrounded by big powers is impossible ...'

A hoopoe bird's song filled the air. It had landed in the quadrangle beside the corridor and hopped about in the moist grass, pecking the ground with its pointed beak. The Abdullahs watched their visitor with interest.

'A kettle of kahwa is all we need to imagine we're picnicking in Gulmarg as we agonize over these questions,' Begum Jahan mused.

'Only our bodies are imprisoned. Our minds are out there, prancing in the sunlit world outside.'

'Sheikh sahib,' Begum Jahan smiled indulgently, 'some days I think—'

Footsteps hurrying down the corridor arrested the conversation. A constable informed them that the superintendent was arriving. Sure enough, the senior officer, baton in hand, followed.

'Sheikh Mohammad Abdullah,' the officer said imperiously, chin jutting out. 'As per the orders of Maharaja Hari Singh, you will be moved out of this camp.'

Husband and wife exchanged a glance.

'Moved? Where to?'

'To a bungalow.'

'A bungalow ... Hmmm.' Sheikh Abdullah pondered. Distrust of the ruler and his administration was deep-seated. He was a child when famine had struck. Since their mohalla was outside municipal limits, they were not eligible for rations. The people of the mohalla had approached the food department which sent an official to enquire. When the officer asked who the leader of the mohalla was, people pointed to Abdullah's older brother, Sheikh Mohammad Khalil, a well-respected resident. The officer took one step towards him and gave him a resounding slap. All were stunned. Abdullah realized then that this was the officers' method of dispensing justice to common people. Now, unconsciously, his left hand moved to his face; the stinging slap still smote him.

'Get ready to leave soon!' the superintendent rapped the baton against his left palm.

'Either way, I remain a guest of the Maharaja. What's the difference?'

'Count your blessings; you will not be in prison any longer.'

'In prison … imprisoned …' Sheikh Abdullah muttered as the officer strode away. He leaned towards his wife. 'It appears to me, Begum, that Hari Singh might have begun to feel the winds of change. Muslim soldiers are deserting the state forces in Poonch and Mirpur. Pakistani irregulars are crossing the border. Jinnah's economic blockade is squeezing the Maharaja. Perhaps he's keen to get the National Conference on his side?'

An unconvinced Begum Jahan rubbed her hands. 'How many times has the Maharaja made promises of a representative government and not kept them?'

'Perhaps he's realized that he cannot suppress a popular movement. Either way, time to move, hmmm?'

Taking his wife's hands in his, Abdullah recited a shayr in his honeyed voice; one which had first revealed his talent at recitation of the Quran in childhood and later won over Kashmir with oration that challenged Hari Singh.

'Safar zindagi ke liye barg-o-saaz
Safar hai haqeeqat hazar hai majaz.'

Quoting couplets was her husband's mode of conveying his thoughts, something she had learned during their brief courtship, most of which he had spent interred in Udhampur from where he wrote to her regularly. And Iqbal was one of his favourite poets.

The essence of life is motion
Motion's real, rest, illusion.

He squeezed her hands. 'The future has arrived, Begum. We must brace ourselves for the challenge ahead.'

9
Jammu (October 1947)

Early evening, Koko Jan washed Masud Ahmed's feet with akk leaves. The milky sap was a good balm for the nicks and bruises that her husband sustained on the nightly excursions he led as a militia leader of the Azad Army. Maharaja Hari Singh was sitting on the fence about joining India or Pakistan, but Poonchis had already decided. Bands of ex-soldiers were fighting state troops and defeating them – not only in Poonch and Mirpur, but even in Muzaffarabad!

Ensconced in a cane chair, Masud Ahmed pulled on his hukkah. The gurgle of water and sweet smoke filled the courtyard.

In the kitchen, Zooni rolled out thick rotis sprinkled with salt and chilli to pack for Masud Ahmed's next foray. He expected to be away for a few days. His absences from home were a mixed blessing. Zooni was spared the exigencies of the marital bed, but was also forbidden from venturing out of the house except to gather firewood. Days were shorter, the jamuns were gone, the chinars were dressing up in their finery mindless of the distinctly non-festive air. And Zooni had started paying attention to Masud Ahmed's declamations. In the sprinkling of arms and ammunition, Murree, Pindi, volunteer forces, Sardar Ibrahim, General Tariq, Bhimber, Muzaffarabad, Zooni hoped to glean something about Baramulla, her hometown, and learn how her family was doing. Thus far, nothing. When she had enquired on this with Masud Ahmed, he had lifted his head like a king cobra and told her to mind her business. Zooni stacked the thick, hot rotis and started to slather each with ghee. The canister of home-made butter was one of the items from the booty that Masud Ahmed brought home regularly from his forays. After all, 'General' Masud was a powerful local leader fighting for the freedom of Jammu–Kashmir from the tyranny of the Maharaja. Zooni did not know about all that, but the quilts had been removed from the trunk, the guns retrieved, and its cavernous hulk was filling up with assorted goods. As she licked ghee off a finger, Zooni snorted: A band of brigands, that's what Masud Ahmed actually led!

Time for departure. The hukkah's gud-gud had stopped, replaced by a rustle of footwear as Masud Ahmed gathered his weapons. Zooni sprang up to hand him food for the journey, Koko Jan lit a four-wicked diya in the nook, and both women stood to attention as he barked orders.

Slinging a gun on each shoulder, the general departed.

The courtyard was radiant in the mellow noon sun of autumn as Koko Jan sat on a low stool applying ubatan on her limbs. The paste of oil-turmeric-gram flour was a luxury she indulged in infrequently. But with Masud Ahmed away for days and fewer household chores therefore, Koko Jan could leave the ubatan on as she stretched out on the string cot, her face shielded by a mulmul dupatta, sparrows twittering around the harsingar tree, bathwater steaming on a cauldron in the kitchen …

'Zooni,' Koko Jan said to her saut who sat on the cot, threading the jasmine flowers the harsingar shed at night into a string.

'Hunh,' Zooni said without raising her head.

'Still thinking of your family? Didn't I share with you what Shahji told me? There is *no* fighting going on in Baramulla. And Srinagar? Why, the Valley is where Hari Singh resides! You think any harm will come to those who live there?'

Zooni sighed. Kashmira would be okay, she agreed. Her sister's in-laws lived off Dal Lake, their houseboat hosting white people, who flocked to the city, as well as local nobility. But the thought of Baramulla, the low-roofed house with her parents, younger brother, buffaloes, sheep and hens and the vegetable patch, was always on her mind. Perhaps because she could no more sit silently by the riverbank and think her thoughts. On nights that Masud Ahmed was away, she snuck up to the rooftop. Under the twinkling stars, everything felt small – the house, their village, the distance to Baramulla. Some nights, she sighted what appeared to be giant glow-worms pulsing on the horizon. Another house or village burning. Distressed, she headed down, feeling even more trapped.

'Zooni, ni?' Koko Jan tapped the cot. When no response was forthcoming, she tried another tack. 'Your Jugnu is late today?'

Zooni examined the torn stem of a jasmine, put it aside and picked another to thread. 'His mother wanted to bathe him. Guess she had the same thought as you.' With raised brows, Zooni pointed to Koko Jan's bare arms and lower legs turning golden with drying paste.

Koko Jan moved closer as she whispered, 'What about their plans for Udhampur? Weren't they supposed to be gone already?'

'Hmmm, Jugnu's father got held up in Laur, Rani said. Imagine selling house and business in this time!'

A chuckle sounded as Jugnu's head popped up over the boundary. Grinning widely, he straddled the wall. Beside him, his mother appeared, a cloth-covered bowl in one hand. Hurrying, Zooni grabbed the boy from his underarms and set him on the packed mud floor.

'For you both.' Rani smiled at the two women, extending the bowl. It smelled of roasted semolina and ghee. A quick look beneath the cover confirmed it was halwa indeed.

'What for?' Zooni asked.

'It's happy news.' Rani's smile widened as she tugged her dupatta forward and tucked it behind her ears. The nun-like headwear did nothing to diminish the charm of Jugnu's mother, whose pomegranate cheeks and fair skin even Koko Jan had remarked upon with undisguised envy.

'Come tell us all about it, sister,' Koko Jan cooed. 'Happy news is meant for sharing.'

Basking in the autumn sun on a cool day had lifted her saut's spirit, Zooni thought as she headed to unlatch the front door. Rani entered, wearing a khaddar salwar-kameez and settled on the cot.

'Jugnu's father arrives tomorrow, finally. You know how anxious we've been for news of him.' Relief flooded Rani's face.

'Here.' Koko Jan scooped some halwa out and held it up to Rani's mouth. 'May Allah grant him a long life.'

'Yes, sister, that's all I wish for.' Rani clasped her hands together, eyes half-lidded as in prayer. 'Parwardigar, keep everyone safe in these times—'

'*Aapa, Zooni Aapa!*'

Jugnu's urgent hailing punctured the solemnity as the women turned to the boy standing like a warrior, feet apart, arms taut, the catapult set to wreak havoc on its target.

'Count, okay?' Jugnu nodded briskly at his engaged audience before returning to concentrate on the wall where Zooni had drawn concentric circles in coal. For every pebble that hit the smallest circle, Jugnu won a point. Which wasn't too often. But since his training began, the boy had at least mastered the technique of hitting the broad target and to avoid spattering the wall.

Zooni kept one eye on Jugnu as the women chatted amiably in Sialkoti Panjabi.

'We leave for Udhampur the day after tomorrow,' Rani said. 'Our Reasi is safe, but the news coming out of neighbouring Mirpur is scary.' Her surma-lined eyes clouded. 'Bhai Bagga says that the area is being cleared of Hindus, Sikhs, Dogras.'

Zooni caught Koko Jan's eye and looked away hurriedly. Both wives of General Masud knew that the loot accumulating in their large trunk was not donated, nor was any militia in the business of brotherhood. Zooni didn't know to lie so she left Koko Jan to offer comfort with pleasantries. The gathering storm was plucking people from their homes; raging rumours had reached Reasi, but the handful of non-Muslim households had been counselled by their Muslim neighbours to stay quiet and let the storm blow over. Bagga, Bibi Pyari's eldest son, had sought out Masud Ahmed some weeks ago. The two had shared a hukkah on the rooftop. After which Bagga had departed, stroking his henna-dyed beard in satisfaction. Meanwhile, Jugnu aimed for the circles, his lower lip jutting out in concentration, the black kohl mark prominent on his forehead. Rani must have dipped a fingertip in her surma-lined eye to anoint her freshly bathed son with a black mark to ward off the evil eye.

Afterwards, the women shared the sweet as Jugnu explored the courtyard. Navratri, the nine-day festival, would soon arrive and Rani was looking forward to being in Udhampur with family.

'In Sialkot,' Koko Jan said, 'when Dassehra and Eid fell one after another, there was great festivity in our city. New clothes, shops full of sweets, phool makhana, Eid sevaiyyan … this year too, Eid is right after Dassehra.'

The cloud of steam in the kitchen caught Zooni's eye. The water must have boiled to half! With her chin, Zooni indicated the cauldron to Koko Jan who examined her yellow-crusted limbs.

'Hai,' Rani said, fingers on her chin, 'I have delayed you, sister Koko Jan! We must get going.' She hailed Jugnu and made to rise. Jugnu raced to the cot, picked a jasmine string and draped it around his neck.

'Na!' Rani shrieked and plucked it away. Jugnu, stunned by the vehemence, dug his face into his mother's kameez. 'Wearing a garland of harsingar,' she explained to the women, 'it's inauspicious.'

A giant roar sounded as Zooni hit the water. She plunged in, the river dragging her down. Thrashing her hands and feet, Zooni struggled to wrest free of the waters. The clamour was endless. Trying to breathe, she fought to surface—

A gasping Zooni sat up in bed.

It was the old memory. She breathed lungfuls of air, reminding herself that she had survived the tumble into the Jhelum, which had swept her along until she got entangled in weeds. That the five-year-old did not drown was considered the handiwork of the River Pir, saint of the river, who floated on the Indus river on palla fish and in whose praise folks sang '*Dama Dam Mast Qalandar*'. Zooni was awake now, but the racket was still on … She hurtled from the bed into the courtyard where Koko Jan stood, mouth open in horror. Bibi Pyari's house was under attack: flaming torches, shouting, wood splintering, shrieking, shots! The two women cowered until Koko Jan grasped Zooni's wrist and pulled her into the shed. Shivering, biting their lips, hugging their chests, they hunkered against the rear door. A child's scream rent the air.

'Jugnu,' Zooni sobbed. She started for the door.

'Don't be *mad*, Zooni!' Koko Jan hissed. 'Think they will spare you?'

Tears coursing down her face, Zooni cracked the door open and stepped gingerly into the yard. Crouching, she climbed the steps to the rooftop on all fours until the neighbour's quadrangle came into view. Clamping her mouth shut with both hands, cowering to stay hidden, she watched, stricken by the sight. Slashed bodies lay on the floor in pooling blood, limbs twisted in aborted escape. Men were ransacking the rooms and making away with household goods. A woman screamed … *Rabba!*

Rani begged with folded hands as Jugnu stood in front of her legs, arms outstretched to guard his mother. A burly man, rifle in right hand, face covered with the end of his turban, slapped Jugnu away with the back of his left hand. The boy spun to the floor. Rani shrieked. He lunged at her neck and started to drag her inside. 'No-no-no,' Rani tried to dig her heels into the mud floor. At the threshold of a room, he stopped and swivelled his neck. Jugnu, arms taut, catapult in hand, was raining stones on his mother's aggressor. The man laughed, let go of Rani who stumbled to the floor, and addressed Jugnu.

'Here!' The man rested his gun against a pillar.

'I will walk to you, slowly. If one stone finds my,' he jabbed an index finger into his forehead, 'you get your mother back. Okay?'

On a harrumph, the man started to strut towards Jugnu, feet planted wide, chest out, a rooster advancing upon a wriggly worm.

Rani sobbed on the ground, whimpering, arms extended in a plea.

Jugnu the warrior, lower lip thrust forward, kohl-mark smeared, eyes burning, kept plucking stones from his shirt pocket and firing. The man walked through the hail, cackling. Until he reached Jugnu. One swift arm snaked out, clutched the boy's neck in a vise, hoisting him up. Jugnu's eyes bulged, his tiny feet thrashed, the flailing arms slackened, the catapult slid to the floor. Then Jugnu was tossed aside like a dead fish.

Zooni bit the heel of her hand to prevent the almighty scream from tearing out of her.

10

Srinagar (October 1947)

Late evening on 24 October, Tiger lay in bed reading Maupassant, *Great Short Stories*, a gift from Victor Rosenthal as he tucked into a Swiss chocolate – another present Victor had brought him. Gulab Bhavan lay quiet, the merriment tonight was at City Palace on the Jhelum where Maharaja Hari Singh was holding Dassehra Darbar, which family and members of staff were attending. Tiger could visualize the resplendent gathering under the richly decorated papier-mâché ceiling, musicians providing entertainment, chandeliers ablaze, silks and brocade, pearls and rubies glittering as the nobility paid obeisance to Father—

His room had gone dark.

Tiger sat up in bed. Indeed everything had! His suite on the ground floor directly overlooked Dal Lake. The lamp-lit promenade, manicured lawns, walkways … all had blacked out. This had never happened before. He gave it a few seconds to revive, minutes … No. The room stayed as dark as a clouded night sky. For no reason, Tiger felt his throat constrict. He gulped. A howl tore through the darkness. The book fell on to his lap as Tiger scuttled against the bolster. Howls filled the room, curdling the night air, freezing his blood. His tongue darted out, he licked his dry lips, he tried to reason his way out of his alarm. It was jackals, that's all, jackals howling as they were wont to; didn't the forest come right down to the back of the palace? Hadn't Father once shot a panther from the main lawn, and the visiting Maharaja of Bikaner shot a bear from his bathroom window? *One bare body against another!* someone had tittered. Tiger chuckled at the recollection, a forced sound that subsided without providing any comfort. In the pitch darkness, the cacophony of the jackals rose and fell, an orchestra that was thriving on the darkness that had seemingly descended upon entire Srinagar. Why were the lights not coming back on?

'Koi hai?' Ashamed at his squeal, he shouted, 'ANYbody?'

No footsteps padded into his room. Tiger manoeuvred his body out of the bed, easing the stiff plaster-cast right leg first until his foot found the carpeted floor. Reaching out, he grabbed the wheelchair and pulled it close. His heart was hammering inside him, from fear not exertion, he knew. Two days ago, news had arrived of serious trouble on the border. Father had ordered Brigadier Jamwal to go to Uri and fight to the last man and the last bullet. He had sent reinforcements that very morning. He had also sent the deputy prime minister to Delhi with two letters. A request for arms and Indian Army troops to help repel the invaders. The other was Father's offer to accede to India on the same terms as those being offered to the Nizam of Hyderabad, the other large Princely State that had yet to choose accession to either of Pakistan or India. But had the brigadier failed to stop the advancing hordes? Were the kabailis in the capital? Had the worst happened?

Gritting his teeth, Tiger tried to steer his body into the wheelchair which he usually got into with the help of two attendants. His hands were clammy, fear sprouting in sweat on his body, the chair slipping and sliding. Again, Tiger tried to haul his bulk on to the seat, gripping the arms as he swivelled his body, the chair shifting despite the carpeting. When his bottom was finally on the chair, he shuddered. Then he started to steer it towards the door.

Inky darkness.

Death and destruction were in Srinagar, our smug world has collapsed, the wheel of destiny has turned full circle …

Rubbish! Get a hold on yourself, Tiger!

The grand Darbar Hall had its own generator, in which case nobody would have noticed the blackout. Was there even a blackout? Perhaps it was just the palace? Besides, it was Dassehra, the auspicious day when good triumphed over evil. What could go wrong? Mother had marked the nine days of Navratri, leading up to it by praying, singing devotional songs, lighting earthen lamps, and practising what she preached by including Harijan girls among the nine young women worshipped on the last day. Tiger felt his spirit bolstered. *Poise,* he reminded himself, his guardian's life lesson. The remarkable Pandit Kak had honed on to the insecurity that afflicted the Yuvraj, an adolescent diagnosed with muscular atrophy, with a stern, distant father and no adequate role model. *The greatest quality one could develop was 'poise', a calm imperturbability in the face of any circumstance*. Now was the time to exhibit that quality, Tiger determined, and wheeled his way into the hallway. It was close to midnight, the Darbar should have ended—

A sudden commotion erupted outside … A flurry of feet … Bobbing light from petromax lamps … Car doors banging …

The kabailis had captured and destroyed the only power house that supplied electricity to the capital, located at Mahura, 35 miles away on the main road from Domel to Srinagar. The invasion was progressing to plan: to celebrate Eid at Srinagar.

Father had returned ashen-faced and grim from the Darbar. Guests had tumbled from the glittering hall into darkness, the entire city shrouded, jackals howling, and pandemonium had erupted. Now Father, Prime Minister Mahajan, and other men were huddled in a closed-door meeting. Mother's large eyes had lit up with relief at the sight of Tiger. But after squeezing him to her bosom, she had set about collecting all the ladies and families of the staff, organizing their feeding, and putting them up for the night. As he watched her calming frightened women and reviving Mrs Batra, the wife of the deputy prime minister, who had had several fainting fits, Tiger understood anew the meaning of poise.

Daylight brought no respite, but more rumours and more panic.

Lorry-loads of tribesmen were hurtling down to Srinagar to massacre the city's Hindus and Sikhs. The kabailis numbered 2000, no 26,000. Mobs of black-turbaned and blanketed men were seen rushing through Uri bazaar. The road to Srinagar was filled with terrified refugees. Tongas were in big demand as people looked for escape routes to Jammu, an astronomical 200 rupees was the going rate for transport. Owners of houseboats on Dal Lake were selling the little cook-boats attached to them since people looking to flee could pole the small craft upstream; heavier boats wouldn't be able to hide in streams or narrow canals. English and American tourists on houseboats and at the Nedou Hotel were being besieged for their European clothes, an effective disguise. The police had vanished from the streets ...

Prime Minister Mahajan was in telephonic communication with Brigadier Jamwal who had had to fall back from Uri. He had ordered the blowing up of bridges to slow down the raiders, but nothing seemed to stop the mountain fighters, who, in the rocky gorges of the Kashmir valley, were in their element. Many state Muslim soldiers had switched sides and were leading the Pathans now. Father and the Cabinet discussed what military action they could take at this last moment to save Srinagar. At disposal was a cavalry battalion, Father's personal guards and a disbanded company of Muslim soldiers.

The situation was perilous.

11

Delhi (October 1947)

At York Road, the tents housing the refugees in his garden now covered every square inch of land. Jawahar had not been able to prevent people from leaving their homes. Liaquat and he had toured West and East Panjab, both prime ministers putting up a joint front in the face of the escalating civil war. They had chastised Muslim leaders in Lahore, laid into the Akalis in Amritsar, but communal feelings had spread to Delhi. From the bathroom window, he watched smoke curling from one of the makeshift brick stoves. Bitterness pooled in his mouth. The Nizam of Hyderabad's countless rounds of negotiations even as Razakars grew more militant daily. Perhaps Vallabhbhai was right: The Nizam was *not* the master in his own state—

'Papu?'

Indu knocked discreetly at the bathroom door. He rolled his shoulders back. He really should be getting back to his guests, the Siamese foreign minister and Governor General Mountbatten—

'Papu!' Indu rapped the door. 'It's urgent.'

He flung the door open. 'What is?'

Indu's forehead was creased as she indicated the foyer with her chin. 'An envoy has arrived from Kashmir, with letters from Maharaja Hari Singh. I'll keep the guests entertained with small talk, but please hurry back.' Saying which, she scurried to the living room.

R.L. Batra, the Maharaja's deputy prime minister, looked like he had frozen atop one of the region's Himalayan peaks. His complexion white, he greeted Jawahar with a mute namaste, two envelopes clasped within his folded hands.

Jawahar read the letters. The foreboding he'd been carrying over the state of affairs of Panjab and Delhi, the volte-face by Junagadh, the recalcitrance of the Nizam of Hyderabad, now rocketed with the contents of the mail. *Raiders were rushing to invade Srinagar, having already entered the state of Kashmir … Requesting arms and Indian troops to repel them* … In the second letter, the King offered to accede to India.

Jawahar spun on his heels and, as unobtrusively as possible, pried the governor general away from the living-room conversation. Waving the letters, he hissed, 'News has just arrived of a large-scale invasion of tribesmen from the North West Frontier Province into Kashmir! And a cry for help from the Maharaja. We need an urgent meeting of the Defence Committee to decide India's response.'

The next morning, 25 October, at 11 a.m., a special meeting of the Defence Committee began. An official report had arrived from General Lockhart, commander-in-chief of the Indian Army, who had been informed by headquarters, Pakistan Army, in Rawalpindi that some 5000 tribesmen had entered Kashmir three days earlier, and had seized and burnt down the town of Muzaffarabad on their way to Srinagar.

Vallabhbhai regarded the committee members, a severe look on his face. 'The invasion has been timed with the clear knowledge that India will have great difficulty coming to the aid of the Maharaja. The road from Panjab is terrible at the best of times; now snow will soon close the mountain passes. Hari Singh's army is distracted with the fighting in Poonch, the road to Srinagar lies undefended and if the Pathans take Srinagar airfield ...' The home minister's scowl deepened.

What was left unsaid hung in the air: Kashmir would be seized by force, regardless of the ruler's decision or the people's inclination.

'We have received information that supports General Lockhart's report.' Jawahar pursed his mouth before continuing to address the committee members. 'An advance guard of tribesmen travelling in trucks has reached Uri after seizing Muzaffarabad, where Muslim soldiers of the *Maharaja's* army shot their commander,' he glanced at the sheet of paper on the table, 'Lt Col Narain Singh, and joined the raiders. Many Hindu and Sikh refugees have reportedly been killed.'

Dickie Mountbatten, presiding over the meeting, clasped his hands together. 'Gentlemen, the Maharaja's indecision has brought this trouble on him.' He hadn't forgotten Hari Singh's convenient fit of colic during his June visit. 'I tried to persuade him to make up his mind—'

'Forgive me, Your Excellency, but it is the policy of the Political Department under the previous Viceroy that is to be blamed!' Jawahar retorted. 'Besides, States and Defence Departments had approved Kashmir's repeated requests for arms and equipment. Yet, nothing has reached them.'

'The weapons still lie scattered in army depots across India,' Baldev Singh added.

Vallabh snorted. 'Held up by pro-Pakistani officers under Supreme Commander Auchinleck?'

'The staff of Supreme Headquarters have been at pains to act impartially,' Dickie felt the need to reiterate. He was aware that Jawa, Mr Patel and the defence minister had little confidence in the commanders-in-chief who, probably, like most British Army officers, preferred Muslims to Hindus, but the Auk was an honourable man tasked with the dispiriting destruction of his beloved army.

Vallabh sniggered. 'Your Excellency, they may *think* they are acting impartially, but they are all, mentally, completely pro-Pakistan.'

Feeling the need to steer the conversation on to urgent ground, Dickie said, 'Our first task is to determine how quickly arms *can* be supplied to Kashmir.'

'An airlift,' Baldev Singh answered. 'We will need sufficient aircraft to collect arms from various depots and fly them into Kashmir.'

The defence minister shared further details, the committee discussed the supply of arms and Dickie's military experience – the reason why Prime Minister and his deputy Vallabhbhai Patel, had asked him to act as chairman – came to the fore. The shortage of military aircraft was solved by the decision to switch British Overseas Aircraft Corporation planes, which had been borrowed for the transport of refugees, to ordinary passenger traffic – this would release Indian civil airways machines. The latter would then be chartered to the government to be flown by Indian Army officers. The commanders-in-chief of the army and air force were directed to give the highest priority to aircraft supplying arms to Srinagar.

Jawahar rose and started to perambulate the room, hands behind his back. From a half-open window birdsong floated, carried on a cool breeze, so welcome after the torrid heat of a prolonged summer.

'Having settled the matter of arms, I think we need to discuss what the future policy of the Government of India will be towards Kashmir.' He was aware that they were caught in the exigency of the moment, but they must plan what action to take to avoid knee-jerk responses. 'It is clear to me that the raids into Kashmir, with arms and trucks, must have had the full assistance of the Pakistan authorities. Indeed, I have information that the invasion was planned at a meeting in Rawalpindi a fortnight earlier.' He came to a stop and turned to his deputy, asking pointedly, 'Vallabhbhai?'

'Jawaharlal had shared with me similar reports he'd received earlier. About a plan to infiltrate Kashmir quietly and seize power once snows blocks the access road to India. And on 9 October, I received an intelligence report, from a fairly reliable source who claimed that Pakistan had deployed over 30,000 armed Pathans along the border with Kashmir.' The home minister's usually sombre demeanour was even more grim as he conveyed that local officials in Pakistan had been told to provide the Pathans with as many guns as they could spare.

Jawahar's lip curled. 'I have no doubt that Junagadh was used as a smokescreen to distract us from the actual target.'

A bitter taste pooled in Vallabh's mouth. As the minister in charge of States Department and a Gujarati, he had taken Junagadh's unexpected accession to Pakistan in mid-September as a personal betrayal. Jinnah's scheming hand was apparent behind the state's about-turn: If the Nawab of a Hindu-majority state could accede, why not the Nizam of Hyderabad? Hyderabad, in the belly of India, was the prize, Junagadh the bait. As for Kashmir, Muslim-majority, contiguous to West Panjab, Vallabh wouldn't complain if Hari Singh chose Pakistan, he had told Baldev Singh. But Jinnah's devious dabbling in Indian affairs had changed Vallabh's stance. So when Mehr Chand Mahajan, the Prime Minister of Kashmir, flew in to confer with Jawaharlal and him on 19 September, and expressed Hari Singh's desire to accede to India, Vallabh had seized the offer. He had directed the defence minister to collect weapons for the Maharaja's army out of Indian stores, sent wireless equipment to Srinagar airport to equip it for winter use, and ordered repairs of the lone route that snaked north from Gurdaspur – intersected by the Ravi, its numerous tributaries rutted the track, hugged the Himalayas, ascended to a dizzying 9000 feet of snow and ice, before it plunged into the Valley.

Now Vallabh struck the table with the flat of one palm.

'It is essential therefore that we offer *full* support to the Maharaja. I see nothing to prevent India from sending armed assistance to Kashmir, whether the state has formally signed the accession or not. Maharaja Hari Singh has written to us of his intention to accede.'

'Sardar, if I may,' V.P. Menon, secretary of the States Department, waded into the discussion. 'It is important that the state's legal status not be in limbo for us to send troops in. Otherwise, Pakistan could just as easily dispatch its troops across the border under the guise of "helping" local Muslims in their supposed "uprising" against the Hindu Maharaja. And Jinnah has an easier task. Srinagar is 150 miles from Abbottabad, down a good road, one that is now largely under the control of the tribesmen. Whereas we have the difficult task of airlifting troops and supplies to a small airport in Srinagar.'

'Where the runway is in danger,' Dickie reminded him, 'of falling into the hands of invaders.'

Vallabh held up his right index finger. 'Even more reason why we should not delay things more! Kashmir, an independent state, has been invaded and has asked for help. Nothing illegal in that. Nothing illegal in India responding either.'

Jawahar nodded. 'I agree with Vallabhbhai that nothing prevents us from sending armed assistance, irrespective of accession.'

He only wished things hadn't come to this pass. After their meeting, he had told Mehr Chand Mahajan that the Maharaja should release Sheikh Abdullah, enable the formation of a popular government under the National Conference, and determine the will of the people with regards to accession. Instead, Hari Singh had sat tight!

'Gentlemen,' Dickie held up a hand, aware he was dealing with two London-trained lawyers. 'One way out would be for Kashmir to *temporarily* accede to India, which then comes to its aid, subject to the proviso that the will of the people would be ascertained as soon as law and order is restored.'

Jawahar shook his head. 'I still have my concerns.'

Kashmir was his ancestral home, a land that held a peculiar hold on him. In July 1945, he had hiked in the mountains with Sheikh Abdullah, revelling in the landscape that could almost be out of a fairy tale. Yet, it was not romanticism for mountains – there were plenty of mountains in India – it was something to do with the solidity and imperturbability of the Himalayas that looked down upon him with the wisdom of a million years. He could trace it back perhaps to his jail term in Dehradun … During that long period of solitude, with no interviews, no visitors, even when he could not see the mountains from his cell, he was ever conscious of its nearness, and a secret intimacy seemed to grow between them.

The wall-mounted clock sounded the hour. It drew everyone's eyes.

Jawahar exhaled. 'My concern is democratic principle. If India accepts an offer of accession from the Maharaja, even provisionally, its motivations would be suspect among ordinary Kashmiris. The only way the Maharaja's government saves the situation is by cooperating with the National Conference and Sheikh Abdullah, the acknowledged leader of his people.'

The committee, aware that time was not on their side, agreed on the guiding principle that accession should be dependent on the will of the people, but also agreed with Lord Mountbatten's view that the Maharaja could hardly be expected to ascertain the people's will amidst an ongoing revolt. In the end, they decided the best course of action would be for V.P. Menon to fly to Srinagar with an army officer to assess the situation on the ground. Meanwhile, the chiefs of staff were asked to examine and prepare plans for possible courses of action, including flying troops to Srinagar.

Late that evening of 25 October, V.P. Menon and Colonel Sam Manekshaw of the Directorate of Military Operations flew to Srinagar on a BOAC aircraft.

12

Srinagar–Jammu (October 1947)

Tiger exhaled his relief. An emissary had arrived from Delhi: V.P. Menon.

However, India was still deciding whether it could send troops legally and V.P. Menon was there to get the formal Instrument of Accession signed. After speaking with Father and the Prime Minister, Menon's advice was blunt: Leave immediately for Jammu and take with you all the valuables you can!

Father vowed to join the state troops on the front lines. But the large-scale Muslim desertions had rendered the forces inadequate to protect even the palace. There was no option but to flee.

Gulab Bhavan went into a frenzy. Since the raiders would loot the palace from its chandeliered ceiling to carpeted floors, all manner of goods, clothes and valuables had to be packed; cars were drawn up in the courtyard, agitated staff rushed in and out of rooms, and Victor Rosenthal helped gather pearls and rubies and assorted jewellery for transport.

At 3 a.m., the convoy began to move. Father was up ahead, driving his own car with Victor at his side and two staff officers with loaded revolvers in the back seat. Mother and the ladies followed in several cars. Tiger was in no position to get into a car because of the heavy plaster cast, so his wheelchair was hoisted and placed in the back of one of the station wagons that Father reserved for his shikar expeditions. Tiger could not help reflecting that the hunters had become the hunted as they abandoned Gulab Bhavan to the howling jackals ...

A bitterly cold wind accompanied the silent convoy that drove slowly, haltingly, out of the capital. It crawled over the 9000-feet high Banihal Pass, leaving the Kashmir valley to enter the plains of Jammu, as the first light of dawn glimmered. Soon, a cream-coloured car joined the grim procession towards Jammu. Swami Sant Dev! Clearly, Tiger snorted, his miraculous powers did not include the capacity to repel the raiders. Finally, the convoy pulled up at Hari Niwas Palace, bordered by the river Tawi, ringed by the Shivalik range, crowned by the triple-peaked Vaishno Devi mountain. The French chateau–styled mini castle was where the Maharaja spent his winter days – evening water polo in the swimming pool, hunting expeditions to Udhampur, the becalming company of Swamiji – until the days became intolerably hot, mandating a return of the ruler once again to his blessed Valley of emerald forests, turquoise rivers and crystal peaks.

Now Father stepped out of the car, loss beaded into his brow, chin wobbling with emotion, and said, 'We have lost Kashmir.'

13

Delhi (October 1947)

Returning to Delhi on the morning of 26 October, V.P. Menon drove straight from the airport to the Prime Minister's York Road residence. With Sardar Patel present, he updated them. Colonel Manekshaw went directly to General Roy Bucher.

'I do not intend to be dramatic, but when I landed, I was oppressed by the stillness all around – as of a graveyard.' Menon adjusted his thick-framed glasses. 'An atmosphere of impending calamity hung over everything. The road leading from the aerodrome to Srinagar was deserted. At some of the street corners, I noticed volunteers of the National Conference, armed with lathis, who challenged passers-by. But the state police was conspicuous by its absence.'

Mehr Chand Mahajan, who had accompanied V.P. Menon and was party to the ongoing discussion in the drawing room, shifted uncomfortably.

'The Maharaja was completely unnerved by the turn of events and by his sense of helplessness. At one stage, he had said he would be prepared to make a present of Kashmir to the Government of India and himself retire to Jammu. I advised him,' Menon cleared his throat, 'for his own safety, to leave immediately for Jammu with his family.'

'Thank you,' Pandit Nehru said, eyes tired and sleep-deprived.

V.P. Menon nodded. The scene at the airport this morning was in direct contrast to that of the evening before: brimming with frantic folk, all looking to escape the Valley one way or another! The woman who had beseeched him to take her two daughters with him on the plane to Delhi, fearful they would meet the fate of thousands of other Kashmiri women. How the girls had sobbed for the entire duration of the flight. Meanwhile, the pilot had confided that in the hotel where he and his crew had their dinner, not a single soul talked and, but for the noise of forks and spoons, the whole hotel was hushed in silence. It was all horribly depressing.

Mehr Chand Mahajan now made his case for saving Kashmir. Of the Kashmir state forces, totalling about 8000 men, one-third were Muslims and these had gone over to the other side with their arms. There were four companies of state forces in Srinagar, while the raiders, who had reached a point only 35 miles away, were said to number 2000 to 3000 – all armed and having some modern equipment and mortars. The National Conference was putting up a fight, but the Muslim League in Srinagar was arming its members. He ended with a plea.

'Give us the military force we need, on any terms ... the town of Srinagar *must* be saved at any cost from loot and destruction!'

'Even if the town is taken by the tribesmen, India is strong enough to retake it.'

V.P. Menon could see that Prime Minister Nehru, keen to do the right thing, was averse to overtly dramatic speech.

'Panditji, the recapture, however, would not undo the damage that would most definitely result,' Mahajan insisted. 'I, therefore, firmly, but respectfully insist on the acceptance of my request for immediate military aid.'

'It is not easy to send troops on the spur of the moment!' An annoyed Pandit Nehru cast a chiding glance at the premier. 'An operation of this scale requires considerable preparation and arrangement; troops cannot be moved without due deliberation merely on demand.'

Mahajan wagged his head. 'Give us the military force we need. Take the accession and give whatever power you desire to the popular party. But the army must fly to save Srinagar this evening or-or else ...' His palms, spread wide, in a plea. 'OR I will go to Lahore and negotiate terms with Mr Jinnah!'

Pandit Nehru's famous temper reared up. He gestured to Mahajan to go away.

A stunned Mehr Chand Mahajan got up to leave.

Before he could reach the door, the Sardar, in a soothing tone, chided, 'Of course, you are not going to Pakistan, Mahajan.'

Just then, a peon hurried over with a piece of paper for the Prime Minister. He read it and announced, 'Sheikh Sahib also says the same thing.'

Sheikh Abdullah had arrived last evening at 1 Aurangzeb Road, and held discussions jointly with Panditji and the Sardar at the home minister's residence. Now he was listening to the discussion from one of the adjoining bedrooms.

Mahajan loudly exhaled his relief. Panditji's attitude appeared to have changed with the Sheikh's assent. He conferred softly with Vallabh, then turned to the Kashmir premier.

'Go and rest at Sardar Baldev Singh's house. I am calling a meeting of the Defence Committee to discuss the matter. We will convey our decision to you before lunch.'

At the Defence Committee meeting that followed, V.P. Menon once again recounted his impressions and reiterated the necessity of saving Srinagar. Then Lord Mountbatten turned to Colonel Manekshaw, who was present with General Roy Bucher. 'Manekji, what is the military situation?'

The colonel squared his shoulders and spoke, 'There are practically no state forces left and the raiders have almost reached the outskirts of Baramulla. At this rate, they could be in Srinagar in a day or two. Unless we fly in troops immediately, we *will* lose the city – going by road will take days, and if the tribesmen enter the city and take the airport, we won't be able to fly in either.'

Lord Mountbatten eyed the other members. 'It would be improper to move Indian troops into what is, at the moment, an independent country. Kashmir has not yet formally acceded. Now that the Maharaja is anxious to accede to India, it means Jammu and Kashmir would become part of Indian territory. *This* is the only basis on which Indian troops can be sent to the rescue of the state to stop further pillaging by the aggressors.'

Dickie steepled his hands. What the others did not know was that Auchinleck had pleaded to be allowed to send British troops to protect the British citizens living in the Valley – a tempting target for the Pathans, undoubtedly. Dickie had considered that improper. *Those people will be murdered and their blood will be on your head,* Auchinleck had accused. Which was true, but Dickie could not afford to let British troops get involved in the first war between the two dominions. If Srinagar was to be saved from pillage by the invading tribesmen, and if the couple of hundred British residents in Kashmir were not to be massacred, Indian troops would have to go in.

'Further,' Dickie tapped the table, 'in view of the composition of the population, accession should be conditional on the will of the people being ascertained by a plebiscite after the raiders have been driven out of the state, and law and order had been restored.'

'The great majority of the population of the valley of Kashmir would be friendly,' Pandit Nehru said, 'but there could be an active hostile minority—'

Sardar, with slight impatience, interjected. 'Sheikh Abdullah will be in a position of authority, which will ensure local Muslim support.'

'So, we have an agreement, gentlemen?' Lord Mountbatten asked.

The Prime Minister's brow was still furrowed.

'Jawaharlal!' Sardar swivelled to him. 'Do you want Kashmir or do you want to give it up?'

A massacre was imminent in the Valley unless Indian troops arrived to counter the raiders. 'Of course, I want Kashmir—'

Sardar turned to General Bucher and Colonel Manekshaw, 'You have your orders.'

The Defence Committee at once discussed the military action required. Since the commander of the state forces had asked for a battalion of the Indian infantry to be sent to Srinagar that day, the 1st battalion of the Sikh Regiment would be sent from Gurgaon. Transport aircraft was the limiting factor, and the operation involved considerable military risk.

The committee then charged the Ministry of States with preparing a draft Instrument of Accession and a draft letter from the Government of India to the Maharaja, recording the conditional acceptance of this instrument.

Later that day, V.P. Menon once again caught a flight – this time to Jammu. He found the Hari Niwas palace in turmoil, valuables strewn around, the Maharaja in deep slumber. Menon awoke him with an update on the Defence Committee's directives. A relieved Hari Singh signed the Instrument of Accession, agreed to set up an interim government, and to ask Sheikh Abdullah to shoulder the responsibilities in this emergency with Mehr Chand Mahajan. He also confided to the secretary of the States Department that before he went to sleep, he had left instructions with his ADC that if Menon failed to return from Delhi, that would mean that everything was lost; in which case, his ADC was to shoot him in his sleep! Leaving a buoyed Maharaja Hari Singh in Jammu, V.P. Menon flew back to Delhi with the Instrument of Accession. In the pre-dawn hours of 27 October, civil and military pilots and ground crew marshalled a hundred civilian aircraft and Royal Indian Air Force planes to fly troops, equipment and supplies to Srinagar. The airlift, unprecedented in scale and speed, astounded even Lord Mountbatten, the erstwhile chief of combined operations and supreme allied commander, South East Asia.

It was done just in time.

Black-turbaned kabailis were set to swoop down upon the Valley, their war cry of 'Allahu Akbar' ricocheting off the Himalayas and Pir Panjal that girded the flat fertile basin of meadows and lakes. Unknown to them, Dakotas packed with black-bearded Sikhs were flying towards Srinagar to open a new front in an ancient war between old rivals. In mid-eighteenth century, Kashmir had been wrested from feeble Mughal hands by the fearsome Ahmad Shah Abdali – until 1819, when the Pathans lost their land of milk and honey to Maharaja Ranjit Singh, the great Sikh ruler. Now, spurred on by Pakistan, tribal lashkars had rallied not only to the cry of jehad for Kashmir but also the chance to go kill Sikhs in the Panjab.

The wheel was set to turn, again.

14

Delhi–Lahore (October 1947)

On 27 October, as dozens of Dakotas deposited Indian soldiers on an airstrip barely adequate for mild civilian air traffic, less than 200 miles away in Lahore, Mohammed Ali Jinnah – Quaid-i-Azam, great leader and governor general of Pakistan – was at Government House, being hosted by Sir Francis Mudie, governor of West Panjab. The two men were in a celebratory mood. Jinnah knew that the tribesmen had reached the outskirts of Srinagar, having routed the Maharaja's army; and, in Hyderabad, a militant Muslim mob had prevented the Nizam's lawyer from flying to Delhi with his signed agreement – both the biggest and the wealthiest Princely States were set to fall in his lap! Mudie, meanwhile, simply hated the Congress. They were enjoying postprandial whiskys when news on the radio interrupted their soiree: Indian troops had seized Srinagar!

The Scotch soured quickly.

Jinnah's visions of a victory parade through the mile-high Valley, basking in the light reflected off the snow-capped peaks of its cradling mountains, collided with the troops-on-ground reality engineered by his bête noire, Jawaharlal. The speedy response to the stealthy invasion was proof to the Quaid of deep collusion between Hari Singh and India. The only justifiable response: War! A midnight call went out to Lieutenant General Douglas Gracey, filling in for General Frank Messervy, Pakistan's commander-in-chief. Two Pakistani brigades were to hasten to Kashmir pronto! The twin mandate: Capture Srinagar and cut off India's road access!

A nervous Gracey turned to Supreme Commander Auchinleck, whose standing order was that in the ongoing division of the erstwhile Indian Army between the two dominions, no British officer was to face off another. Jinnah's order would have made the British commanders-in-chief of the Indian and Pakistani armies, Generals Frank Messervy and Rob Lockhart, clash. The Auk caught the morning flight to Lahore. He found Jinnah surrounded by the governors of NWFP and Panjab and assorted army officers, all belligerent. Auchinleck and Gracey tried to persuade Jinnah to step back.

When the Quaid remained obdurate, the Auk issued a grim forecast. 'The British officers will be forced to quit. In which case, the Pakistani Army will just fall apart.'

Jinnah scoffed at the notion. But the threat hung in the air and sobered him. Accompanied by his two loyal governors, he went to confer with the ailing Liaquat Ali Khan.

Auchinleck proceeded to update London about the explosive situation in the subcontinent. After which, he called Delhi to update Governor General Mountbatten. Who was chairing another Defence Committee meeting where vigorous plans were being made to defend the Valley: a full brigade being dispatched by air to Srinagar and numerous civilian aircrafts ferrying reinforcements.

Again, just in time.

The Auk insisted that Indian and Pakistani leaders meet face to face to avoid a further conflagration. Jinnah, luckily, agreed to a meeting in Lahore the next day. Would Nehru be willing?

Dickie Mountbatten extricated Jawa from the committee meeting and popped the crucial question. Jawaharlal Nehru, keen to avoid full-on war, ruminated for a bit before agreeing to fly to Lahore.

On this day, 28 October, the rift between India and Pakistan looked like the Jhelum river did in parts as it traversed the Himalayan state: narrow and bridgeable. Jinnah was convinced that the Muslims of Kashmir would vote overwhelmingly in favour of Pakistan. And Jawaharlal was committed to a plebiscite to determine the will of the people. Dickie and the Auk exhaled.

A little too soon.

At a Cabinet meeting later in the day, ministers disapproved of their leader's plan. Vallabhbhai was emphatic. 'For the Prime Minister to go crawling to Jinnah, when we are the stronger side and in the right, would never be forgiven by the people of India!' Even the mild-mannered and entirely diplomatic V.P. Menon cautioned, 'This would be another Munich' – alluding to France and England's 1938 policy of appeasement in the face of German aggression.

A perplexed Dickie turned to Gandhi to understand the truculence. 'I would be prepared to go see anyone, anywhere and at any time, if it would help public interest,' he said.

The apostle of ahimsa, shaken by the violence of Partition, which had played out like a contemporary enactment of the Battle of Kurukshetra, sighed. 'I feel the same way.'

The Cabinet nixed Nehru's flight.

The Jhelum swelled to a spate – unseasonal, incessant.

15

Kashmir (October 1947)

Since Indian aircraft were patrolling the skies above Kashmir, the earliest Akbar Khan could cross the bridge at Kohala was at sunset. In the gathering dark, the Jhelum below shifted like a silvery beast that had slithered down from the hulking Himalayas. In the passenger seat, Malik's right leg twitched incessantly. This annoyed Akbar, but since they would be in the vehicle together for the time it took the Major to assess the on-ground situation in Srinagar, the situation in the car must be endured. Malik had insisted upon coming; the charge against him was grave. The thousand men on the critical Kathua road, despatched to prevent Indian reinforcements, had instead returned home! Because their rifles had broken down. Apparently, the rifles Malik had supplied were not military-grade but country-made. When Akbar had stormed to Malik with the news, the militia commander had insisted the fault lay at Akbar Khan's end: Somebody had switched the rifles and made a neat packet. Since there was no point frothing at each other in the manner of rabid dogs, the two men had embarked on this joint trip.

The director of weapons and equipment had recently been inducted into the Prime Minister's Liberation Committee as its military member. Liaquat Ali Khan was monitoring the situation arising out of Kashmir's accession to India and India's military intervention. Pakistan must answer the intervention, *unofficially*, for now. It would be called 'Operation Gulmarg'. Meanwhile, the news that on 27 October Sardar Ibrahim had formed the first provisional government in Muzaffarabad had lifted the spirits of all Pakistanis. With Kathua out of action, Akbar Khan was keen to secure the Srinagar landing ground—

The screech of an owl brought Akbar back from his rumination. Out of the corner of his eye, he saw Malik, sullen, sunk in his seat.

A man's name is as good as his word! Malik had thundered. He would prove the allegations against him were false. The rot was in the director's unit … on and on the militiaman had roared, his limp getting more pronounced as he swivelled vigorously with every step forward.

The man was a raving lunatic, Akbar had concluded. Still, he might be of use.

With the Jhelum on his left, Akbar drove up north in silence. The area was unusually quiet – no one in sight, the far-off village huts with no light … Where was the war?

Twenty-five miles on, approaching Muzaffarabad, located at the confluence of Jhelum and Neelam, it was as if a curtain lifted! On the one single road connecting Muzaffarabad to Srinagar, a cavalcade was on. Tribesmen, answering the call to jehad in Kashmir, had descended in multitude. Buses, lorries, trucks, all manner of ramshackle transport on four wheels, all full to the brim, heading to free their Kashmiri brethren. Akbar and

Malik watched as they wedged their car past vehicles packed with forty, fifty, in some as many as seventy, tribesmen, lying on the roofs, sitting on the engines, hanging on to the mudguards! They were men of all ages, greybeards to teenagers; few were well-dressed, many with torn clothes, some even without shoes but all were tall and imposing and fired up. Akbar could see all manner of weapons: British, French, German, Frontier-made rifles, long and short-barrelled pistols, shot guns even. Then there were those with only daggers, no firearms at all – the intent was to capture those from the enemy.

Akbar could not contain his awe. 'Like their ancestors of yore!'

Malik fixed him a stare before turning to look straight ahead.

'What?' Akbar asked. 'Didn't their forefathers similarly pour in through the high mountain passes of the Frontier?'

'So?' Malik grunted.

'So, behold the grand spectacle: Here again are the rugged mountains, and here are the descendants of the same men looking much the same, clothed in much the same manner and plunging forward into the unknown much the same!'

'Their forefathers came to conquer.'

'Which proves my point: Kashmiris are our brethren; they belong with us.'

Finding a clear spot, Akbar pressed the accelerator, skirted the convoy and surged forward. At Uri, fifty miles from Muzaffarabad, the bridge was down. Destroyed two days prior by the retreating state troops as they were pursued by the tribesmen, a man informed them. He pointed to a mile-long diversion which the locals had cut into the hillside overnight which had enabled the tribesmen to pass.

Soon dawn was creeping over the horizon. Akbar yawned. The sun's rays were parting the mist, the landscape unveiling one of its famed picture postcards: emerald meadows circled by pearly peaks, geese flying in formation across a turquoise sky, golden chinars—

A wailing disrupted the quiet. On a rickety old bridge over the Jhelum, a clutch of women stood. A baby was tossed in the air and a woman leaped into the water after it. Malik bolted upright. Akbar watched stunned as the rushing waters swallowed the child and woman.

'Stop!' Malik shouted.

As Akbar braked, Malik swung open the door and jumped out of the moving car. He sped towards the bridge, tottering, staggering, dragging his limp leg, one arm aloft. 'TARA!' he yelled, 'stop, STOP, Tara!'

A woman in a pink salwar-kameez stood poised at the edge, hair that had escaped her long braid whipping around her fair face, her nosepin glinting in the sun.

Did Malik *know* this woman? Akbar screwed up his eyes as he watched Malik hurtle down the bridge which swayed with the man's exertions. A child shrieked as a woman lifted him by the shoulders and swung him over the bridge. Meanwhile, several other children clung to their mothers' legs amidst a rising cacophony of wails. *La haul vila kuvat!*

Having parked the car, Akbar Khan bounded in the direction of the bridge. Ahead, Malik had woven his way through the forlorn women to the one who teetered over the river. He reached for her shoulder; she whipped her head around, screamed and slipped. Malik watched the water swallow her and clutched his head. A perplexed Akbar was at the riverbank when he sighted two tribesmen rushing up, gesticulating at the women, who, sighting the black-turbaned men, grabbed their children and scurried to the edge. Like raindrops, the women began to fall into the raging river. The tribesmen pointed their weapons and shouted as they grabbed the women. Shoving a gun in their faces, they tried to force them back from the edge. Malik, enmeshed in the mass of women, stood like a statue – eyes vacant, mouth slack. Women writhed, children clasped to their bosoms, as the raiders cajoled and threatened. Gunfire. A woman shot in the back.

Drawing his gun, Akbar sped to the bridge.

'WHAT are you doing?' The sight of a uniformed man seemed to have made an impression. In Pashto, one of the tribesmen explained that he was trying to prevent the women from killing themselves. Clearly, the women thought that fate worse than suicide – in the brief interval that Akbar had engaged the tribesmen, more women had jumped into the Jhelum.

'OFF! Off the bridge,' Akbar commanded the tribesmen. 'Where's your officer?'

The raiders shrugged, complained and explained as Akbar Khan herded them off the wooden bridge. The tribesmen had raided the neighbouring villages, killed the men, looted the possessions, including women, some of whom had escaped and were now flinging themselves into the river. There was no officer commanding the men.

After he had packed off the tribesmen, he urged the women to return to their homes. It was patently false advice, he was aware: Their houses were burned down, ransacked, their menfolk dead …

But it was war, Akbar pursed his mouth, and retreated to resume the drive to Srinagar, a shell-shocked Malik in the passenger seat. Jang-e-azeem had disabled the man, obviously. And the star-crossed love Akbar had heard of had unhinged him completely; like a Jhangi Ranjha, he saw his beloved Heer Sial in every woman!

Wondering where he would catch up with the tribesmen, Akbar gunned the accelerator.

16

Srinagar (October1947)

On 31 October, Sheikh Mohammad Abdullah, with the support of the Indian government, was sworn in as head of the administration.

Srinagar was festooned with banners and buntings as the Sheikh went to the old palace on the bank of the Jhelum, Sher Garhi, where the Sher-i-Kashmir had been officially recognized. Later that day, he addressed a rally in Lal Chowk. A squally wind had not deterred people. Even tongas and bullock carts parked at the periphery were jam-packed. Abdullah swelled with happiness and pride at the sea of bobbing caps sporting the National Conference insignia, a white plough against a red background. The volunteer force had a formidable task in front of them. After Hari Singh's unseemly flight, the city administration had collapsed. Law and order must be maintained in the Valley, shops must stay open, people must go about their business without fear.

'In this time of national crisis, Kashmir must be the beacon,' he began.

National Conference volunteers cheered as their leader, prisoner of the Maharaja just five weeks ago, was now the acknowledged leader of the city. 'All around us we see the tragedy of brother killing brother. At this time, Kashmir must come forward and raise the banner of Hindu–Muslim unity.'

He patted down his fez, glad he had had the foresight to conceive and implement a volunteer force in the short time since his release from prison. Ten days after he'd been let out, he had addressed a public meeting and first appealed for 10,000 volunteers to form a 'peace brigade'. Reports were reaching the city from the state borders that necessitated the formation of a volunteer corps to maintain peace, and protect hearth and homes, irrespective of creed or community. Even Pandit Nehru had suggested they create a local militia and promised that the Indian Army would provide rifles and basic training for the defence of the city and other towns in the Valley. Srinagar was quiet, but restive in the face of refugees pouring in. The aircrafts bringing in reinforcements were departing full of men, women and children with their pitiful belongings.

Abdullah inhaled deeply. 'In Kashmir, we want a people's government. We want a government which will give equal rights and equal opportunities to all men – irrespective of caste or creed.'

Dark clouds scudded across the sky. He frowned. The Peace Brigade was keeping guard, patrolling the streets of Srinagar, watching approaches to the city. All would be okay, dark clouds were not a bad omen, just a harbinger of rain. He resumed his oration.

The Kashmir government will *not* be the government of any one community. No! It will be a *joint* government—'

Applause erupted, the crowd anticipating their leader's words.

'—of the Hindus,' he paused to allow the approval to chime down, 'the Sikhs … And the Muslims!'

The rally erupted.

Sher-i-kashmir ka kya irshad: Hindu, Muslim, Sikh ittihad!

What is the message of the Lion of Kashmir: Hindu, Muslim, Sikh unity!

17

Kashmir (October1947)

Baramulla, where the mountains fell away to yield to the gate of the Kashmir valley, looked as if an earthquake had struck it!

Shops were empty, doors and windows missing, brick, stone, paper littering the ground, fires still burning. The blown-up buildings must be the handiwork of the retreating state troops, an attempt to block the road to Srinagar, barely 35 miles away. But the air of a city struck by a typhoon could only be because of the advancing tribesmen. Everywhere Akbar Khan looked were signs of looting and destruction. So it was true what he'd heard: Major Khurshid Anwar had promised a booty to the tribesmen as their reward for fighting in Kashmir. Since there was no other remuneration, the tribesmen were ransacking and carrying off all they could.

As he drove down the bare road, smoke laced his windpipe.

Where was the fighting happening? Where was the front? Now and then, Akbar sighted someone sneaking away. Had the tribesmen reached Srinagar where they had planned to celebrate Eid on 26 October? After all, the coveted city lay down this road. But no such news had reached Pindi when Akbar had left on the 29 October …

A few miles on, he sighted men sitting around a fire. A kettle hung from a horizontal log over the flames, a man chopped onions, another sat on a rock tucking into a thick naan. At the sight of the approaching car, a man in uniform walked up. Akbar parked and stepped out.

'Captain Alamgir,' the man introduced himself. He was short, with a pleasant, open face and a rather luxuriant moustache.

'Where's everybody?' Akbar questioned with a furrowed brow.

'The lashkar, you mean?'

'The tribesmen, yes. And their commander, Khurshid Anwar.'

'Some of the lashkar went forward. Quite a few retreated.'

'*Re*-treated? Why?'

Alamgir stroked his moustache.

'Speak up, Captain! I'm General Tariq.' Akbar felt Malik's enquiring gaze on him, but he ploughed on. 'Baramulla is devastated. Where's everybody? Any news of the Indians?'

'Sir,' Alamgir straightened up. 'We came up from Kathua, reaching yesterday. By that time, the lashkar had been looting the town for two days. Muslims, non-Muslims, they spared no one.' He lowered his voice. 'It seems commander Anwar was not happy with their recklessness; why alienate local Muslims? He told them not to destroy government property. But the tribesmen were out of control. So Khurshid Anwar sent for tribal leaders to instil discipline into their men.'

Akbar Khan swore. Khurshid Anwar was a loose cannon, even Shaukat Hayat Khan had conceded that. The tribesmen were some of the best fighters in the world, having encountered Alexander, Chingiz Khan, Timur Lang, and remaining unconquered. Here, they had covered 120 miles at lightning speed, destroying all in their path, and this Khurshid Anwar had squandered the chance to conquer Srinagar!

'What happened at Kathua?' Malik asked the captain.

Captain Alamgir eyed the general's companion dressed in civvies. 'We were a thousand strong,' he shrugged.

'So? Why didn't you fight?'

'I could, with my weapon.' Finding that General Tariq was listening to the conversation, Alamgir elaborated. 'But many rifles didn't work. These were ex-servicemen like me, INA, and they were given useless guns. So they left. I heard of the action planned in the Valley and decided to come here with my men.' He gestured with his thumb to those at the fireside. One man was walking up with cups of steaming tea which he handed to the three men.

Malik persisted. 'The faulty rifles—'

'Frontier-made,' Alamgir said on a sip of the sweet fragrant tea. 'But many men had functioning rifles, too. It seems that a consignment came from Panjab Police, which was not military-grade rifles.'

Malik raised a brow at Akbar Khan. The arrangement had been for Malik to supply the rifles to Panjab Police, who would then issue them on. If all of those rifles did not reach the men for whom they were meant, might Panjab Police not have switched some for poor-quality Frontier rifles which could be bought for one-hundred rupees whereas the going price for a military rifle was a thousand rupees?

Having finished his tea, Akbar Khan rolled his shoulders back, disregarding Malik. *If* Kashmir was to be part of Pakistan, somebody had to make it bloody *happen*!

'Captain Alamgir, will you be willing to go forward if needed?'

Akbar explained that he was heading to Srinagar to reconnoitre. The captain assented. 'Wait for my message!'

Akbar was revving up the car when Alamgir poked his head through the open window. 'We heard there was a local man on a motorcycle who led the tribesmen down a wrong path,' he shouted over the idling engine. 'When they realized his treachery, they executed him in the town square.' Saying which, he withdrew, clicked his heels together and saluted. 'General.'

Smoke rose from several village huts in the distance as they drove into Baramulla.

'*General,*' Malik sniggered as Akbar drove, 'I hope I stand cleared of the charge of supplying faulty rifles.'

A grim Akbar looked straight ahead. Both Malik and he had been proved right. Not only were there too many cooks brewing Operation Gulmarg, they were using third-rate spices as well!

Smouldering rubble, blackened walls, deserted homes, a defaced convent atop a hill, the town centre ... flies swarmed around an electric pole to which a corpse was nailed by his hands, a notice stuck to his forehead, his body riddled with bullets.

'Why Tariq?' Malik asked.

'Tariq, from twelve centuries ago. Upon landing on the coast of Spain, he burned his boats, thus abandoning the only means of going back to his country.' Akbar sucked his teeth. 'I may be no Tariq, but I am similarly inspired.'

'Ameen,' acknowledged a solemn Malik.

'Ameen,' replied Akbar. An hour or less of daylight before they plunged into darkness. For all he knew, the fighting could be somewhere up in the hills ... The road itself could be in enemy hands... He slowed down, headlights off, picking his way in the gloaming.

Malik had piped up.

'Mountains behind,
valley ahead,
No boats to burn,
no men to churn,
Thus leads Ta-*riq*,
Ameen, A-*meen*.'

Not content with his ridiculous ditty, Malik whistled the tune now, tapping a knee in accompaniment.

Akbar stayed silent, a tiny muscle in one corner of his mouth jerking agitatedly, as the car headed to Srinagar. Ten miles or so ahead, he sighted tribesmen sleeping around a fire. Further on, dark figures crouched along the road. Nobody attempted to stop him. Another hour and the lights of Srinagar were visible in the distance. The sound of firing reached them. They were close to the front. Even Malik had perked up in the passenger seat at the sight of wounded men being carried away. Another half a mile, and shells were landing on the road. They were at the fourth milestone, on the edge of Srinagar. Akbar parked by the roadside. A quick chat with a clutch of Pathans informed him of the enemy roadblock ahead. Having got mired in the marshy area at the perimeter, they had launched a direct assault, and faced the full blast of Indian fire – rifles, Brens, machine guns, mortars. The attack had failed, and the Pathans had halted action for the night.

The particular group of tribesmen were Mohmands, Akbar deduced as he looked for shelter. They lacked the experience of Mahsuds or Wazirs, who would have been more cautious. Malik waved. He'd found a clump of chinar trees set back from the road. They parked beneath and tried to rest. It was cold and eerily quiet.

'Akbar Khan,' Malik's voice rang out.

'Shhh!' Akbar hissed. 'Want to alert the Indians?'

'Can you see the trees?' Malik whispered.

'Considering we're right beneath …'

'Can you see what's in them?'

'*In* them?' Akbar leaned his head out of the window. He examined the clump towering above them. It would be majestic in daytime, but now—

'The women in the trees – see them?'

Sighing, Akbar leaned back into the seat. *Women. Again.* Did the man ever catch a break?

A rumble awoke him. Mist hovered high above the ground, snowy peaks glistened in the dawn light, bulbuls twittered in the chinar trees. Malik, eyes bright, was awake, too. A fighter aircraft sliced the sky like a scythe. A burst of machine gun ripped through the air. A bomb was dropped … Another … Then another. The aircraft flew low, skimming the chinar tops. No one fired back. Akbar and Malik held their breath.

The aircraft would return. Time to get to business.

Malik had a manic look about him – had the man slept at all? Leaving him in charge of the car, Akbar set off to explore the area with a pair of binoculars and a map, staying low. Aircraft returned for renewed assault, but they were easy to dodge; besides, a single individual was never a worthwhile target. His reconnaissance showed the approaches to Srinagar were all covered in water, enough to restrict movement to the main road or even the few paths off it. The outer perimeter of Srinagar was many miles long and irregular. Indian posts were few and scattered; likely no more than three battalions altogether. In spite of the aircraft and the troops, the tribesmen were still roaming around the perimeter and the landing ground, freely and undaunted. If they infiltrated Srinagar, it would be impossible to eject them. Panic would ensue. Kashmir state troops had already given up, the Indians would be more concerned with protecting the airfield, their only route to India.

But *how* was an entry to be made?

Akbar mulled over this as he wove his way through the thicket reverberating to the drone of aircraft, the whistle of bombs, the rat-a-tat of guns. The tribesmen needed boats to cross the water. But locals on the outskirts had disappeared – finding boats and guides might take too long. Meanwhile, every day lost would result in more Indian troops on the ground. So, it was back to the main road again, the site of last night's attack. His survey of the enemy's roadblock had shown no concrete pillars, bunkers or heavy obstacles, only a barbed wire construction covered by gunfire. It could stop unprotected men and lorries, but an armoured car? A single one would ram right through.

Akbar sped back. A couple of armoured cars could reach Srinagar from Pakistan in twenty-four hours. There was not a moment to lose!

18

Srinagar (November 1947)

The *Mayfair* houseboat, at a quiet spot on the backwaters of Dal Lake, moored against a grassy bank where an old chinar spread its bountiful branches, had caught Margot Parr's eyes when she had first arrived in the Valley in early September. Delhi was roiling with excessive heat and humans, and an escape to the mountains had seemed just the solution. A passably good road led to Lahore, the city she was covering for human-interest stories for readers back home in America. An earlier Delhi feature had been such a big draw that her editor had commissioned a parallel Pakistan piece; and though Karachi was the capital of the new Muslim nation, Lahore was where the action was.

Now, as she lounged on the deck of the houseboat in a thick overcoat, smoking a cigarette and watching bulbuls cavorting in the flaming red tree, her mind went back to the unusual conversation she had had with an English journalist in Lahore a fortnight ago. 'Flee Srinagar!' Larry Collins had warned, refusing to give any explanation. He had returned from Karachi, having failed to interview Jinnah, was in a foul mood and piss-drunk, and Margot had ignored his advice entirely. Until last Friday, when Srinagar had gone dark and panic had set in. While other Europeans and Americans had sought to flee, Margot had tried to get on the road to Muzaffarabad. No luck, so she had stayed put in the capital and managed to report on action that other intrepid reporters had totally missed! Margot Parr was the only reporter on ground when the Maharaja fled with a convoy of forty-eight trucks carrying carpets, jewels and artefacts, as tribesmen from the North West Frontier Province swooped down upon the Valley, and volunteers of the National Conference tried to secure the city with lathis and makeshift roadblocks. Since telegraph lines were out, she had hurried to Nedou's to send stories through the pilots who had flown in and for three straight days, her byline informed the world of all the events before other foreign journalists managed to hitch a ride on Indian planes from Delhi. But they were lagging. Besides, Margot had an inside eye on the newly installed government of Sheikh Abdullah because the owner of *Mayfair*, Ali Dar, was an NC activist.

A rustle of feet alerted her to Gul, heading in her direction with her breakfast. Margot blew a final smoke ring before stubbing out the cigarette in the marble ashtray.

'Good morning, Miss Margot!' Gul chirped.

'Good morning, Mister Gul.'

Giggling, the five-year-old deposited the walnut tray with a pot of tea, toast topped with softly done eggs, and a single stem of a white chrysanthemum in a slim brass vase. Margot grinned. After Gul had figured that the Memsahib was taken in by the abundant flowers of the Valley, he tried to bring a different one daily: a clutch of zinnias one day, tuberose on another, foxgloves, lupins. These were not bought from a boat laden with flowers for sale – Gul had no money – but foraged from fields and meadows, making them special. Now, Margot picked up the chrysanthemum, plump as a baby, and expressed her admiration. 'Fabulous!' Gul blushed before spouting an exact copy of the word and scampering off to the living room to refresh the fire in the metal stove. The boy had a mimic's talent and often repeated her words verbatim, bolstering the pidgin English he'd picked up from previous guests.

Bless Kashmira, Margot exhaled, as she did daily upon sighting her perfectly done meal. Thereafter, on the road, scrounging for stories, she would live off fruit and nun cha returning for a late dinner. Right now, she would enjoy a hot cup of English breakfast tea. As she cradled her teacup and inhaled the fragrant brew, she watched Kashmira cross the cookboat to the houseboat, her face wearing the worried expression she had donned since the evening when news of the kabailis had arrived. Margot knew what Kashmira was seeking: news of her parents in Baramulla. Hindu and Sikh refugees who had poured into the Valley told horror stories of the destruction and loot caused by the tribesmen. But Kashmira's parents were Muslims, like the kabailis, so they should have been spared, right?

'Kashmira,' Margot said in a cheery voice, indicating the lounge chair across from her, 'sit, please.'

Kashmira refused, as always, preferring to stand. She bit her lower lip before asking hesitantly, '*Any* news?'

'No,' Margot smacked her lip. 'I'm meeting the Indian commanding officer today and I hope to get some information. Did Ali's contacts—'

Margot stopped. Kashmira had started shaking her head. With a quick bow, she stepped away from the verandah to go assist Gul.

Ali Dar could not understand what Hassan's problem was. Finally, the people had their own leader in the government, and yet, his younger brother and other members of the Muslim Conference were still complaining.

'Sheikh Abdullah has been sworn in under the Maharaja! Mahajan is still the Prime Minister! Then what kind of freedom or people's rule is it, tell me?' Hassan jutted his chin at his older brother.

Ali waved a dismissive hand. 'That's just protocol. The fact is Hari Singh has fled, leaving us to govern the city, the Valley and the state—'

'The state! You know what's happening in Poonch? Mirpur? Sardar Ibrahim has already formed the Azad Jammu and Kashmir government!'

Ali shrugged expansively. 'One upstart doesn't change things. Who *is* Sardar Ibrahim against Sheikh Abdullah, the people's leader? For how long has the Sheikh struggled with us ordinary Kashmiris? Now who is organizing food and defence in the city? Hmm? Your Ibrahim?'

Hassan gulped. 'Bhaijaan, please see reason. We are Kashmiri Muslims; our rightful place is with our brethren in Pakistan, our home should be in Pakistan.'

Ali had not missed the softening in his younger brother's voice, or the use of Urdu. Moving forward, he draped an arm around Hassan's shoulders and drew him to the bank, away from the cookboat's earshot. The aroma of fresh bread wafted through the air. Softly, Ali said, 'You are right, now that we are rid of Dogra tyranny, we Kashmiris must decide where Kashmir should be: with India, Pakistan, or free. Sheikh Abdullah doesn't rule out independence, and Prime Minister Nehru has promised a plebiscite once we are rid of the raiders—'

'Tch!' Hassan shook his head. 'The *raiders* are our Muslim brothers who have come to help liberate us from the Maharaja's tyranny!'

'*Really?*' Ali hissed. 'Do you know what those savages have done to Baramulla?' He cast a quick glance to see if Kashmira was listening. She must be serving salty tea and kulcha to Ammi, Safina and Gul. 'NC volunteers in Baramulla are saying that the lashkar didn't spare *any*one, Muslim or otherwise! All they are interested in is loot! While here in Srinagar, Muslim, Hindu, Sikh, all are trying to keep peace.'

Hassan shrugged his brother's arm off, a dark cloud on his face. 'Keep *peace*?' He spat out the word like it was some bitter berry. 'You know in the border areas in Poonch, state troops are trying to get rid of all ex-servicemen living there. Shooting people, setting fire to homes ... The Maharaja's plan is to allow the surplus Sikhs of West Panjab to settle in Kashmir. Bring non-Muslims into J&K and change the population in their favour.'

'Oh, brother, these are all wild rumours—' Ali chided gently.

'Rumours, all rumours,' spat Hassan before he strode off angrily towards Gagribal.

With one arm extended, Ali called after him, 'Have some food before you leave.'

But Hassan was hurrying away without a backward glance. Ali sighed. The Muslim Conference was churning out such wild rumours that fear was gathering in the Valley, like a thunderstorm. And arming its cadre with weapons supplied by the Muslim League. They knew they could not rival the popularity of Sheikh Abdullah, so their men were a nuisance even as the National Conference was trying to keep the peace in a volatile valley.

19

Jammu (November 1947)

Masud Ahmed thought it best that Koko Jan go to her parents' in Sialkot until things settled down in Reasi and take Zooni with her. His work with the Azad Army kept him out most nights, and though Reasi was Muslim-majority and would soon be part of the newly formed provisional government, Dogra troops had begun attacking Muslims – apparently Hari Singh was directing operations from his palace in Jammu. Either way, it wasn't good for women to be home alone without their menfolk.

The wives had packed a bag each, finished the butter and milk at home, stored away the grains and flour, swept the rooms and kept everything ready for locking, but Masud Ahmed had not returned to transport them. Having left on one of his night-time adventures, he was to return in one night. However, it was the fifth night now and fear was gnawing the women's insides. As was the urgent summons from Afshana Bibi: *A bus is coming to transport women, children and the elderly to Pakistan until the turbulent time passes; those who want to leave should be ready by*

9 p.m.; they would travel in the night to avoid attracting attention. Since the Maharaja fled Srinagar for Jammu – or was it Delhi? – the entire state was in turmoil. Koko Jan had heard that Sialkot had been emptied of all its Hindus and Sikhs, kafilas of whom were streaming into Jammu from Pakistan. From Masud Ahmed they knew that Pathans had swooped into Muzaffarabad and Baramulla, and carried away all they could, including women. At Zooni's worried look, Ahmed had rebuked: *Don't the Gujjars know kalma? Those who can recite it are being spared!* Mist-laden winter air exhaled rumours: State troops were killing Muslims wherever they could find them! Tauba tauba. India had sent a force of its bearded savages to tackle the Pathans and they would soon be in Jammu to quell the Azad Force ...

Zooni and Koko Jan sat in the bedroom, bags packed; Koko Jan biting her lower lip, Zooni cracking her knuckles as a cold wind howled in the courtyard. Should they, shouldn't they? The women had argued back and forth.

'If we left and Masud Ahmed returned to find the house vacant?' Koko Jan had asked.

'Better than him returning to find us dead, or worse, raped?' Zooni had countered with a meaningful glance. Their neighbour's house stood charred like a clay oven.

'But this night journey ... Will it be safe?'

'Who knows?'

'But Afshana is going on it, all the Chaudhurys are, and Naseeba and Beena; and even Beena's husband, who refuses to fight like Shahji and is otherwise healthy, is going to Pakistan.'

Unable to sit, Zooni checked her bag once again: three khaddar salwar-kurta, a sweater her mother had knitted, her catapult—

A honk. Koko Jan sprang like a startled doe. Zooni grabbed both their bags, squared her shoulders and stepped out. Harsingar perfumed the courtyard, and weighed Zooni's heart.

Her saut locked the door, still mumbling. 'When our husband returns and can't find us, my letter will tell him we are in Sialkot, no?' Koko Jan knew a smattering of the alphabet, had scribbled a note and left it on top of the trunk in the storeroom. She cast an anxious glance at the sky, wound her wool shawl tight around her head and neck, her face as lovely as the night jasmine.

The bus rattled through the dark, the door loose on its hinges, headlights diffusing the hovering mist. A cold draft wafted over the heads of passengers packed tight like chickens in a butcher's coop – as if all of Reasi had emptied itself into the bus. Zooni, cramped in the back, holding on to Koko Jan who perched on her lap, had sighted trunks, holdalls, utensils, goats even, as the two women had ploughed their way into the bus. Folks were abandoning their homes!

A rustle, a clearing of the throat, a bleating occasionally broke the silence of the packed bus, fear their amorphous co-passenger. The bus jolted, Koko Jan slid forwards, before Zooni grabbed her, fingers digging into her soft belly, the nutty smell of Koko Jan's morning ubatan in Zooni's nostrils. Passengers heaved as one wave and settled again. Pinching her eyes, Zooni tried to determine where they were. She could hear the Chenab gushing nearby. The intermittent howl of jackals meant they were nearing the jungle—

The bus shuddered to a halt.

Passengers exchanged glances. 'What happened,' somebody squeaked.

Zooni arched her neck. Had the driver jumped out? The passengers' breath clouded the still bus as speculation mounted.

The bus door yanked open, boots mounted the steps and two troopers appeared, their rifles pointed at the passengers. A scream tore through the bus.

'Out! Out!' the policemen shouted, swivelling their guns.

'Hai!' a woman cried.

'Out!' a policeman shouted. 'Or we shoot you all here!'

Zooni and Koko Jan sank into the seat, trying to hide behind the riders in front. As the trooper took aim, a man darted from his seat, followed swiftly by another until people started to trickle out, dragging their baggage.

'Leave belongings behind! Just yourself; out! Hurry, we don't have all night!'

Half the bus had emptied. Zooni peered into the darkness. Suddenly, from out of the thicket, jumped a posse of men brandishing naked swords! They fell upon the passengers huddled outside, slashing at them like they were stalks of corn. Most collapsed to the ground without realizing their throat or abdomen had split open, blood, entrails pouring out of them. Zooni bit down on her lips, there was a whimper from Koko Jan, then wailing erupted in the bus. As the remaining passengers cowered in their seats or sank to the floor of the bus to hide, the troopers opened fire. Gunshots ripped through the bus, bullets darting like glow worms, followed by deafening screams.

Diving to the floor, Zooni and her saut curled tight like twin foetuses, their breath caught in their breasts. In time, the cries started to die down and the shooting became irregular. Rivulets of blood coursed near them. Silence, inside the bus and outside. Zooni was trying not to gag on the thick, musty smell of blood. Boots descended; the bus heaved back up.

'All dead?' A voice enquired. Someone ascended.

Crouched on the floor, Zooni sighted a bearded man who surveyed the bus as he wiped his sword with a cloth. Ahead, a leg twitched. The man swung his sword down. A piercing shriek, then quiet. The man went back to cleaning his weapon. 'Oye,' he beckoned someone over.

A trooper joined him.

'Some more rainfall,' the burly man ordered.

A spatter of bullets later, the men exited.

Zooni did not know if she was alive or dead until Koko Jan went limp in her hands. No sound, no word, only Koko Jan's warm blood coating Zooni's hands, mingling with the smell of oil-turmeric-gramflour in her nose.

The men peeled away into the dark night. Jackals yowled, crickets chirped, the river gurgled. Zooni waited until she could discern no human sound. Moving Koko Jan off her stiff body, Zooni crept out, her salwar-kurta sticky with blood, and stumbled into the thicket. Mindless of the bramble or the jungle animals, she walked towards the sound of the river. From the corner of an eye, she caught the light but waded on. She could smell the spray of the river. A shout went up, several male voices, then a crashing through the jungle.

Zooni had reached the edge; below the river tumbled on its way.

'Oye, catch her!'

'She has nowhere to go ...'

A sniggering laugh.

The spray rinsed her hands and face and hair and clothes, the water murmured; it had cradled her as a child ...

Zooni flung herself off the cliff.

20

Srinagar (November 1947)

Abdullah awoke with a start. He had fallen asleep at the table, his neck now complained, and a yawn broke out of him. A light, like old silver, that presaged dawn filled his room. Standing up, he padded to the window. The Valley lay in its blanket of mist, guarded by hulking mountains. He felt a tremor down his back. Barely a day since the tribesmen had almost broken through. Brigadier General Sen said in his briefing that around 700 men had attacked an Indian patrol less than 5 miles from the airfield. The Indian soldiers were severely outnumbered, six to one, and came under heavy mortar fire, which resulted in multiple casualties. Abdullah had ordered his volunteers to stay extra vigilant and watch for anybody looking to enter Srinagar. The enemy was audacious and hungry, and skilled at mountain warfare …

The light had turned roseate, revealing snow-clad peaks. As if on cue, birdsong erupted.

It was good that Sardar Patel had turned up for discussions accompanied by the defence minister, Baldev Singh. Because of the battle with the tribals, they had met at Srinagar airfield itself. Brigadier General Sen had lured the tribesmen by withdrawing his men closer to the airport, then punishing the enemy with heavy firing. But to hold the city, he needed more troops, and fast. Hearing which, Sardar had firmed his jaw and Baldev Singh had promised reinforcements. Following this, two battalions of troops had arrived by air.

Abdullah exhaled. Outside, the sun was rising, lighting up chinars and deodars, dazzling fields, dispersing the mist. Wild geese flew against the orange ball, their feathers radiant in the sun rays. It was a new day and there was much to be done.

He was having tea when Ramzan, an old comrade rushed in, his face sunken with more than the effort of guarding Srinagar. To avoid upsetting Begum Akbar, Ramzan lowered his head and whispered urgently into Abdullah's ear. *Y'Allah*! He felt like somebody had dunked him into the crystalline waters of the Jhelum. Two volunteers dead. *Killed!* Not by Pathans, but *Indian soldiers*! Abdullah gulped. He indicated that Ramzan take a chair, then nodded to his Begum, who rose and stepped away quietly.

With a pained expression, he enquired, 'How?'

Ramzan bunched his mouth, sighed, and started. 'Last night, a group of our volunteers was returning from a patrol in the Budgam area. It was dark, and as they approached Srinagar, a voice rang out enquiring who the party was. Our men thought it was a lashkar and took flight. But they were fired upon and … And two men killed. It was a 1Sikh outpost.'

Ramzan paused and wiped his forehead with a palm.

Abdullah shook his head, trying to tamp down the frustration bubbling within him. 'Ali Dar and Feroze Wani?' he enquired again.

Ramzan nodded mutely.

Two bright young men, full of vigour and hard work, such exemplary young leaders of NC volunteer corps. Ali Dar was a family man too, with an elderly mother, two young children and a hostile younger brother. This was a disaster. Outside, the sky had abruptly darkened.

'The bodies? Where are they?'

'The army unit buried them in the trenches—'

'WHAT in God's name!' Abdullah sprang up. This was wrong on so many levels! An insult to the dead men and their living families, to be hastily buried without prayers or farewell, without any information … If news of the unprovoked killings got out, the city could erupt!

'Leave it with me,' Abdullah said abruptly to Ramzan before striding out of the room to request an urgent meeting.

'Please accept my deepest sympathy,' Brigadier General L.P. Sen said, 'on this unfortunate incident that has cost two lives. But this was the result of a genuine mistake—'

'*Mis*-take?' Abdullah asked pointedly.

The brigadier leaned forward, elbows resting on his knees as he tried to close the distance between their two chairs. 'An honest mistake. A picket's job is to challenge anyone approaching its position. Now, if the volunteers had answered the challenge raised, instead of fleeing, the 1Sikh sentry would not have opened fire.'

Abdullah locked eyes with the general. 'How do I explain to the people that the men sent to protect us are the very men killing us? Hmm?'

Brigadier General Sen wagged his head slowly, framing a response that would not inflame the Sheikh.

'This puts us in a very difficult position. Indian troops cannot act like the tribesmen—'

'Excuse me, but we aren't!' the brigadier interjected.

'I have two dead men in Srinagar, killed by Indian soldiers, *not* kabailis. How do I explain this to the Valley?'

With a bang the rain cloud burst, spewing water. The sudden downpour, as if the Valley was weeping, filled his ears. Window curtains billowed, then sodden with rain, went limp on the sill.

'A genuine mistake,' the brigadier reiterated, raising his voice to be heard above the din of nature.

Abdullah scoffed. 'We should fear the day when deaths are passed off as mistakes.'

L.P. 'Bogey' Sen licked his lips. 'I understand entirely.' It was critical that Sheikh Abdullah accept his explanation and calm down; dissident elements would make capital of the incident … 'Which is why I have already moved 1Sikh away from its position at the south-eastern end of Srinagar. The battalion is now redeployed in the Rifle Range area, to the north of 1Kumaon, astride the Srinagar–Baramulla road. You can offer this as example of our corrective action.'

Abdullah grunted. 'Please have the bodies exhumed so we can carry them to the families—'

A commotion was heard from outside, raised voices, sullen slogans, anguished cries. Both men sprang up from their chairs, Sheikh Abdullah leading the way to the window that overlooked the entrance to the house. A large crowd was assembling outside, despite the rain. At the front of the procession, carried on shoulders, were two bodies in white shrouds!

Abdullah's anguished eyes darted to the general.

The men had clearly got to the buried bodies of the NC volunteers and paraded them through the main road in protest. Anger radiated outwards, slogans of azadi sounded, and

Abdullah knew that sympathizers of the Muslim Conference had seized this opportunity to browbeat the new government, committed as the MC was to acceding to Pakistan. But there was genuine anguish in the crowd, too, as it reeled with shock, and Abdullah's mind went back to when he had just returned from college and a religious clash had occurred in the streets of Srinagar. A Hindu girl was purportedly lying dead in her house by the second bridge, her family too afraid to step out for fear of their Muslim neighbours. Two whole days had gone by. Abdullah headed to the house. In time, a boat passed down the Jhelum river, a body wrapped in white placed upon a plank. Crowds followed the boat's passage along the riverbank, jeering and taunting: *Abdullah is a kavog!* Dressed in his black student's jacket and red fez, Abdullah took the body to the cremation ground even as his fellow Muslims ridiculed him as a low-caste burner of corpses.

It had been over twelve hours since the men had died. The bodies needed to be washed and dressed for burial before twenty-four hours were up. His eyes moist, Abdullah's gaze roamed restlessly over the swelling crowd.

How would he explain to the families of Ali Dar and Feroze Wani how their sons had died? If he hadn't asked for help from India, wouldn't the young men still be alive? In the days ahead, as the Valley became a battlefield, would more men get killed, their deaths explained away as 'mistakes' …

21

Srinagar (November 1947)

The raiders had an enormous advantage over the Indian troops flying into Srinagar.

Even as 161 Infantry Brigade was being hastily inducted in the Valley, the premeditated advance meant that the raiders were well entrenched to invade Srinagar, despite the prolonged looting spree in Baramulla. On the morning of 1 November, when Lt Col Harbakhsh Singh of 1Sikh flew into the Valley as deputy brigade commander, his commanding officer, Lt Col Ranjit Rai, had been killed near Baramulla; Brigadier Janak Katoch had been wounded and airlifted to Delhi; 1Sikh, compelled to pull back, was surrounded by 2000 tribesmen barely 10 miles from Srinagar, and it was uncertain if the Srinagar airfield was still in Indian hands.

As the plane crossed the Banihal Pass into the Kashmir valley, from the cockpit, Singh observed smoke shrouding neighbouring villages – the handiwork of the kabailis. Was the airfield still in Indian hands?

'Do a trial run over the landing strip,' he instructed the pilot as they approached the plateau of the airfield. 'Without touchdown.'

No immediate hostile reaction. But remote gunfire punctured the air.

Upon landing, Singh swiftly learned that only one company was defending the entire airfield. The gunfire sounded closer now. An army officer hurried up to inform him that about 200 raiders had been intercepted near the perimeter of the airfield! A platoon was engaging them in battle. They had a mere thirty riflemen. How long before the raiders broke through …

A thick cloud of red dust engulfed them as another aircraft landed.

Through narrowed eyes, Singh watched a mountain gun being off-loaded from the aircraft. Men were shouting to be heard above the din of the engines as a young Sikh supervised the unloading. He strode towards the crew.

'Ja-*bar*?'

The officer was his nephew with the Patiala State Forces! He was delivering two mountain guns, property of Indian Army on loan to Patiala during WWII. Which could not be more propitious, Singh realized.

'Can your men assemble the guns?'

Second Lt Jabar Jan Singh shook a rueful head. 'We are under strict orders not to participate in the hostilities in Kashmir.'

Singh glared at the young man. 'There is fighting going on near the perimeter. A mere infantry platoon gallantly facing a much larger force of raiders.'

A sheepish Jabar examined his shoes before pulling a note out of his pocket and handing it to his uncle.

Harbakhsh Singh read the written order, signed by the commander-in-chief of the Patiala State Forces, the Maharaja himself. Folding it with care, he put it in his pocket. 'You realize what happens if the raiders get the upper hand here?' He turned his neck to stare at the periphery where Indian troops huddled in defensive position. 'Hunh?'

His crew would not be able to fly in that eventuality; Jabar went to convince them. But they stayed disinterested.

More aircraft were landing and the growing swirl of dust and din was disorienting, Singh observed. He pursed his lips.

Fighting the Japs in Malaya during WWII, Harbakhsh Singh was wounded, operated, fitted with a silver plate to cover a gash in the cranium, endured a gruelling time as a prisoner of war, escaped to Singapore, returned from the threshold of death – all this to fiddle his thumbs whilst the Valley burned? In 1936, when he had joined the Sikh Regiment, the first instruction given to him was: *In this battalion, we give you a rope; you either pull yourself up or hang yourself!* Singh squared his shoulders. And marched to the men, calling them to attention.

'Under the powers I enjoy as a force commander in battle,' he leaned into the men to make himself heard without shouting, 'I order you to assemble your guns and follow me.'

It was a field service regulation that an order by a superior could be altered by a field commander on the spot, provided the latter could justify it later. '*Should* you disobey my order,' he said, looking each man in the eye, 'I *will* have you court martialled and shot for showing cowardice!'

The havildar with the gun detachment quickly assented. But, he gulped, the guns were without their sights and useless, therefore.

Singh waved a dismissive hand. 'Not a problem. See,' he pointed to the perimeter where the raiders were assembled. 'The distance is so short your men can fire directly through open sights.'

The startled detachment, having no choice, started to execute the CO's orders. Harbakhsh Singh stood back and observed as artillery began booming, shattering the air, exploding in giant clouds above the raiders, sending them fleeing.

Srinagar airfield was still in Indian hands.

With the airfield secured, Harbakhsh Singh turned his attention to the Brigade Headquarters, moving from the din of the airfield to a double-storeyed house half a mile down the road to Srinagar. There, he checked on the latest situation of 1Sikh. They were firmly placed on the high ground outside Pattan, ten miles from Srinagar on the Baramulla road, but surrounded by 2000 kabailis! Reinforcements and ammunition were urgently needed. Ammo could be free-dropped from the air, but reinforcements ... Singh pondered over the situation as darkness fell around them. After the ferocity of the day, an eerie quiet had descended in the Valley. The crisp air reminded him of his trek in the Kashmir valley a dozen years ago. He was on leave from the Mohmand operations against the NWFP tribals—

A sudden brain wave hit him!

Wasn't one of the infantry companies with 1Sikh, recently evacuated from Pakistan, made up of gunners who could do with a gift of mountain guns? Singh sprinted back inside and instructed a colonel to tie the guns behind jeeps and transport them at daybreak.

After which he tried to get some sleep. But the thoughts bouncing in his head kept him awake, the stars in the inky sky reminding him of night operations undertaken against the

Pathans. Breakfast at 10 p.m. and a night march to the picket in order to catch them napping. He had started his soldierly career fighting the Pathans and here he was, facing off against them again …

After three hours of sleep, Harbakhsh Singh left HQ before dawn for a recce of Srinagar. The thick mist unveiled stricken refugees everywhere, bundled in woollens, laden with personal belongings, hurrying southwards, fear carved into their faces. Patrols were sending reports of raiders in large numbers hiding in nullahs south of the airfield. This had spooked soldiers enough to result in an unfortunate shoot-out killing two locals. Securing the city was an immediate priority!

Singh decided to withdraw 1Sikh from Pattan for the defence of Srinagar. Avoiding wireless, which could be intercepted by the enemy, he asked Wing Commander Mehar 'Baba' Singh – a daredevil with a bushy beard – to fly him over 1Sikh position to drop his message for withdrawal. The new position was to be Milestone 4 on the Srinagar–Baramulla road: Shalateng.

On the morning of 4 November, Singh left by jeep to meet the 1Sikh battalion during their withdrawal.

When he arrived, soldiers were pulling tongas – the locals claimed the ponies had run away – loaded with heavy equipment and spare ammunition, running at the double. Great improvisation! The banks of the spill channel at Shalateng ran across the road, which was excellent high ground to deploy the machine guns. Singh instructed each party where to take position.

The raiders, meanwhile, assumed the Sikhs were withdrawing for good. They halted at Zainkut village, half a mile from the Sikh position, Srinagar in their sights. On the night of 5–6 November, they opened fire at Shalateng, which the Sikhs replied to. But the raiders withdrew by morning. From the leisurely pace of the Pathans, Singh gauged that the kabailis had been lulled into believing that the Indians were on the defensive. Meanwhile, 4Kumaon had been flown into the Valley and Singh had deployed them behind 1Sikh, in an abandoned race course. Unknown to the raiders, the Indians were awaiting their chance …

Which arrived on the morning of 7 November.

Through the night, the raiders had been closing in on 1Sikh. What they didn't know was that some armoured cars had just arrived in Srinagar. Singh instructed the armoured cars to approach Zainkut village directly behind the raiders' and in front of 1Sikh. He asked the air force to concentrate their patrolling in that specific area. After which, Singh gave the word.

GO!

1Sikh attacked the raiders' frontally. When the Pathans tried to get on the high ground of the spill channel, they were mowed down by machine gunfire. They tried to shelter in the haystacks on the ploughed maize field. But Indian aircraft spotted them and fired into the hay, setting the field afire.

Caught in a cleft stick, the raiders were rendered helpless for the first time.

As the Pathans wondered about their next course of action, armoured cars appeared blazing from their rear. Singh ordered 4Kumaon to attack the enemy base at Zainkut. He watched as the raiders fled pell-mell, jumping into the Jhelum river or the adjoining lake. In twenty minutes from the word GO, the battle was won! Singh exhaled. Srinagar was secured. With it, so was the airfield, the only route available to move army troops into the Valley.

At the end of the day, the Indians counted some 300 bodies. A journalist who had been bravely milling around the scene requested Singh's permission to keep a miniature sarangi he had retrieved from one of the raiders as souvenir.

The Battle of Shalateng – short, intense, decisive – had turned the tables on the enemy.

22

Srinagar (November 1947)

Margot shuffled down the boat deck, huddling in her wool overcoat. It had served her well in the biting cold of Berlin during the war, but seemed inadequate against the chilly wind that swept down from the icy peaks. She had no reason to be out in this bracing weather when a fire was spitting warmth inside. And the deck, wet from rain, was slippery. But Margot needed to think and the heat made her brain blurry. So, she smoked and shuffled to and fro, wood planks squeaking in sympathy. A fortnight since Ali Dar's death – no, *killing* – and the *Mayfair* continued to be under a pall. Margot hadn't seen Kashmira once since the unfortunate news, even as her food continued to arrive like clockwork, courtesy a neighbouring houseboat. The sound of Kashmira crooning, plaintive and oddly melodious, Kashmiri songs that drifted from the cookboat or the floating farm as she went about her chores, had died down. Even the smell of woodsmoke wasn't wafting … who was feeding the family? Occasionally, young Safina sniffled about in the shadows of the cookboat, whilst Gul looked lost and woeful as he sat under the chinar petting a stray kitten. Only Hassan was visible, spitting and hissing like a kangri fire pot going kaput.

Margot blew smoke into the misty air and watched it mingle with the vapours. With the ongoing struggle in Kashmir, her assignment had swelled exponentially – there would be enough work until year end. By which time, all houseboats typically emptied out, the tourist season well and truly over. With the violence, the end of the Raj and the exodus of foreigners, the economy had sputtered to a halt. The flower-seller, who would paddle by in his shikara, had yesterday begged to offload his entire stock of daisies, dahlias, zinnias and roses for *one* dollar! In winter, Ali had worked as an embroider to supplement the household income. The mantle had now fallen on Hassan, younger brother and man of the family. Margot pursed her mouth and plucked a scrap of tobacco from her lower lip. Hassan was a bit of a loose cannon, ricocheting about as he railed against Sheikh Abdullah, National Conference, India, Pandit Nehru. He was in Baramulla on 12 November when the Indian Prime Minister had visited Srinagar and addressed the people in the poor, brutalized town. Margot was there, covering the event, when a sole heckler repeatedly interrupted Pandit Nehru's speech. Hassan was allowed to vent until NC volunteers decided they had had enough.

With a shake of her head, Margot stopped by the ashtray to stub out the cigarette. A flash of brilliant blue cut the vaporous air as a kingfisher dived for fish. She knew what she had to do. Hand over in advance the full rent of the houseboat plus meals until spring: a princely sum of two dollars per day. With three rupees to a dollar, Margot was living better than any New York socialite, with a four-room houseboat, servants, and meals of quail and wild duck! By March 1948, the issue of Kashmir would be resolved and Kashmira would have had money to tide over the coldest winter of her life.

Showered and dressed, Margot walked down the planks that connected the houseboat to the cookboat. She was aiming for informality – a brief detour en route to a meeting to drop off her rental money, an advance of four months, no big deal. Creaking, which was set off with any pressure on the wooden planks, alerted the inmates and Safina's head soon popped out. Her face was puffed, eyes swollen. Margot's mouth quivered as she tried to muster the right tone. '*Is* Kashmira receiving visitors?'

Safina stayed blank. Language was an issue. Ali and Hassan both spoke English. Margot tried to simplify, supplementing her delivery with expressive use of both hands. 'Can I … see Kashmira?'

Safina held up a palm before diving back in. She returned quickly and beckoned Margot inside.

It was her first time in the cookboat, which was dingy, dark and dank, so removed from the palatial houseboat barely fifty yards away, which had a living room, dining room, two bedrooms with bathrooms, was flush with overstuffed armchairs, walnut tables, carved cupboards, carpeted floors, wood-panelled walls, gauzy curtains, reading lamps, a radio, a phonograph and a pot-bellied stove that crackled invitingly. The cookboat was decrepit! Her solitary luxury smacked her and Margot felt a deep sense of unease – the kind that pitted her stomach when grandmaman recounted stories of her childhood amidst the poverty of a Haitian Creole household. Margot sucked her teeth.

In a small room, which likely served for cooking and washing, Safina indicated a rickety chair for the guest. Margot, tall as any man, perched on it. A creaking of wood and a shuffling of feet, Kashmira emerged from the dark adjacent room. She blinked her eyes, a hand raised involuntarily as a shield, before slumping on the thin rug. Margot promptly dropped to the floor and sat with her knees pulled up, as she had first learned to do when visiting Mahatma Gandhi in Delhi after his prayer session.

Margot cleared her throat. It struck her that she wouldn't be able to communicate with Kashmira since neither spoke the other's language. 'Gul?' she enquired. With his smattering of English, the boy could help.

Safina sighed and trudged off. Kashmira sat listless, head bowed, eyes lowered. When she first met her, Margot was struck by the singular face, as if the picture-postcard beauty of Kashmir had transposed itself on a human being: complexion like fresh snow, cheekbones like cliffs, greyish-green eyes that changed colour like the quicksilver Jhelum. In the confined space, Margot's nose registered the rank odour coming from Kashmira's unwashed body. In the doorway, a drop of water coalesced before it fell. On Safina, who came in, dragging a reluctant Gul with a leaky nose and tear tracks down his grimy face.

'Mister Gul,' Margot hailed in a cheery voice, 'hello!'

Gul wrapped his arms around his bony chest, refusing to look up.

'Broar,' Safina explained, angrily pointing to her brother. 'Broar … Mao … jabran.' She made her hands into claws and mimicked a cat scratching.

'Ah,' Margot nodded. She had sighted Gul petting the kitten aggressively – clearly it had not appreciated his misplaced affection. From her bag, Margot withdrew the envelope with cash and held it forward. 'Gul, this is my advance rent for Kashmira.' She looked from the boy to the mother who had not looked up since joining them, her head tilted downwards like a broken flower on stem. Margot shook the envelope. 'Rent. Advance. Till March.'

Gul looked up and cocked his head. 'You stay in ... in ...' he searched for the word, then spat, 'chilai kalan?'

It was Margot's turn to look puzzled.

'Chilai kalan is our deep winter,' a man's gruff voice explained as Hassan sidled in from the doorway. 'Which scares even locals. You are here till March, Miss Margot?'

He stood with the light to his back, which made his hooded eyes and shadowy face hard to read.

'Ye-es,' Margot drawled, adopting a casual air. 'I expect the issue will be resolved by then.'

'Yes! We would have thrown Sheikh Abdullah back into jail or kicked him to India.' Hassan breathed heavily through his nostrils. 'I will take that.' He extended a hand for the envelope.

Ideally Margot would have wanted to hand it to Kashmira, in the absence of her brother-in-law. But he was the head of the house now. Hassan grabbed the proffered cash, nodding his head. 'You are a guest, Miss Margot, so I should not say this, but what you wrote was not right, you know. *Baramulla Brutalities!* The lashkar is here to liberate us, not loot us.'

'Really?' Margot cocked her head. 'Then why did Baramulla look like an army had invaded the town?'

'Army has invaded Srinagar! Don't you see?' Hassan's extended arm questioned her. 'Indian army killed Ali, have you forgotten?'

Margot wouldn't go down that path. Besides, Gul's lower lip was trembling and Safina looked like all the colour had fled from her face. Hassan might want to rake his family's terrible misfortune, but Margot would not rise to the bait.

'I'm planning a visit to Jammu. Perhaps you can help arrange a meeting with Sardar Ibrahim. A chance to see what's happening in Muzaffarabad—'

'Yes, yes, I help. I help you meet the Muslim Conference leaders and the leaders in Muzaffarabad, so you can write, eh, write about our side of the story. Tell your readers how the people of Jammu and Kashmir want to join Pakistan, not India, not Nehru, not Gandhi! Stop praising Nehru and Abdullah in your reports, they are devils! Shaitan!'

Margot kept an impassive face. Safina was casting anxious glances at the room beyond. Probably where the grandmother sat. The elderly woman was blind, not deaf – Hassan really was an idiot. Margot made to get up.

'That story about Sherwani,' Hassan clucked, 'pure hokum.' He pulled a folded sheet of newspaper from under his loose overcoat, shook it out and read with effort. 'A sort of Robin Hood character, from the stories the townspeople told me … his *martyrdom* … he was fast assuming the stature of a *saint*.' Hassan paused, his face like he had tasted poison, and he smacked the paper with the back of his right hand. 'Why you lie, Miss Margot?'

Margot wanted to leave, but Hassan Dar was blocking the doorway.

'My party people tell me my houseboat guest write lies. Why, they ask? Why, I ask?'

'Don't presume to tell me how to do my job!' Margot snapped.

Hassan's eyes narrowed. 'You live under my roof and you abuse me!' His voice had risen as he flung the paper, thrust his hands inside his coat, retrieved the envelope of cash and thrust it at Margot. 'Take your money, take and leave!'

The man was stark raving mad. Margot put the envelope back into her purse, and quietly and politely reminded him that she was booked to stay until December, cash for which she had already paid. She knew that money had already gone into the unexpected expense of Ali's funeral. And Hassan Dar wasn't earning any income …

His face darkened. Fuming and muttering under his breath, Hassan stomped off.

Margot blew air out of her mouth. She turned to say bye and saw Kashmira was whispering to her daughter. Safina frowned, then turned to whisper in Gul's ear. With her chin, she indicated Margot. Gul gulped.

'Miss Margot,' the boy sniffled. 'Mouj say … her family in Baramulla,' he licked his lips, 'was dead … by kabaili.' He paused, his chest heaving. 'My M-Moul … dead by Indian Army…' Gul turned to his sister and whispered urgently in Kashmiri. Safina insisted. He tilted his head at Margot. 'So, my Mouj trust who?'

Kashmira had raised her head and was watching Margot, her eyes jade-green in a face white as ice.

Margot, wearied of Germany and her reportage of WWII, had come to India to witness the birth of a new nation. Europe had appeared heavy with death of an era, India seemed on the threshold of a new life – something she had got increasingly convinced of as she interviewed Gandhi and Panditji, and met ordinary Congress workers. But, in that instant, facing Kashmira, all of Margot's certainties were stripped away and she felt déjà vu creeping up – it was war, once again, brutal and hopeless.

23

Delhi (November 1947)

Vallabh placed a small box on the table.

'This was taken off a *raider* in Kashmir.' He opened it to reveal two small bottles of pills to Jawaharlal. 'Kit for sterilizing water – standard issue for Pakistani soldiers. And still Liaquat Ali Khan and Pakistan want us to believe that they were not behind the invasion!' He snorted.

Jawahar had walked over from his York Road residence, as was his habit when he needed to discuss something. Vallabh was aware of Lord Mountbatten's efforts to arrange a meeting between Jawaharlal and Liaquat Ali Khan to settle the Kashmir issue diplomatically.

'You can take this box as a gift for Liaquat.' Vallabh curled his lip.

Jawahar sprang up and started to walk the length of the spacious room, pivoting at the door which opened on to the verandah, shut against the winter chill. The scenes from Baramulla were vivid in his mind – a picturesque town torn asunder as if by a typhoon, rubble everywhere, everything looted, even doors missing from houses and shops! The Christian mission had been ransacked, nuns brutalized by 'great black wild beasts', as a mission priest had described. It was all a taste of what Pakistan meant. Jawahar shook his head.

'After my Baramulla visit, I am convinced that no vote can be held until every single raider is expelled.'

But Vallabh knew Lord Mountbatten thought that the United Nations could be a possible mediator for Kashmir between India and Pakistan. Even Liaquat had floated the idea of asking the UN to consider the question of all three disputed states – Kashmir, Hyderabad and Junagadh. But Junagadh was in the bag already! Its dewan, Shah Nawaz Bhutto, had cabled saying he would hand over power to the Indian government. Setting up an Arzi Hukumat in Rajkot with Samaldas Gandhi as its president, and moving forces into neighbouring Babariawad and Mangrol had put the ring right through the bull's nose. And Hyderabad, after the drama of the preceding months, had finally signed a year-long standstill agreement with India. Vallabh's nostrils flared in quiet satisfaction. Liaquat's UN idea was part of Jinnah's plan to stick a dagger into India's heart by using the hilt of Junagadh to keep Hyderabad independent. Foiled. Now, even the kabailis in Kashmir were on the run.

Manibehn popped her head through the open door and enquired about tea. Jawahar thanked her, but refused. Meanwhile, Vallabh looked hopeful. But his daughter shook her head and slipped away. Vallabh sighed. He couldn't blame her. His colon, which had flared up on news of Junagadh's betrayal, had finally settled.

'How was the meeting with Lord Ismay?'

Now that Lord Mountbatten was away for the wedding of his nephew with Princess Elizabeth, his chief of staff, Ismay had sat down with Jawahar for two hours, trying to convince him to sit down with Liaquat.

'We did not start the fighting, I reminded Ismay.' Jawahar rolled his eyes. 'Besides, His Excellency knows that I am convinced that the whole business has been very carefully planned on an extensive scale. After Kashmir, the next objective would be Patiala, then East Panjab, then Delhi itself. "*On to Delhi!*" is the cry all over West Panjab.'

Vallabh patted the shawl around his shoulders, freshly spun by Mani who worried about his health in Delhi's winter. His Excellency liked newfangled ideas and the UN was one such. Earlier, Mountbatten had persuaded Jawaharlal to make a broadcast to the nation that a plebiscite would be held under UN auspices. Usually the PM shared those texts with his deputy, but that particular day, 28 October, a busy Jawaharlal had not sent the text before 8.15 p.m. When Vallabh read it, he found the commitment unnecessary. He tried to contact Jawaharlal to suggest an edit, but the Prime Minister had left for the Broadcasting House. So, he deputed Vidya Shankar to hasten and ask Jawaharlal to delete the offending phrase, 'under UN auspices', but to retain the commitment made at the time of accession, namely that the wishes of the people would be ascertained. By the time his confidential aide reached the Broadcasting House, the PM had already begun his broadcast.

Jawahar's voice brought Vallabh back.

'… I made it clear to Ismay that a meeting was desirable *in principle*, but there was no hurry.' Jawaharlal perched on the sofa across from Vallabh. 'Things are going well in Kashmir, and deferring the discussion with Liaquat will only strengthen our hand …'

Vallabh nodded. It was in their interest that the matter was resolved without outside mediation. 'My sources tell me that even Liaquat is keen on seeking every means of settlement with India, even though the extremists in Pakistan are pushing him the other way.'

Jawahar probed his chin, his eyes on the pill bottles on the table. 'Well, the upcoming Joint Defence Council meeting will be a good opportunity for him to execute that sentiment.'

On 26 November, Liaquat Ali Khan arrived in Delhi. Still recovering from his illness, he sat in an armchair with a blanket for warmth. It was the first time the two leaders were meeting since 30 September, and after the invasion of Kashmir – this was one of the issues for discussion along with others leftover from Partition. Dickie Mountbatten was hoping to get some breakthroughs when a 'Most Immediate' letter from Jawaharlal Nehru was brought in. Which surprised Dickie, since Jawa was expected at the meeting!

Enclosed were two telegrams, and Jawa's note: 'In view of what Mr Liaquat Ali Khan has said in these telegrams, I see no particular advantage in my discussing the Kashmir situation or indeed any other matter with him.'

Dickie could not believe the contents of the two telegrams. It was as if Liaquat had decided to dig a hole in his own lifeboat! He had accused Sheikh Abdullah of being 'a quisling and a paid agent to disrupt the Muslims of Kashmir', the Government of India of trying to mislead the world, of evasion ... contradiction ... tyranny ... and of attempting to eliminate the whole Muslim population of Kashmir! One telegram was addressed to Prime Minister Attlee himself, requesting the setting-up in Kashmir of an impartial and independent administration immediately.

Dickie pursed his lips, trying to quell the anger boiling up in him. Weeks of work had gone into arranging this meeting, and a wan Liaquat had arrived as if arisen from his deathbed – for what?

'You've been criminally foolish to jeopardize this chance at negotiation!' Dickie berated him.

After which, he turned on the charm to convince Jawa to join the meeting.

Upon arrival, a terribly annoyed Jawaharlal Nehru started off by categorically stating that the Dominion of India had gone to the assistance of Kashmir when called upon, not only by the ruler but also by Sheikh Abdullah, the leader of the biggest popular party in the state. 'Further,' Jawahar rapped the table. 'I have no doubt that if we had failed to respond with help, the present Government of India would have been overthrown, to be replaced by an irresponsible and extremist government which,' he glared at Liaquat Ali Khan, 'would probably have declared war upon Pakistan!'

The Pakistan Prime Minister shifted in the armchair before speaking in a strained voice. 'The Government of Pakistan has had their position greatly weakened by not taking strong action against India … I am personally being abused in the vernacular press for failing to support Muslim interests.'

'Gentlemen,' Dickie addressed the two leaders, 'thank you for airing your initial thoughts. Now we *must* address the business at hand, the first of which is how to divide the Raj's sterling balances and international debt.'

The meeting turned into a series of meetings, the two leaders meeting four more times over next two days. Back and forth, back and forth, they traded charges – *Kashmir, the 'K', was integral to Pakistan … The ruler had asked India for help … As had the Nawab of Junagadh, to Pakistan; yet, India had sent its forces to invade! ... Pakistan had sent the kabailis into Kashmir! ... Shouldn't the same rule apply?* – steered by Mountbatten until each exhausted side conceded some ground.

Eventually, the proposals were scripted by Lord Ismay with an official representative of each dominion: Mohammed Ali for Pakistan and V.P. Menon for India.

Pakistan should use all their influence to persuade the rebel 'Azad Kashmir' forces to cease fighting, and the tribesmen and other 'invaders' to withdraw from Kashmir territory as quickly as possible. India should withdraw the bulk of their forces, leaving only small detachments of minimum strength to deal with disturbances. The United Nations would design and supervise a plebiscite. Terms for the return of refugees were agreed upon, and Pakistan got 550 million rupees of reserves.

A relieved Lord Mountbatten thought the deal was sealed. Even Mr Patel, who could be obdurate over the issue of Pakistan's share, had signed off a larger share of reserves than expected. 'That ought to show Pakistan that India was not out to throttle her,' he said magnanimously.

The relief was ephemeral.

Dickie, having brought the shutters down on the British Raj and partitioned the subcontinent, should have learned by now that perverse sceptres loomed in the background – Jinnah in Pakistan, zealous Hindus in India.

Shortly afterwards, Sardar Patel and Baldev Singh returned from a visit to Jammu with stories that raised the temperature of the Indian Cabinet. Tribesmen in large numbers were waiting on the border in West Panjab for more raids. Liaquat Ali Khan, after leaving Delhi, had assured the Pathans that Pakistan would never give up Kashmir. But what really made the Indian ears burn were stories of the wholesale massacre of non-Muslims and the widespread selling of Kashmiri women. Edwina, returning from relief work in West Panjab, had heard similar tales of woe which she had shared with Jawaharlal Nehru.

Meanwhile, in Pakistan, Liaquat Ali Khan, whilst touring Sialkot, heard ghastly stories of the massacre of Muslim men in Jammu, and the abduction and rape of Muslim women. In Rawalpindi, Azad Kashmir leaders condemned the new proposals. And an apoplectic Jinnah dismissed Mountbatten for having 'become a Hindu'!

India explored ways to ratchet up its military offensive.

Pakistan enlisted its army regulars to boost the proxy war.

The first Indo-Pak war had officially begun.

24

Lahore–Rawalpindi–Datiyal (December 1947)

In the abandoned cowshed with its charred pillars and sunken ceilings, the only thing of beauty that still stood was the old banyan. Its trunk was wider than the combined girth of two buffaloes standing side by side, its aerial roots more numerous than the stars twinkling on this overcast winter night. Malik, wrapped in a thick loi, scrutinized the tree from below. His eyes flitted from branch to branch, parsing the thick leaves, looking for a sign, some sign ...

It was good that nobody was there to observe him.

Akbar Khan had declared him a shaidayi when their Srinagar trip had ended. The director had not even meant to condemn him with faint praise, but Malik's heart had rejoiced. What else was he but shaidayi, crazy, mad in love? He was reminded afresh that the militiaman who arranged weapons of mass destruction in Panjab, now Kashmir, was the sepoy whom Tara had loved. That sepoy had died with Tara ... Or so he thought... For Tara had shown herself to him, on the bridge over Jhelum, in the chinar tree outside Srinagar, fleeting, teasing, elusive, much like Tara was … *is* … Her eyes alight with mischief … Malik peered at the banyan with laser eyes: Why wouldn't Tara show herself? He had been gazing at the trees of Laur since his return, hoping for a sighting, with no luck until this dusk when he thought he heard her laughter in the banyan. He had been meditating under the tree since then. Early on, the glow worms kept him company, but now, past midnight, his bottom was sore from the rough-hewn jute seat, his eyes fatigued, his head beginning to loll …

Say, sepoy, did you miss me?

In the three years he'd been away, Tara had blossomed like the kachnar flower. How was he to impress her? *Care for a fag?* The phrase popped out of nowhere.

She tittered. *You have returned an Angrej, is it?*

I've returned after licking the Angrej's enemy! In my spare time, I picked up gitter-mitter, he said, hoping to make her laugh at their colloquial term for the English language. Now he spoke to impress; she listened to be impressed.

Stand firm. Dig for victory. The need is great, time is short.

A pull on a cigarette.

Rats as big as cats. Yes, sir! Whiz-bang. Flaming onion. Bum fodder.

A spiral of smoke.

Careless talk costs lives. Mr Hitler wants to know! Whirra-whirra-whirra-phut-phut-phut!

With his free hand, the gabbling sepoy took her palm and placed it on his groin. It throbbed and grew beneath her hand. He babbled on, his eyes on her—

A screech and Malik shot up. He spun his head wildly, the cowshed, the open yard, the tree … a pair of eyes intent upon him … but no Tara.

Ullu da patha! Malik mimicked Tara as he berated himself and the son-of-a-gun owl above for waking him from his dream. He'd given up smoking when Tara disappeared from his life. For she had *literally* disappeared: He had hunted the compound where Tara died, but found no trace of her. Malik wiped his eyes.

Cigarettes had been plentiful during the war, which was where he had picked up smoking and a smattering of Angreji. 'Care for a fag?' he now asked the tree jocularly, seeing Tara's eyes widen, a smile on her lips. Malik sighed. *Tara*. He shook his head, fingers itching for a cigarette, then turned his head to gaze back at the tree. Swear on god! There was Tara in the tree, swinging her legs from a branch, smiling down at him. Malik shot up. Hoarsely, he asked, 'Is that *you*, Tara?'

'Forgotten me, already?' Tara's giggle burst through his heart and Malik staggered back.

'Forget you? No, never!'

'Then why didn't you save me in Muzaffarabad?'

'I tried, I did, but it wasn't you!'

'It was my sister. So many of my sisters dead because of you, Sepoy Malik.'

'*Me?*'

'Of course. Your weapons killed them.'

Malik clutched his head.

'They're all here with me, in this tree.'

'I-I c-can't see them …'

'Think they will show themselves to you? Trust their killer?'

'No-no-no, Tara, no,' Malik sobbed.

'For so long even I couldn't show myself to you. Hai, I thought, what had happened to my sepoy! But then, in Muzaffarabad, I saw something in you change … you can save the women, Sikandar.'

At the sound of his name from her mouth, Malik collapsed on the floor streaked with hay. 'But the women are dead!'

'Adiya, people think Tara is dead. But you know better.'

Malik gulped anxiously. 'Don't leave me, Tara!'

'Save my sisters, Sikandar, go! You'll find me waiting there.'

Go where? War was raging in Kashmir with Pakistan having entered the battle proper. Daily, extraordinary news arrived, and Malik didn't know what to believe. Gilgit-Baltistan had declared independence from the Maharaja's rule, much like the provisional government in Muzaffarabad. Tribesmen were moving towards the mountain passes of Zojila and Burzil to threaten the Srinagar valley. In Bagh, the state garrison had been liquidated. More Indian troops were continuing to arrive in Kashmir. From Jammu, an Indian brigade was moving westwards to Mirpur, which had been overrun by Pakistani soldiers and Pathans. Civilians were being massacred, men killed, women abducted …

Malik pulled at the strings of his spiderweb for specific information. Following which, he went to Pindi to seek out Akbar Khan, who didn't need him since ammunition was no longer an issue. 'You will not have to do it with sticks alone any longer,' Akbar had mimicked General Messervy, the commander-in-chief of Pakistan, 'I am going to help.'

Malik's sources said the director was in town to attend a conference with the Prime Minister. Malik waited outside Circuit House to meet him. Late afternoon, Akbar Khan came out looking pleased with himself. Surprised to see Malik, he offered him a ride since he was heading to Jhelum.

Jhelum. Malik's ears pricked up. Alibeg was on the old Mughal Road that connected Panjab with Jammu and Kashmir, two miles northeast of Jhelum ...

As they drove south, a blustery wind picked up, smacking dry leaves on the windscreen. Akbar drummed the steering wheel, clearly happy with the conference.

'Is it true then,' Malik cleared his throat, 'that the major scene of operations is now in the area westwards from Jammu?'

'Why do you ask?' Akbar kept his gaze on the road.

Malik licked his dry lips and continued. 'The government in Muzaffarabad government has set up a camp for rescued women, I hear. At Alibeg. Women abducted by Pathans and rescued from them?'

Akbar narrowed his eyes. 'Go on.'

'So, I want to help.'

'Help how?'

'Help at the camp. From what I hear, the camp's commander is Pathan, the camp guards are Pathans, and they have to secure the camp from raiders who are fellow Pathans.'

'So?'

'So, there lies the problem. I assume you want to safeguard the women?' Malik cocked a brow.

Akbar Khan screwed up his mouth. 'Yes. We are keen on an exchange of refugees: Muslims trapped in West Jammu for non-Muslims in the Muzaffarabad region.'

'Exactly. As a Panjabi, and an ex-soldier, I would be a good candidate for the camp commander position at Ali—'

'—at Datiyal, four miles from Govindpur, the district headquarters of the provisional government. Alibeg is overcrowded and overrun. Some of the women and children are being transferred to Datiyal camp after they have been questioned and their statements recorded in the presence of the area deputy commissioner. For those who wish to go to India, arrangements are being made for their exchange. Women who wish to make a home with their husbands will be returned to them.'

Taken aback at the speed with which his tentative proposal had been accepted, Malik nodded wordlessly.

'Why wait then?' Akbar said as he braked abruptly beside a roadside vendor and bought a paper bag of rewaris. Offering the sesame-coated jaggery toffee to Malik, he said, 'Congratulations on your new job!'

Munching on the rewaris, the two men nursed their thoughts as they sped past abundant fields of wheat, corn, tobacco, lentil. At Jhelum town, Akbar swung on to the old Mughal Road towards Alibeg. Crossing the river, they entered an expanse of fruit orchards and vegetable plantations. The grey winter day was changing to twilight, birds in the sky and people carrying firewood or water pitchers were hurrying home. Soon, light from kerosene lamps dotted their approach.

'When all this is over,' Akbar said, 'I want to know the story of how a Jangi became a Jhangi. Warrior to love-struck lover of Heer! For now,' he snorted, 'here is the Datiyal camp.'

Which was how one chilly December evening, Sikandar Malik, erstwhile sepoy and militiaman, found himself in front of a rambling house for the benefit of rescued women.

25

Srinagar (December 1947)

Hassan was missing. Or deliberately absent.

He had been huffing and puffing around the boat, keeping odd hours, sneaking in late, leaving early, angry, always angry, muttering about Ali, Abdullah, Azad Kashmir, azadi. It had been ten days since the family had seen him or the envelope with cash their tenant had given in advance. Safina had turned the cookboat upside down, shaking rugs, flinging quilts, tossing utensils until, clutching her hair, she had screamed and screamed. No money meant no food: Bilquis, Safina and Gul were living off watery gruel, the last few days' meals had been flour mixed with water, whilst Kashmira herself had been living on air since Ali went. A listless Kashmira started to mutter.

To him we do belong, to him we shall return.

Over and over, like rolling prayer beads. She would have continued in this trance-like state if a great sighing, like the ice cleaving, had not pierced her daze and had her catapult to the boat's prow, spring across the planks, and freeze to a stop – oscillating with bare feet in front of the floating garden.

Snow, that had fallen steadily and frozen part of the lake and whitened the mountains, had accumulated on the garden. With no one shovelling the ice, the reed bed was creaking under the weight, ready to collapse into the water from which it had arisen. Grabbing a shovel, Kashmira dug like a maniac, smacking ice with the shovel blade, gouging the frozen bed, then sweeping the loose chunks into the water. Again and again, over and over, not registering the sweat sprouting on her body, or the alarmed looks of her children who watched her zealous progress, or her bare feet turning blue, her hands stiffening, frigid air clogging her lungs as she trowelled the snow. Finally, the shovel slipped from her grip before her icicle-like body plodded back to the cookboat.

Inside, an almighty shivering seized her. Safina rubbed the soles of her mother's feet, trying to pump blood back into them as Gul, under her instruction, massaged Kashmira's forehead, hands and cheeks. When the trembling didn't ease and the feet looked like they'd never thaw, Safina sent Gul to fetch the tenant. It was midday, but Miss Margot was fortunately at home. Fortunately, she was also big and strong enough to scoop their Mouj in her arms and march with her to the houseboat living room where Kashmira was deposited close to the blazing stove and swaddled in blankets.

When Miss Margot learned about the missing Hassan and money, she instructed Safina to fetch Grandma Bilquis and set her up in the other bedroom. Safina looked unsure. Miss Margot said the new arrangement was only until their mother awakened. Gul huddled next to Kashmira, watching anxiously as her eyelids flickered in her state of fugue.

Outside, snow continued to fall, sheathing once again the floating garden's turnips and melons and greens with its white shroud. Inside, Kashmira appeared comatose, but in her mind she was the young bride, newly arrived from Baramulla into the Valley where her house and farm were both on water!

Since the poles had rotted, one of the floating farms was in danger of collapsing. Ali showed his bride what a floating farm was. Poplar poles, seven or eight metre long, were the foundation of the raft upon which they built a radh, a floating garden. As he gathered fresh poles for replacement, Ali teased her, 'Landlubber, at least sing to me as I work!'

Shyly, Kashmira trilled a lol-gevun, as she sat on the prow of their shikara and watched her husband work. The sun made him look radiant: brown eyes and reddish-brown hair like a bottle of honey. Plump pink lotus flowers ringed them, their large flat leaves fanned in a green carpet, bulbuls cooed in the blazing chinar trees as kingfishers dived and emerged, shaking water from their flashy feathers. Frequently, as he worked, Ali smiled with his eyes at his bride, and Kashmira knew she was in paradise. Afterwards, Ali started building a new floating farm with her, teaching her how to weave weeds together into floating mats that would be the base. He gathered plants of the lake together with their roots and intertwined them on the poles. Then he added layer upon layer of pruned weeds. In two years, as they watched over it, the raft swelled in thickness.

'When will it be ready?' Kashmira asked, a hand supporting her belly, pregnant with Safina.

'When it is sufficiently strong to take the weight of a man, it's ready'. Ali wagged his head. Then he turned to her, the gold flecks in his amber eyes sparkling. Before he scooped her up in his arms and stepped on to their floating reed farm, Kashmira squealing in surprise. 'And when a man can carry his wife on to it, it becomes their personal floating garden!' Laughing, he deposited her amidst red roses! Unknown to her, he had been tenderly cultivating a patch of koshur gulab for her. The thorny bushes blossomed for barely a fortnight, with petals soft as pashmina, while requiring care through the year. It was an extravagance, Kashmira had chided. It was love, Ali had declared.

Kashmira flailed in an attempt to rise afresh. No snowfall would steal from her that floating garden with velvety roses which Ali had built for her! Bitter winters had stolen two babies from her – one in the womb, one barely born, before Gul arrived. Kashmira writhed as she fought off chilai kalan. Margot soothed her back. Kashmira moaned through the night, floating between two worlds: newly pregnant with Ali and newly widowed with two children and a mother-in-law; an orphan with no parents, no brother, no sister – *No*. She had no news of Zooni. But Zooni was in Reasi where Muslims were safe from kabaili attacks. Zooni, her younger beni, might well be alive. Just like the flower garden Ali had gifted her. Still alive …

Two days later, Kashmira had recovered enough to sit up, supported by bolsters, as Safina fed her by spoon soupy yakhni, fragrant with curd and ghee, brimming with succulent mutton. Margot had had a grocer unload a shikara-full of groceries to restock the cookboat pantry.

Smiling feebly at her children, Kashmira noticed Gul's mud-stained clothes and snot-smeared face as he rekindled the stove; Bilquis's toothless mouth moving silently in prayer as her cloudy eyes searched the air; Safina's red-rimmed eyes and blistered lips and chapped hands. As her daughter fed her,

Kashmira noticed her limp hair, the colour of her father's and equally bountiful, but diminished in the weeks since his death. Safina's bent head revealed bald patches, the size of lemons. Kashmira's grief had made her oblivious to her children's. But she was no Habba Khatoon spinning verses of sorrow in memory of her husband.

Kashmira stalled Safina's hand as it scooped yakhni, and asked her to finish the rest.

'I've eaten already,' Safina insisted.

Kashmira acknowledged that with wide-open eyes. 'Never a yakhni bowl my daughter couldn't polish off!'

Which made Safina giggle. Gul, feeling left out, bounded up to them. The mother wrapped her arms around her children, burying her head in them, registering their matted hair and reeking bodies, long overdue for a bath.

They were Ali's legacy … hers to preserve.

26

Datiyal (December 1947)

The house was built like any sizeable village home, a large living room, a couple of bedrooms, a storeroom, kitchen and courtyard – which was where any comparison with a normal village home ended. Housing some 150 women and children, it stank like a pigsty. A hillock of garbage graced the entrance, insects crawled over the floors.

It belonged to Abdul Aziz, who had hurried over after Akbar sent word with a sentry. A tall, soft-spoken man, he was called thekedar sahib. Owner of a farm, several orchards and a brick kiln, he paid all the expenses for running the camp. Malik eyed the man suspiciously. The whole world had gone to seed – even the weather had turned cold, wet and miserable – then who was this Muslim man looking to protect unfortunate Hindu women? Women who had the look of cattle meant for slaughter, massed as they were elbow to elbow, eyes vacant, unkempt hair and clothes, their heads buried between their knees or slung back against a wall. A few lay on beds of hay, unconcerned with the crying of children or of other women, the dark rings under their eyes showing they weren't getting much sleep. One laughed periodically, in a hard, uncaring manner, as if possessed by a djinn.

Malik would never forget how the women had eyed him when he walked in with Akbar and was introduced by Abdul Aziz as their camp commander. In the dim light of the kerosene lamp, the women, gaunt, lifeless, appeared like skeletons in rags. Despair had seized him.

That night, Malik had tossed and turned in the cot which he placed in the verandah outside the living room. A bitterly cold wind rustled the hay that served for a mattress, strands swirling in the courtyard like churails ... *Churails* ... Didn't they sit in trees and snare innocent men? Malik looked up at the couple of trees in the courtyard, lemon and mulberry. No Tara there, no other women either. Was Tara angry because he had equated her to a churail? Or because he thought churails were witches or ogresses – *how like a man!* Was that his thought or was Tara speaking? In his mind's eye, he could see her laughing, that chipped front tooth making her smile so winsome ...

Tara, he sighed, and snuggled beneath his loi. He imagined the lice crawling out of it on him, and shuddered. He knew bombs, grenades, rifles, war – how was he to help these women? To quell his dismay, Malik searched the night sky twinkling with stars for an answer.

The same way you would help me, Sikandar.

Malik wasn't sure if he heard her or dreamt it, but Tara's voice was in his head when he woke up. Which was good. For in the clear light of day, things were worse. Human excrement and other waste was piled within the compound, rank with the smell of urine. Men could use the open to defecate, not women. Trying not to gag, he tied a cloth around his mouth and nose, and set about cleaning the filthy courtyard, assessing the situation as he went. Blood-filled rags from wounds and women's menstruation; no soap or detergent for washing bodies, clothes, utensils; unclean vessels and drinking water; unsheltered firewood soaking in the winter rains; septic wounds, malnutrition, fever, dysentery …

As he swept and scrubbed and collected garbage, he heard a woman reciting the kalma in the manner of a military commander barking orders. Her staccato was picked up by other women, the unholy chorus worse than the rattle of gunfire.

A woman wearing a saree approached him, her head covered with the shawl she had draped around herself.

'Malik ji,' she said, 'I did not meet you yesterday, my daughters were exhausted …' She switched from Dogri to Urdu and started afresh, '… and slept with their heads in my lap. We arrived early last evening. I am Durga Mehra. My husband was the district commissioner in Muzaffarabad.'

The woman had a stately bearing, calm face and determined eyes.

'I'm sorry to hear that,' Malik mumbled.

A brief nod and Durga grabbed a long-handled broom. 'My husband died in the line of duty. We do not mourn martyrs.' She started to sweep from the other end.

Malik felt small. An able-bodied man, he had got disheartened so quickly. And here was an educated, high-society woman; the widow of a senior officer, executed by the kabailis no doubt; a mother; who looked life in the eye and was unafraid of menial work! Such courage. Silently, Malik bowed to her. As a man, his interaction with the camp women was constrained, partly because he didn't know Dogri. Durga Mehra would make an excellent ADC to his camp commander.

In the two months since she had lost her husband, Durga Mehra had managed to travel from Muzaffarabad to Mirpur via Rawalpindi, keeping her four children, two young boys and two teenaged girls, safe and her honour intact. It was no small deal. The kabailis had shot Mr Mehra, set their house on fire, and forced them to flee barefoot with just a bedsheet and a guptee, the walking stick concealing a sword within. The tribesmen were abducting women, forcing them to convert, taking some as 'wives'. Many a lustful eye had roamed over her, many Pathans had tried to separate her children from her, but Durga Mehra had conducted herself as the widow of a senior officer would and demanded the dignity that was her due, sword-stick in hand. Reminding every upstart Pathan who waylaid her that she was the wife of a man they had shamelessly killed, she wore the mantle of a martyr's widow with pride, and consoled herself with prayers from her beloved *Gita*. Counting on the kindness of strangers, drawing out the humanity of a Pathan chieftain, throwing her weight around when needed, she was painstakingly making her way to India. She slept fitfully, but kept her nightmares to herself: the snakes in her garden the morning of the raid; her husband's receding back as he strode off to answer a summon for help; her son questioning why she wasn't flinging herself off the Domel bridge to save her honour like other women … Resolve was Durga's close companion. If there was danger of molestation, she would use the guptee to reunite the family in heaven, for where else could patriot and martyr Gyan Chand Mehra be?

After a talk with the camp commander, Durga took charge of helping the camp women. Fluent in several languages, she switched from Dogri to Panjabi to Urdu to Kashmiri as she coaxed the women to assemble, and suggested a prayer meeting every morning and evening. Some nodded. A few protested. 'We are not Hindus any more!'

'That's fine. Singing hymns will not make you Hindu again. If you don't want to sing, that's also okay. Tell a story. The children need distraction, too.'

Durga squatted on the cleaned living room floor, layered with fresh hay. She invited the women to sit in a circle around her. When she sang, ably assisted by her children, some women began to repeat her hymns with leaden voices. By the end, a few faces had relaxed a little, the children had gone off to sleep in their mothers' laps, someone had hesitatingly shared a story. *When they fled Mirpur, her father got separated from them while her mother, two younger brothers and she were seized by the raiders and taken to Alibeg Camp. There, one of her younger brothers was trampled by a camel and he died in agony.* Kusum's bony chest heaved as she sobbed relentlessly. Over the days, the trickle of women in the evenings changed to a gush as more women spoke, their grief was un-bottled, and they wept in one another's arms. In time, women volunteered for tasks like cooking and cleaning and washing. The laughter in the camp started to arise from children's pranks and creative ways to convert the humble wheat flour into delicacies using the one radish or carrot or turnip that the boys had foraged. But more women continued to stream into the camp – terrified women, women who ripped their clothes off, women who cried to be reunited with their Muslim husbands because who else would accept them now …

Meanwhile, Malik went about securing the mansion. Locating a village mason, he buttressed the boundary wall at the rear. He reinforced the wooden gate with planks sourced from Abdul Aziz's old barn. He instructed the boys to keep their ears open for news about Pathans showing undue interest in the camp. The first few days, Malik had looked hungrily at the trees hoping to sight Tara, but she had kept herself invisible; besides there was too much work to be done. In the freezing nights though, wrung with fatigue, as he lay on his cot, he smelled roses. Which was ridiculous. Except, rose was the attar that Tara favoured.

Late one afternoon, as the winter sun attempted to fill the camp courtyard with light, Abdul Aziz arrived with a woman with golden hair. Stiff as a bamboo pole, dressed in a coarse khaddar salwar-kurta a size short and a man's sweater, she sat unblinking on the string cot as the thekedar spoke to the camp commander. A fisherman had found the woman floating in the icy Chenab. Just his luck he thought, to come across another corpse of another unfortunate woman who had flung herself into another river. It being winter, fishing was poor, yet fishermen were reporting an altogether different catch. But this corpse was floating on its back, it wasn't bloated, it didn't stink – so perhaps it wasn't dead yet? He took it home; his wife ripped the wet clothes off it and wrapped it in a wool blanket. They watched over it for days, unsure if it belonged in their hut or in the ground, but daily the fisherman came back with a good catch of palla! Palla fish in December, who'd ever heard? So his wife made fish fry one day, masala fish the next, tikka, pulao … Until his wife had to repeat recipes. After two weeks, the body sat up in bed. The fishermen and his wife fell at her feet.

'Why?' asked Malik. There was nothing remarkable about her, except she was tall as a man with hair the colour of hay.

'*Why*, you ask?' The fisherman squinted. 'Don't you see? A woman who survives a freezing river, who daily brings the unseasonal gift of palla fish, who wakes up from a death-like sleep ... how do you think it happened?'

Malik shrugged. Abdul Aziz patted his beard as he listened attentively. Meanwhile, a clutch of women had gathered around them in the courtyard. They stared at the new specimen in their mix, whispered and gesticulated. The fisherman looked from Malik to Aziz before slapping his palms together. 'The River Pir! Who rides the waters on palla fish? Zinda Pir, Jhulelal, Khwaja Khizr – what do *you* call him?'

Of course, Malik was aware of the old man with the flowing white beard worshipped as the saint of rivers in Hind–Sindh. And the popular dhammal in his praise: *Dama Dam Mast Qalandar*. He cast a look at the woman who sat unmoving through the recountal.

'Does she speak?' he asked.

The fisherman raised his palms skywards.

A group of camp boys bustled into the yard, laughing and tucking into fruit they had nicked off trees. They were allowed to roam the neighbouring villages to barter. The villagers did not know to knit or sew; Abdul Aziz got the camp women to knit their wool into sweaters. In return, the villagers gave them buttermilk, jaggery, millet, rice. As they ran errands, the camp boys got a chance to do what normal boys their age did: climb trees for walnuts, apples, lemons. When they ventured into orchards, Abdul Aziz heard complaints right after. Upon sighting the thekedar, the boys dived amongst the women, hiding their stash.

Abdul Aziz returned his attention to the young woman. She had perked up, her eyes on a mischievous face peering from behind his mother. The boy tucked into a walnut, a catapult clutched in his other hand. Aziz sighed and patted her head. There was hope … He beckoned to Malik and the two men started towards the main gate. In a low voice, Aziz spoke about trouble with a particular Pathan raider-husband whose Hindu wife was sheltering in the camp. After pleading his case for days, the man had graduated to threats. 'Stay vigilant,' Aziz cautioned.

'I need more guards, you know' Malik asserted. 'Two policemen are not enough to secure an empty mansion, leave alone rescued "wives"!' After all, the men belonged to the Pakistani police.

'Brother Malik, I'm trying to recruit some able-bodied villagers. But many are convinced that the women should return to their rightful Pathan husbands … Others are scared. Who wants to tangle with Pakistani soldiers or tribesmen?'

Malik watched him go, then secured the gate. Abdul Aziz wasn't winning a popularity contest any time soon but he was a rich man, owner of orchards, and he was using his own money to aid the afflicted. The villagers might disagree with him, but they could not fault the thekedar for following Allah's writ.

27

Delhi (December 1947–January 1948)

On the road from Muzaffarabad to Srinagar, midway sat Uri: shaped like a bowl, its walls made from steep hills. Indian forces had taken control of the town by early December. Pathans, however, in the fashion of mountain goats, were staked out on the surrounding cliffs, able to snipe and shoot at will.

Snow arrived. As did a visible change in enemy battle formations – the tribesmen now had Pakistani troops assisting them. On 11 December, they rained gunfire upon the hamlet of Bhatgiran, halting traffic coming into town, placing Uri under siege. Two days later, 1Sikh Battalion, attempting to clear out the enemy, was ambushed. More lives were lost in the Battle of Bhatgiran than in the time since 1Sikh's arrival in Srinagar on 27 October.

Blood anointed snow.

Ahead, as days rolled into weeks, which snowballed into months, opposition to Indian troops would come not just from frontier fighters, but also from the tricky terrain as winter closed in. Blinding snowstorms changed the landscape, masking folds and gullies under a flat white blanket – what was solid ground, what was thin air? Troops from areas with no snow, Rajputs and Madras Engineers, twisted ankles and bruised shins – how to put one foot after another on hazardous ground? With the snow six-feet deep in places, platoons encountered unusual problems – how was 3Garhwal, with an average height of five feet, to progress? Avalanches, fast and furious combinations of snow and large loose boulders, slid down mountain sides, pummelling men, piling to heights of forty feet and severing links. Men had to work against their instincts, and learn that warming themselves by placing their booted feet against a stove could result in frost bite and possible amputation. Troops airlifted overnight from plains to the Himalayas realized their battle dress was inadequate. Poshteens, knee-length leather coats lined with fur, were bought and worn; and kangris tucked within, the portable fire pots smouldering against winter's harshest stretch, the dreaded chilai kalan. Yet, the kabailis, supported by Pakistan, persisted with fighting. So Indian commanders had to apportion considerable energy to keep troops warm and mobile in sub-zero temperatures.

The war for paradise was pure hell.

Indu served her father his morning coffee with hot milk. He looked preoccupied as he sat at the dining table and she wondered which problem he was tussling with – refugees, Hyderabad, Kashmir, Bapu's health – but gave up, there were too many to consider. She deposited the coffee pot down loudly, and the noise served to rouse him. He reached for his cup and started to sip. Suddenly, his ears pricked up.

'Hear that?' He cocked his head, trying to ascertain the bird. It was early morning, the garden still to surrender to the sounds of the refugee camp.

'Sounds like a mynah, Papu' Indu said.

He shook his head. 'No, it's something different.' On another sip, he reflected, 'You know how the mynahs in the hills sound different from those in the plains, less noisy?'

Indu grinned. 'Not everyone gets trained in bird calls because of extended stints in Almora jail!'

'Hah!' Jawahar laughed. His mind journeyed to those days in jail, as recent as 1943 and yet, it seemed aeons ago. He'd never imagined he might long for the quiet of prison. 'You know,' he took an appreciative sip and turned to Indu, 'once I sighted a new and lovely bird in the Almora jail grounds, and with no one to refer to, I asked a jail official if he knew anything about birds. "Well, yes," he replied, "I know the crow!"'

Father and daughter burst into guffaws.

Indu was glad she had managed to make him laugh. The situation in Kashmir was vexing enough, and news of the setback at Uri had put Papu in a dark mood for days. The Banihal Pass was completely snowed under and workers were clearing it on a daily basis. And the Pakistan Prime Minister and Papu had had a lacerating follow-up in Lahore, arguing and exchanging accusations until dinner. She sighed. It was all a terrible mess.

Papu had finished his coffee. He tapped the table in rhythm to some thought.

'What's on your mind, Papu?'

Jawahar sighed. 'Vallabhbhai sent me his resignation.'

A gasp from Indu, her eyes wide.

'Our approaches are different, especially on Kashmir, and however much we respect each other, I cannot have my freedom restricted.' Jawahar tightened his mouth. Intelligence reports said that Hindu loyalists of Hari Singh were conducting propaganda against Sheikh Abdullah and in favour of the dissolute Maharaja. But Vallabhbhai had dismissed those as mere rumours. 'I firmly believe the interim government under Sheikh Abdullah should be in full charge, with the Maharaja as the constitutional head. Mahajan cannot continue to be Prime Minister. I appointed Gopalaswami Ayyangar to handle Kashmir affairs, but Vallabhbhai's view is that Ayyangar must function under the Ministry of States.' He shrugged. 'Ayyangar is a constitutional expert with intimate knowledge and experience of Kashmir and should be given full latitude. I really do not see where the States Ministry comes into the picture, except that it be kept informed of steps taken.'

'So …' Indu licked her lips, 'what happens now?'

'I offered to resign in turn. But Vallabhbhai wouldn't hear of it. We met with Bapu later …' He left the rest unsaid and poured himself more coffee.

The warm nutty aroma of coffee was inviting. Indu pulled her cardigan closer as she reached for the coffee pot. Bapu was the mediator; he would figure a way out—

'Even Bapu is unhappy with Vallabhbhai for withholding Pakistan's share of reserves.'

Oh!

'Vallabhbhai has refused to transfer any money that he says Jinnah could use to help kill Indian soldiers in Kashmir, not a penny!' Jawahar locked eyes with his daughter over the rim of his cup. 'Vallabhbhai has a point. He did link the disbursement to Kashmir where Pakistan is up to all kinds of mischief. On the night of 23rd December, some 6000-strong lashkar attacked our garrison in Jhangar, outnumbering our troops thirty to one! Now I hear that twice that number of insurgents are massing to attack Uri – you know what happens if the town falls?'

Indu cradled her coffee cup as she weighed her words. 'The road to Srinagar is vulnerable again.'

Jawahar gave a nod. 'I have already warned Liaquat that India will not tolerate insurgent bases in Pakistan. This way, the tribesmen can continue fighting a proxy war for months and months and years!'

'Which will drain our strength—'

'— with little burden on Pakistan.' Jawahar rapped the table and stood up. His mind was made up. 'We have no option but to strike at these lines of communication in Pakistan territory.'

Jawaharlal Nehru summoned Major General K.S. Thimayya to Delhi and gave him a clear order that were Uri to fall, Indian forces should obliterate the bases of insurgents inside Pakistan. Worried by Jawa's plans, Dickie Mountbatten fired off a missive to the British Prime Minister, warning him that the two dominions would go to war unless Attlee flew to the subcontinent immediately. Meanwhile, British officials kindly disposed towards Pakistan, in the fashion of Winston Churchill, sent SOS calls about India's heightened military presence in the Valley.

As the tumultuous year of 1947 wound down, two things happened.

The insurgents who had gathered to attack Uri vanished into the vaporous air. Had they been recalled because of the inclement weather or India's aggressive posturing?

The Indian Cabinet, having decided that India should appeal to the United Nations, accusing Pakistan of helping the raiders, despatched its application to the Security Council on 1 January 1948.

Would the new initiative in the new year settle the old issue of Kashmir? Would the brand new UN, which had risen from the ashes of WWII, with the noble aim to resolve conflicts between nations, find a radical solution to suture the fissure between two brothers? Or would realpolitik, as ancient as the Mahabharata, triumph?

28

Datiyal (January 1948)

It was the first week of January, and the winter monsoon had made the camp a wet and sickly place. Sniffles and coughs wracked lungs and the air. Malik had doubled down on the cleaning, stressing the importance of hygiene as he spoke with the women. Initially, they ignored him or hid their faces in their chunnis. But Durga's evening gatherings had encouraged more inmates to speak. Amidst weeping and wailing and telling their stories, the women were finding some solace. Durga had divided chores amongst them: bathing the weak, combing hair for lice, grinding wheat and rice, cleaning the lone toilet, collecting garbage, cooking, mopping, washing, sweeping ...

Meanwhile, India and Pakistan were still at war, and distressing news arrived frequently from the Alibeg Camp. A former gurdwara – it was a prison now – was housing civilians and soldiers, and instead of hymns, stories of suffering radiated out: soldiers beheaded, young boys axed, starvation diet of two chapatis, ground glass mixed into the wheat flour, women fed better, but shamefully raped ... Vultures routinely circled the air. Malik emptied the bucket of soiled water and sat down on his haunches, tired. Dysentery was wreaking havoc on some women; Abdul Aziz was trying to bring a doctor to the camp. Meanwhile, the women were retching and shitting, and Malik had isolated the ill in the ante-room next to the large living room.

The sky darkened abruptly. 'Not more rain,' Malik groaned, glancing at the bulbous black clouds above. A shout. The lone policeman on the rooftop was pointing in the distance. 'A party of Pathans armed with spears and axes and … one gun … headed this way, I think.'

Malik sprang up and darted to the wall against which his cot was inclined. From behind it, he withdrew the ancient muzzle loader. He hadn't had to use it thus far, but today might be different. Since Abdul Aziz's warning, a couple of incidents had happened to make Malik nervous. First, a worker of the provisional government had visited, in the guise of enquiring about the welfare of the women. But the way his hungry eyes scoured the women, Malik had understood his intent. The workers were not above tribesmen in eyeing the camp women. Thereafter, he had consulted with Durga, who advised the women to be clean, but look unkempt. Following that, some Muslims from a neighbouring village had come to the camp with clothes and money. The women who accepted the clothes endured the tall talk of the men – *it was zakat, the duty expected of all Muslims to be charitable* – but a woman named Madhu had taken one look at them and squirrelled away into the storage room. Later, Malik learned from Durga that the persistent Pathan was bent upon reclaiming the young Hindu woman he had abducted and claimed for his wife, converting Madhu to Zulekha.

Loading the rifle, Malik bounded to the courtyard. Just yesterday, the other policeman had taken leave to visit his family in Jhelum; surely, the timing was suspect. A loud rattle sounded at the gate. Malik herded the women inside, ordered them to shut the windows and be silent as if they'd smelled a snake; he locked the doors.

Meanwhile, the policeman on the rooftop was engaging the Pathans. 'We said already, didn't we, that there is no such woman in this camp. Go look at Alibeg—'

Loud protests from outside. *Zulekha, yes … Madhu was her Hindu name …*

'No, brother, no such woman is here. Only Hindu women in this camp, all afflicted with dysentery.' The policeman clucked.

Oye, enough of this! Tell the camp commander to open this gate and we will find Zulekha—

Shaking his head, the policeman cautioned. 'Go away, brothers. These women are under the protection of the government in Muzaffarabad.'

A clamour erupted. The men appeared to be clambering up the boundary wall, which wasn't higher than them, six feet or so. Malik watched with narrowed eyes, rifle at the ready. A turbaned head appeared over the wall, then another. Malik shouted a warning, then fired the gun above their heads. Gunshot crackled like lightning slashing the darkened sky.

The men tumbled back. Answering fire. The policeman ducked and scooted back. There was renewed pressure on the gate – fists thumping, feet stamping. It was solid wood, but would it hold? A man was on the wall and about to jump in. Malik fired at him, the man toppled back. Above, the policeman crouched forward on his elbows to glance below. He held up two fingers, then waggled them. So two Pathans had fled. There were three more. A roar and a gunshot and the policeman keeled over.

'Kanjaro!' Malik fumed, eyeing the rooftop anxiously. Was the man alive?

Now, it was Malik against three Pathans, but only one of whom had a weapon. Malik took position behind the tandoor. A Pathan crept up the wall; Malik aimed. Another man straddled the wall and fired his musket at Malik, the bullet whistling past his ear, deafening him. The two Pathans jumped into the yard and strode towards the living quarters. Malik shook his head trying to dislodge the buzzing rapidly filling his ear. He blinked his eyes – the men, blurry as their salwars, swung and their rough leather juttis scraped the floor. Malik stacked his shoulder against the oven and dragged himself to a sitting position. Squeezing his eyes shut, he blinked rapidly. His vision cleared: The intruders were at the threshold – but one of them was leaning back, then the other, crying out in pain, grabbing their heads. Stones pelted their faces, finding the eyes and foreheads, and the men howled in agony. Malik let off a series of shots near their dancing feet. The men turned and scrambled to the wall, struggling to ascend. He let them escape.

In the verandah, the windows had been flung open and women's heads were pressed against the iron bars. In the right window, beside the living room door, a woman crouched, a catapult in her hand. Beside her stood the boys, stones in their fists and stones lined on the windowsill. Zooni. The woman with golden hair was strong, Malik knew. She was the one in charge of the chakki and, since no woman had her strength, she ground the wheat and rice, quietly, working alone. She seldom spoke, but the boys crowded around her, learning from her how to aim their catapults better, bringing down so many lemons from the lemon trees in the yard and in the village that the camp inmates were regularly eating dollops of kimb chutney. Krishna, a Dogra woman, taught the others how to first roast the lemons on a fire, then mash the citrus pulp with jaggery, chillies and walnuts for a sweet, sour and spicy relish.

Now the boys whooped in delight, jigging with joy. The women, petrified before, raised hands to their mouths or bosoms in relief. Only Zooni sat as motionless as a statue. Malik touched his right ear, his fingers came back bloodied. A nick. Leaving his rifle, he bounded to the rooftop. The policeman had taken a shot in the arm – wounded, but alive. Malik scooped up the man, exhaling his relief.

Slingshot against a musket – who would have thought?

29

New York City (January 1948)

The tall windows looked on to a parking lot. The lake must be somewhere, Abdullah mused as he scanned the stretch. With the war over, the Sperry Gyroscope plant at Lake Success was no longer manufacturing weapons and had space enough to house the new United Nations – the 'peace factory', a local had quipped.

Sheikh Abdullah, head of the administration in Jammu and Kashmir, was in the US as a member of the Indian delegation to present its case on Kashmir to the UN Security Council. The notion that a weapons factory was the UN's temporary location – its designated home was being constructed on the bank of the East River in Manhattan – distressed the Sheikh. As did the missing lake. Images of the Dal swam in his mind, shikaras navigating planks of ice, which reflected the snow-laden boughs of bordering willows and chinars, a kangri tucked within each boatman's pheran ... He sighed at the memory. Here, despite the freezing cold, central heating allowed everyone inside to be coatless. His eyes took in the wide road, the flying cars, the landscaped expanse. There was nothing a free people could not achieve: build a great country, win a war, donate land to the UN … New Kashmir must uplift every single oppressed Kashmiri—

The opening of a door alerted him. An Englishman in a three-piece suit wearing a tight-lipped smile stood in the open doorway. Abdullah strode towards him. The tall man with a high forehead and round glasses was the commonwealth secretary, Philip Noel-Baker, who was also leading the British delegation. He appeared to be in a hurry. After inviting Abdullah inside, Noel-Baker cleared his throat and launched a broadside.

'I must make it clear that HMG believes that the Pakistan Army has *not* violated the sanctity of the boundaries of Kashmir, *nor* were the raiders sent by them.'

Abdullah was taken aback. Sir N. Gopalaswami Ayyangar, leader of the Indian delegation, had lodged a protest against the raids carried out by the tribals through diplomatic channels. Even Jawaharlal Nehru had brought the same to the attention of Clement Attlee and Stafford Cripps!

Smiling, Abdullah leaned forward, and started to explain what he knew to be the truth. He spoke plainly, but the Englishman pinched his lips as he listened.

Shrugging elaborately, Noel-Baker asked, 'Surely you will agree that because it contains a majority of Muslims, Kashmir quite properly belongs to Pakistan?' His demeanour was that of a school teacher not used to being contradicted by a pupil.

As Abdullah pondered how to make Noel-Baker see his viewpoint, an old memory surged into his mind. It was after he had completed the FSc and was hoping to join medical school with the support of the state. However, he was disappointed when his name was not on the list of the twenty-two candidates who had been selected. Seeing him crestfallen, his older and wiser brother, Maqbool, had enquired as to the cause. After which, he'd given him a sound scolding. 'If candour is all that you are going to offer the authorities, be prepared to spend the rest of your life in the rut in which you were born. The worldly wise, with an eye on the future, soften their seniors with gifts. Why don't you take a shawl or two, and quit harping on principles?' But Abdullah could not make himself obsequious to those in power. Since he didn't know to bow and scrape, he was branded as insolent and disobedient.

Now, Abdullah wondered if he should have got a gift of a fine Kashmiri shawl for Philip Noel-Baker, a doshala the Englishman could gift his wife? Abdullah came from a family of pashmina traders, after all. And Kashmiri shawls were known all over the world for their matchless quality. When the mighty Tipu Sultan sided with Napoleon Bonaparte to challenge the might of the British Empire, he sent with his envoy a Kashmiri shawl of great beauty as a gift. Apparently, Napoleon was so struck by its exquisite workmanship that he presented it to his beloved Empress Josephine. Who, in turn, was so smitten that she started to collect dozens of pashmina shawls—

Noel-Baker cleared his throat and made a show of checking his wristwatch.

A shawl would have been a good idea, Abdullah conceded; the warmth of soft pashmina might have thawed the Englishman. Instead, Abdullah offered him his beaming smile. And restated what he had voiced earlier at the assembly.

'The post-Partition situation, the Kashmir controversy … surely, you must see that the British are responsible for the circumstances.'

'The Partition plan was sponsored as a British Act of Parliament, you are correct.'

Noel-Baker spoke as if addressing a gathering from a podium. His frosty voice rained words down like hailstones. 'It is vital, therefore, that we ensure that both the dominions, India and Pakistan, continue to be peaceful.'

Noel-Baker again glanced at his watch and stood up. 'I am afraid I *really* must get going.'

The plane would be landing soon.

Abdullah still could not believe the news. Despite the solemn condolence session held by the Security Council for a person who had no official status. Such was the stature of Mahatma Gandhi. And now, Abdullah sniffled, Gandhiji was no more. The news of his martyrdom had hit hard, the delegation suspending deliberations as it hurried home. Abdullah had met Gandhiji in Delhi before departure – frail from the fast unto death he had undertaken, the Mahatma was using his body yet again to bridge the rupture between brothers. Eventually, the sum of fifty-five crore rupees was paid to Pakistan, and the fast was broken. But somebody had been angered enough to kill him …

Abdullah wiped tears from the corner of one eye. He had first set eyes upon Mahatma Gandhi at Aligarh Muslim University, where students had invited the Mahatma to speak. The whole country was on fire with the spirit of freedom he had unleashed. Gandhiji was not a fiery orator. It was his simplicity and informality that won them over. Since then he had stood like a human barricade on the path of hate. Now, with him gone and the communal fires raging …

Abdullah rested his forehead in his right hand. The lights had been dimmed inside the cabin – snores of varying intensity rode the pressurized air which smelled of cigarette smoke and caffeine – but he could not sleep.

Things had not gone well at the UN. The leader of the Pakistani delegation, the very competent Sir Mohammad Zafarullah Khan, their foreign minister, had flourished his skills as a barrister. By repeatedly harping on the trauma of Partition, he had manipulated the scope of the discussion. Which resulted in allegations and counter-allegations bandied by India and Pakistan. Ineffectual. When it was Abdullah's turn to speak, Zafarullah Khan had interrupted him, alleging that Abdullah was a puppet in the hands of Jawaharlal Nehru!

Abdullah snorted.

'I am proud of my friendship with Jawaharlal,' he had declared to the Council, his six-foot-four frame trembling with emotion. 'But if I have to choose between that friendship and the interest of the people of Kashmir, I know what I would choose!'

Zafarullah Khan had British backing. And the British refused to see that the first anti-Partition front had opened in Kashmir, which had a majority of Muslims. Because that fact flew in the face of the two-nation theory so beloved of Jinnah and the British! Kashmiris dressed similarly, shared surnames, and it was difficult to tell a Kashmiri Hindu apart from a Kashmiri Muslim. Because they all had the same roots. One of his own ancestors – a Kashmiri Brahmin – had converted to Islam and taken on the Islamic name Sheikh Mohammad Abdullah. But the British, whom Napoleon had best described as a nation of shopkeepers, never lost sight of their personal interests. Hence, their support of Pakistan, their bridge to the oil-rich Arab nations!

Abdullah exhaled sharply.

As he had told Begum Jahan before leaving: Hamari kashti majhdhar mein hai. And the whirlpools were getting bigger.

30

Datiyal (February 1948)

Zooni was making a new catapult for Jugnu, who, at six years of age, wanted to learn to use a slingshot to bring fruit down from trees. She had asked him to search fallen tree branches for a natural fork – one which formed a symmetrical V, as she indicated with her fingers; *fallen*, she reiterated, because it would be dry already. Now, with Jugnu hovering beside her – he had returned with a mulberry forked branch which Zooni had sliced to the right size for his small hands – she chiselled the frame with a stone. Durga watched from the other end of the string cot as she darned a thin quilt.

'You know his name isn't Jugnu?'

When Zooni looked up, mouth pursed in concentration, Durga resumed her questioning, 'Why do you call all the boys Jugnu?'

Zooni returned her attention to the catapult. She knew what Durga was doing: trying to draw the unfortunate girl out, so Zooni would offload her story and start to speak as many other inmates had. But what could Zooni say? She was a Muslim hiding amongst Hindu women; already her name had drawn a few raised brows. Besides, she didn't recall what happened after she flung herself into the river and woke up in a fisherman's hut … Just the feeling of being cradled by water. Muslim *and* a freak! Some women might just faint. Her parents and brother were gone, Zooni was certain, and she must reach Srinagar to find Kashmira and family, hopefully alive because the Valley hadn't fallen – Durga said the Indian Army had arrived just in time, and now she was trying to reach her parents there. A silent "Hindu" Zooni was the safest bet. This way, she could also mourn Koko Jan in peace without having to divulge the story of her saut. Masud Ahmed, Zooni didn't care for: The night bus ride had taught her the nature of the night-time adventures men like her ex-soldier husband were having—

A rat-tat-tat sounded at the gate. The crow perching on the boundary wall took flight, cawing his displeasure as the policeman-guard looked through the slatted window. Soon, the thekedar walked in, an uncertain look on his face. Drawing up a cane moorah, he sat beside the cot and addressed Durga. 'Behenji, I have come with news, and, in keeping with our times, I have both good news and bad.' He sighed. 'Which one would you like first?'

Durga tucked the needle into the quilt and said softly, 'The bad, first.'

Abdul Aziz patted his beard solemnly. 'Gandhiji has been killed!'

A cry escaped Durga before she clamped her mouth shut with both hands. With her chin digging into her chest, Zooni focused on sanding the V-frame, catching the interaction from the corner of her eyes.

'Yes, very sad,' Abdul Aziz swung his head. 'Reason is leaving us … But we must hold on to hope, which is why the good news, too. The time has come for you to leave for India.'

Durga, eyes moist, bent her head gratefully.

Zooni, with lit-up eyes and tremulous mouth hidden, slicked the mulberry branch with renewed vigour.

'An exchange of refugees is planned between our two countries. I will come back with the date, but you must ready your family and the other women who wish to go to India.' He cleared his throat. 'Zooni Bibi, do you wish to leave as well?'

Zooni's head went up. Wordlessly, it bobbed, repeatedly.

Abdul Aziz acknowledged her response with lowered eyelids before turning to Durga. Jugnu darted to the cot to determine the progress of his catapult, arcing water from a puddle he had sped through. Muddy stains sprouted on the thekedar's face and coat. Using his loose turban-end to wipe his cheek, Aziz spoke carefully. 'Behenji, when the day comes to leave, you must exercise great care. Certain raider-husbands are bent upon reclaiming their wives ... They may try to kidnap them. And,' he cast a sideways glance at Zooni, 'some vengeful ones are seeking the Bibi with gold hair, as you know.'

Durga brought her hands together. 'Thank you, thekedarji, for the good news and the warning. We will start planning our journey.'

Next, Abdul Aziz sought out Malik and the two men headed to the rooftop for a chat. A thin winter sun had made the morning bearable as it dried the grounds and starched the washing strung on two lines in the courtyard. Pigeons grunted on the rooftop. Boys played with a spinning top in the covered verandah, and the whiff of cooking rode over the malodours of phenyl and fetor.

'So, Zooni, keen to get home?' Durga smiled as she darned again, the needle flying.

'Home? I want to go to Srinagar and meet my sister.'

Durga nodded. 'We must evade the men who will try to stop us leaving. You know what they are saying—'

'Ghodi, with the mane and height of a horse. Daughter of a woman who copulated with a horse, no, she's an ogress, churail, afriteh …' Zooni snorted.

Durga raised her brows, surprised by the passion and volubility. 'How did you know?'

'The boys keep me informed.'

'Your army of Jugnus!' Durga patted the quilt down and examined the result of her needlework. 'Men can be such spiteful children. Imagine being terrified enough of a gentle old man like Bapu to kill him …' Her throat caught. 'And here I was thinking that we Indians are better than these barbaric tribesmen.' She sniffled. 'Never mind, they spread these ugly stories because they are afraid of you. Which is why,' Durga bit the thread from the needle, 'we must have a plan.'

Akbar Khan swung the car on to the old Mughal Road to Datiyal Camp. Since the Inter-dominion Conference in Lahore, where the operation to rescue abducted women had been agreed upon, the first exchange was expected. The Red Cross was helping with the initiative, and Akbar wanted to check on the camp's preparedness. He drummed the steering wheel; a thought niggled at him. Rape as a weapon of war was as ancient as the concept of war itself. And yet, the brutality that he was hearing of was not something soldiers were trained in at Sandhurst! Women with breasts and arms chopped off, branded with the names of their rapists, tattooed with dates of attack … It was the one common sore point between both governments, arousing much passion and recrimination. Jawaharlal Nehru wanted to bring the Hindu and Sikh women back like the Hindu god Ram had brought Sita home. Liaquat Ali Khan had put his Begum in charge of the women's rehabilitation—

The car juddered. Akbar gripped the steering as he navigated the chain of puddles that was the rickety road to the camp. The camp gate had been bolstered; several upright planks had added to both its height and bulk. Hmm. Having parked the car, Akbar leaped over a puddle, steadied his cap and banged on the gate.

Inside, it smelled like a hospital ward, which made him wrinkle his nose. At least it was better than the stench of a pigsty from the last time. His arrival had brought a few curious women to the windows who watched him with hooded eyes. Some in the covered verandah looked up from their sewing-knitting. Scrawny children were at play in the courtyard. And Sepoy Malik, emptying a soiled bucket, raised one hand in greeting. At first glance, the camp looked less filthy, despite the foul weather.

The two men stepped out. Grey skies threatened rain as Akbar smoked and made his enquires.

'We need more of everything: food rations, clothes, beds, medicines, soap …' Hands clasped behind his back, Sepoy Malik trudged alongside Akbar.

Akbar Khan nodded. Conditions at Alibeg continued to be grim, but, according to Abdul Aziz, the sepoy had worked magic at Datiyal. Women were no longer fainting, or babies dying from starvation or the cold. Since bedding was limited, Malik and Aziz had scoured wheat straw to spread on the floor and begun a barter trade with the neighbouring villages: rations for knitted wool. Apparently the women sang evening hymns, too! And from what the camp commander was relaying, women refugees keen on returning were in the majority and already preparing for the journey ahead. Perhaps he had underestimated the jhangi—

'What news from the front?' Malik enquired having finished his update.

'Chacha Nehru went to the UN crying, "Help! Help! Raiders in my house."' Akbar blew smoke and gazed into the distance. 'Who are the Indians trying to fool, hain? They haven't asked for the UN to intervene to ascertain the wishes of the Kashmiri people. No. Only to accuse us of aggression and demand that the UN throw the raiders out!'

A flock of birds wheeled and circled in the air. Vultures, most likely, Malik surmised. With 4000 prisoners in Alibeg, and no arrangements for cremation, corpses were rotting in the fields or floating in the Jhelum.

'What does the UN say?'

'Zafarullah Khan, the Pakistani delegate, rubbished the claims of the Indians. It helps that the British see our viewpoint.'

'So, the war will go on.' Malik nodded.

'Yes, the struggle continues. But with heavy snow in Kashmir, the action is in Jammu. Azads and tribesmen are resisting the Indian Army, but the Indians retain possession of the road. We have reached a stalemate of sorts.' Akbar shrugged and tossed the cigarette into a puddle.

Powdery snow began to fall.

Malik narrowed his eyes. 'Nothing much to be done in the winter months.'

'The Liberation Committee is—'

'*Lib*-eration Committee?'

'The overall struggle is being organized by GHQ Azad *and* a Liberation Committee to assist them. Collecting resources, organizing the various sectors, etcetera …' In his mind, Akbar Khan was mulling over the bureaucracy that had beset the committee; they were obsessing over matters of procedure, administration, politics, instead of overseeing a war! Justice

Din Mohammad, the president, was a retired judge and the meetings had started to become like a court in session. Ordinary reports and statements had the air of allegations – which, in the absence of any cross-examination, were then accepted. So, people were occupied with defending themselves instead of focusing on the war effort. What had that Azad Major said? *Din Mohammad sits like a constitutional judge upon an affair that is utterly irregular*. Akbar snorted.

Malik looked at him intently. 'Have you,' he asked carefully, 'heard of Field Marshall Masud?'

Akbar Khan didn't know whether to laugh or glare, and as he was contemplating that, Malik's face split wide open.

'Field marshall!' Akbar Khan guffawed.

'*Field marshall*, exactly!'

'What next rank will they promote themselves to?'

Around Poonch, two rival commanders had set up headquarters, both submitting reports to GHQ Azad – one signing himself as captain and the other as major. Then, they promoted themselves to major and colonel. Then to colonel and brigadier … and so on, until both were field marshalls now. Seeing which, the defence minister, with no other title left, had come to adopt the rank of captain general. It was distinctly un-English, being inspired by the Germans!

Akbar Khan shook his head, trying to dislodge the absurdity of it all.

'What?' Malik asked.

'Oh, yaar, where to start and where to stop!' He sighed.

'Well, let me tell you one.' Seeing Akbar Khan's raised brows, Malik quipped, 'You forget, I had a vast network of operatives …'

Akbar Khan, duped by the devoted camp commander, had quite literally forgotten the sepoy's erstwhile role. 'Go on,' he urged.

'The GHQ, I hear, was asking for some bold ideas to win the war. And it received one. From a former air force warrant officer. A file landed on the GHQ desk, neatly typed, illustrated with blueprints. What it offered was an ambitious plan. One,' Malik wagged an upright index finger, 'under which, not only Kashmir, but *all of* India could be invaded and conquered. Ask how?'

Akbar Khan donned the awestruck expression of a country bumpkin.

'A glider-borne invasion. Only two-*thousand* gliders required!'

Akbar Khan hooted his derision. 'I have an even better story!'

Snowfall picked up; the two men hurried towards the camp in the cascade.

'This bold plan,' Akbar Khan shouted over the swirling wind, 'was concocted by a refugee from India. He had studied German rocket technology and had a plan to build long-range rockets.' Malik's eyes widened appreciatively. 'GHQ pooh-poohed him. But our man, he convinced GHQ with his militant zeal. So they gave him a workshop and other facilities he asked for. After six weeks came the final showing. Of course, our genius inventor had a prototype to show: twenty-foot long … bullet-shaped … solid piece of … *wood!* And … and … listen,' as Malik began to cackle, 'not to be discounted, the bullet was painted green, complete with a white crescent and star at the base!' Akbar joined Malik's cackling.

As they neared the gate, Malik said solemnly, 'General Tariq?'

Akbar Khan looked askance.

'You want to win the war? Release these plans to the Indians.'

As Akbar Khan frowned, Malik added, 'They will die laughing first!'

31

Datiyal (February 1948)

The evening of departure arrived. One hundred and four women and children would leave Datiyal Camp to board a train to Amritsar, India. Several inmates had remained unconvinced about the journey. Was it safe? What if they were abducted by other tribesmen? Would they find their families in India? Would the families want them, now that they had been despoiled? Could they re-convert from Islam? The commissioner would permit only those women to travel who were 100 per cent certain they wanted to leave. Amongst those were Zooni, Madhu, Krishna, Kusum, Mehri and her son Bitta-Jugnu, the elderly Pritam Kaur, Durga Mehra and her four children. A policeman would accompany the refugees to the Red Cross truck, which would transport them to the railway station in the dark.

The night was chilly as the group assembled in the courtyard. A half-moon slid in and out of thick clouds. A sombre Malik counted them, again, knowing that Pakistani soldiers would assess each person before allowing her to board the truck. Durga had instructed Madhu, Krishna, Kusum, and her two daughters to undo their plaits and leave their hair open, and walk like older women. Wrapped in shawls and ill-fitting clothes, this was one dowdy group of women.

With folded hands, Malik saw them off. 'We wish you a safe journey to your land and hope you're united with your families. Please forgive all the mistakes that have happened at our end.'

'Malikji,' Durga stepped forward, 'I know I speak on our behalf when I say that you have been like a brother to us all.' Heads nodded, to a chorus of weeping and sniffling. But Durga wasn't done. From her satchel, she took out a knife, pricked the tip of a finger, and drew a tilak on the camp commander's forehead with her blood. Calmly, she proceeded to rip a scrap from the pallu of her sari, then tied it around Malik's right wrist.

Overcome with emotion, Malik cupped his face in his palms.

Several trucks were transporting women to the train. Durga counted as each Datiyal inmate boarded a truck – Pakistani soldiers peering at each face, scrutinizing each woman, sniffing at Zooni – and boarded last. In her truck were her children, along with Zooni, Madhu and Krishna. Red Cross workers were overseeing the operation, a few soldiers guarded each truck; so far so good. But before Durga could exhale, the truck halted and two men climbed in. One was dressed in salwar-kameez, the other as a soldier. They had a word with the driver, the truck started, the men surveyed the passengers.

Madhu clutched Durga's hand, trembling, and muttered, 'You must save me. It is *him* – "my husband"! He is here!'

In the dark, Durga couldn't discern which man was the raider-husband. But the Pathan began addressing them directly. 'Do you know all that I have gone through because of this girl?

My whole family has turned against me. But I want to hear from her lips what she chooses.'

Durga gulped. The whole truck seemed to hold its breath. Madhu whimpered.

Giving Madhu's hand a reassuring squeeze, Durga said, 'She is in the truck going to India, she has already spoken through her actions.'

The man shook his head, rubbed his jaw, and gazed out. The soldier continued eyeballing the inmates. 'Are you going to Hindustan?' he shouted. 'The Indian Army is suffering from smallpox. You will die!' The truck trundled through the dark. *How much longer to the train station*? An owl flew low, its flapping wings eerily loud in the still of the night.

'Zulekha?' The Pathan addressed his 'wife'. 'Speak, Zulekha … tell them … Tell them how I rescued you from drowning, and took you home and married you in front of the Qazi and—' He broke off, beseeching her from where he sat beside the driver. 'Abducted girls are being sold in Jhelum city for 10–20 rupees. But I-I …'

The truck came to a stop. They had reached Sarai Alamgir from where the refugee train would depart.

Durga felt a vice-like grip around her upper arm as the young woman levered herself up.

'My name is Madhu, not Z-Zulekha,' she sniffled, 'please let me go home.'

The raider-husband stood up, his shoulders sagging. 'Behenji, she is in your care. Please make sure she reaches safely.' Saying which, he descended from the truck.

Madhu collapsed in relief. Durga patted her and gathered her children, and, as they made their way to the platform, she couldn't believe the danger was truly over. The train was already full of refugees from the Alibeg Camp. They walked through compartments, peering for space in the unlit carriages. Someone struck a match – all the berths were crowded, so they moved on. Finally, Zooni found one empty berth and they crowded on, under and around it. They had barely settled down when a wailing woman stumbled into the compartment and thrust her baby into their midst. Zooni, tucked into a corner on the floor, grabbed the baby. Madhu flung out her blanket to hide the cowering woman as a Pakistani soldier blundered in, a torchlight in hand. For a moment they were captive in the glare before the soldier decided to hurry on.

Hours passed and more people crammed into the train, which was due to leave at four in the morning. There was a strong smell of tea in the air. Durga and her companions sat trussed together, her sons dozed, her daughters huddled in sleep and as the moon slid out of hiding, Madhu was still wide-eyed, Zooni was tucked behind Kusum, and Krishna snored softly. Durga hoped the others had all managed to board—

A soldier's face was bearing down upon Durga, eyes glistening, a dagger gleaming in his hand!

'*Ghodi!* Where's she? Where's the woman with horse hair?'

It was the soldier who had boarded their truck.

'Tell me, or I will stab you!'

Durga, afraid to breathe, watched the dagger inch its way towards her eyes.

In the moonlight, the soldier glowered at the others in the compartment, his eyes scanning passengers for a light-coloured head of hair.

The next instant, the man buckled, yelped, the knife in hand slackened, a woman shrieked, then more women joined the screaming. Scrambling for a foothold, the soldier lurched his way out of the compartment, screams chasing him as he ran.

The moon had again slid back into the clouds as the women, sobbing and crying, rearranged themselves. Durga was breathing heavily. The train lurched, a horn blared, wheels groaned. And a collective sigh rolled through the carriage, the women exhaling their relief. From beneath the berth, Zooni's hand snaked out; Durga squeezed it. Zooni's kick to the man's groin had been most timely.

As the train clickety-clacked out of Sarai Alamgir, a faint glimmer shone on the horizon. Durga clasped her hands in prayer: On this new day, Lord Ganesh, may we begin a new life in India. Beneath the berth, Zooni slid the knife against the wall, tucked her long legs back, and let the train rock her to sleep, a sleep which was perfumed with tea leaves. Daily, Durga had made Zooni soak her golden hair in strong black tea for hours.

The train sped towards Amritsar.

Meanwhile, back at Datiyal Camp, Malik wept like a river that had breached its bank. All those tears bottled up since Tara's death oozed out of him, stealing sleep from his eyes. When the sky blushed pink, he saw women in the lemon and mulberry trees in the courtyard. Amazed, he sprinted up the steps to the rooftop. As far as his eyes could see, in the fruit orchards and farms and scrub, women sat in trees, swinging their legs, laughing, chatting, even as vultures huddled on several other branches.

'Khasma nu khani Partition!' Tara sighed.

'Hain!' Malik whirled.

Tara stood beside him, head cocked. 'Squeezed this new nation out of their bodies, didn't they?'

Malik, standing arms akimbo, surveyed the land in the foothills of the Pir Panjal mountains, oscillating his head in awe. Seeming to remember something, he turned urgently to Tara. 'So they *trust* me now?'

Tara smiled, the morning rays glinting off her nosepin. 'You've only just begun, Sikandar. You have a long way ahead of you … Seven seas across … They will call you Mr Malik.'

'*Mis*-ter Malik?'

Tara nodded, eyes dreamy.

Malik went pale, the tilak of crusted blood stark on his forehead.

'And wherever you go, you'll find me, Sikandar. I made a promise, and I intend to keep it.'

The sun had risen, the land awash in its golden light. A scene was unfolding – Malik watched with narrowed eyes.

In a field of tall mustard where the smell of young mango blossoms wafted, Tara swayed on a rope swing that floated back to where Sikandar stood to push her. She laughed and he indulged her. Back and forth she went, between her beloved and the sky, higher and higher. Men stole up on them, hooded men armed with scythes, spears, swords and guns – men determined to rid Laur of kafirs …

From her bosom, Tara plucked the Mills Bomb her Sepoy Malik had brought back as war souvenir, looked back.

I will meet you yet again, Sikandar.

And pulled the pin of the grenade.

32

Rawalpindi (February 1948)

In Pindi, Akbar Khan felt he could cut the air with a knife, it was so thick with rumours.

The first inkling that all was not well was when a senior officer casually asked why he had been absent from GHQ. Surely, Akbar thought, now that the war over Kashmir was well established, his senior officers were not unaware that Akbar Khan was serving as military adviser to the Prime Minister himself on the Liberation Committee! To serve which purpose, he had been relieved of his duties at GHQ. The initial need for secrecy had been lifted because General Messervy, commander-in-chief of Pakistan Army, was helming the war effort now.

Akbar pondered over this problem at his desk, the warm room infiltrated by the sounds of typing, the rustling of papers, lively chatter – so removed from the freezing rain, faulty guns and fighting on the frontlines.

Lately, he had begun investigating why stores and rations dispatched from Rawalpindi were reaching the front so infrequently. He had found clothing, blankets and other materials generously contributed by Pakistanis being sold openly in the Pindi markets. And Azad Government had furnished evidence of certain officials visiting the territory for expressly administrative issues, but engaging in private deals in timber instead!

Akbar's requests for assistance had been held back and delayed often … the corruption was deep. Perhaps a plan to stab him in the back?

A knock and the orderly popped his head in. It was time for his meeting with the American journalist.

Akbar had clean forgotten about the interview request from Margot Parr, promised by Sardar Ibrahim on his behalf. He sat up in his chair and tried to focus on the immediate task. No sooner was his guest – an extraordinarily tall woman with a commanding presence – seated, that she started firing questions.

'Would you say it's official then, Pakistan's entry in the war? Kabailis tell me that it is faith and faith alone that is handing them these victories.'

As he hedged that question with the usual spiel about the brotherhood of Islam, Margot Parr shot off more questions. *Where were the tribesmen getting their weapons from? Why was there a cardboard victory arch over the main highway leading from Pindi to Kashmir? And why were Pathans waving green flags bearing the star and crescent of the Muslim League?*

The woman had done her homework. Not that anything was hidden in Rawalpindi – one just had to walk around to size up Pakistan's support. Akbar stalled. 'Perhaps you would like to speak with the refugees who have crossed over into Pakistan from Jammu and Kashmir? Surely your readers will be interested in their stories?'

'Oh, absolutely. We must. Also, I would like to interview a few tribesmen. Readers appreciate an all-round perspective.'

'The tribesmen?' Akbar pretended surprise. Margot Parr's bright eyes studied him. With her short hair and winsome smile, it would be a mistake to take her for a rookie.

'Well, yes. You see, I did manage to speak with a couple, and their answer was simple. We are all Muslims, in Kashmir to help our Muslim brothers, they said.'

Akbar Khan raised his eyebrows politely. 'Miss Parr, now that you have already met the tribesmen, what is your personal opinion?'

'My personal opinion is nobody's business, you'll agree. But my *professional* opinion is a work in progress: The more I learn, the better informed I am. I was in Baramulla, you see.' She dug into her bag and held up a cigarette. 'Do you mind?'

Akbar Khan stood up. Retrieving his Zippo lighter, he leaned forward and snapped it open. An intense aroma of tobacco, clove and sandalwood entered his nostrils – whatever perfume the woman used was as bold as her.

'It was a pile of rubble, really; blackened with fire …' Margot settled back in her chair and blew a smoke ring. 'Baramulla reminded me of those picturesque Italians towns decimated during the war in Italy.'

Akbar Khan frowned. 'WWII?'

A rap at the door. A summons from his senior officer. Akbar Khan seized the chance to end the meeting. As he excused himself, he suggested the orderly see Miss Parr out.

'Ma'am, please be careful,' he added as the journalist gathered her bag, lit cigarette dangling from one corner of her mouth. 'The tribesmen are dangerous … Perhaps, it's not my place to advise—'

Margot Parr plucked the cigarette from her mouth. 'It's not.' She took a long puff before releasing a perfect smoke ring that floated to Akbar Khan. 'So don't.' A click of heels, and she was gone.

On the grounds that he had been absent from service, Akbar Khan was informed that he had earned no salary for the past three months. Three months in which he had been working for the Prime Minister himself! Further, the selection board had decided to pass him over for promotion!

Back in his room, as he fulminated over the turn of events, Akbar realized that his mandate had been to carry on the struggle for three months. That time period had passed. And there was no imminent danger on the front. The Uri sector was under heavy snow; the situation was mostly static elsewhere; Pakistan's claim in the UN had won great support. It was time to return to the army.

He would ask the Prime Minister to relieve him.

33

Srinagar (March 1948)

In the moonlit bedroom, the warm air heavy with lovemaking, Margot Parr smoked as her companion, coiled like a foetus, snored beside her. Larry had returned from the UK via New York and New Delhi, full of news and himself. The man's network of connections was akin to the complex mosaic of the royal families of Europe. If Larry was to be believed, the ongoing war between India and Pakistan wasn't going to get resolved anytime soon. The UK's interest lay in keeping Pakistan happy. Muslims, antagonized by Britain decamping from Palestine, were watching the country closely. Noel-Baker was of the view that in order to secure the Middle East, Britain needed Pakistan on its side. Besides which, an Islamic Pakistan would serve as the much-needed buffer against Communist Russia …

A brisk wind knocked at the rickety glass windows. Spring was in the air, pinkish-white blossoms tufting almond trees. Margot, having arrived when the chinars were turning russet, had seen three seasons in Srinagar already – how long could she stay? With a possible stalemate at the UN, if Larry was to be believed, there wouldn't be much justification for staying on. Besides, her editor had begun dropping hints …

Larry coughed in his sleep, which awoke him. Turning on his back, he slid up against the bedrest, his hand reaching for Margot's half-finished cigarette. She handed it to him and he took a deep draw, watching her with half-lidded eyes. 'You look ravishing in the moonlight, my dear.'

'You don't.' Margot plucked her cigarette back.

'No?' Pushing a forelock back, he quipped, 'I've been told on good faith that I remind ladies of a certain Hollywood actor – you know I trust female judgement.'

'Let it never be said that Larry Collins undersold himself.'

They had first met in Berlin: he, an English reporter of acclaim; she, an American novice. The attraction had been immediate. She was single, he was twice divorced and twice her age almost, and nothing beat the allure of lovemaking as bombs dropped around them. Generally regarded as one of the best war correspondents, Larry Collins had cut his journalistic teeth in the dying days of WW1, reported on the inter-war developments in Russia and Europe, been arrested, deported and re-arrested by the Gestapo, and finally freed from solitary confinement by the Allies.

'Got any whiskey?'

With her chin Margot indicated the wall across.

A naked Larry padded to the cupboard that protested as its doors were opened.

'There should be a soda siphon somewhere,' Margot flicked her fingers absent-mindedly.

A source in Pindi helped her with liquor supplies. This time though she had also bagged an item that, in the Valley, had become as valuable as cashmere in Paris: Salt. At Rs 20 a seer, hardly any household could afford it – if any was at all available in the market. Every dish depended upon the use of salt, and Margot had observed Gul's reluctance to eat since the houseboat had entered saltless days. When serving food, Kashmira apologized profusely, but Margot shrugged it off. She had survived war on bland bread baked from chaff – a memory stirred, her mouth wobbled, she pulled the shutter down. Besides, she raked fingers through her hair, there was no dish that a side of liquor didn't improve! But Gul's visible thinness, the bulky sweater could fill two of him, and trauma over his father's death, bothered Margot. And lately, the cookboat had another mouth to feed: Kashmira's younger sister, a refugee from Reasi, had arrived. So Margot had lugged a seer of salt from Army rations, Pindi. The cigarette stung – it had burnt down. Margot stubbed it out.

Larry handed her a glass of whiskey, neat like she preferred, and settled against the bed, sipping his drink with soda.

'What news from Delhi?'

'Well, Nehru is brimming with confidence with the latest Indian victory in Jammu—'

'Naushera?' In Pindi, Margot had heard disgruntled voices bemoaning the lashkars who had fled in the face of Indian artillery.

'Nehru is jubilant that the Indian side was led by none other than a Muslim, a Brigadier Usman. Pathans and Pakistanis might have launched a holy war, but Nehru, mind you, is also waging war, a secular one. Nothing tickles his fancy more than Hindu–Muslim bhai-bhai!'

'You think this war over Kashmir will go on?'

Larry shrugged. 'The two dominions didn't wait two months to go to war with each other. How long did the British manage to prevent that? Perhaps there *is* some weight to the argument that the Indians and Pakistanis need the English to keep them in order.'

'What tosh, Larry!' Margot lit another cigarette. 'You British taught Indians to fight amongst themselves to *your* benefit.'

'That's how empires rule. But the end of empires is never pretty. WW1 brought about the collapse of four multinational empires: the Russian in 1917, followed by the Ottoman, Austro-Hungarian and German empires in 1918. Old ethnic groups demanding new states, new homelands, new borders and boundaries. The old order changeth, yielding to new, eh? Nationalism, democracy – how does the new system of organization hold up to the Empire?' Larry lifted his glass in a token of 'Cheers'!

'You mean dismantling large blocks of territory to draw the boundaries of new, independent states? States like Pakistan and India? Which came about only because the English first made slaves of Indians and taught them to fight one another?'

'My point exactly. The British did keep the Indians from killing one another.'

Margot clucked her tongue. 'Ah, I forgot. The superior English mind, right? That can civilize the natives, improve their lot, raise them to the point where they can govern themselves. But India and Indians, under Gandhi are in such a damned hurry to get their freedom! Pray, enlighten me. What makes a young man from Surrey or Yorkshire or,' she looked pointedly at Larry—

'Shitterton.'

'Shitter-ton … *Shit*-ter-ton! Wherever … think he is superior to the *natives*? What is it but privileging white skin? The US, UK's foremost colony, did this with white dominance over natives and Blacks.'

The moon had vanished, plunging the room into darkness. The wind had picked up, rocking the boat like it was a cradle. Which reminded her of childhood summers spent on cypress pirogues. The daughter of a French Creole mother from Louisiana and an Irish father from New Jersey, Margot understood all too well the white racist Anglo-Saxon logic. Stories passed down from her Creole and Black ancestors told of how Free Blacks were re-enslaved once United States purchased the state of Louisiana from the French in 1803. So much for the 'Blessings of Liberty' guaranteed by the American Constitution! Margot flicked on the papier-mâché lamp by her bedside.

Larry continued to sip his whiskey. Nothing ever seemed to stir him. But his body showed his trauma when he slept, curled into himself like an infant.

'Men's egos bring us to wars. And in every war, the first casualty are women and children.' Margot thought she had seen enough shit but images of Baramulla women with chopped noses and ears, because the raiders were in too great a hurry to remove the gold ornaments, stalked her …

'War is evil.' Larry sucked his teeth. 'Which is why Churchill said we must draw a veil over all the horrors of the past—'

'Larry, the zealot!'

'Well, if it helps, Churchill was against us scuttling out of India.' Larry held a palm up.

'Pax Britannia!' Margot chortled. 'But listen,' she sat up grinning and crossed her legs. 'When I was denied permission to cover the D-Day landing in Normandy on account of no penis, I smuggled myself on a hospital ship and posed as a nurse. You know that? Well, at dinner once, I overheard a major suggesting to his superior that the Allies drop supersized condoms marked 'medium' into Germany. The psychological toll would weaken the Nazis and pave the way for an Allied victory!'

Larry hooted.

A giggling Margot rolled back into bed. 'One hell of a dick-measuring contest!'

With a glint in his eye, Larry swigged his drink, and leaning forward, grabbed Margot's left foot, and cradling it in one hand, started to massage the sole with the other, circling his thumb in firm spirals down to the heel, eliciting moans from Margot.

'On the subject of dicks ...'

Two days later, Larry had left for Pindi to meet Liaquat, and Margot sat sunning herself on the roof of the houseboat. A bright day when the Dal shimmered, light dazzled on icy peaks and clumps of snow on the bank, kerosene tins that plated a distant roof glittered like silver, and Gul played on the bank with chicks that had newly hatched while bulbuls sang in willows decked in fresh green leaves—

Raised voices alerted her.

Lifting her head, Margot sighted Hassan Dar stomping out of the cookboat. He had surfaced after the worst of winter was over and skulked around often. Now, Gul looked apprehensive as his uncle approached him. Hassan's shrill voice shattered the idyll as he thrust his large hands at the boy. The rapid-fire delivery reached Margot who, with little comprehension of the Kashmiri language, watched with a frown. Suddenly, Hassan pounced on Gul and tried to pluck the chick. Gul thrashed about before fleeing to the cookboat, the chick secure in his hands. Waving a threatening fist, Hassan stomped away.

Fucking fascist! Margot knew she could not interfere but the memory of another small child had resurfaced. A girl who brought her coarse bread made from chaff, bread that saved

Margot but condemned the partisan family that had given her shelter in fascist Italy to severe punishment. Margot clamped her suddenly tremulous mouth behind a curled fist. Meanwhile, Gul had cautiously stepped on to the houseboat, tears streaking his smudged face. She had to investigate. Fetching a round tin of the sticky toffee the boy loved, Margot greeted him cheerily.

Gul sucked on the toffee and, caressing the chick in his lap, explained what had transpired. Hassan had accused Gul of being a sissy who could only play with chicks and would never lift an arm against the enemy. Meanwhile, his aunt Zooni was learning to use the rifle at the women's self-defence camp! Such shamelessness!

'Pitar thinks he can hurt my chicks,' Gul sniffled. 'Wait till he sees my *big* bird.'

Margot narrowed her eyes.

'Want to show *me* this bird?'

Gul tipped his head. 'Can I trust you?'

Margot nodded solemnly. After which, Gul deposited the chick back in its coop, grabbed a stinking cloth bag and led Margot along the lake into a thicket. Abounding with tall chinar and oak trees, the area grew more shaded as Gul led Margot zigzagging into a forest. Until the ground dipped to a ravine ringed by pines, chestnuts, deodars. In the hush, Margot could hear her heart beat.

Raising one reassuring hand, Gul instructed. 'Miss Margot, don't be scared.' Then he started to make a robust rattling sound, which she couldn't believe came from within the boy's thin chest. As the sound amplified, Gul threw his face upwards, his eyes scanning the sky.

There was a flapping and a large bird swooped down from a pine. From his bag, Gul dug out a long bone and tossed it on the ground. The raptor swept down and started to gouge.

Margot gulped. A snapping beak, up close, was terrifying! Vulture sightings were aplenty in Jammu, Panjab, Kashmir, wherever corpses were rotting. Beady eyes, talons, enormous wingspan, but *this* vulture had icy-blue down. Was it a juvenile, one that had separated from its pack?

Finished with feeding, it raised its long neck, fixed a stare at Gul and Margot before it soared up and away with a vigorous flapping.

Gul turned to look at Margot, his face radiating pride, astonishment and joy.

Margot let out her breath. 'I must admit, Mister Gul, you had me there.'

Gul giggled, slipped a hand into Margot's, and started to lead the way back. Trying not to appear nosey or apprehensive, Margot made casual enquiries. Gul had found the bird a month or so back, lying on the forest floor, not moving, weak. He brought it water and bones that Mouj discarded and in a couple of weeks, it began to fly. Once Gul heard the bird make that sound whilst hunting, he began to mimic it. Since then, it had become easier to train Boi than the chicks or the cat, Gul grinned.

'Boi?' Margot frowned.

'Boi for brother, Miss Margot,' Gul explained helpfully.

Margot smiled, wrinkling her nose. It could be a girl, but that wasn't important. Since Ali Dar's passing, his son had been actively seeking companionship from animals. Now he was calling this raptor his brother. But this was no ordinary bird; the fact that it was responding to Gul meant it was likely not an adult. Still, it was some kind of Himalayan vulture …

Margot resolved to find out more and to keep an eye on Gul, meanwhile.

34

New York (March 1948)

The snow lay two-feet deep. Tiger was still mesmerized by it. He had landed in New York late on the evening of 31 December and seen snowfall for the first time. It was strange that the heir of Jammu and Kashmir state, renowned for its snow-capped Himalayas, should first witness snow in a strange country halfway around the world. But Tiger had never spent a winter in Kashmir.

It was his third month in America – an astonishing country as he was discovering. There was an air of freshness; people were informal and friendly; and the staff at the Hospital for Special Surgery was curious and kindly about the patient, whose arrival had been published in the *Daily Mirror*. And New York, with its huge buildings thrusting up into the air, the tops oft-lost in the swirling snow of blizzards, was a great city. The radio programmes went on for eighteen hours, from six in the morning to midnight, with a bewildering array of music, plays, talks, news and sports commentaries! Dr Philip D. Wilson, one of the most distinguished orthopaedic surgeons in America, had infused confidence in him. Yet, despite the medical treatment and the diversions, the fact remained that he was still a cripple, unable to move on his own, dependent upon sponge baths and bedpans. Some days, as he sat soaking the sun in the solarium on the sixth floor – a large glass-panelled room with potted plants – while snow fell outside, he was beset with those same doubts ...

Would he ever be able to walk again, or was he condemned to be a helpless cripple for the rest of his life? What would become of the state of which he was born heir apparent? Would he ever see India again, or his parents?

Unbidden, the mantra his mother had taught him for the worship of Goddess Durga rose to his lips. She had also given him a small picture of the eight-armed Singhavahini riding a lion, which he had clutched during the long laborious flight from India and which he turned to whenever despondent. His—

'Good morning!'

The soft-spoken greeting brought a smile to Tiger's face. Mr J.E. Brown was his tutor in economics and political science. Three days a week, he arrived from Columbia University to give him lessons, something Tiger enjoyed very much.

'How are we feeling today?'

Mr Brown approached the quiet corner Tiger had chosen as he was wheeled up for his instruction. The distinct Central European accent of his tutor made Tiger wonder why he went under an assumed name. His doubts were cleared soon enough.

'Very well, thank you,' Tiger replied with cheer, unconsciously mimicking the gung-ho attitude of the Americans who surrounded him.

'Good, good.' Mr Brown took the empty chair, opened a textbook on the centre table, deposited a rolled-up newspaper and briskly resumed the ongoing lesson on capitalism. 'The way to learn is to always interrogate what's happening around you. Economics is not an ivory tower field; it is directly related to how the world works. Look at today's paper,' he opened the *New York Times*, shook it open, and started to read from the front page. 'Tensions continue between the government and the opposition in Costa Rica.' Smacking the paper with his right hand, he handed it to Tiger. 'Headline. Here. Read it yourself.'

Tiger scanned the article about the ongoing civil war in Costa Rica. *President Calderon's government ... allied to the Costa Rican Communist party ... promoting social reform ...*

'So... what do you think?'

Mr Brown, hands clasped around one crossed knee, observed him keenly. When his pupil looked unsure, he asked, 'You don't think America has any role in this civil war? The opposition, rebelling against a democratically elected Left-leaning government interested in social reformation – does it have outside support, perhaps? Hmm.'

'You mean to say the Costa Rican opposition has the support of the US?'

Mr Brown unclasped his hands and tapped his chin with his right index finger. 'What is the item most in demand in any war?'

'Weapons?' Tiger said hesitantly.

'Munitions, yes! And who are the biggest munition manufacturers in the world?'

'America?'

Mr Brown beamed as he held up one hand first, 'Demand,' then another, 'Supply,' and made them meet mid-air. 'The munition manufacturers need a market for their wares; the South American neighbours are a lucrative market. The CIA has a habit of supporting the opposition against Left-wing leaders. A Communist agenda does not sit well with American capitalism.'

Tutor and pupil sat in quiet contemplation, a whoosh penetrating the solarium as the wind outside suddenly gusted, hurling snowflakes like grenades.

Tiger remembered when Sheikh Abdullah had visited him. The Kashmir dispute in the United Nations was on the front pages of all major US newspapers. The wily Zafarullah Khan seemed to be getting the better of the Indian delegation, much to Tiger's exasperation! Sheikh Abdullah had said the British were leaning in favour of Pakistan because of their own interests. And the US was happy to follow the UK's lead. The tribal invasion had developed into a full-scale war, in which the state forces and the Indian Army were pitted against the tribals and regular units of the Pakistan Army. In which case, Tiger thought with furrowed brow, would the US look to Kashmir as a new market for selling weapons? It was a very distressing thought—

'Well,' Mr Brown sat up perkily, a jaunty smile on his face. 'The study of economics is not meant to weigh us down. Let's continue with our discussion – and dissection, eh? – of capitalism.'

Tiger nodded. 'Mr Brown, a question first, if I may?'

The tutor held both palms upfront.

'What is a Leftist such as yourself doing in a capitalist system?'

The barest flicker of sadness before Mr Brown quipped, 'Being a fierce critic, of course!'

Later, as Tiger lay in his hospital bed listening to pop music, Captain Ranjit Singh arrived with a letter. His companion – one of Father's aides who had accompanied him from Jammu and was resident in the adjoining room – looked crestfallen though he was trying to mask it.

'From your father,' he said, tipping his head.

'What is it?'

Instead Ranjit gestured with his chin. 'Read it. Let's hear the news from home, eh?'

Father wrote regularly with news of the progress of the military campaign, and some news of the Bombay races. Tiger was aware the Indian offensive was gradually succeeding, but the process was much slower than Father had hoped for. The performance of his horses provided some distraction to Father. Tiger's own letters to him were full of the Security Council proceedings regarding the Kashmir dispute. Now, he opened the letter hurriedly.

Sheikh Mohammed Abdullah was appointed as prime minister of an interim government in the state of Jammu and Kashmir on 5 March 1948, and a new Kashmir Cabinet had taken oath … Mehar Chand Mahajan had left the state …

Tiger looked at Ranjit. The captain had been aware of the contents of the letter – presumably from Brigadier N.S. Rawat, the senior Gurkha officer of the state forces, who was Tiger's second companion on this American journey. Licking his dry lips, Tiger returned to the letter in his hand. When he had finished reading, he folded it back and dismissed Ranjit.

In Jammu, it would be spring. Mother would be active in the refugee relief work, visiting one camp after another, distributing rations and clothes deep into the night. And Father… Father would be maintaining his usual composure, wincing inwardly with news of each reversal. And while writing the last lines in the letter, his eyes would have been moist.

The Constitution of India is also being framed. I have no idea of how this is going to affect us beyond the fact that before very long, princely rulers will disappear even in name.

35

Srinagar (March 1948)

A woman without a nose. Another missing her ears. Several with bandaged necks, in an attempt to get the skin to cleave to bone again. Some with stumps for hands …

Durga swallowed again, forcing herself to look at the women, at each woman who was sheltering in the house, Dar-ul-Aman, House of Peace. Refugees from Baramulla – they were Sikh and Pandit women, who had survived the slaughter of October. Six months later, their bodies wore the signs of the ordeal. Greeting the women with a smile, hands folded, Durga wove her way through the living room. She had seen the worst of humanity in her trek from Muzaffarabad to Datiyal. The months in the camp had revealed all the misfortune that could befall women – or so she had thought.

Masking the sniffle that arose by rubbing her nose, Durga entered the kitchen. Bibi Charan Kaur looked up from kneading a mound of flour, the sleeves of her sweater ruched at the elbows, and paused wrestling with the atta. The lobes of her ears split at the bottom like trouser legs. A Pathan was about to plunge a knife into her throat when she had torn off the heavy earrings herself. All her life the matriarch had worn those silver hoops, laden with dangling silver balls, which had given her distended lobes. But what use were those when her whole family – husband, three sons – was butchered? Dry-eyed, Bibi Charan Kaur had narrated her story to Durga when they first met. Now, wordlessly, she acknowledged Durga and returned to her kneading.

The inviting aroma of ripe apricots wafted from the pantry. Durga went to check on supplies. Salt was perennially short … Rice needed stocking up … A week's supply of flour and oil … Fruits were abundant, though – Durga made sure her father's orchards did not neglect the refugees. Her palm stilled over the basket of walnuts.

When a bedraggled Durga had walked into her childhood home with her raggedy children, Mai had dropped her teacup and screamed. As she clutched her chest, the scream became a honking with the onset of an asthmatic attack. News of the killing of the district commissioner of Muzaffarabad had reached them, alongside stories of the brutalities unleashed by the kabailis. Sorrowfully, they had assumed that their only daughter, whom they had raised like a prized kosher gulab, had wilted in the storm. Relieved at her return, they wanted her to relax and rest and eat, and try to forget her trials. But a week of lying in bed and being served hand and foot had only made Durga morose. Memories of the Muzaffarabad house had flooded her mind … The fortifications her husband had erected in front of their bungalow … His anxious face as he rushed on his border visits … The discovery of snakes about the house … When she forced herself to nap, weird visions woke her up. In one, she was visiting the temple, but stumbled and dropped the plate of offerings. In another, a snake fell on her youngest son as he dozed. The more she lay in bed, the more tired she became. Until—

'Mrs Mehra?'

Durga stepped out, patting her hair, a long braid which she curled into a low bun at the nape of her neck.

Freda Bedi stood in the kitchen wearing her usual pleasant smile. She was the wife of B.P.L. Bedi, who had drafted the 'New Kashmir' manifesto which conveyed Sheikh Abdullah's ambitious vision for social transformation.

'Namaste.'

Durga and Freda headed out to the terrace. Since neither felt like sitting, they then went for a walk in the garden where the brown grass was dotted with clumps of violets and yellow crocuses.

Within days of Durga's arrival, Freda had sought her out and Durga suspected her mother must have put her up to it. At first sight, Durga had wondered what she would have in common with the blue-eyed blonde whose nation had brought this entire calamity upon India and Kashmir. But Freda had shared her experience in Baramulla, where she had gone with a group of volunteers to help the survivors, many of whom were now housed in Dar-ul-Aman. Freda said that listening to gory stories of locals, seeing the destruction first-hand, scraping dry blood off the chapel floor had made her lose her appetite and sleep, and take to bed.

Upon hearing which, Durga had felt an immediate kinship with her.

In a week though, Freda said, she had bounced back: *17,000 refugees in the city needed help!* Now, she helped run twenty-three relief centres, was a member of the Women's Self Defence Militia, and assisted her husband in his work.

Durga had jumped at the chance to join her, despite Mai's protests. With Freda, she had marched to Srinagar's main square which had been renamed Lal Chowk, where red flags of National Conference fluttered as men and women worked together for New Kashmir. Freda had shared the story of Durga's incredible escape in their newsletter to inspire other women and to counter false Pakistani propaganda. Durga had helped other women at camp before; she could do so now as well. Robbed of their families, traumatized, the women felt helpless. But women bound by suffering could band together to improve their lot. Which was how Durga had landed at Dar-ul-Aman.

'So,' Freda said, 'how are things progressing?'

'Most women are turning up for the evening prayer and story session. And a couple of them are very good with needlework and have begun embroidering a shawl each. Rano, the young Sikh woman who was abducted? She has a way with children ...'

'Hmm?' Freda urged.

'I think we can start a small school for the children in Dar-ul-Aman!'

'Excellent idea!'

Durga nodded. 'The children have seen so much hate so close ... It is time we show them light.'

'A leprous daybreak,' Freda muttered.

Faiz, who oft visited Durga's parents during his sojourns in Srinagar, and who was a friend of the Bedis, had lamented the dawn of freedom in a mournful ghazal. Durga sighed. The refugee train that had deposited her in Amritsar was terminating at Kurukshetra. That famed battleground of Mahabharata had become the site of the largest refugee camp in independent India.

'Leprous indeed,' Durga agreed.

A tortoiseshell butterfly floated in front of them.

Durga lifted her face to the blue sky. 'But we've been given a new day to seize.'

36

Srinagar (April 1948)

At Gol Bagh, the assortment of women in pheran-poch, sari-shawl, salwar-kameez – scarves, pallus, chunnis firmly tucked – pumped their legs and flapped their arms as their instructor barked commands. Dressed in military uniform, he was leading them in physical exercise, which was the first essential element in the training of the Women's Self Defence Corps, WSDC. This would be followed by a parade, followed by weapons training. The ever-present threat of kabailis, the horror stories circulating, the sightings of women cleaved of their noses and ears, had roused residents of the Valley to the realization that no woman was safe. The least they could do was to prepare their womenfolk in the art of self-defence. Which was why Gol Bagh had, of late, become a Zanana Bagh: no sundry male entered the park unless he was an instructor or from the Indian Army or the Salamati Fauj, the Valley's militia to secure peace.

Zooni had been coming for a month now, having joined the corps on arrival when Durga Mehra had alerted her to it.

Zooni's fantastic work with a catapult meant she would make a great markswoman, Durga was convinced. *Besides, a gulel might scare away a Pathan or two, but it could not win wars or defeat enemies – didn't Zooni know?*

Zooni had swallowed the bitterness that sprang within her at the question. *Oh, Zooni knew, she knew so very well.* In Baramulla, the kabailis had set fire to her home, burning all to cinder. Kashmira said Ali had found three human skeletons and a charred barn. What had riled the Pathans so? Mouj and Moul had no money, no gold, no ornaments … had the lack of booty drawn the wrath of the raiders? To kill with such abandon – where did this cruelty come from? Little Jugnu swam in her mind then; Jugnu firing pebbles at his burly assailant in order to save his mother – that memory raked Zooni's eyelids day and night, the faces of Jugnu and her Boi mingling with each other. Zooni had failed her family. Zooni had failed Jugnu. Not only had she not trained him well enough to be a skilled marksman, she had also raised his hopes that a catapult would protect him and his mother. No, Zooni needed no convincing. If a weapon would help her protect her family, she would learn to fire that weapon. But Kashmira did not agree. Kashmira was aghast. How could Zooni join in training from the very men who had killed Ali Dar?

'All of Srinagar is sending their daughters,' Zooni had pointed out. 'And the trainers are members of Salamati Fauj as well.'

'The fauj is as bad as the Indian Army,' Kashmira had countered hotly.

Zooni had exhaled, her breath rising and falling with agitation. She had shared only cursory details about the past few months: Masud Ahmed had gone fighting and never returned, the enemy had killed the older wife, the refugee camp had saved Zooni …

Then she had said quietly, 'I have seen men like these kabailis. The only reason I am here is because Koko Jan took my bullet, too.' Seeing Kashmira's eyes widen, Zooni drove home her point. 'The kabailis killed our entire family in Baramulla … Mouj, Moul, Boi, gone … all gone! So, if tomorrow the kabailis turn up at *Mayfair* houseboat, I want to be able to keep us safe.'

After that, Zooni had showed up daily at Gol Bagh to learn and practice, and Kashmira showed her disapproval by never enquiring about the training.

The women had finished their parade and broken into groups for weapons training. Learning to fire the .303 rifle, Zooni, with Kanta Misri and Usha Koul, was top of the class in marksmanship. A new instructor had arrived to work with them specifically. Watching him now, Zooni was reminded of that first day when another instructor had fired that first shot: Most women cowered in fright, a couple even fainted, but Zooni was frozen. Watching the women's reaction, the instructor did not laugh. He sat them down and took them through the various parts of a rifle, a Salamati Fauji translating alongside in Kashmiri. Then he demonstrated how to hold it. After which he asked them to pick up a hockey stick each and hold it like it was a rifle. Days later, women who felt ready to hold a weapon were given rifles without rounds. After which, some had graduated to learning to shoot.

Daily, as she walked from *Mayfair* to Gol Bagh and back, Zooni observed Indian Army patrolling bridges, roads, checkpoints and figured that many soldiers in the Valley were Masud Ahmed's 'bearded savages'. And Zooni learned that as chaff with wheat, rice and barley, there were worthless men – be they Muslim or kuffar. Slow to start, Zooni had proved herself an ace student.

'Zooniji,' the new instructor approached her, having assigned exercises to Kanta and Usha. 'Myself, Havildar Fateh Singh.' He pointed to the target, 'Aim for the bulls-eye, three shots in quick succession.'

He was one of Masud Ahmed's 'bearded savages' and he *spoke* Kashmiri? But Zooni had no time to register the unusual. Squaring her shoulders, pressing the butt of the gun into her right shoulder pocket, she took a deep breath, aimed and fired. When she finished and looked up, one shot had succeeded; the other two had strayed to the right. Zooni clenched her jaw. The instructor did not miss her reaction. With hands on his waist, he asked, 'Do you know what you're doing wrong?'

Zooni shook her head mutely.

He stepped up to her. 'Take your stance.'

She could smell the maleness on him as he towered over her. Months spent in Datiyal with other women had obscured the odour that she associated with her husband. Zooni tried not to flinch.

'Fire!'

He repeated the order twice thereafter, giving Zooni more time between each shot.

When Zooni looked up, the result was same as with the first round, but the instructor looked satisfied.

'Your first shot hit the bulls-eye, both times. The following two did not. Why?'

Zooni blinked. *Was she doing anything different?*

'Remove the rounds. Then fire three shots again.'

When Zooni was about to pull the trigger the third time, a burly hand layered hers, a deep male voice commanding, 'KEEP the finger squeezed!' As if Masud Ahmed had snuck up on her! She shuddered.

Immediately, the instructor stepped back, palms raised. 'My mistake.'

Hands on his waist again, he cast a look around before bounding to grab a rifle. Standing parallel to her, he said, 'There are *five* principles to firing a rifle. One: Take aim. Align sight with target, keeping both eyes open.' Then he illustrated what he meant. Straightening up, he continued. 'Two: Control your breathing. One deep breath, exhale half of it, hold your breath as you squeeze the trigger.' Again he demonstrated the correct technique. 'Three: Hold your aim. Focus, minimize movement. Four: Squeeze the trigger. Do *not* shake the gun; only use a slow steady pressure until the gun fires.'

Nodding at Zooni, he made her go through the four steps with deliberation.

When she finished, he said, 'So far, so good. Your problem, Zooniji, is the last step. Step five: *Follow through*. Now, after the bullet fires, if you jerk the gun even slightly *before* the bullet leaves the barrel, you will miss your aim. Which is why your first shot both times is on target. But you are impatient with the following. Now, I want you to keep the finger squeezed on the trigger each time you fire. Okay?'

Zooni licked her lips and nodded.

'Let's try again.'

The hubbub of women's voices, gunshots, orders; the spring song of bulbuls, mynahs, sparrows; the swarm of bees humming around the nearby apricot tree – Zooni tried to leave it all behind as she concentrated on the target board, superimposing the face of a cackling monster on the silhouette, the night rent with Rani's pleas ...

Over the following trials, Zooni had mixed luck, averaging the bulls-eye half the time.

'You can aim, Zooniji, there is no doubt about that ...'

Havildar Fateh Singh bunched his mouth and probed his black beard. He studied the target, riddled with shots, to unlock the puzzle. Meanwhile, Usha Koul had one arm raised high and he went over to answer her summons.

Zooni, at a loss, studied the ground. Green grass studded with familiar bluebells. The whiff of fruits in the crisp morning air. The soil ready for sowing rice. Mouj and Moul removing weeds, some song of Lalla on their lips, watering, ploughing … in time, green tendrils would emerge— Military boots swam into view. Zooni's head snapped up.

'When you take aim,' Havildar Fateh Singh asked, 'do you have an image in your mind?'

Jugnu. Zooni saw Jugnu. Setting her mouth so it would not quaver, she gave a brief nod.

'A specific image? A very *specific* memory?'

At the barest tilt of her head, his eyes lit up with comprehension. 'O-kay. Can you hold that image for longer?'

No! Absolutely not! Zooni did not summon the image of Jugnu – it popped into her head when she took aim, but she cast it out. As the conflicting emotions played out on her face, the instructor spoke softly.

'You took up arms for a specific reason. Let that reason guide you.'

Zooni looked at the instructor's face for the first time, locking eyes with him. She noticed his forehead framed by the arch of his khaki muslin turban, the intense eyes, the nose straight like the trunk of a poplar, the full lips set in an arch of whiskers … how *could* he know?

'Hmm? Try again, shall we?'

This time, when Zooni took aim and Jugnu's image slid into her mind – Jugnu, his trembling lower lip stuck out in defiance, with squared shoulders and widely planted feet as he attempted to save Rani – she let the image fix itself in her open eyes. Once. Twice. Thrice.

When Zooni lifted her head, the instructor was clapping his hands. 'Very good! We continue our lesson tomorrow.'

At the Shia mosque, Zooni parted from the group of WSDC women and headed to Gagribal. It was late noon and the area was quiet. Tourists had not returned to the Valley even as the snow had melted, the days were bright, and peaches and apples bloomed on trees. Kashmira worried about how the houseboat would survive after Miss Margot left. The American reporter had been kind, but she could not stay in Srinagar forever—

A figure slid out from behind a willow tree and jumped into her path. Hassan. What a nuisance the man was. He stood blocking her path and as Zooni tried to dodge him, his arm snaked out and grabbed her wrist.

'What were you doing with the balwallah kuffar?' Hassan hissed.

Zooni looked into his furrowed, bitter face. 'Why do you speak like a Pathan?'

He shook her arm. 'Answer me!'

Relaxing her wrist, Zooni rotated it towards Hassan's thumb. Which loosened his hold, allowing her to quickly retract her arm.

'None of your business,' she answered a bewildered Hassan.

'Ali's sal fraternizing with the enemy is *my* business. It is a stain on the Dar family name. You're a half-widow. I forbid you to be out and about like some indecent woman!'

'For-*bid* me?'

Hassan waved a threatening index finger. 'Watch out, woman, or I will take away my niece and nephew before you ruin our family further!'

Hamlavar khabardar! Aggressors beware!

A chorus of slogans sliced the air. Accompanied by drumbeat and marching feet. Hassan paled.

Hum Kashmiri hain tayyar!

The sounds were getting closer. Hassan swore before tossing his head and hurrying away.

He had barely turned the corner when a parade came into view. The men carried assorted long-barrelled matchlocks, country-made rifles, hockey sticks on their shoulders as they swung their arms and shouted slogans about fighting looters and aggressors.

Ladengay hum, looteron aur hamlawaron ke sath!

Half-widow! Hassan acted as if the women of the family were his wares, to display or stow away at will. And he was not even a husband: fire the stove, splay your legs. Before Masud Ahmed, the only man Zooni knew was Moul, who sang to his sheep as he herded them, washed kohlrabi and lotus roots for Mouj to pickle, showed Zooni where the grassy uplands were above the wood line, where the best trout was to be found in the rapids of the Jhelum below Baramulla, what all fruit a catapult could bring down!

On that bittersweet memory, Zooni resumed her walk. Sparrows and starlings hopped in the dappled spring light. One of Moul's songs rose to her lips. She started to hum.

Come, O Gardener,
Create a new spring,
Make the gul bloom,
And the bulbul sing.

37

Srinagar (April 1948)

Pashmina was currency.

Kashmira untied the bundle of embroidered cotton cloth, wound tight against silverfish. Within it was another bundle. As she unravelled the multiple folds of muslin littered with dried bitter flowers and medicinal herbs, her nose pricked at the tart odour. Then, her hands stilled. In the recess, lay six yards of pashmina tucked into a neat rectangle. It was no ordinary saree, the base fabric having disappeared entirely, the fine wool covered in delicate, filigreed sozni embroidery.

Kashmira caressed the embossing with one hand, the silk threads gleaming like jewels in the dim light of the cookboat. *If you ever need money desperately, cut a shawl out of this and sell it to the shawl peddler. Remember, this is equal to gold.* Ali's smile as he had gifted her the insurance currency was secure in the knowledge that they would see their old days together. Why would a master embroiderer fall on dire times?

But that eventuality had arrived.

Kashmira needed money. After Hassan had pilfered the initial advance, Miss Margot had repaid her. But prices were as high as the Himalayas and Kashmira had an additional mouth to feed. Zooni, thanks to Allah, had joined them. But her younger beni was learning to fire guns, which did not earn any money …

Kashmira bit her lower lip. The brilliant flowers, leaves and berries in lilac, rose, emerald, auburn, nudged the flesh of her palm, coarse from tending to the vegetable garden, cooking, cleaning, darning the children's increasingly frayed garments. She nestled the duffe daar kani sozni, her mouth wobbling with the effort not to cry. Abruptly, she grabbed the big scissors that lay at the bottom of the trunk. Sentiments were foolish; hadn't Ali himself said, '*Pashmina is currency.*' Sniffling, she started to unfold the saree.

'*Kashmira!*'

Zooni popped in through the doorway, neck darting about as she tried to ascertain what was happening.

'Don't!' she cried out, concern lacing her voice.

Kashmira shrugged. 'We have to eat.'

Zooni dived to the floor. 'Wait. There's a chance to earn money.'

With a furrowed brow, Kashmira waited for her sister to elaborate.

'So, Durga Mehra, you recall? Yes? At her relief centre, she's started a sadan to train refugee women in domestic crafts, lessons in hand spinning and embroidery. Accompanied by a monthly cash payment!'

'To learn, you get paid?'

'And to teach.' Zooni nodded briskly. 'Technical training and income – to help all Kashmiris impacted by the war!'

'I don't need training,' Kashmira said quietly.

'Precisely! Who will train the women, you think?' Zooni's eyes sparkled.

Kashmira pursed her lips. 'I haven't picked up a needle to embroider in months.'

'True. But an embroiderer doesn't lose her skill. Even the ustad acknowledged that.' Zooni pointed her chin to the window beyond which Kashmira's mother-in-law was visible on the tiny deck of the boat, her face raised to the sun.

Kashmira knew what her beni was referring to. In the first winter of her marriage, Ali had encouraged her to practice a certain movement of holding the needle and passing it through the cloth to learn a particular stitch. Six months of daily practice and Kashmira had perfected the stitch. After which, she worked alongside her husband. When she finally completed embroidering her first sozni shawl with her favourite chinar leaves, all by herself, Ali had showed it to his mother. Her mother-in-law had examined the shawl in the bright light of late spring, probing the embossing, looking for errant thread work, irregularities in pattern, until she had looked up and instructed, 'Fit 500 stitches per square centimetre of cloth.' A perplexed Kashmira had looked from her mother-in-law to her husband until realization had dawned: The renowned 'ustad' of the Dar family was none other than her mother-in-law!

Since master embroiderers were meant to be men, Bilquis had let her husband take the credit as the shawls brought in fame and money either way. A life devoted to fine needlework had made Bilquis purblind. But not before she had taught her special skill to Ali, and then Kashmira.

'Hmm?' Zooni urged.

'I can't. I can't let people think that Ali's embroidery was my work.'

'Because his wife can embroider, too?' Zooni snorted. 'Men with thick fingers and coarse hands can create sozni, but women know only how to darn! Come, Beni, people are fools to believe that. *You* need money and *you* have a skill to sell. Besides, the refugee women will have difficulty learning from a male … Our pain is still raw.'

As Zooni firmed her jaw, Kashmira watched her sister. Zooni pursed her mouth and started to rummage through the trunk. She plucked an old pashmina shawl, the colour of pearly rice, light as an iris, and inhaled its smell before taking it to Kashmira's face. That old shawl, which Bilquis had used and softened with wear, was as soft as butter and fit to swaddle children. Kashmira clutched the shawl, fragrant with her babies, even the infant who didn't survive, and buried her face in it. After she lost two babies, she had dressed Gul as a girl to deflect the evil eye … Gul, whose cheeks had sunk in … Who grieved for his father by befriending strange animals … Whom Hassan sneered at … Who had the hands and temperament of a fine embroiderer like his father and his granny …. Unlike Safina, who was a younger Zooni. Which made Kashmira giggle.

The sound surprised her. She hadn't laughed in months.

38

Delhi (April–May 1948)

The ice field stretched luminous in front of them, its white brilliance mesmerizing. Jawahar inhaled deeply. The three-and-a-half mile trek up to Zojila had stiffened his legs, after which ascending the Gumba ravine had clear knocked the wind out of him! Another satisfied breath as he took in the sight, snowfall obscuring his vision with big fat flakes. Exhilarated, he felt on top of the world. At 17,000 feet, he was indeed! With a nod to his friends, he proceeded ahead. Since they had started, the weather had changed for the worse, fresh snow masking the terrain. A thin crevasse. He could jump over it. Jawahar leaped. But instead of firm ground, he felt weightlessness. A hollow was swallowing him up … He was falling, falling, falling!

On a gasp, Jawahar awoke.

The glacier he had trekked in Kashmir the summer of his marriage and nearly lost his life to! A rope had saved him.

Swinging his legs off the bed, Jawahar sought his slippers with bare feet. Kashmir was on his mind and in his nightmares – perfect.

Softly, he began to perambulate his bedroom and line his thoughts.

London had played dirty at the UN. Bapu had never been keen on the idea of the UN mediating. *If India and Pakistan come to a settlement, the big powers at the UN will have to endorse that settlement*. Bapu, who had always advocated that the people of Kashmir should be asked whether they wanted to join India or Pakistan, had used his last prayer meeting to talk about Kashmir. *The ruler will be dead one of these days, but the people will remain*.

Bapu's wisdom returned to Jawahar in snatches of conversations, snippets from years of togetherness, lingering in the lessons he had taught … tears filled his eyes. It was Bapu who had first shown him that his life could have meaning in the service of a cause. Accepting Bapu's leadership, and the civil disobedience and jail-going which had followed, had made a man of him.

Jawahar rolled his shoulders. In the months since Bapu's passing, the issue of Kashmir had got mired in the UN …

Noel-Baker's attitude was prejudicial to the continuance of friendly relations between India and the UK – Jawahar had conveyed that much to Prime Minister Attlee. After which, the British Cabinet had modified its stance: Pakistan should deny assistance to the raiders and should refrain from bringing any Pakistani troops into Kashmir, and while Sheikh Abdullah's government need not be replaced, it should include members of rival parties. Following which, the Kashmir government had released Ghulam Abbas – the imprisoned leader of the Muslim Conference – so he could confer with Pakistan. But Jawahar would not legitimize Muzaffarabad by permitting it to be a part of the government. He need not have worried. Liaquat had rejected the proposal entirely, once again calling the Sheikh a 'quisling and puppet of the Congress'!

Birdsong began to sound through the open window. Time for his yoga. Jawahar headed to the toilet for his ablutions.

Sheikh Abdullah was keen on another alternative – an independent Kashmir, guaranteed by both India and Pakistan. It was certainly one way he could continue to head Kashmir. Jawahar was aware that Abdullah had spoken in private to the Americans at Lake Success as he sought their backing for his independent state. Unconvinced that the idea was workable, Jawahar had nonetheless broached it with Liaquat.

'It will solve nothing!' the Pakistan Prime Minister had rejected. 'And will only leave Kashmir as a hotbed of inter-dominion intrigue.'

Jawahar ran the water and watched it pool in the sink. An independent Kashmir could end up falling in the crevasse between India and Pakistan, jeopardizing its people.

Defence Minister Baldev Singh and General Roy Bucher sat across from Jawaharlal Nehru in his study at Teen Murti, the Prime Minister's new residence. Baldev Singh had just finished his briefing. With the capture of Jhangar and Rajauri, the threat to the lines of communication from Jammu to Naushera had been neutralized. And with the snows melting, it was time to plan for the spring offensive. However, the Princely State of Hyderabad sat like the proverbial elephant in the room.

'Razvi thinks our troops are occupied.' Baldev Singh stroked his beard. 'He is counting on the Indian Army not being able to launch a parallel offensive in Hyderabad ... *If* we wanted to.'

Jawahar caught the meaningful look. Hyderabad was not honouring the Standstill Agreement it had signed with India. Razvi, the Nizam's chief rabble-rouser, was making increasingly incendiary speeches. The government had drawn up a contingency plan, Operation Polo. But that plan was to be actioned solely against the extreme emergency of Razvi carrying out his threat of murdering Hindus with his Razakars. Flipping open a tin a of 555 cigarettes, Jawahar withdrew one before standing up.

At the window, he collected his thoughts as he smoked. Vallabhbhai's illness had certainly emboldened Kasim Razvi, whose goons were daily forecasting the demise of both the Prime Minister and his deputy. Below, Indu was herding her boys indoors, the midday sun having lit up the garden like a tandoor. By all accounts, Vallabhbhai was recuperating well in cooler Mussoorie. There were days he wished he could walk across from his York Road bungalow to Vallabhbhai's to discuss affairs, as they had done in the past—

Bucher cleared his throat, which drew Jawahar back to the table.

'We can advance on Domel and thereafter remove the non-Muslim population from Poonch city. So long as Poonchis, Mirpuris and Muzaffarabadis offer resistance, it will simply *not* be possible for India to overrun these areas.'

Bucher held Jawahar's gaze. The two had been in many a pickle together: facing down a bloody mob in Bihar, surveying refugee kafilas from air, fighting to keep a grip on Delhi post-Partition. Now, Roy Bucher was the first commander-in-chief of the Indian Army looking at war on two fronts: Kashmir and Hyderabad.

'It's not our intention to invade every nook and corner!' Baldev Singh turned to the general. 'Gilgit, for one, is out of reach. But surely, Palandri and Mirpur can be captured with the present strength of our forces.'

Jawahar stubbed the cigarette on the ashtray on his desk.

'Our problem is tactical. We are a large army facing a group of irregulars. Our operations requiring large troops are proving ineffective against raiders who hover about and make a nuisance of themselves. We should aim not to capture and hold ground, but to destroy the enemy's will and cohesion.'

Baldev furrowed his brow. 'General, do we have any intimation of Pakistan Army's movements into Kashmir? From your counterpart, Gracey?'

Bucher arched an eyebrow. 'Not to my knowledge, no.'

Jawahar looked from his defence minister to his chief of army. 'Swift blows at many places, and no time given for reformation and recuperation. I want us to focus on Uri: quick occupation of Domel and Kohala to bottle up the raiders that remain behind. Mopping up can follow at leisure.'

Turning to Baldev Singh, Jawahar asked, 'We already have infantry units present in areas not far from Hyderabad. Correct?'

The defence minister nodded in assent.

'Let's position them closer such that an armoured brigade can be deployed quickly in case of an emergency. But don't make haste. *No*, precipitate action that might suggest we are launching war. Tell the troops to proceed in a deliberate manner. The news of such a movement will spread like wildfire in Hyderabad and convey our message that India means business.'

Bucher scraped his chair back. 'A two-pronged offensive then: frontal attack along the Uri–Domel road, and a diversionary attack towards Tithwal and from there to Muzaffarabad.'

'We seal it at the Defence Committee meeting,' Jawahar concluded.

39

Srinagar (April–May 1948)

Zooni steadied the .303, the butt snug against her right shoulder which screamed with agony.

One more shot. If she hit the bulls-eye, the prize was hers. Three packets of salt! She took a deep breath and exhaled half of it. Her shoulder was thudding, pain radiating like heat rays from a throbbing sun. The rifle kicked hard, and six weeks of daily practice had left her shoulder raw and bruised, the tang of gunpowder lodged deep in her throat. Even the day was feeling the heat of the competition: summer in spring, the sky a dazzling blue, heat sticking the baggy kameez to her back, a bee droning somewhere above ...

The assembly of onlookers at the army cantonment in Badami Bagh – the women of WSDC, their trainers, a senior officer from the Indian Army – hummed with anticipation. Usha Koul and Zooni Gujjar were the two contestants left in the final round of rifle shooting. They had shot four rounds each, Usha had missed the bulls-eye once, and it was all down to the fifth and final round.

Zooni had to win!

Usha didn't need the prize – her family owned apple orchards, surely they had enough salt in their mansion of a house? And surely, they didn't have a Hassan who visited their houseboat on the pretext of meeting his purblind mother and filched salt on his way out! Since the war, Pakistan was withholding salt from Kashmir. Like Hassan, it believed it could defeat people by depriving them of the essential condiment.

Ignoring the pain, keeping the half-breath in, Zooni focused on the target. Her family clouded her mind: crestfallen Kashmira, wide-eyed Gul, the habitually pinched face of Safina. Zooni exhaled in frustration.

This wouldn't do. If sighing won competitions …

Once again, she steadied herself, jammed the butt tight and close, registering but rejecting the pain, inhaled, focused on the target ahead, and released half her breath. Zooni went as still as a bare cedar in winter, sound retracted, only the silhouette remained … a face came into focus … a monster … hooded eyes and sneering mouth … Hassan.

She squeezed the trigger, right index finger maintaining a steady pressure, the rifle immobile as a tree trunk, and watched the bullet leave the barrel. A joyous cry went up. Zooni let her arms slacken.

The salt was hers.

Two days later, Havildar Fateh Singh found himself answering a summons from Lt Col Harbakhsh Singh, commander of Sri Garrison. With a click of heels, Fateh Singh delivered a crisp salute and stood to attention. The commander looked up from studying a map spread out on his desk.

'At ease. Did you train the WSDC winner, Zooni Gujjar?'

'Sir.'

'What can you tell me about her?'

'S-*ir*?'

The commander fixed his eyes on him. Information on the young woman said she had arrived in Srinagar as part of the refugee exchange programme. Her deceased brother-in-law, a member of Sheikh Abdullah's NC, had died at the hands of 1Sikh in an unfortunate incident. Hassan Dar, the dead man's younger brother, was a member of Muslim Conference and had returned from Muzaffarabad – a troublemaker whom they were keeping under watch. The defence and maintenance of law and order in the Valley was a primary task of Sri Garrison.

'If Zooni Gujjar was a sepoy training under you, what would you say?'

Fateh Singh cleared his throat. 'Sir, she is hard working, punctual, has not missed a single day of training, and a fast learner, yes.'

'Fast learner. How so?'

'She had a problem with successive firing. Once I showed her the correct technique, she improved quickly.'

Harbakhsh Singh smoothed his whiskers with his right hand.

The family background was not ideal, but from what he had witnessed during the competitive shooting, the woman showed the ability to be a top-notch sniper. In the ongoing war, the Pathans had a natural edge – skilled as they were in mountain warfare. 161 Infantry Brigade used locals for assistance with terrain and roads. But a local expert at both terrain and shooting would be invaluable. With the snows melting, the war was ratcheting up again, more battles lay ahead … the one who held the heights would win the war.

'Havildar, I want you to start training Zooni Gujjar in long-range shooting, 500 metre and beyond. Train her as you would a sepoy.'

'Sir,' Fateh Singh nodded, trying not to show his bewilderment.

'You look unsure?'

'No, sir, no.'

'Speak up, havildar! Do you fear a lack of motivation from her?'

'No, sir!' Fateh Singh shook his head. 'Zooniji, Zooni Gujjar, is very motivated. I-I believe her family was killed in Baramulla. I am not sure …' he searched for the right words, 'how … how comfortable she is in the presence of men.'

Lt Col Harbakhsh Singh's face went dark. 'Havildar! Have you been behaving yourself?'

'Si-iir!' Fateh Singh fumbled. 'What I mean … Zooni Gujjar is like other women, unused to male company, is all.'

The commander nodded. The best snipers in WW2 were women, drawn from the countryside. It was generally believed they demonstrated more patience and greater endurance than their male counterparts. 'Our women have faced the brunt of this battle. Which is why we have the WSDC. It is your job now to convince Zooni Gujjar of her full potential.'

'Sir, a question? There is Usha Koul, as well …'

'The Kouls are not shepherds. The kabailis did not kill them either. But the kabailis brought the battle to Zooni Gujjar's house.' The commander tapped the table with his right thumb. 'All war, havildar, is personal.'

40

Srinagar (May 1948)

The crowd listened attentively, faces tilted to the man in a knee-length achkan, white cap and white tang pajama who spoke to them from the gallery. Pandit Nehru, a rosebud in the third buttonhole, hands clasped behind his back, paid tribute to soldiers – young and old – and commended the residents of Srinagar on their defence of the city last October.

Seated in the gallery behind, the bespectacled Sheikh Abdullah, in a matching sherwani and loose pajama, and his trademark fez, along with members of his Cabinet, dignitaries of the Valley, and Maulana Azad, who had accompanied the Indian Prime Minister from Delhi, listened to the address. Indeed, the People's Militia, which started off as the Salamati Fauj, had instilled calm in the residents, kept peace among all communities, and galvanized even the women! The difficult days the Valley had endured – kabailis creeping up on Srinagar, the constant fear of being overrun, eating bland boiled maize because of a shortage of rice and salt, living in the dark with no electricity, sheltering refugees staggering into the Valley, their tales of woe sparking the dry grass of tension – had united the citizens against a common enemy. The Valley had burst into revolutionary fervour, like daffodils that erupted to herald spring! Ten thousand volunteers, with no uniform, shoes or weapons even, except their courage, armed with wooden, red-painted staffs, some musty single-shot rifles and pellet guns used to shoot pigeons. Until the Indian Army started training them with modern rifles.

With a satisfied smile, Abdullah inhaled deeply and smiled at Begum Jahan seated beside him. It was a beautiful May morning – the final day of the week-long celebrations of Kashmir's independence. A sky, as blue and bright as the bountiful lakes of the state, splayed with multi-coloured buntings; the numaish ground, bordered by trees abundant with sweet-smelling fruit, packed with eager citizens; the gallery full of dignitaries who had accepted the invitation to celebrate freedom. A sourness surfaced. Jinnah had declined to even respond. The Sheikh swallowed.

A painful memory inserted itself.

Of a time when Maharaja Hari Singh had police guards placed at each of the seven bridges of Srinagar. And every pedestrian was forced to raise his hands and hail, 'Maharaja Bahadur Ki Jai!', before crossing the bridge. Fines were levied on those who refused to do so. Flogging stations were set up for those who refused to pay. Abdullah pursed his mouth. Locked up in jail, he had wished he could cross the bridge and get flogged repeatedly to showcase Hari Singh's manic cruelty!

The ground erupted with applause.

Seated to his right, Maulana was wagging his head. Absorbed in his thoughts, Abdullah had missed what Panditji had said – no doubt the Kashmiri was connecting with his fellow Kashmiris. Jinnah, meanwhile, could tolerate nobody except

Jinnah. Anyway, it was none of the Sheikh's concern! He sat up. Their goal was a self-sufficient Kashmir. Hands steepled in his lap, his mind unspooled his priorities, the changes that had to be made to bring Kashmir into the modern age …

The lot of the poor peasantry had to be improved via redistribution of land and waiving of rural debt – debtors were trapped in a vicious circle having paid in cash or kind multiples of the original dues. Education was crucial, a university must be established, the Kashmiri script must be adapted to enable typing, and schools must impart education in Kashmiri and Dogri. Kashmiri handicrafts, shawls, carpets, papier-mâché needed to be marketed to the rest of India and the world through a government arts emporium …

A rustle. People were stirring. Panditji was turning from the dais, smiling.

Lunging forward, Abdullah reached his side and started to lead Panditji to the grounds where troops awaited to give the Indian Prime Minister a guard of honour. But first, an inspection of the People's Militia. A banner in the hands of two young militiamen proclaimed: *We will defend our motherland with our young blood*.

As Abdullah and Panditji descended on to the ground, a man sped over, a young boy running in tandem. Releasing the boy to wait for the Indian Prime Minister, the man melted into the militia unit. Dressed like a boy scout with a beret and a scarf around his neck, the boy awaited until Panditji had come to a stop in front of him. Then he did a flourish with his tiny baton before clasping his right hand to his forehead in a smart salute. Panditji, masking a smile, saluted back with proper formality.

After the inspection of the militia, Panditji walked keenly to the Women's Self Defence Corp who were assembled smartly: Dressed in salwar-kameez, a dupatta draped around their chest and secured firmly at the waist, a rifle on their shoulders. Krishna Misri, a WSDC leader, answered Panditji's queries as she walked beside them. She also narrated how all female members of her family had stored bags of powdered chilli peppers and hundreds of large stones. 'We were instructed to spray those should the kabailis reach our courtyard!' She paused to introduce a tall woman with golden hair, who had won the shooting competition of Mukta, the first women's battalion.

Smiling broadly, Abdullah extended his right arm. 'Indeed! We are using Zooni Gujjar's sketch for the WSDC pamphlets to inspire others.'

A satisfied Panditji in tow, they reached the oval in front of the Military Hospital. A hundred men of 1Sikh who had borne the brunt of the fighting in the Valley, led by Harbakhsh Singh, recently promoted to brigadier, presented the guard of honour in full dress.

The final event of the day was a boat procession down the Jhelum river.

With Maulana seated to Abdullah's left and Panditji to his right, the trio took in the gaiety. People watched from the riverbanks, hanging off trees, from shikaras and dungas; buntings of colourful triangular flags were strung across gates, between pillars and electric poles; drum beats and shehnai sounds rippled through the air.

A slogan rent the air:

Sher-i-Kashmir ka kya irshad?
What does the Lion of Kashmir say?

Shouts followed:

Hindu, Muslim, Sikh ittihad.
Hindu, Muslim, Sikh, united we stay!

Bapu had always maintained that Kashmir was the real test of secularism in India. Indeed, Kashmir had acceded to India on the basis of that promise. Abdullah narrowed his eyes as white clouds scudded across the blue sky. A chilly wind had picked up as dusk approached over the swelling crowd, the air thick with joyous slogans. The battle with the kabailis was still underway, the so-called 'Azad Kashmir' wanted no truck with his government, the Muslims of Jammu had thrown their lot with Pakistan – innumerable challenges lay ahead.

The essence of life is motion.

As that favourite shayr of his swam into his mind, Abdullah squared his jaw, brought a smile back to his lips and turned his attention to his guests.

41

Srinagar (May 1948)

My mother-in-law was a sour woman who could curdle milk.

The peal of women's laughter floated to the terrace where Zooni and Margot awaited Durga Mehra. Through the open window, Margot observed the women embroidering and bantering. She did not understand what was being said, but the refugee centre was doing something right, clearly. Even Kashmira wore a smile as she supervised the needlework of a young woman who was threading her needle intently, the tip of her tongue peeping out.

Zooni, meanwhile, sat upright, hands locked in her lap.

Kashmira would not like the news, Kashmira might forbid her even. But, Zooni bit her inner cheek, she had already accepted the offer to accompany the brigade as guide and sniper. She would be paid a salary, Kashmira could do with the money. Besides, Zooni was good, she had won the shooting competition – *a sharpshooter*, Havildar Fateh Singh's chief had commented, and this was her chance to kill kabailis. *You will die!* Kashmira would yell when she heard the news, her eyes as deep as a summer forest. Perhaps. Which was why Zooni had brought the white reporter woman along to meet Durga Mehra. Margot had been so excited with the pamphlet she had torn off a lamp-post in Lal Chowk. It showed members of the Women's Self Defence Corps marching with their rifles, in the foreground a woman aiming her rifle. Margot had not missed that woman's likeness to Zooni Gujjar and wanted to interview Durga Mehra – at whose suggestion Zooni had joined the WSDC and become its poster woman! – who was carrying out such fantastic initiatives with refugee women. Hassan had not missed the likeness either, stomping into the cookboat, flashing kohl-lined eyes and hurling threats.

Zooni inhaled loudly. To distract herself, she watched sparrows take flight as a crow swooped into the garden. She had something very specific to ask of Margot Parr—

Durga Bibi had stepped on to the terrace and was speaking with the journalist, who stood a head higher and had a camera slung around her neck. Behind them, she could sight Kashmira thread a hook needle and begin to embroider with deft strokes. A stab in Zooni's heart. A memory of Mouj darning their clothes. Zooni closed her eyes tight. Kashmira was the daughter with Mouj's beauty, family and neighbours had agreed. That didn't bother Zooni, but Moul, feeling a need to compensate, sought her out often, seeking her help in naming their sheep and goats and one buffalo. Zooni's mouth quivered. The kabailis had set fire to the barn in Baramulla, trapping the animals inside. How they would have suffered—

Through the blinking of her eyes, Zooni saw Kashmira hold up an almond pattern. 'See: The aari kari technique covers a much larger area than needlework in the same time.' Kashmira urged the women to try a motif of their choice.

Yambarzal. Booen. Pamposh. Daenposh …

As the women debated amongst daffodil, chinar, lotus and pomegranate, Zooni caught sight of Durga's questioning brow.

'Yes, yes,' she replied in haste, having missed what was said.

Margot, forehead puckered, sat down whilst Durga Mehra gestured for Zooni to begin.

'So,' Zooni licked her lips, 'I-I have a … a proposition … which Durga Bibi will translate to you for me. If you agree, it will be a great help to me. If you disagree, you must never speak about this to anyone.' She pinched the skin at her neck and paused.

Following Durga's translation, Margot nodded her head.

'Soon, I will be going to battle with the Indian Army as guide and sniper. I know you have looked out for my sister's family since Ali's death. Can you watch them in my absence? When I return, I will share my story with you. You can print it and make money for your newspaper and yourself.'

As Durga translated, Zooni tried to read Margot's face. But the white woman kept her face bland, her eyes flitting from Durga to Zooni.

The chuckle of a chakor sounded.

Durga turned to Zooni. 'She asks: What happens if you die?'

Zooni shrugged. 'It cannot be worse than if I had not turned up at all, right? One less mouth for Kashmira to feed? And Miss Margot can still write a story, not a triumphant one perhaps, but the story of *Kashmir* through the family of *Kashmira* … also, she can help spread the word about our *Mayfair* houseboat and get my sister some good clients?'

As Durga turned back to Margot, Zooni massaged her hands. She would not worry half as much, but for Hassan. The wretched man would have *Mayfair* join Pakistan or Muzaffarabad in case the Valley did not. And the way he kept sneaking around the boat, prying on Kashmira, bullying little Gul, smouldering like a cowpat, hissing azadi, army, Abdullah ... Besides, Miss Margot was fond of Gul, and lately, he had been spending a lot of time in the houseboat, looking through the many books on *Mayfair* left by houseguests and tourists over the years. Gul had been coming to Dar-ul-Aman with Kashmira, attending the school, while his mother trained the women in embroidery. Most evenings, he could be sighted on the terrace of the *Mayfair*, kitten in lap, book in front as he gazed at the pages as if he were memorizing the Quran. Which irked Hassan even more. Afraid to step on to the *Mayfair* and reach Gul, he would take off on Bilquis or Safina – order them to fry him a fresh trout or fetch him green tea with saffron. Really, the man was insufferable!

The fragrance of tea wafted over. Inside, a couple of samovars were steaming and women were taking a break from cooking, embroidering and teaching. Zooni decided to look for Gul, while Durga and Margot headed inside for nun cha.

Margot watched Durga pour the pink tea into a cup and top it with crushed almonds. Zooni's unusual request wouldn't be burdensome. Hassan was irksome, but he suffered from the gora syndrome, which cast her as someone not to be messed with ... the rent was paltry ... Zooni's first-hand tales of battle would be a definite coup! There was one niggling matter though.

Back on the terrace, Margot took small sips of the fragrant nun cha. Salt in tea was still unexpected. Durga Mehra updated her on the various activities of the sadan, how training the women in domestic crafts was a way to empower them since she hoped to be able to sell their wares, in time. She was hopeful that Sheikh Abdullah's progressive government would be able to rebuild Kashmir – the recent Kashmir Day celebration had lifted everyone's spirits! Finally, Durga returned to the question of Zooni's request.

'Eight months on the *Mayfair* now, and I haven't met more kindly people. I am happy to help. I've indeed been keeping an eye on little Gul; it helps that he's really keen to learn English.' Margot then divulged her concerns about the vulture that the boy had befriended and trained of sorts, whom he fed routinely and called Boi.

'Hmm,' Durga leaned forward. 'Can you describe the bird?'

Margot mentioned the downy blue fur, which appeared to be the vulture's most distinguishing feature. Crunching on an almond bit, she frowned. 'A raptor for a friend makes me uneasy … whoever heard of it?'

Durga was amused.

'It's not entirely unheard of, Miss Parr. Are you familiar with the Ramayana?'

Margot nodded wordlessly.

'Well, then you might recall that when the evil Ravana tried to abduct Sita from the jungle, Jatayu tried to protect her. Jatayu was a friend of her husband, Rama.'

'And Ja-ta-oo was a vulture?'

'Not just any vulture. The Himalayan griffon. From the same family as Gul's Boi.'

'Well, I never!'

'Vultures have a bad reputation, especially now … I have never seen so many as I saw on the trees around Datiyal Camp, hooded scavengers, sometimes too full to eat. But really, who is to blame: them or us? They are merely cleaning up after us.' Durga sighed.

'Keep an eye on Gul, Miss Parr, especially in Zooni's absence. But the vulture may not be your problem.'

42

Chowkibal (May 1948)

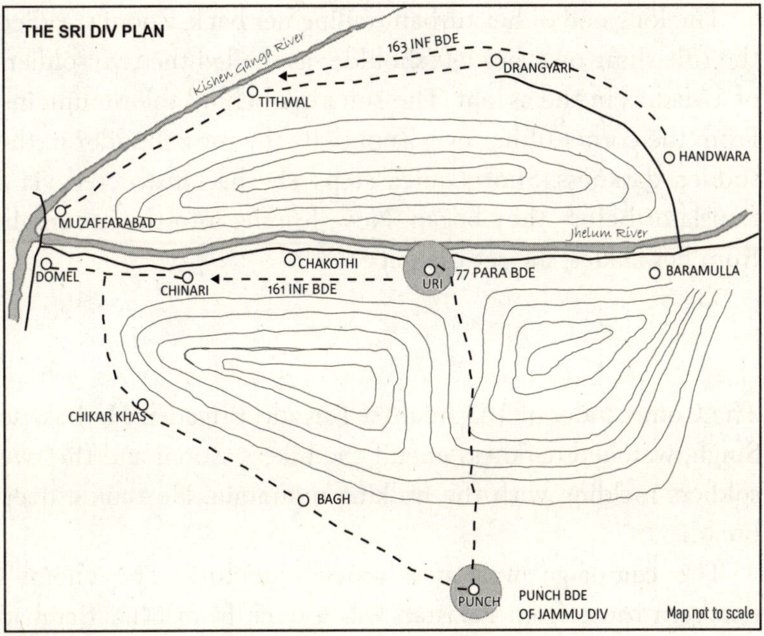

Grey clouds scudded across the darkening sky as Zooni headed off from Chowkibal with two soldiers. Tasked with reaching Nastachun Pass, located above 10,000 feet, where the enemy was firing from a vantage point, the team had to take out the snipers and determine why the Indian picket that had left earlier wasn't responding to wireless communication. They moved swiftly up the grassy hill dotted with flowers. Scarlet tulips brushed against the marchers' legs, depositing purple streaks on the men's pants and Zooni's salwar, white irises getting crushed under the tread of military boots and Zooni's rough leather shoes.

The distance to the pass was just over a mile, but the climb was 5000 feet. The track was a sliver – serpentine and slippery.

The long end of her turban trailing her back, Zooni steadied the rifle slung over her left shoulder as she led the two soldiers of 1Madras in the ascent. The sun sank behind the mountains. From the corner of her eye, Zooni saw the men shudder in the sudden darkness. Short, quick steps, she had instructed via a translator before they began. Now, leaning into the mountain from her ankles, she set the pace.

The Commander of 163 Infantry Brigade, Brigadier Harbakhsh Singh, watched darkness engulf the hikers, Zooni and the two soldiers melding with the hulking mountain. He took a deep breath.

The campaign was at a crucial juncture. The enemy's northern route from Pakistan was a track from Muzaffarabad to Tithwal across the Neelam river to Nastachun Pass and then on to Kupwara, Sopore, and finally Srinagar. Major General Thimayya was leading a frontal thrust along the Uri–Domel road. But a regular Pakistan Infantry Brigade was in position in

Chakothi, midway between Muzaffarabad and Uri, supported by Azads and tribesmen. It was essential therefore to create a diversionary threat. Brigadier Harbakhsh Singh had been given that charge. He was to push in the direction of Tithwal, so the enemy would believe that 163 Infantry Brigade's advance was the main threat.

Speed being of essence, Singh had decided that their best chance lay in surprising the enemy by taking the most difficult, hence least expected, route – under cover of darkness. D-day, 18 May; capturing Chowkibal, base of the dreaded Nastachun Pass, was the first objective.

Twenty-four hours later, fifteen miles from Chowkibal, they had got the enemy fleeing. The Garhwalis had attacked frontally, while 1Sikh and 1Madras, in a night advance, had cut off the raiders from behind. But wireless communication with the advance Indian picket at Nastachun had fallen silent … which was where Zooni came in. None of the other soldiers would be able to hike up to the pass in such a short time. Even in May, Nastachun was freezing, with ice on the ground. It was also notorious for a piercing and ceaseless wind. Precisely the kind of weather that would trouble the Madras troops. Meanwhile, 1Sikh was seven miles behind in Panzgam leading a house-to-house search of a village from where the enemy had fled, leaving behind a large dump of supplies. Havildar Fateh Singh – Zooni's designated superior for the campaign, and the only one who knew that their local guide and hunter was not a young male but a female – was in Panzgam, but the hike couldn't wait …

Silently wishing the trio luck, Brigadier Singh turned to working out artillery support for the attack planned for the next morning.

The men had begun to struggle, their breathing getting laboured as Zooni kept a relentless pace.

At the start of the campaign, a sand model of the terrain had been prepared and shared with the battalions to familiarize each person with the ground over which they were to operate. But the model did not account for freezing wind that stung their eyes, howled in their ears, lunged at their feet. For Zooni, the mountains were home. She had climbed the 1000-feet-high Takht-i-Suleiman as a child, hiked regularly to Gulmarg where Moul's family dwelled as shepherds, trekked via Pahalgam to the caves of Amarnath in the summer when Mouj made money guiding pilgrims – but her two companions?

The increasingly bare ground was icy, the track rutted and pebbly, each step forward a calculated risk that the mountain would not serve up a patch that would send them sliding down. Doggedly, heads down, they pushed against the wind and the incline, the fog of their breaths leading them.

Brigadier Singh wanted the pass cleared quickly and Zooni knew she could scale the height in an hour by herself. But the men were necessary in case there were too many Pathans ahead—

A sudden cry arrested her. She swung her neck.

One of the soldiers had slipped and slid down the incline. Loose stones clattered after him. The other soldier was frozen in his path. With a finger to her lips, Zooni motioned him to stay still. She held her breath and concentrated on listening to the mountain. The wind whistling, plucking at her clothes, smacking strands of her hair in her face … and then a sigh … like the mountain had shrugged … that grew to a ro-o-o-AR.

'HOLD on!'

Zooni flattened herself against the incline, clutching anything that gave her hands a grip. The thunder came closer and closer. An avalanche. They would not survive.

With an almighty fury, it boomed past, missing them by a few feet. But, as Zooni blinked, she realized the soldier who had slipped earlier had caught the whiplash of the avalanche. He was crying out in agony. Zooni indicated to the second soldier to go to the aid of the first. With luck, he might be able to carry him back to Chowkibal. Not waiting for his objection, she resumed her ascent.

Meanwhile, Brigadier Harbakhsh Singh and the battery commander debated how best to take the field guns, 25-pounders, up the non-existent track to Nastachun Pass. The guns had to be in position by first light of 21 May in order to support the attack on the pass by 1Madras.

The track ahead, from Nastachun to Tithwal, through the Tangdhar valley and across the Neelam river, was unmetalled and unmotorable. For Major Thimayya's planned frontal offensive to succeed, it was crucial that the enemy think that the diversionary attack under Singh was the main threat. Which was why Singh had started two days earlier to arrive in Muzaffarabad such that the enemy, based in neighbouring Domel, would have to weaken its position in Chakothi–Chinari to counter his forces. That would open up the way for the frontal attack to push through the depleted enemy positions and reach Domel.

The gunners argued about ways to best move the big guns up a narrow, circuitous and slippery path. Could they dismantle the guns? Carry them all the way up? With soldiers unfamiliar with the terrain?

Moving the guns would be a miracle of sorts. Assuming Nastachun Pass could first be secured ahead. Once again, the brigadier wondered how close Zooni's team was to reaching the Pass. 163 Infantry Brigade could not afford any delay …

As his mind hopped from one impediment to another, and doubt reared its tentacles within him, Singh turned to his favourite prayer. Three hundred years ago, when Guru Gobind Singh took up the sword of righteousness against Mughal oppression, he had recited a pledge. Which was also the motto of the Sikh Regiment that had nurtured Singh. Eyes closed, he now recited the words to himself.

> *De Shiva bar moh ehe, shub karman te kabhun na taro,*
> *Na daro ar son jab jaie laro, nishchey kar apni jeep karo.*
> Oh Lord, grant me this boon, may I never falter from doing good,
> Never fear going to war, may I determine to win.

The Guru's vow was Singh's, too. Like the Guru, Brigadier Singh was determined to win.

At the top of the ridge, where the mountain dipped and rose, a kotha nestled in the bowl, its roof piled high with snow. The log and mud house could be of any of the pastoralists from her family. Except, this stood abandoned in summer, not winter, and the advance team were believed to have picketed there. The family must have descended and melted into the forests like other villagers. Panzgam had been eerily empty … But a brief glow came from within the kotha. The soldiers knew better than to light a petromax lamp, which would present a wonderful target to the enemy. In which case, had the Pathans seized the hut? Were they listening to the wireless? Were the soldiers alive or dead?

It was good that the brigadier had not communicated anything about the team heading to Nastachun. And the Pathans probably believed that no one would be foolhardy enough to ascend in the dark.

Steadying the rifle in her hands, Zooni crouched low and scuttled over in the direction of the shed. From behind a bend, she could see the small window. There was no movement inside, no shadows on the walls. No sounds either, except for the howling wind.

Quiet as a leopard, Zooni inched to the hut, gun at the ready as she pushed open the door with one foot. It was light and swung with ease. Two Pathans were curled up on a mattress on the floor. A third, on sentry duty, sitting against a wall had fallen asleep, head lolling, the gun upright in his hand. He was the first one Zooni shot. In the time it took one of the sleeping Pathans to register the fired shot, she had put a bullet through his forehead and fired one into the heart of the other. Then she took stock of the shack. Two Indian soldiers had been slaughtered; the wireless set destroyed. A doorless entrance to another room in the wall across from the Pathan who had been on guard duty. Zooni minced her way forward. The room was smaller, bare, except for a blanket on the floor and a hearth with dead embers in it.

Zooni exhaled and stepped out of the kotha. She would make the descent in less time than the ascent—

A gust tore into her, slamming shut the door of the hut behind her. Zooni was blinking her eyes when a bank of snow hurtled down, the kotha offloading five feet of snow from its roof. Her surprised cry was muffled as the snow knocked her over and drowned her out.

The pass went quiet again, sighing now and then when the wind gusted.

43

Delhi (May 1948)

Late at night, Dickie worked on a memorandum that he intended to send to Jawa, Patel and Rajagopalachari. Having returned from Mashobra, Simla, to the furnace of Delhi, he appreciated the late hour, and was using the precious time to work on the document and his genealogy maps. He was on the item 'Ministerial Backing of Civil Servants' when Edwina popped her head in his study. Her exhausted look meant one thing alone. 'Can't sleep?'

'Nembutal not helping.' Edwina sighed and crept in.

She really shouldn't be driving around in the terrific heat which gave her those blinding headaches. But Dickie knew better than to voice that.

'Working on your precious family maps again?'

'In addition to composing some final thoughts for the Government of India. I have done so much thinking on the future of India that it would not be right not to put down some thoughts before leaving.'

'Hmmm.'

Edwina walked to the French windows to stare at the darkness. It would be nice to have her husband's head for a change, which filed things into neat compartments: farewell tour, diplomatic duties, rides with Pamela, entertaining guests with games, relaxing with a movie or his damned geneology tables … She couldn't even make a sedative work on her feverish mind!

Watching her blow air out of her mouth, Dickie said, 'It was a 110 degrees today. The good news is that we won't have to suffer the heat for too long.'

21 June was the day Dickie's nine-month governor-generalship would end. But the thought made her miserable. In her mind's eye, she was walking with Jawa amongst strawberry bushes on a terraced hillside. Their joint excursion in Mashobra had been altogether lovely, and short.

'How was your dinner?' Dickie asked.

Edwina turned to an armchair and settled in, legs crossed, drawing the nightgown tight against her chest. The air conditioning was gelid. 'Jawa brought Krishna Menon along and we chatted till late. You just missed them.'

Dickie nodded.

Pamela and he had left for the YWCA ball, knowing how much Jawa and his wife doted on each other in the nicest way. His hand stilled. It was remarkably lucky that among his many defects, god did not add jealousy in any shape or form. Indeed, he liked and admired Jawa, and was doing all that was possible to stitch up the two biggest problems facing the young nation: Hyderabad and Kashmir. Success would, undoubtedly, burnish his legacy, too. He had dispatched his press attaché with a personal invitation for His Exalted Highness the Nizam of Hyderabad to visit him in Delhi. Alan, though, had returned with a firm 'No' from HEH – apparently the man hated flying!

Thankfully, though, Walter Monckton was returning to assist HEH. Clearly, the Nizam, aware the governor general would be departing soon, had recalled his legal counsel from London. Dickie might still get his agreement. As for Kashmir …

Twiddling his pencil, he asked Edwina, 'What if I told you the only solution for Kashmir was to partition it?'

Edwina was feeling flighty, restless, and blaming it on menopause, but the mention of partition made her sit up.

'I've discussed it in principle with Jawa and asked V.P. Menon to prepare a plan for dividing the state. Liaquat is expected in India soon and I intend to discuss the proposal with both leaders.'

As Dickie waited for her response, Edwina recalled the evening in April when the Mountbattens had taken a guest to an Inter-Service Tattoo – an evening bugle signal recalling soldiers to their quarters – against the background of Purana Qila. A magnificent light and sound show, but her mind had kept inserting alternate images. For in that very Qila, just a few months before, had huddled thousands of Muslims who had fled their homes, terrified of their non-Muslim neighbours.

The refugees of Panjab's partition were still housed in camps at Kurukshetra and Panipat, upwards of 30,000 people. The rescue and repatriation of abducted women was going on. She had hugged and comforted them, witnessed the tattoos inked on their chests and limbs and foreheads, haggled with the administration for improved sanitary conditions, arranged relief – there was *so* much that still needed to be done!

'Hmmm?' Dickie arched a brow.

'An-*other* partition?' Edwina said.

Dickie puckered his mouth. The UN talks had got off to an unpromising start – a disillusioned Jawa even claiming the organization was an American racket! Which had led to a building of resentment against the British. Dickie had reiterated to HMG that Noel-Baker's attitude was endangering the whole structure of goodwill between Britain and India. Indeed, he had telegraphed Attlee to warn him that India might just tilt towards Russia. Now, the Security Council's commission was to visit the subcontinent to mediate between India and Pakistan. But the two dominions remained dissatisfied.

'The UN Commission is not expected until after we leave,' Dickie shrugged, 'and I really feel I ought to make one final effort to settle the Kashmir problem directly between the two governments.'

'Hunh,' Edwina grunted. Dickie could exit with a clean slate, all neat little partitions and dominions, but her work was not done. India needed her; heck, *she* needed India. She had found herself here, found her purpose, found Jawa who understood everything about her ... She had not wanted to come, now the thought of leaving was more scorching than Delhi's devastating dust storms—

'I expect Mr Patel might support the plan, considering he wasn't very keen on Kashmir to begin with.' Dickie squared his shoulders. 'I'm sending Bucher off to Dehradun on the thirty-first to sit down with Patel and get his blessings.'

Dickie's words reached her, but Edwina's thoughts were with Amrit Kaur discussing the riots in Delhi, a fortnight after the Partition of 1947. Late at night, they heard that the Prime Minister had gone out to investigate a riot and had not returned. The two women had searched the dark streets until they found him by the roadside, calming a mob armed with knives. Was that when she first realized how fond of him she had become? She sighed. Jawa and she had promised each other that nothing either of them did or felt would be allowed to come between them and their work. *That* was that.

Through the ajar door, a Sealyham terrier hobbled in.

'My little darling,' Edwina murmured as she scooped him up. Her beloved Mizzen had been with her from Adsdean, her first house after marriage, through the war years, and now India. She stroked his shaggy coat and he settled his bearded jaw in her left palm. He was too old to quarantine in the UK upon return and would pine for her. In a quandary, she had consulted Jawa and decided to have Mizzen put down. Her mouth trembled. A scraping of a chair. Dickie had stood up.

'To bed, shall we?'

At two in the night, he looked astonishingly well rested. Edwina masked a sniffle as she patted the Sealyham, who was now snoring softly in her lap.

Dickie walked to his wife to help her up. Draping an arm over her shoulder, he started to lead them out of his study. 'The Nizam is bedevilled by the bloody fanatics in his state, but hopefully sense will prevail …'

Dickie spoke his thoughts aloud as they walked down the hallway. Edwina, swamped by a terrible sense of loss, studied her palm that rose and fell gently with Mizzen's every breath.

44

Chowkibal (May 1948)

Icy wind smote Havildar Fateh Singh as he made his way up the mountain, steep as a bayonet. Brigadier Singh had given him permission to proceed ahead as the company wrestled with moving guns uphill.

His heart was hammering, not due to exertion. Not for this Udhampur lad, who hiked the 7000-feet Patnitop for casual sport. Zoo-ni. Zoo-ni. Zoo-ni. The staccato of his heartbeat. The two soldiers who had accompanied her had turned back halfway. Zooni would have reached the pass. But she did not know to operate a wireless. The only reasonable course of action was for her to return to base. Unless the Pathans had waylaid her. He clenched his teeth. Her disguise as the whiskerless local lad, Zain, held because Zooni was habitually quiet and Fateh Singh watched over her …

The Japani in Malaya had been cruel, often using POWs for target practice. But their code of conduct also included self-sacrifice, hara-kiri, being the preferred option instead of surrender. The Pathans, however, seemed intent only upon plunder and rape. Villages razed to the ground and deserted, trembling villagers fleeing to the nearby jungles. When 1Sikh located them, the villagers wailed at the sight of the Sikhs for the Pathans had forewarned that the 'bearded savages' would eat them up alive! Tales of woe were manifest upon women's scarred bodies—

A loose rock made him stumble. Forcing himself to focus on the ground, Fateh Singh trod on.

When Zooni was singled by the brigadier for the hike, the havildar had tried to caution her. 'You can refuse,' he had argued, aware of the danger inherent in the mission. But Zooni had stayed silent.

'How do you know you will be safe?'

'I don't.' Zooni had shrugged.

And Fateh Singh had watched helplessly as she marched to Chowkibal, while he led the search in Panzgam.

Now he consoled himself once again with the same words he had reiterated to himself earlier. Zooni had survived perils that no ordinary human should: gushing rivers, mass shooting, freezing waters ... there were people that Rab watched out for personally, and Zooniji was one of those. Reassuring himself thus, the havildar continued uphill.

The picket revealed five corpses, all male. No Zooni. Fateh Singh perambulated the shack and searched the perimeter with no luck. Where could she be? Sheltering in the doorway, the havildar blinked at the ferocious wind that slapped his face. Until he registered the large pile of snow that lay to the left of the door. Slipping off his backpack, he attacked the pile with his bare hands. He dug feverishly through four feet of snow when his hand found a body. Scrambling to remove the layer of snow, he found Zooni fast asleep, gun nestled beside her!

Scooping her up, her backpack intact, Fateh Singh trudged into the shack.

After removing a blanket from the backpack, he spread it on the floor of the ante-room and deposited Zooni upon it. Her turban had slipped from her head and she was unconscious, but breathing. Quickly, he set to reviving the fire in the hearth. After which he blocked the window with the backpacks of the dead soldiers, staving off the whistling wind. Next, he rubbed Zooni's palms and soles. Slowly, her eyelids fluttered open.

In time, she sat up with his help.

The havildar draped his blanket around her and suggested she let her damp cold clothes dry out. With his back to her, he tended to the fire.

As she shrugged out of her coarse woollens, a relieved Zooni explained how the wind had banged shut the door and offloaded the piled-up snow upon her. Which had then buffered her against the cold as she slept soundly!

Meanwhile, Fateh Singh had got the fire going in the hearth. From his knapsack, he removed a small iron pan which he filled with snow and set to heat, crooning as he worked.

She watched him, a tenderness welling in her heart, a heart which had withered in the arid reality of her marriage. 'What are you humming?'

'A song.'

He gave her a sheepish smile. At the POW camp in Malaya, the Japani guard was most irked with the young Indian soldier's routine humming. *Why happy, he would glare, why*?

Zooni liked how his eyes smiled, too. 'What is it about?'

'A-a-about a woman …' Zooni having opened her braid, golden hair framed her face and splayed out on the blanket she had wrapped around her. 'With silver skin and golden hair.'

Zooni's neck retracted with incredulity.

Fateh Singh paused, surprised. He met her eyes directly, seeing the disbelief in them. *Did she not know?*

The tea was bubbling in the iron pan, its sweet hot fragrance filling the tiny shack. Havildar Fateh Singh poured the brew into two metal cups, served one to her, and raked the coals, sending sparks shooting. Since he had barricaded the small window the air within was losing its bite. Retrieving his emergency ration, he offered her a panjiri laddoo.

Zooni shook her head.

'It will revive you, Zooniji,' he insisted. 'My mother makes it every winter, it's very nourishing. Brigadier Singh's mother must also be preparing these. Which is why he thought of panjiri laddoos for emergency ration, and ordered the Sikh battalion to prepare them. Who taught the Madras battalion, in turn. Easy to carry—'

'Halve it, then,' Zooni cut into his nervous prattle. 'And we can share.'

After which, Fateh Singh sat across from her to sip on his tea and keep one eye on the door. The homely scene – food, warmth, safety – dislodged something within Zooni. Her eyes were hot, moist.

Nothing in the front, nothing behind. The first words Masud Ahmed had said to Zooni after he wed her. Not that Zooni disagreed with that estimate – *Willow rush or lotus root?* other girls often teased her as they filled out and Zooni only gained height – but it was the summary dismissal in her new husband's words that stung. Now, this man gazed upon her as if she were Habba Khatoon. If that was not surreal enough, a man and a woman sat sipping tea amidst five corpses as wind smacked the kotha with drifts of snow and war raged outside. Her mind took her to the winter nights of her childhood, the family in one room beneath quilts, nestling against kangris, listening to

Mouj's stories, falling asleep to the gurgling of Moul's hukkah … the apple tree grazing the earth with its fruit in autumn, the Jhelum dropping its level in winter, the family sowing rice and maize right about now! Baramulla, she sighed. *Rows of ruins*. Kashmira said that was all that was left of their hometown. Zooni's lips trembled. She raised the tea mug to hide behind it and saw Fateh Singh watching her as if at worship.

'Zooniji.'

'Hmmm.' She gazed into his eyes.

'With silver skin and golden hair, *you* look like a princess.'

Zooni snorted. The havildar was an innocent.

Fateh Singh pinched the skin at his neck. 'Swear, Zooniji.'

'Come,' she beckoned.

Fateh Singh scooted closer, sloshing tea. They sat in proximity, sipping, gazing into each other's eyes, the fire crackling. Before Zooni cast her cup aside, exposing a shoulder as pristine as fresh snow. Fateh Singh's eyes widened.

Gathering the ends of the blanket in her hands, she invited the havildar into her embrace.

'I-I …' He gulped, stricken like some deer. 'I've never been with a woman.'

'Neither have I,' she muttered huskily, 'woman or man.'

A flicker of confusion. Before realization dawned in his eyes.

'Like Adam and Hawa,' Fateh Singh exhaled in Panjabi. Before he lowered his mouth to the dip in her neck.

45

Kohala (May 1948)

Stray dogs, lounging in the shade of a blooming jacaranda tree, watched with disinterest as the men carried out fortifications.

The old mule track from Kohala to Bagh, a length of 50 miles approximately, had to be made into a road fit for trucks. A tall order. Akbar Khan scratched his chin as he watched the progress of the Pakistani sappers. The local Azad government was providing the daily labourers. About a thousand men, working with enthusiasm and zero wages. Still. The road would take a long time to complete. Akbar Khan's brigade, stationed in the North West Frontier Province until April, had been ordered up to Pindi, from where parts of the brigade were dispatched to Muzaffarabad, Tithwal and Kohala. Indian troops were expected to make a push along the road from Baramulla and Uri towards Muzaffarabad.

As the din of gravel being poured on to the track rose, Akbar recalled what General Gracey had said.

'If Pakistan is not to face another serious refugee problem, if India is not to be allowed to sit on the doorstep of Pakistan, if the civilian and military morale is not to be affected to a dangerous extent, it is imperative that the Indian Army is not allowed to advance west beyond the Uri–Poonch–Naushera line.'

India had begun a summer offensive that could no longer be ignored. The Pakistan government had therefore decided to send some troops into Kashmir for self-defence. They were to avoid a direct clash with the Indian Army unless they had to prevent any sudden breakthrough to the Pakistan borders by the enemy.

Akbar strode to a sapper who was supervising the stones being worked into the muddy track by the men. A mechanical road-roller would make short shrift of the labour. He frowned. Dark clouds on the horizon. Rain would be unseasonal and unwelcome, converting the mud to slush!

He snorted, impatient.

When the enemy's blow fell, how could he reduce the impact of that fall? It was a question that had preoccupied General Tariq – when on the battlefield, Akbar Khan was determined to reprise the heroism of his twelfth-century role model. The tribesmen were unpredictable, he knew, and the Azads were mostly civilians with little previous military experience – an inadequate force against a mighty enemy. An enemy that thought it could trample them like an elephant. But … a thought had struck him. An old tale he had heard about a gnat that got into the elephant's trunk to avoid being trampled.

Ha! Haha! General Tariq had slapped his thigh with gusto then and driven south to Kohala, and ordered this roadwork.

He could use the tribesmen and Azads to harass the enemy flanks when they moved forward, diverting some of their force away from the road. He would keep his men in the high mountains on the right flank, therefore. But the men would need supplies, which was possible only if they had a road on the right flank, from Kohala to Bagh.

Hence, the roadwork. Akbar flicked one end of his moustache with his index finger

Now the men, having broken for lunch, proceeded to sit in the shade of tall jacaranda trees laden with purple flowers. Wiping sweat, they bantered with each other. Eager dogs surrounded them for morsels. Sweet fragrance wafted from the apple orchards by the Jhelum's bank. The bucolic scene was deceptive, Akbar knew. Early summer, and the sun was baking already. No wonder the enemy was rearing – the stalemate offered by snow was long over.

Five days later, on 20 May, news arrived that the Indian advance had begun the previous night: west towards Uri *and* north towards Tithwal. By midday, the news became quite alarming. A message from the battalion commander said that Indians had crossed Uri! And the Azads, having taken the first shocks, had withdrawn and scattered away!

Akbar Khan requested for permission to move to the Chakothi front immediately.

46

Tithwal (May 1948)

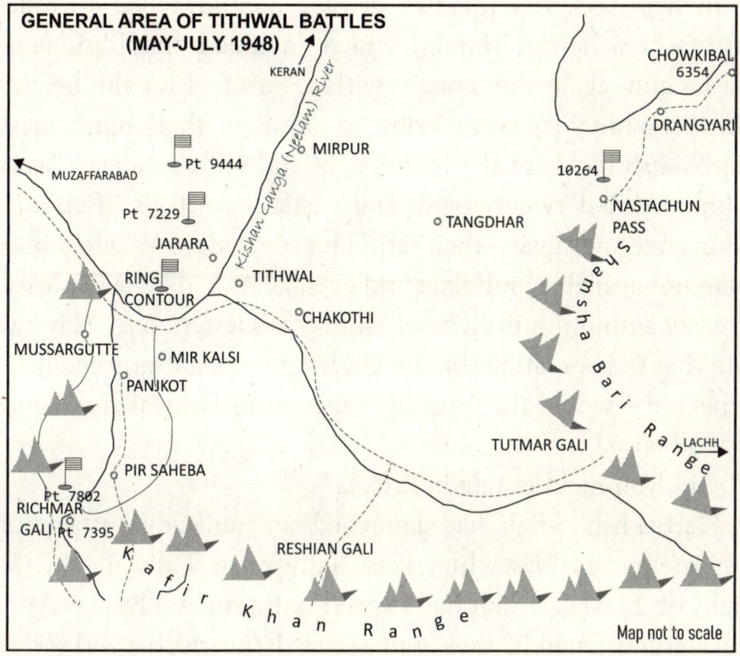

The morning of 27 May. The sun, high and hot. Through his binoculars, Brigadier Harbakhsh Singh could see men in uniform on the ridge of Pir Sahiba. Regular Pakistan Army. 161 Infantry Brigade had captured the Tithwal sector; now, the battle was on for control of the dominating heights.

In the open area where he stood, he began to give orders for further advance along the track running through the Neelam defile below. It was a deliberate move; one he wanted the enemy perched high on the adjoining mountain not to miss. Sure enough, machine-gun fire ripped the air as a hail of bullets descended upon him. The brigadier didn't flinch.

'*Sahib*,' the lance naik in charge of his protection party raced over, positioning himself between the brigadier and the fire. 'Shelter behind me or you might get shot.'

In five days, 163 Infantry Brigade had advanced 40 miles over a treacherous terrain, which included the formidable Nastachun, against an enemy with a sure feel for the heights like a mountain goat's. Trying to simulate their nimbleness, Harbakhsh had kept the troops light and self-contained. Every soldier carried twenty-one panjiri laddoos – balls of roasted flour, ghee and sugar – their ration for seven days. Where ponies were not available, buffaloes and even goats had been deployed to carry ammunition. General Thimayya's letter on 21 May had said that the operations on the Uri front were not proceeding as expected – would the brigadier push on to Tithwal and secure it at all costs?

Did Rommel hesitate in Eritrea?

Harbakhsh Singh had launched an audacious attack on the enemy via Nastachun Pass, halfway to Tithwal. On the night of 22 May, 1Sikh had carried out a night advance. After a hazardous march, they had secured the ridge overlooking Tithwal by 9 p.m. on 23 May. Rattled, the enemy fled across the river, throwing reserves of ammunition and equipment into the rapids.

War did not forgive hesitation. And the brigadier could lead from the front only because of the morale of his troops. His heart swelling with pride and affection, Harbakhsh Singh held the lance naik by the arm. 'Bachcha, I am not scared of this fire; you don't worry!'

The enemy machine guns at Pir Sahiba were well out of range from where they stood, and the bullets were fully spent by the time they reached him.

Harbakhsh turned his attention to the column of troops and animals advancing along the track below in full view of the enemy position. On purpose, the column had proceeded slowly since midday. The show of extra caution was intended to lure the enemy into moving its strength to the lower slopes of the ridge to oppose the 'attack'. Now, daylight was dying. Since the column had been clearly checked out by the enemy, Harbakhsh gave orders to slowly withdraw to Tithwal. Let the enemy believe the Indian attempt had failed!

As they reached camp just after last light, the brigadier wondered how the Sikh patrol, sent earlier, was faring with its goal of securing Richmar Gali. The high ground southwest of Tithwal had to be secured to ensure safety of the area against any counter-attack from the direction of Muzaffarabad. With Tithwal secured, the thrust towards Muzaffarabad could resume. He pored over a map. A battalion column, supported by a section of mountain guns, from Tithwal to Muzaffarabad, by the shortest route over the top of ridges … Eighteen miles … once having arrived at the top of the watershed, the ground according to the map appeared to be level—

A goat bleated.

In the dull glow of a desk lamp, the brigadier stroked his brow as he studied the plan.

Woodsmoke floated in the crisp air. Men bantered casually. The Brigade Administrative Column, with its motley crowd of porters, ponies, donkeys, buffaloes, cows and goats had finally caught up, tired and famished, having run out of rations. Harbakhsh Singh smiled. The large quantity of enemy food captured at Tithwal would be put to good use.

The 1Sikh patrol had reached the base of Richmar Gali after a hard day of precipitous climbing.

Zooni, trailed closely by Havildar Fateh Singh, had tried to find the best route, but the ground was difficult and ascending constantly. Two men had taken bad falls, another limped awkwardly. Junior Commissioning Officer Naik Singh had decided to set up a base for the night, therefore. The patrol had reached only half way to its objective; assault was planned at first light the next morning. A message was sent to the brigadier, who had ordered the rest of 1Sikh to also join up with them.

The night was dark, but a half-moon hung in the sky, bathing the peaks in moonlight. Exhausted, the men rested beneath their blankets, munching on their panjiri.

Zooni watched the men, still amazed at how quickly they fell asleep. Fateh Singh, who had taken position nearby had joined in the chorus of snores. In the first few days she was reminded constantly of Masud Ahmed – masculine smells, antsy energy, farts, the men an amorphous mass of maleness. But faces and names had begun to emerge. Jarnail with no facial hair: ribbed by others because of his name when he was just a junior-most sepoy. Avtar, who rolled the big mole on his nose: always ready with a joke. Subedar Mal Singh, who carried a neat little axe, the blade coloured red because it had tasted enemy blood—

Someone moaned as he shifted position. One of the men who had taken a fall. Ajaib. Zooni watched Naik Singh tend to him. Ajaib swore and asked for some rum.

'JCO saab, you planning to take it back home with you?'

Zooni had begun to fathom the Panjabi the men spoke; all of whom were Jat Sikhs, Fateh Singh had told her.

'Nange auna te nange jauna,' Naik Singh chuckled. 'There is nothing any of us is going to take back with us. Here.' He offered a bottle to the soldier who took a healthy swig.

Zooni wouldn't have minded one herself. The climb was easier on her, but the days of hiking were leaving her sore. Her shoulders ached routinely. Besides, she woke up extremely early every day to get her ablutions done before the men stirred.

The soldier smacked his lips. Someone belched. Amongst assorted male sounds, Zooni drifted to sleep.

I will drink your blood, pehnchod! I will skin you alive and use it to line my jutti!

Zooni awakened to frenzied swearing.

One of the men was sitting upright, staring at the dark, eyes wide open.

Fateh Singh hurried to him and shook him by the shoulders. To no avail. The cries got more shrill, more fierce, the whites of the soldier's eyes visible in the moonlight. The next instant, a slap rang out. The spell was broken. The JCO, having administered the slap, sat down beside the man who had sobered up just as quickly. Naik Singh patted the man's shoulder. 'Get some sleep, son. You will get your fight tomorrow.'

When Fateh Singh settled back, Zooni enquired softly. Mindar was a fresh recruit – one of the few who had survived the ambush at Bhatgiran, where a large number of 1Sikh soldiers had been killed in December.

After that, Zooni couldn't sleep. Kashmira's last conversation played in her mind.

'When will you be back?' Kashmira's hands had stilled over the heart-shaped paddle of her shikara, the boat laden with chillis and roses.

'When the war is over,' Zooni had shrugged.

Kashmira's eyes had clouded. 'Only the dead see the end of war.'

The thought of staying alive hadn't crossed Zooni's mind. Did the soldiers think about it?

She watched Fateh Singh sleep, his whiskers ruffling with every exhalation. After their night of lovemaking, he hadn't treated her any differently. Which she liked. His eyes betrayed him, though. Now and then, she would catch him looking at her and find herself reflected in those brown eyes – like the willows mirrored in the limpid waters of the Dal. A son of the soil, he fought to defend the motherland. The soldiers called the brigadier their Mai Baap, and did exactly what he asked them to do. Did the brigadier think about the lives of his men … and who thought of the brigadier's life? His sahib? And the sahib's sahib …

Zooni sighed. Fateh Singh's Ma must worry. As must the brigadier's wife, back at home. Like Kashmira, who didn't want her beni to leave. Like Koko Jan, who worried over Masud Ahmed … but Koko Jan was dead.

Which reminded Zooni why she was with 1Sikh. Her mission would start pre-dawn. She shut her eyes.

Before sunrise, JCO Naik Singh sent Zooni and a forward observation officer ahead to find a vantage point to fire at the enemy whilst the patrol worked its way up. The Mountain Battery was in position at Tithwal. The rest of 1Sikh would reach by the evening. The objective now was to capture all three high ridges – Richmar, Pir Sahiba and Mir Kalsi, proceeding north.

Early morning, the Sikh patrol reached Richmar Gali. Just in time. For the enemy's dawn patrol walked right into them! From her vantage position, Zooni didn't waste a single bullet. The enemy, outnumbered, tried to put up a fight. With cries of 'Bole so nihal, sat sri Akal,' the Sikhs pounced on them, killing five enemy combatants. Through the day, the enemy made attempts to retake the height overlooking Richmar Gali, but were repulsed. They were never in strength, fooled by the expectation of another Indian attempt along the Neelam defile. The next morning, with the full strength of 1Sikh, assault commenced on Pir Sahiba. The advance was along a knife-edge, nested with enemy light machine guns. Every inch of ground had to be fought for. Spurred by the ghost of Bhatgiran, the Sikhs bore into Pakistan Army troops of the 3/12 Frontier Force Rifles.

Subedar Mal Singh was attacking an enemy with his axe, when a Pathan emerged from behind a boulder and aimed at the subedar. Zooni had him in her crosshairs. But before she could fire, Fateh Singh had launched himself on the Pathan with his bayonet. Zooni fired. The Pathan swerved to avoid Fateh Singh and escaped. Zooni reloaded her rifle. Several enemy heads popped up from behind the boulder! An enemy post! The forward observation officer called for artillery support. Zooni fired. In the hand-to-hand combat below, the Sikhs danced with the enemy. Gripping her gun tight, Zooni waited for the right moment to pull the trigger. Again and again. Screams and shots pierced the air. Stones flew as the ground was raked.

A dense shattering sound. A grenade blew up, scattering the men like debris. Ajaib was hurled against the cliff and fell like a cloth doll.

The late afternoon sun descended to crown distant firs and glinted in her eye. Zooni shifted position. And gasped.

An enemy with a light machine gun had popped his head and had started shooting below. Sparks of fire as bullets erupted. Zooni aimed her rifle at the enemy's head encased in a helmet. Aiming for the sliver of skin visible beneath his left eye, she fired.

The gun went quiet.

Zooni raised her head. The enemy had collapsed on his gun. Not too soon. Below, the bodies of several men, 1Sikh and the enemy, lay tangled. Her eyes pricked.

Fateh Singh had crumpled on a rock, blood leaking out of him. He appeared unconscious.

47

Muzaffarabad, Chakothi (May 1948)

Accompanied by two staff officers, Akbar Khan reached Muzaffarabad around 7 p.m. Grimly, he motored the car down a road clogged with goats and sheep being herded by frenzied families to the safety of Pakistan. Ahead, on the road to Chakothi – midway between Muzaffarabad and Uri – he encountered two platoons of Frontier Scouts. But they were going in the wrong direction. He flagged them down and learned they were on their way out!

'You are paid government servants!' Akbar Khan lashed out.

The men stayed sullen. A few tribesmen with loaded rifles sidled up to watch what was going on.

Lowering his head close to the Scouts officer, Akbar hissed, 'Don't forget, you are subject to martial law … I order you *back* to the front!'

Instead, the men hopped on their feet like bashful new brides, refusing to budge. The tribesmen exchanged looks.

Akbar pursed his lips, stood arms akimbo and surveyed the lot. These were trained men, who, in the days of the British, were famed for their fighting skill. Now, they were blatantly refusing to do their duty, having suffered practically no casualties! No. No! He could not allow this. He looked at the tribesmen. Wordlessly, an understanding passed between them. In the next instant, the Pathans had pointed their rifles at the Scouts.

'Lay down your arms!' Akbar Khan commanded. They were deprived of their lorries and told to await further orders.

Placing the officer under arrest, Akbar decided to take him forward along with him.

At Chakothi – where a regular Pakistan Infantry Brigade was in position, supported by Azads and tribesmen – the battalion commander and others were still in good spirits, though the general impression was that the situation was not very hopeful. But Chakothi was also where they had made a stand in November. Akbar Khan patted the commander on his shoulder.

'We have to defend at all costs. Let's go over the ground in daylight.'

He took his party uphill and settled for the night in a ditch which offered protection from the biting air. Stars took over the night sky, but Akbar could not sleep. Over the snores of his comrades, he could hear the Jhelum river nearby. Any other time, the moist soil would be ready for the sowing of maize, farmers ploughing their fields, removing weeds and stubble. Instead, it was the season of war, the enemy proliferating like harmful weed …

The only way to deal with weed was to kill it. On that thought, Akbar Khan turned on his side and went to sleep.

At first light, the spray of machine-gun bullets awoke him. What the hell! Peering from the ditch, he surveyed the area.

Sure enough, they were situated above a supply point. More enemy aircraft followed, raking the ground, ripping through the sky. A lorry, packed with ammo, caught fire as he watched. Akbar narrowed his eyes. A curious sight on the horizon … a figure clad in a white sheet huddled atop a hut. A Pak soldier? As a low flying aircraft approached, the man shot up and charged at the aircraft, the sheet billowing behind him. But as the aircraft neared, the wannabe matador had an abrupt change of heart. He jumped off the roof. In the nick of time! For the hut was aflame.

Akbar slumped back in the ditch. He did not know whether to rant or hold his head in his hands. He settled for slow, long exhalations. Enemy aircraft strafed the area continuously, sparing nothing: trucks, huts, soldiers, civilians.

Finding the first gap, Akbar Khan darted to the battalion HQ.

The brigade intelligence officer had brought from GHQ Azad whatever information was available about the enemy. It appeared that ranged against them, on both sides of the river, were two brigades supported by considerable artillery, some light tanks at Uri, and the Indian Air Force, of course.

Akbar requested for another battalion to take his strength up to two. And a lashkar of tribesmen. However, the disparity in strength was still great … he could not enter into a straight trial of strength with his small force. If he took a purely defensive position, sooner or later it would be overcome.

With a furrowed brow, Akbar consulted his staff officers and the battalion commander.

Ultimately, it was decided to use the two elements that were their strength: tribesmen and heights. The Indians were apprehensive of the Pathans, aware that they were born mountain fighters. Draw Indians away into the mountains on the flanks, scatter them sufficiently, disable an effective breakthrough.

'One problem, though,' Staff Officer Kamil dissented. 'We *have* no tribesmen in the area.'

Akbar nodded wordlessly. And the Bagh road would not be ready for some time. He gazed at the emerald mountains piercing the blue sky. A vulture, or maybe an eagle, glided above. He clapped his hands and turned to the men.

'The lashkar will be coming. Meanwhile, some regular troops will have to act as tribesmen.'

The men listened, their faces creased in various degrees of doubt.

Akbar Khan stared at them. 'Think the Indians will know the difference?'

48

Srinagar (June 1948)

Margot Parr, having decided the brilliant sunshine was too good to waste, was bathing in the tepid waters of the Dal as ripening apricots perfumed the air, shikara paddles hummed, and willows swayed like lazy dervishes.

From the deck of the cookboat, Bilquis muttered at the unseemly sight. Water spirits that lurked underneath, among the lotus roots and winding weeds, were known to reach up, wrap their tentacles around a bare ankle and drag down the insolent bather. As she sorted rice, Bilquis's hand felt for grit and stones, while her blurred eyes regarded the Englishwoman swimming for pleasure.

Singing to herself, Safina polished kangris. Summer was the only season when those were not in use. Indeed, granny Bilquis would demand hers when the rains began and she felt cold in the evenings. *In Kashmir, you can afford to be without a kangri only for a few days!* Safina smiled at the sight of her toothless granny, in a cotton pheran, a thin shawl draped on her shoulders, looking out to the water. Miss Margot, though, she watched with some awe. What was it like to be a woman and walk the world like a man? Unafraid to expose your limbs? To host a man in your bedroom? To smoke with abandon? Drink … Safina had so many questions, no answers. But since the arrival of Zooni Mass, Safina could see that there were other ways to be a woman …

At her aunt's encouragement – *If Srinagar fell, she should know how to defend herself!* – and despite Mouj's reservations, Safina had joined the Bal Sena, the children's army. Nearly a month since her brave aunt had gone to battle. Daily, Safina prayed for her safety, and then added: 'Help Zooni Mass cut the kabailis like weeds.'

On the grassy bank, Gul was hunched over a picture book. It was about a monkey called Curious George who had so many questions and did so many silly things that he made Gul giggle. Miss Margot, gifting him the parcel of books she had arranged from American friends in Delhi, had said: *Have yourself a great adventure!* Gul's cheeks were rosy as apples in the burgeoning sunlight as he studied the pictures and tried to recall the sentences Miss Margot had read aloud to him, his right index finger pausing over each word. Mouj had taken the shikara with vegetables to the market and promised to bring his favourite rolls encrusted with almond and poppy seeds—

A scream shattered the idyll.

Hassan had grabbed Safina by the wrist and was trying to pull her upright. Safina resisted, digging her heels in.

'Join the Bal Sena, will you? Dragging our family name in mud!' Hassan's snarls sliced the midsummer's day. Bilquis began to berate her son. Margot's head popped up amidst lily pads. Gul clutched the book in both hands like it was a shield.

'You badd bakhat, you orphan! You think you can do what pleases you?'

Hassan was lunging at Safina with both hands now. She thrashed about the kangri she was clutching. In the tussle, it smacked his forehead. Hassan yelped. Safina screamed. Bilquis began to hurl fistfuls of rice in the direction of Hassan, along with imprecations.

'Photyi shoosh! May your lungs burst! Drayi holhaej! May you get chicken pox!'

Hassan clasped his forehead with both hands. Safina ran, the cookboat rocking, and cowered behind Bilquis. With long strokes, Margot was swimming to the boat. A lump was forming on Hassan's forehead. Glaring at the women, he spat loudly before swivelling and storming off to the lake's bank.

In anticipation, Gul was scurrying towards the houseboat. But Hassan was swifter. Snatching *Curious George* from Gul's tiny hands, he flung the paperback away. It landed like a mangled butterfly on the green grass – the bright yellow front cover torn from the book's spine. Gul started to howl. Hassan snarled, grabbed the boy and, tossing him over one shoulder, started to stride away.

Margot gulped, ingesting water, still twenty yards from the bank. She thrashed her arms, increasing her speed. Safina was watching open-mouthed, Bilquis muttering incoherently.

Gul started to pound his uncle's back with his fists. A stinging slap as Hassan whacked the boy's bottom. Gul wailed.

'Gul! Gul! *Guuul!*'

Miss Margot was shouting and treading water.

Tears flowed down Gul's cheeks. Miss Margot was waving her hands … Miss Margot was saying something … Miss Margot was trying to fly … *Fly*?

Gul stopped sniffling. He threw his face upwards, neck arching, eyes scanning the sky, and started to make a rattling sound.

'Naakaar! Awful!' Hassan scolded.

But over and over, Gul produced that sound, his tiny throat like some wayward trumpet as he struggled over Hassan's shoulder.

Hassan clamped a hand on his right ear.

Which was perhaps why he did not register the flapping overhead before a large bird swooped down upon him. Clasping its talons on his head, the raptor started to strike Hassan's forehead with its large curved beak.

In the next instant, Gul slid to the grass.

Hassan spun wildly, his hands scrabbling as he tried to protect his face, protect his eyes, protect his temples, trying desperately to dislodge the griffon from his head, howling, howling, howling his guts out.

49

Dehradun (June 1948)

Staff in hand, Bapu walked briskly, leading a growing gaggle of men, as the air rent periodically with cries of 'Inquilab zindabad!' Women watching from the edge of the unpaved road held up their babies for Bapu's blessing. They had earlier sprinkled water on the path to prevent dust from churning, and thrown leaves and flower petals to cushion the feet of people marching with Bapu to Dandi. Winding his way from one village to the next, covering ten miles in a day, stopping to rest only late in the evening, Bapu led his disciples in prayer with the villagers who hosted them for the night, after which he explained the inequity of the salt tax levied on them by the British. They were marching in the name of god, he asserted. Reporters following the ragtag marchers watched in awe as the initial group of Gandhi and several dozen swelled to several thousand, and correspondents flew in from around the world to send reports back home. In this march of this frail man, the Westerners found a Biblical allegory – of Jesus journeying to Jerusalem. Someone found a donkey to follow in the wake of Gandhi. Finally, 241 miles later, when Bapu witnessed the Arabian Sea snaking into the Gulf of Cambay to lap at the mouth of his destination Dandi, he declared: *Either I shall return with what I want, or my dead body will float in the ocean.*

A vice-like grip on his heart.

Now the flower-bedecked funeral cortège swam into view. Bapu's face, the only visible part of him in the sea of rose petals, his nostrils stuffed with cotton, a bereaved Vallabh trying to keep his neck erect even as it threatened to snap with grief—

An anguished cry.

Father?

Vallabh's eyes blinked. The Himalayas in the distance. A twitter of sparrows. Mani, sitting on the edge of her chair, watching him worriedly. Vallabh sucked his teeth.

'A dream?' Manibehn enquired softly.

'Nightmare.'

Manibehn stood up, poured some water into a glass and served him. Vallabh sipped some before returning it. Almost three months of rest and recuperation in the hills as advised by doctors – time in which ancient memories had stirred in his mind like dry leaves rustling in an empty courtyard. One of those Western reporters had called him John the Baptist to Bapu's Jesus. Vallabh was a forerunner of sorts. When Bapu was planning his Dandi march, Vallabh had begun visiting villages on the planned route to alert and mobilize them. Alarmed, the British had arrested him at village Ras and sent him to Sabarmati jail. They believed they had crushed the march before it began. Vallabh snorted. After Dandi, the whole of India had erupted – people swarming to beaches to make salt and court arrest! From the corner of his eye, he saw Mani's look of interest as she smoothed her lap.

'Was Bucher on your mind, Father?'

General Roy Bucher had visited the day before as Lord Mountbatten's emissary. They had chatted in his office for an hour after lunch. On the table was a proposal to partition Kashmir: Western Poonch, Gilgit, Chitral and most of Baltistan to go to Pakistan.

'Bapu … And the British, early days … But Bucher is British, too!' Vallabh rested his forehead against one palm, fingertips tapping.

Manibehn knew her father had been against the idea of referring Kashmir to the UN. Not only had the dispute been prolonged, but the merits of India's case had been completely lost in power politics.

'Lord Mountbatten is convinced that an agreement between India and Hyderabad is about to materialize. So, he wishes to "solve" Kashmir as well before his departure.' Vallabh turned to his daughter.

Years of worrying over India had given Father a forehead which mirrored the fields he had ploughed as a boy. She had listened to the news on the radio with him. *In Hyderabad, a war-like situation was developing after the state stopped Bombay officials from entering Nanaj, an enclave of Indian territory within the state*. No wonder Father didn't share Mountbatten's conviction.

'What was Bapu saying to you?'

Vallabh narrowed his eyes.

'In your daydream?'

'Ah! I recalled Bapu very vividly on his salt march. But the thing is that I wasn't even *with* Bapu on that march, as you know, Mani. But my mind conjured it up with all possible details … women with babies, marigold petals under the feet of the marchers, the blue waters of Khambat … and then, then

I was sitting beside Bapu on his final journey to the cremation ghat.' Vallabh pursed his mouth.

Manibehn nodded. She was there with Father when Dr Bhargava had bent over Bapu's blood-stained body and confirmed that he had died.

Vallabh gazed at the expanse in front of him. 'I am reminded of another incident. From early on in our association, 1922, when Bapu was jailed by the British for six years. He left saying that a mason experiences no difficulty in completing a structure in accordance with the plan of an architect.'

Father was the mason who had completed Bapu's plans. Manibehn clasped her careworn hands together as she studied him. Bapu had departed and on Father's shoulders, sheltered by a khaki shawl she had spun, rested unfinished plans. The heart attack had spurred him on instead of slowing him down; Father, the runner-up, refusing to trail for long the Great Soul that had already flown. Manibehn's throat caught.

Vallabh did not miss the moisture in Mani's eyes before she hurriedly looked away. A slow cart lasted long, but he could feel the hand of Yama on many days. His time was approaching, but there was much to accomplish still. Vallabh firmed his jaw. Bapu's assassins had gone on trial on 27 May 1948. Meanwhile, in Kashmir, like Oliver Twist, the military commanders always asked for more, their estimates of requirements were constantly changing. The prolonged fighting in Kashmir was straining military resources, which the Nizam and his Razakars were taking full advantage of.

A light breeze rippled the folds of his dhoti. Enough of sitting in the wheelchair! Vallabh hoisted himself up, Mani lunging to his side.

'You know, Mani,' Vallabh steadied his legs, 'people think I am anti-Muslim, but that is not the case at all. I am quite ready to guarantee the safety and well-being of Muslims all over India. I told Bucher I would not oppose some form of settlement over Kashmir, but if any boundaries were to be agreed, they must be capable of being recognized on the ground. A settlement on Kashmir is conditional on Hyderabad coming to terms … and I don't think Lord Mountbatten is going to get a satisfactory acceptance of the Indian government's proposals from the Nizam.'

They walked side by side, slow steps, heads down.

'A teacher once criticized me for choosing Gujarati instead of Sanskrit. "Every Hindu student in this country should learn Sanskrit, he said,"' Vallabh snorted.

Manibehn grinned.

'"You would be out of a job!" I told him.'

Vallabh paused to watch a flock of birds cross the sky. Lord Mountbatten would depart in less than three weeks. He meant well, but good wishes seldom trumped ground reality. In the face of the Nizam's constant vacillation, there was only one course left to take.

50

Tithwal (June 1948)

Truce period.

After the failure of their attack on Mir Kalsi peak, the enemy had taken up position on the opposite side of the Indian picket. Both positions were level and equally exposed to each other. And the soldiers learned they could not even pee, without attracting a bullet. A wholly unnatural situation, which nature itself resolved. A white towel on a twig was raised to allow men, Pakistani and Indian, to answer the call of nature. Slowly, an understanding evolved. Both posts allowed an hour off in the morning, another at meal times, and an odd half-hour for tea or a VIP visit when no shots would be exchanged. A Himalayan detente to attend to normal life chores.

Which was how the truce period came about. When he visited the picket, Brigadier Harbakhsh Singh marvelled at the gentleman's agreement!

The men wounded in the battle of Pir Sahiba, having lost a lot of blood, were revived by life-infusing blood plasma. Some of them had recovered, whilst Havildar Fateh Singh and JCO Naik were airlifted to Delhi for further hospitalization.

Major General Thimayya's frontal thrust along the Uri–Domel road had come to a standstill. Meanwhile, Singh's brigade could not progress to Muzaffarabad because of the heavy enemy concentration in front of Tithwal. For once, both Pakistan and India were on the same page: Stalled.

The brigadier decided to carry out a final reconnaissance.

Tithwal camp lay in a deep hollow with dizzying mountain heights to the west, south and east. To the north was the Neelam river, where the enemy was gathered in strength. Enemy gunfire from across the river was ineffective – their shells shooting overhead or hitting the shoulder of one or the other hill. The only chance open to them was to move enemy guns across the river. Harbakhsh Singh seized this chance.

He gave orders to his men to blow all the suspension bridges across the Neelam river on the way up and down to Tithwal.

In late June, as the summer sun blazed and bumble bees droned, as hillsides were dotted with yellow barberry and wild pink roses, as soldiers armed themselves with guns and air warning systems, the two armies of Pakistan and India were perched on peaks bisected by a flowing river, having battled each other to a standstill.

51

New Delhi (July 1948)

The garden, drenched by a monsoonal shower, sparkled in the evening light. The zoo that had come up at Teen Murti in a short time – parrots, pigeons, peacocks, dogs, a deer – gave Jawahar relief as much as it amused the children. Birds and animals had sustained him during his days in prison. In Bareilly, there were pigeons; in Naini, red-billed parrots that nested in the crevices of the barrack walls. Some days, if he sat absolutely still, a squirrel would clamber up his leg and pause to watch him with unblinking eyes—

'How did it go with Mr Korbel?' Indu asked anxiously before turning to watch the ayah coax the children to stop playing and get ready for a wash before dinner.

Jawahar harrumphed. The UN diplomats had arrived in Delhi, having learned from Zafarullah Khan, the Pakistani foreign minister, that three brigades of the Pakistan Army were fighting in Kashmir. Not surprisingly, their whole case had been built on deceit and falsehood throughout. And yet, Josef

Korbel, the Czech delegate, had had the nerve to suggest that India, as the stronger party, make some concessions!

'I let him know that we are a secular state, which is not based on religion. Unlike Pakistan, a medieval state with an impossible theocratic concept. One which should never have been created had the British not backed Jinnah's foolish idea!'

On a squeal, Rajiv sped towards them, the ayah scooping up Sanjay and a few of the children's toys.

'Nanu, Nanu,' he clambered onto his grandfather's lap. Jawahar wrapped his arms around Indu's older boy who was about to turn four years old.

'It's time for your bath, you know.' Indu shook her head.

'Not before one story from Nanu.' Rajiv swivelled his neck to Jawahar, who mussed up his hair.

'Okay, one quick one before your mother sends me in to bathe as well.'

Which made Rajiv giggle. Indu, trying not to smile, waved to the ayah to proceed indoors.

'A dog story or a monkey story?'

Rajiv's eyes lit up. 'Both!'

Jawahar shook his head. 'One, we agreed.'

'Monkey, then.'

'This is from when I was in Bareilly jail. Some of the other prisoners would keep animals as pets; it was lonely, you see. Once, a baby monkey had lost its way in the barracks. He was caught and tied to a post with a string around his neck. The baby started to cry. Its piteous shrieks brought the family of monkeys to the barrack walls. A large monkey snarled,' Jawahar bared his teeth, 'and barked,' Jawahar rasped. Rajiv's eyes widened as he hung on to every word. 'The prisoners started to brandish sticks to scare him off ...' Jawahar swung his forearms in menacing motions. 'But the monkey vaulted straight on to the men, hopping onto their heads, smacking their sticks,' Jawahar mussed his grandson's head in playful swipes, 'sending the men scattering like so many twigs!' Rajiv gasped. 'Now, the monkey bit through the string, and gathering the baby in his arms, swung back to the barrack wall and a-WAY!'

Rajiv clapped his hands in approval. Jawahar chuckled. Indu smiled, arose and wiggled her fingers at her son. 'Alright, time to go.'

Jawahar watched his family head into the house, the sandstone aglow in dusk, birds arcing the sky. A koel cooed. His mind journeyed to Dehradun where, jailed in solitary confinement, he would wait for the koel to call out, its music filling the prison yard and his heart with joy. Otherwise, the dominant birdcall was that of the brainfever bird, quite rightly named for its insistent shrill trill, which became tiring very quickly. When permitted out of his cell for exercise, he would get to see the Himalayas – imperturbable, solid, serene, they grew more beloved with each solitary day as they beheld his varying humours and soothed his fevered mind.

Jawahar sighed, mulling over the tortuous path of the Kashmir problem.

The battle between Indian and Pakistani troops was seesawing, no decisive victories, and now with the monsoons, fighting was stalling again. The partition maps drawn up by V.P. Menon at the behest of Dickie had to be shelved because Liaquat had taken ill. The UN commission should come down in favour of India … All rationale indicated that the intruder and the aggressor could *not* be considered equal. He rolled his shoulders back. Hyderabad, meanwhile, was acting more provocatively with every passing day. And Vallabhbhai, who had returned to Delhi, was livid at intelligence reports that attempts were being made to smuggle arms and ammunition into Hyderabad through an Australian by the name of Sidney Cotton. Cotton's gun-running base was Karachi, where the government had begun to cash a portion of the Government of India securities which Hyderabad had offered to Pakistan as loan! This, despite Laik Ali's solemn promise that no portion of the securities transferred to Pakistan would be cashed while the Standstill Agreement was still pending. Jinnah's meddling was keeping both Hyderabad and Kashmir on the boil!

Jawahar shot up and started to pace.

Challenges, multiple challenges, as they sought to build a new India … But they had also accomplished some goals. Almost 600 Princely States had been integrated into the Indian union, save two. The credit was Vallabhbhai's. And yet, there were those who were trying to drive a wedge between the Prime Minister and his deputy. They differed sharply, Jawahar had always admitted as much, yet, both had a mutual confidence in each other's integrity. And the memory of Bapu kept them together … Their refugee problem was of a magnitude unheard of ever before in the world. But they had progressed to a point where kafilas settled in camps were being rehabilitated: workshops set up for minor trades – weaving, spinning, dyeing, soap-making, woodwork, handicrafts; educational and recreational facilities being provided; refugees being relocated in evacuee lands … Sadness swamped him. Edwina had devoted her energies to the refugee work, over which they had both bonded and connected so deeply. He had even asked her to stay back and carry on with her work. But Edwina had reminded him that he had told her to be practical. Jawahar sighed. There was little satisfaction in wisdom! He forced his mind back to the present. The Constituent Assembly had begun work on drafting India's Constitution to ensure individual freedom and economic opportunities for all its citizens—

Papu!

Indu hailed him from the arched doorway. He responded with a raised arm. Snatches of the children's voices drifted down the steps, mingling with the chirruping of crickets in the vast gardens. The peacock called out. Jawahar turned to catch it shake its feathers that glinted in the gloaming, before it sashayed down the side of a mirror pool in which pink lotus flowers floated. Kamala, his wife, was named after the flower – perhaps why it had become his favourite and why he had named Indu's firstborn after it: Rajiv. Jawahar cast a look at the extensive gardens, a blend of East and West ... In the midst of a similar garden, Bapu had broken his last fast at Birla House. When Maulana Azad and Jareb Zahid Hussein, the High Commissioner of Pakistan, and Ganesh Dutt, on behalf of the Mahasabha and the RSS, renewed their pledge to end violence, and Bapu finally broke into his impish smile, the room had erupted with joy. After which, the ashram did a typical religious service, with readings from scriptures of several religions, ending with Bapu's favourite Christian hymn: *When I survey the wondrous Cross*.

Maulana and he had taken turns holding the glass of orange juice, while Bapu sipped slowly. Less than a month later, Bapu was dead. The great man who had taught him never to hate and never to fear, was no more ... but his teachings were with them.

So, he had told the tumultuous crowd gathering at Birla House upon Bapu's death: *A man like Gandhi came once in a thousand years*. As cyclists and scooterists turned up their lamplights to cut through the darkness, Jawahar mounted the compound's gate to speak to the stunned multitude. With moist eyes and a wet kerchief stuffed in his sherwani pocket, he confessed how his hopes had been blasted by the killings in the wake of Partition—

A child's delighted shriek interrupted his recollection. His family was waiting for him … In the face of myriad challenges, one thought sustained him: A country that could produce Gandhi had to have something great and vital in it.

Jawahar bounded up the steps.

52

Srinagar (July 1948)

A hazy summer afternoon.

A million pinpricks on the Dal's water. A hoopoe bird tweeting its three-beat song. The smell of fried batter in the humid air on the deck of the *Mayfair* where Bilquis snored as she napped on a thin quilt, a cotton scarf shading her face from the sun. With Miss Margot having left for the US, Kashmira had decided to give the houseboat a thorough cleaning. Zooni had returned from battle a week ago with nary a bruise to show. But her recounting had got the journalist excited enough to record everything, quiz Zooni for hours, work furiously, her typewriter clacking through the night like some night heron. And then she hopped on a plane out of Srinagar.

'I'll be back,' Miss Margot had waved. 'The war ain't going anywhere!'

Which was both good news and bad. Her return would mean continued income, especially when visitors had vanished from the Valley. But, Kashmira sighed as she shifted her bottom on the wooden deck, keeping the sun firmly on her back, it also meant ongoing war ... Shading her eyes with one hand, Kashmira scanned the boat deck. Gul, who had offered to dust *Mayfair*'s assorted library, was sitting cross-legged, a book open on his lap, surrounded by a moat of books and periodicals. She smiled indulgently: Her boy would become an ustad in the time it took him to finish dusting! A yawn escaped her. It was the batter-fried pumpkin flowers they had all so cheerfully demolished. Kashmira looked to the cookboat where Zooni had gone to make mint buttermilk drinks – *They cool everything down, didn't Mouj say that*?

Resting her back against a pillar, Kashmira let her eyelids droop.

Soon she would have to get up and start preparing dinner – a special one with mutton yakhni and lotus root and kohlrabi. At the sadan, Durga had managed to sell two shawls to a white reporter – after keeping a portion for the kitchen, she had distributed the remaining cash amongst the women who had worked on the shawls. Kashmira liked the feel of the rupees in her hand; it allowed her to treat her family to an occasional feast. A memory of spiced yogurt simmering in the thick-bottomed pan in their Baramulla kitchen stirred ... the scent of burning chinar leaves in late autumn ... Moul sucking on his hukkah ... purple markings on Bilquis's inner thighs where the kangri had cooked her blood vessels ... mint in her nostrils—

Kashmira opened her eyes to a glass of buttermilk under her nose.

Zooni offered it to her with a grin before sitting down to drink hers. She gave a sidelong glance to the girls giggling at the front of the houseboat, Safina and two of her friends sitting on the steps, feet dangling in water. Every now and then, a squeal escaped the trio before they shoved one another or dissolved into laughter.

'Remember when we were that age?' Zooni asked.

Kashmira nodded.

'Of course, you were Mouj's helper, always darting to fetch one thing or another ...' Zooni screwed up her nose. '*A mother without a daughter is like a boat without oars*. That's what Mouj would always say. I wonder what she truly thought of me.'

'You were Moul's oar ... You climbed the hills in no time, knew which goat or sheep was sickly, used the catapult to keep them safe from the wolves ...' She looked away into the distance. 'Now, the Indian Army thinks similarly.'

Since Zooni's return, the Valley had been abuzz. But Zooni had spoken to no one but Miss Margot, collected her salary and handed it to Kashmira, and returned to WSDC. But Kashmira knew how her beni tossed and turned in the night before sleep finally came. During the day, her eyes flitted about like a sparrow, ever alert. Her shoulders must hurt, because she flexed them for relief unconsciously. It was good though that Zooni's reputation as a sharpshooter had grown in the Valley. That would teach Hassan not to show up again with evil intent. Kashmira tightened her mouth at the memory of the day he had tried to snatch Gul in her absence, when Gul's 'Boi' had drawn so much blood, the grass was streaked red when Kashmira had returned. A fortnight later, Hassan had showed up again, his face heavily bandaged, kohl-lined eyes spitting fire as he had harangued them from the bank, watching the sky warily.

Tell your half-wife of a sister, I will be back! When the Azad Kashmir army has thrown out Abdullah and the Indian Army. I will come back with General Masud, eh? General *Masud! Tell Zooni her husband has a brand-new wife and she should get ready to wipe her slippers!*

After which Hassan had disappeared again – gone for good, Kashmira prayed.

But Gul, with great pride, had narrated to his Zooni Mass the story of Boi's attack on Hassan. And Kashmira had been forced to divulge Hassan's threats.

Zooni had listened as she cleaned her rifle. 'When the wolf comes too close, the shepherd must know how to keep the sheep safe. That was the first lesson Moul taught me when we took our herd grazing.'

Now, having finished the buttermilk, Kashmira sucked her teeth as she raised an index finger in the air. 'Turn!'

Zooni frowned.

Placing her hands on her sister's shoulders, Kashmira propelled Zooni around until she had her back. With a firm grip on the shoulder blades, she started to massage the knots in Zooni's neck.

A moan escaped Zooni. She let herself relax. With half-open eyes she watched the kingfisher darting amidst the abundant lotus flowers, the bees buzzing in Kashmira's rose garden, the distant shikaras laden with flowers … war seemed far away … but no! Just last week, she was battling the enemy to prevent access to the roads that led to the Valley! She sprang upright, surprising her sister. And shot off a query before she could be questioned.

'Kashmira, are you enjoying going to the sadan?'

'Un-hunh.'

The company of other unfortunate women made her feel less alone. Then there was the embroidery. Crafting a clutch of almond-shaped patterns – paisley, the English called them; or a bunch of booyne leaves in the russet hues of autumn – chinar; or the slender-necked nargisi – narcissus. All of this absorbed her mind such that it forgot the passage of time.

'Know what?' Kashmira said with a lilt in her voice. 'When the English customers came to look at our shawls and Durgaji asked me to explain the intricate work, I parroted Ali's salesman speech! The one he would use when displaying his silk samplers for orders. Durgaji then translated for the customers!'

As Zooni chuckled, the memory of Ali washed over Kashmira. When she embroidered, it was as if she were conversing with her husband. *Auburn here, are you sure? Not red? A lotus you say, not hyacinth?* Lately, Ali had been whispering to her: Shawl is good, try a wall hanging next, a jungle scene, embellish it with animals, mystical birds, flowers …

Meanwhile, Bilquis had sat up and looked disoriented. The sun had moved, leaving her in the shade. With a tap on Zooni's back, Kashmira levered herself up and headed to her mother-in-law.

Rotating her neck, Zooni admitted the massage had helped. Fateh Singh swam into her mind. He had written a letter from Delhi which the brigadier had sent over for her with an orderly. She had taken it to Durga to read: Fateh Singh was recovering and would visit her soon in the Valley. Thankfully, Durga had not asked any questions. Zooni did not know what she felt, so how would she answer? A balwallah kufar, as Hassan and many others called the Sikh men … One of whom had killed Ali … and what exactly did Fateh Singh himself think? Did he fancy her as some Habba Khatoon gathering purple crocus for saffron and singing poems of love? No, probably not. She had battled alongside him … was he in love with her? Was *she*? What *was* love?

What Kashmira felt for Ali?

What Mouj and Moul shared?

Zooni didn't know. She only knew that he was with her all the time, the crinkles of his eyes when he smiled, the arch of his turbaned forehead, his slim strong fingers as he positioned her rifle grip, the way his nose wrinkled in thought … he slid out from behind her eyelids at whim … much like Moul—

Excited voices roused Zooni from her reverie. Safina, hands on her waist, was teasing Gul: How many books had he finished dusting exactly, hunh? As Gul giggled, Safina started to tickle him. Gul squirmed. Safina ran. Gul deposited the book on the moat, leaped out, and started to chase Safina. The two ran circles around the books, shrieking. Kashmira, meanwhile, had moved Bilquis so that she soaked the mellow evening sun as she smoothed her mother-in-law's thin long hair with a wooden comb.

As they watched the children, a smile spread across the faces of the three women.

The fierce noon sun was a mellow ball of orange on the horizon. So much had changed in less than a year, so much loss … and yet, here were the children, laughing, playing, their joy a sparkling silk thread coursing through the sorrow of life's shawl. Zooni inhaled sharply as Moul whispered in her ear.

The invaders always arrived in Kashmir and never left. Some stayed as lambs, others as wolves. It is for a shepherd, however, to ensure that his sheep can graze safely.

Epilogue

The see-sawing war between India and Pakistan, the on–off negotiations, the high jinks at the United Nations ultimately led to a ceasefire mediated by the UN Security Council on 31 December 1948. A year later, a formal ceasefire line came into effect, giving one-third of the state to Pakistan, the rest to India. Western Jammu, Gilgit, Baltistan had sided with Pakistan from the start; eastern Jammu and Ladakh with India. What remained in balance – the Kashmir valley – remains contested to this day.

Meanwhile, the wedge of Pakistan Occupied Kashmir secures Pakistan's long border with India. Tithwal (now Teetwal) has become the last town on the Indian side; the Neelam river is part of the LOC (Line of Control) between the two nations, renamed Kishenganga in India; a bridge across the river connects both nations to allow families split apart by the LOC to meet occasionally.

What of our principal characters?

Vallabhbhai Patel suffered a second heart attack and passed away on 15 December 1950. In homage, Prime Minister Nehru declared a week of national mourning.

A year later, Akbar Khan tried to overthrow Liaquat Ali Khan's government and was jailed. Liaquat himself, blamed by the Pakistan Army for the ceasefire with India, was assassinated shortly thereafter.

Back in Kashmir, Tiger/Karan Singh was appointed regent, replacing Maharaja Hari Singh. Sheikh Abdullah went on to secure special provisions for Kashmir in the Indian Constitution: Article 370 recognized the state's autonomy and allowed Kashmir its own Constitution. But all didn't go well. In 1953, the Sheikh was dismissed and imprisoned, primarily for nursing the idea of independence for Kashmir. He languished in jails for almost a decade.

Meanwhile, communal violence flared up frequently in the state. Jawaharlal Nehru, recognizing the discontent of the Kashmiris, freed Sheikh Abdullah from jail in 1964 and conferred with him on a possible solution. He even agreed that the Sheikh should visit Pakistan to meet President Ayub Khan. Whilst Sheikh Abdullah was in Pakistan, Jawaharlal Nehru passed away on 17 May 1964.

Seizing the opportunity, Pakistan infiltrated the LOC and tried to foment an uprising against India in Kashmir, under the code name 'Operation Gibraltar'. Like Akbar Khan in 1947, the Pakistanis were still seeking inspiration from the eighth-century Muslim conquest of Spain. In the ensuing Indo-Pak war of 1965, Lt Gen. Harbakhsh Singh played a key role as the western army commander and was awarded the Padma Vibhushan upon victory. The war of 1947 came a full circle.

The two nations have gone to war over Kashmir on a total of three occasions: 1965, 1971, 1999. The first proxy war initiated by Pakistan in 1947, via the kabailis, has become a standard operating procedure for sustained warfare in non-war times. Meanwhile, the Indian Army has sustained its presence in the Valley. Each nation holds a part of Kashmir, but desires the whole – above all the Valley of lily-covered lakes with its increasingly blood-soaked land.

On 6 August 2019, India revoked the special status granted under Article 370 of the Indian Constitution to Jammu and Kashmir, thereby rescinding its autonomy.

What about the Kashmiris?

The promised plebiscite never happened.

Which brings to mind what a Kashmiri woman, when advised to leave the besieged city of Poonch for the safety of Jammu in 1948, had replied. 'We will, but only when the army does. Our homes are here and we do not intend to go until you do – and we do not think you ever will.'

Acknowledgements

The signature tune of Manhattan is its sirens – ambulance, fire truck, police car – a sound so insistent you cannot but fold it into the background of Big-Apple living. During the singular silence of Covid, the sirens acquired a new meaning, a fresh urgency, a haunting. I was working on the first draft of *Kashmir*, through fear and uncertainty that bedevils a time of plague and a new writing project. The trees outside my window kept me company, bare branches yielding tender leaf buds that turned to lush foliage that matured to flaming russet crowns come Fall. Like the Kashmiri chinar which greeted invading Persians the autumn they first entered India, duping them into thinking they were riding into a blaze!

Another companion was the poetry of Agha Shahid Ali, 'Lenox Hill', in particular. In which he describes his mother waking from surgery at Lenox Hill hospital in Manhattan, the sound of sirens reminding her of the screams of elephants as they were pushed off steep cliffs by the sadistic conqueror, Mihiragula.

> The Hun so loved the cry, one falling elephant's,
> he wished to hear it again. At dawn, my mother
> heard, in her hospital-dream of elephants,
> sirens wail through Manhattan like elephants
> forced off Pir Panjal's rock cliffs in Kashmir …

Plane trees and poetry were my portal to Kashmir from Manhattan as I sifted the threads of loss and longing, cultural memory and motherland, history and abyss, in my attempt to stitch together a narrative that does justice to the story of Kashmir. Which is ancient and current, layered and complex, deep and unsettling. I have given it all the love and care and attention to detail that a storyteller can bring to bear; still, any shortcomings discerned are entirely mine. As the wise Islamic artists say: Only God is perfect.

Whilst researching and writing The Partition Trilogy, I had two specific goals. One was to put faces on the ones who lived and loved and lost in that cataclysm, especially women who suffered the worst and were obscured in the interstices of history. Second was to faithfully, with great historical accuracy, render our leaders as flesh and blood characters. I bring the subaltern, the aam admi and aurat, out of the shadows and on the same stage as Vallabhbhai, Jawaharlal and Dickie (Mountbatten), my three political protagonists. This device allows me to show the life-altering impact in Lahore/Hyderabad/Kashmir of decisions being taken in Delhi.

The women in *Kashmir* – Durga, Kashmira, Margot, Zooni – are inspired by real women who, with great resilience and courage, negotiated conflict and violence to keep their families safe. In particular, Zuni Gujjar/Zoon Gujjari was a real-life activist and sharpshooter, about whom not much is known otherwise. So I fleshed her out from skeletal research because the world needs to know the kickass Zooni!

My large-canvas historical trilogy, undergirded with rigorous historical and archival research, would not have been possible without the libraries that have supported me, beginning with the Singapore National Library, followed by the Hong Kong Public Library, and now the New York Public Library; the countless writers whose books have informed me (some of whom I have been able to acknowledge in the Select Bibliography); the beta readers and final readers whose suggestions have made the manuscript stronger – a special shoutout to Minoshka Narayan and Sheila Kumar.

As always, my gratitude to the entire team at HarperCollins India.

The only true magic in this world is love. *Ishq Bulleh nu nachave*. Thank you for the magic, my loves, Malvika, Prasanna, Nyx.

With *Kashmir*, the Partition trilogy comes to a close. I end this saga with the hope that the books will give you fresh stories about a time period that has deafening reverberations today. Stories you can share, laugh and cry over, shatter the silence with. A good story can save us. Scheherazade knew this, as did the forebears of my craft who started their trade around the first fire. The Partition Trilogy sure saved this writer. I now pass you the baton.

Select Bibliography

Abdullah, Sheikh. *Flames of Chinar*. New Delhi: Viking, 1993.

Azad, Maulana Abul Kalam. *India Wins Freedom: An Autobiographical Narrative*. Bombay: Orient Longman, 1959.

Bazaz, Prem Nath. *Kashmir in the Crucible*. Bombay: Pearl Publications, 1969.

Bourke-White, Margaret. *Halfway to Freedom*. New York: Simon and Schuster, 1949.

Brown, Judith M. *Nehru: A Political Life*. Yale: Yale University Press, 2003.

Campbell-Johnson, Alan. *Mission with Mountbatten*. London: Hamish Hamilton, 1951.

Carter, Lionel, ed. *Partition Observed: British Official Reports from South Asia*. 2 vols. New Delhi: Manohar, 2011.

Chaudhuri, Nirad C. *The Autobiography of an Unknown Indian*. London: Macmillan, 1951.

——— *Thy Hand Great Anarch! India, 1921–1952*. London: Chatto and Windus, 1987.

Chopra, Prabha, ed. *Sardar Patel and the Partition of India*. Delhi: Konark 2010.

Collins, Larry, and Dominique Lapierre. *Freedom at Midnight*. New York: Avon, 1975.

Cohen, Maurice. *Thunder over Kashmir*. Hyderabad: Orient Longman, 1955.

Corfield, Conrad. *The Princely India I Knew: From Reading to Mountbatten*. Madras: Indo-British Historical Society, 1975.

French, Patrick. *Liberty or Death*. London: Flamingo, 1998.

Gandhi, Indira, and Jawaharlal Nehru. *Two Alone, Two Together: Letters between Indira Gandhi and Jawaharlal Nehru, 1940–1964*. Edited by Sonia Gandhi. London: Hodder and Stoughton, 1992.

Gandhi, Rajmohan. *Patel: A Life*. Ahmedabad: Navjivan, 1990.

Gopal, Sarvepalli. *Jawaharlal Nehru: A Biography*. 2 vols. London: Jonathan Cape, 1975–1979.

Guha, Ramachandra. *India after Gandhi: The History of the World's Largest Democracy*. New York: HarperCollins, 2007.

Hajari, Nisid. *Midnight's Furies: The Deadly Legacy of India's Partition*. New York: First Mariner Books, 2016.

Hodson, H.V. *The Great Divide: Britain-India-Pakistan*. Karachi: Oxford University Press, 1971.

Hoskote, Ranjit, tr. *I, Lalla: The Poems of Lal Ded*. New Delhi: Penguin Books, 2013.

Hutheesing, Krishna Nehru. *We Nehrus*. New York: Holt, Rinehart and Winston, 1967.

Jha, Prem Shankar. *Kashmir, 1947: Rival Versions of History*. New Delhi: Oxford University Press, 1996.

Khan, Akbar. *Raiders in Kashmir*. Karachi: Pak Publishers, 1970.

Khan, Nyla Ali. *Islam, Women, and Violence in Kashmir: Between India and Pakistan*. London: Palgrave Macmillan, 2010.

Khan, Yasmin. *The Great Partition: The Making of India and Pakistan*. New Haven and London: Yale University Press, 2007.

Khilnani, Sunil. *The Idea of India*. London: Penguin Books, 2003.

Khosla, G.D. *Stern Reckoning: A Survey of the Events Leading Up to and Following the Partition of India*. New Delhi: Oxford University Press, 1989.

Korbel, Josef. *Danger in Kashmir*. Princeton: Princeton University Press, 1966.

Krishna, B. *Sardar Vallabhbhai Patel: India's Iron Man*. New Delhi: HarperCollins, 1996.

Lamb, Alastair. *Kashmir: A Disputed Legacy, 1846–1990*. Karachi: Oxford University Press, 1992.

Mahajan, M.C. *Looking Back*. London: Asia Publishing House, 1963.

Mathai, M.O. *My Days with Nehru*. New Delhi: Vikas, 1979.

Menon, V.P. *The Story of the Integration of Indian States*. London: Longman, Green, 1956.

Menon, V.P. *The Transfer of Power in India*. New Delhi: Sangam Books, 1981.

Moon, Penderel. *Divide and Quit*. London: Chatto and Windus, 1964.

Moraes, Frank. *Jawaharlal Nehru: A Biography*. New York: Macmillan, 1956.

Morgan, Janet. *Edwina Mountbatten: A Life of Her Own*. London: HarperCollins, 1991.

Mountbatten, Pamela. *India Remembered*. London: Pavilion, 2008.

Munshi, K.M. *The End of an Era: Hyderabad Memories*. Bombay: Bharatiya Vidya Bhavan, 1957.

Nehru, Jawaharlal. *The Discovery of India*. Delhi: Oxford University Press, 1985.

———*Selected Works of Jawaharlal Nehru*. 1st series. 15 vols. Ed. Sarvepalli Gopal et al. New Delhi: Orient Longman, 1972–1982.

———*Selected Works of Jawaharlal Nehru*. 2nd series. 55 vols. Ed. Sarvepalli Gopal et al. New Delhi: Jawaharlal Nehru Memorial Fund, 1985–.

Noorani, A.G. *Article 370: A Constitutional History of Kashmir*. New Delhi: Oxford University Press, 2015.

Pandey, Gyanendra. *Remembering Partition: Violence, Nationalism and History in India*. New Delhi: Cambridge University Press India, 2003.

Schofield, Victoria. *Kashmir in Conflict: India, Pakistan and the Unending War*. London: I.B. Tauris, 2003.

Sen, L.P. *Slender Was the Thread: Kashmir Confrontation, 1947–48*. New Delhi: Orient Longman, 1969.

Shankar, V. *My Reminiscences of Sardar Patel*. Vol 1. Delhi: Macmillan India, 1974.

Singh, Harbakhsh. *In the Line of Duty: A Soldier Remembers*. New Delhi: Lancer Publishers & Distributors, 2000.

Singh, Karan. *Heir Apparent: An Autobiography. Vol. I*. Oxford: Oxford University Press, 1982.

Snedden, Christopher. *Kashmir: The Untold Story*. New Delhi: HarperCollins India, 2013.

Symonds, Richard. *In the Margins of Independence: A Relief Worker in India and Pakistan*. Oxford: Oxford University Press, 2001.

Talbot, Phillips. *An American Witness to India's Partition*. New Delhi: Sage Publications Pvt. Ltd, 2007.

Talbot, Ian, and Gurharpal Singh. *The Partition of India*. Oxford: Oxford University Press, 2002.

Von Tunzelmann, Alex. *Indian Summer: The Secret History of the End of an Empire*. Henry Holt and Co., 2007.

Whitehead, Andrew. *A Mission in Kashmir*. New Delhi: Penguin India, 2007.

Wolpert, Stanley. *Shameful Flight: The Last Years of the British Empire in India*. Oxford: Oxford University Press, 2006.

Ziegler, Philip. *Mountbatten: The Official Biography*. London: Collins, 1985.

About the Author

Manreet Sodhi Someshwar is a bestselling author of nine books, including the award-winning *The Radiance of a Thousand Suns* and the critically acclaimed *The Long Walk Home*. Hailed as 'a star on the literary horizon' by Khushwant Singh and garnering endorsements from Gulzar for two of her books, Manreet and her work have featured at literary festivals. Her articles have appeared in *The New York Times*, the *South China Morning Post*, and several Indian publications. Manreet lives in New York City with her husband, daughter and cat.

HarperCollins *Publishers* India

At HarperCollins India, we believe in telling the best stories and finding the widest readership for our books in every format possible. We started publishing in 1992; a great deal has changed since then, but what has remained constant is the passion with which our authors write their books, the love with which readers receive them, and the sheer joy and excitement that we as publishers feel in being a part of the publishing process.

Over the years, we've had the pleasure of publishing some of the finest writing from the subcontinent and around the world, including several award-winning titles and some of the biggest bestsellers in India's publishing history. But nothing has meant more to us than the fact that millions of people have read the books we published, and that somewhere, a book of ours might have made a difference.

As we look to the future, we go back to that one word—a word which has been a driving force for us all these years.

Read.

Harper Collins | 4th | HARPER PERENNIAL | HARPER BUSINESS | HARPER BLACK | हार्पर हिन्दी

HarperCollins *Children'sBooks* | HARPER DESIGN | HARPER VANTAGE | Harper Sport